PRAISE FOR JANICE CANTORE

"Questions of faith shape the well-woven details, the taut action scenes, and the complex characters in Cantore's riveting mystery."

BOOKLIST on *Burning Proof*

"In *Burning Proof*, Cantore proves her skills as an author with multilayered plots, all with an underlying focus on faith. Her twenty-two years of experience on the police force lends her riveting police-crime drama totally suspenseful, authentic, and memorable."

CBA RETAILERS + *Resources*

"[In] the second book in Cantore's Cold Case Justice series . . . the romantic tension between Abby and Luke seems to be growing stronger, which creates anticipation for the next installment."

ROMANTIC TIMES on *Burning Proof*

"This is the start of a smart new series for retired police officer–turned–author Cantore. Interesting procedural details, multilayered characters, lots of action, and intertwined mysteries offer plenty of appeal."

BOOKLIST on *Drawing Fire*

"Cantore's well-drawn characters employ Christian values and spirituality to navigate them through tragedy, challenges, and loss. However, layered upon the underlying basis of faith is a riveting police-crime drama infused with ratcheting suspense and surprising plot twists."

SHELF AWARENESS on *Drawing Fire*

"*Drawing Fire* rips into the heart of every reader. One dedicated homicide detective. One poignant cold case. One struggle for truth. . . . Or is the pursuit revenge?"

DIANN MILLS, *bestselling author of the FBI: Houston series*

"This hard-edged and chilling narrative rings with authenticity. . . . Fans of police suspense fiction will be drawn in by her accurate and dramatic portrayal."

LIBRARY JOURNAL on *Visible Threat*

"Janice Cantore provides an accurate behind-the-scenes view of law enforcement and the challenges associated with solving cases. Through well-written dialogue and effective plot twists, the reader is quickly drawn into a story that sensitively yet realistically deals with a difficult topic."

CHRISTIAN LIBRARY JOURNAL on *Visible Threat*

"[Cantore's] characters resonate with an authenticity not routinely found in police dramas. Her knack with words captures Jack's despair and bitterness and skillfully documents his spiritual journey."

ROMANTIC TIMES on *Critical Pursuit*

"Cantore is a former cop, and her experience shows in this wonderful series debut. The characters are well drawn and believable, and the suspenseful plot is thick with tension. Fans of Lynette Eason, Dee Henderson, or DiAnn Mills and readers who like crime fiction without gratuitous violence and sex will appreciate discovering a new writer."

LIBRARY JOURNAL on *Accused*

"Cantore provides a detailed and intimate account of a homicide investigation in an enjoyable read that's more crime than Christian."

PUBLISHERS WEEKLY on *Accused*

"Janice Cantore's twenty-two years as a police veteran for the Long Beach Police Department [lend] authenticity in each suspense novel she pens. If your readers like Dee Henderson, they will love Janice Cantore."

CHRISTIAN RETAILING on *Abducted*

"[*Avenged*] offers plenty of procedural authenticity and suspense that will attract fans of Dee Henderson."

LIBRARY JOURNAL

"Cantore . . . delivers another round of crime, intrigue, and romance in her latest title."

JOYCE LAMB, USA TODAY on *Avenged*

"Set in a busy West Coast city, the story's twists will keep readers eagerly reading and guessing. . . . I enjoyed every chapter. *Accused* is a brisk and action-filled book with enjoyable characters and a good dose of mystery. . . . I look forward to more books in this series."

MOLLY ANDERSON, *Christianbookpreviews.com*

"*Accused* was a wonderfully paced, action-packed mystery. . . . [Carly] is clearly a competent detective, an intelligent woman, and a compassionate partner. This is definitely a series I will be revisiting."

MIN JUNG, *freshfiction.com*

"*Abducted* is a riveting suspense . . . [and] the many twists and turns keep the reader puzzled. The book is a realistic look into the lives of law enforcement officers. *Abducted* is one book I couldn't put down. Can't wait to see what Carly and Nick might be up to next."

PAM, *daysongreflections.com*

CATCHING HEAT

CATCHING HEAT

COLD CASE JUSTICE

JANICE CANTORE

TYNDALE HOUSE PUBLISHERS, INC.
CAROL STREAM, ILLINOIS

Visit Tyndale online at www.tyndale.com.

Visit Janice Cantore's website at www.janicecantore.com.

TYNDALE and Tyndale's quill logo are registered trademarks of Tyndale House Publishers, Inc.

Catching Heat

Designed by Jennifer Ghionzoli

Edited by Erin E. Smith

Published in association with the literary agency of D.C. Jacobson & Associates LLC, an Author Management Company. www.dcjacobson.com

Catching Heat is a work of fiction. Where real people, events, establishments, organizations, or locales appear, they are used fictitiously. All other elements of the novel are drawn from the author's imagination.

Library of Congress Cataloging-in-Publication Data

Names: Cantore, Janice, author.
Title: Catching heat / Janice Cantore.
Description: Carol Stream, Illinois : Tyndale House Publishers, Inc., [2016]
 | Series: Cold case justice
Identifiers: LCCN 2016016021 | ISBN 9781414396705 (softcover)
Subjects: LCSH: Policewomen—Fiction. | Private investigators—Fiction. |
 Murder—Investigation—Fiction. | Cold cases (Criminal investigation)—Fiction. |
 GSAFD: Mystery fiction. | Christian fiction.
Classification: LCC PS3603.A588 C38 2016 | DDC 813/.6—dc23 LC record available at
https://lccn.loc.gov/2016016021

Printed in the United States of America

22   21   20   19   18   17
7   6   5   4   3   2

ACKNOWLEDGMENTS

I'D LIKE TO ACKNOWLEDGE the help of Detective Stephen Jones (ret.), Officer James P. Barringer, and Commander Lisa Lopez; the encouragement of Don Jacobson, my agent; and the overall support of Kitty Bucholtz, Marcy Weydemuller, Cathleen Armstrong, Kathleen Wright, Wendy Lawton, and Lauraine Snelling, my writing friends, for always being there to listen to the ideas as they bounce around—some good, some not so good—and to always tell the truth about what is what.

And thanks to Erin Smith, my awesome editor, and all the great people at Tyndale that I am blessed to be able to work with.

"Vengeance is mine, and recompense,
for the time when their foot shall slip;
for the day of their calamity is at hand,
and their doom comes swiftly."

DEUTERONOMY 32:35

PROLOGUE

"THIS LOOKS LIKE a fairy-tale cottage, one you'd see painted on the cover of a kids' book." Abby Hart turned toward Robert "Woody" Woods as they reached their destination. "Trouble is, in those books something bad often lives in the cottage."

Her partner laughed. "Think an ogre lives here?" he asked as they stepped out of the car.

"If this were fairy-tale Grimm, you can bet that's what we'd find."

She stood by the car door for a minute and took a deep breath, enjoying the fresh air. It had rained yesterday, but today was gorgeous—seventy-five degrees, puffy white clouds dotting a brilliant-blue sky with a gentle breeze rustling leaves on the trees. She turned as the patter of paws caught her attention. A medium-size shepherd trotted up to her, wagging his tail. Abby missed her own little dog, Bandit, and bent to scratch the shepherd's head.

"Hey, cutie, you live here?"

Woody joined her, and for a moment they showered the dog with praise.

"Nice dog. Collar, no tag. Wonder where he belongs."

"He's a little on the thin side. . . . I wonder." She looked toward the house. "We can ask, but first let's find out about the odd guy that used to work here."

They left the dog and walked toward the house. Around them birds chirped, and she noticed a hummingbird feeder hanging from a branch on one of the oak trees.

Abby knocked on the door and stepped off the porch to wait, noting that the dog had followed and was watching her, tail wagging. She'd try to remember to ask who owned the dog—if they came up empty on their search, that was. They were asking about a cold case, and you never knew if you were going to touch a nerve, unearth a buried clue, or receive blank, empty stares.

She took a police tactic out of habit, moving to one side of the door as Woody stood on the other. She had been part of the West Coast's federal cold case squad since November and was now working with Woody and PI Luke Murphy. But she'd known and worked with Woody for years before that. He'd been her first training officer in uniform and a good, solid friend for the fifteen years since. Though he'd retired from the PD, Woody eagerly jumped aboard the cold case squad and Abby was happy to be teamed up with him.

She was about to knock again when the door opened. From the corner of her eye, she caught a blur of fur and realized that the dog had fled, tail between his legs. Frowning, she turned to the tall, dark-haired and bearded man who had stepped partially into the doorway but stayed in the shadows.

"Sergio?" Abby asked.

"*Sí. El jefe*, he send you?" Through his thick accent, his tone was guarded, suspicious, and it set Abby on edge. But there could be a lot of reasons he was nervous.

"Yes, I'm Detective Hart, and this is Investigator Woods. The owner told you we'd be coming by to ask you some questions?"

"About Chester?"

"Yeah, what kind of problems did he cause?"

He shrugged. "I don't know where he is."

"What can you tell us about the man?"

He shook his head, looking for all the world like he didn't understand the question. Abby squinted, trying to read his face in the shadows.

"We're not from immigration," she said, hoping he'd stop being obtuse. "We're looking for a witness to a crime that occurred near here a few years ago. Maybe it was this Chester."

She glanced at her watch. They were scheduled to meet Agent Orson for an early lunch after this contact, and at this rate they would be late.

"Your boss told us you fired him. Do you remember anything about him?" Woody asked, trying a different tack.

"*Sí*, I fire him, but I don't know where he go."

He looked bewildered again, and Abby got impatient with the shtick. And with the sun hitting her in the face, this was a position of disadvantage. She was ready to move on but wanted to be 100 percent certain.

"Maybe you have employment paperwork we could look at. Would you mind if we came inside to talk for a few minutes?" she asked, praying the man wouldn't pretend he didn't know what that meant. His employer had told them that most employee records were kept with Sergio. She hoped he'd have something that would provide a more detailed work history about Chester than they had so far.

Thankfully, Sergio nodded and stepped aside, motioning for

Abby to enter his home. Abby stepped up onto the porch and into the house, Woody behind her.

Sergio let them enter and closed the door. Abby turned to look at him just as he brought his elbow up and struck Woody full force in the back of his head. Woody went down hard.

Shock gripped Abby by the throat, and she dropped her notebook to reach for her gun.

Too slow.

Sergio knelt on Woody's back, flipped open a switchblade, and held it to the fallen man's neck, just below the ear.

"Don't move or I will kill him," he ordered, voice calm, with no trace of an accent. Keeping the knife pressed to Woody's neck with his left hand, he held out his right hand. "Hand me your gun by the grip."

Abby hesitated as Sergio pressed with the knife and a drop of blood pinched out.

Face flushed, she tried to think, tried to see a way out of surrendering her weapon.

"Now. The gun. Hurry."

Knowing Woody would bleed out in bare minutes if Sergio pressed any harder, Abby carefully drew her weapon and handed it to Sergio. He took it and thankfully removed the knife from Woody's neck and stood upright, pointing her .45 at her. As he backed up, Abby knelt to check on Woody, who started to get up. He put a hand to his neck where Sergio had drawn blood and rose to his knees. To Abby he seemed okay, if a little shaky from the blow to his head.

"Kudos to you two for finding me after all this time. I've stayed well hidden but never lost my paranoia. Does Victoria know?"

Neither Abby nor Woody answered.

"Does she know?" he demanded.

"She will, when we take your butt in," Woody said, the timbre in his voice telling Abby he was more than a little shaken up.

"You don't get it. You think I'm the monster. You're wrong. She's the killer, and if she finds me, she'll finish the job. I can't let that happen. I can't let you tell her that you found me." He extended the gun their direction.

All Abby could think was *Welcome to fairy-tale Grimm.*

CHAPTER

1

THREE WEEKS EARLIER

"**PLEASE STATE YOUR** name for the court."

Abby had to admit to almost feeling sorry for the woman sitting before the judge today. Less than a year ago, Kelsey Cox had retired as a deputy chief after a thirty-year, trailblazing law enforcement career. And here she was in a prison jumpsuit, no makeup, bad hairstyle, and looking so painfully thin, Abby winced. She also sported what looked like a fresh black eye. Someone in jail had most likely recognized her as an ex-cop. Abby wondered if that was why Kelsey insisted on the fast track for her confession. If so, she understandably wanted to get out of the city jail and into a state facility, where there were fewer chances of being recognized. She was set to confess to murdering and then concealing the body of Buck Morgan, Abby's father, more than twenty-seven years ago.

Yeah, Abby thought, *I almost feel sorry.*

Cox cleared her throat. "Kelsey June Cox." She stared at the microphone she spoke into, seemingly oblivious to anyone else in the judge's private chamber. This had been one of Kelsey's demands—along with the plea to speed up the process and have her hearing as soon as possible—that she be able to give her statement in private, with only a few people present and no questions except from the judge. All in exchange for a mere fifteen-year sentence.

Sure, I'm getting a confession, Abby thought. *But why do I feel as though in our effort to close this, we've dealt away justice—real justice?*

She looked over at Walter Gunther, Long Beach's police beat reporter. She'd fought to have him here in a simple demonstration of petulance. It was one battle won in a lost war. As glad as she was that he was in her corner, she wished it were Luke Murphy by her side, giving her support.

"Please proceed with your statement, Ms. Cox, about what occurred on the night of June 16, 1988."

After a sip of water, Cox began. "On that night, I left work late, after 10 p.m., and returned to my home on Granada, in Long Beach, to hear two men arguing." Her voice was thin and reedy, not the same one Abby remembered barking orders when Kelsey Cox was a supervisor in patrol.

"I shared the home with Gavin Kent. He was a fellow officer and my fiancé. I recognized him as being part of the argument, but it was only when I stepped out onto the patio that I saw who the other person was. It was Buck Morgan." She paused to take a drink of water. Her gaze flickered briefly to Abby, then back down to the mic.

"Was Buck Morgan an acquaintance?" the judge asked.

"Buck Morgan was known to me as one of the owners of a restaurant that had burned down, the Triple Seven. The fire had occurred two nights previous, and it was assumed by everyone that Morgan had died in it."

"Did someone die in the fire?"

"We found three bodies. At the time we thought them to be Buck Morgan, his wife, Patricia, and Luke Goddard, their cook."

The judge scribbled some notes.

"When you stepped out onto the patio, did the two men see you?"

"No, uh . . . I mean, I think Gavin saw me, but I was behind Buck."

"What was the argument about?"

"I only caught bits of it—it really didn't make sense, and like I said, I thought Buck was dead, and that concerned me. What if he had faked his death? It occurred to me that he might be a killer; he might have killed his wife, the cook, and set the fire . . ."

Abby was almost up out of her seat. Beside her, DA Drew gripped her hand, and Walter shook his head. Face hot, heart pumping, Abby slowly settled back into her chair. For the first time Cox steadily looked her way, expression blank.

Abby fumed. Gavin Kent was the one who burned down her father's restaurant, killed her mother. Of course her father had a reason to be arguing with him. What was it Kelsey was going to confess to? A bad hair day and taking it out on Abby's dad?

The judge cast a frown Abby's direction and then nodded for Cox to continue.

"I didn't really know what to think, or what was happening, but I could see that Buck was trying to get Gavin to go somewhere with him. Fearing for Gavin, I moved in behind Morgan."

"Did you have a weapon?"

"I'd left my duty weapon in the house and I didn't want to waste time by going back to get it. I grabbed a shovel—we were having work done in our backyard and there was one handy. Morgan was getting more animated. Gavin was vulnerable—he'd hurt himself and was not 100 percent."

"How had he hurt himself?"

"Helping with the yard remodel."

Abby could not hold back a snort. Gavin Kent had been wounded in a gunfight, shot by her father, after Buck had witnessed Gavin kill Abby's mother. Her dad then killed the drug dealer Gavin had brought with him. After that he ran out of ammo and had to flee the restaurant for his life.

Another angry glance from the judge, and she forced herself to nod an apology.

"What happened then?"

"I just reacted. I saw Morgan move toward Gavin, and I swung the shovel and hit him in the head as hard as I could."

＊＊＊

Abby left the courthouse angry and frustrated. She remembered when she was a kid in foster care, in the weeks right after her parents' murders, filled with anger. She used to pound big rocks into smaller rocks and pretend she was pounding the people who had murdered them. It had been a long time since that anger—rage, really—had surged so completely through her. A rage that made her want to pound something—or someone. What Kelsey called a confession was a farce.

A social worker back then had given Abby a Bible verse from the book of Deuteronomy. It took years before six-year-old Abby completely understood the verse, but when she did, it became a lifeline and something that eased her anger. *"He gives justice to the fatherless and widows . . ."*

"Hey, Abby, hold up."

She stopped and turned. She'd tried to ignore Gunther but wasn't angry enough to make the old guy chase after her. Besides, he wasn't the one who infuriated her.

"Trying to give me a heart attack?" He caught up to her, breathing hard, bending over, and putting his hands on his thighs to catch his breath. "You stormed out of there and made the judge mad," he said after he straightened up. "Hope you don't have to try any cases in front of him right away."

"I don't know what I expected in there. I didn't want a trial any more than the DA did—too risky with the shaky evidence we have—but somehow what Kelsey had to say just didn't sit right with me. She wanted my dad to be the bad guy, threatening Gavin Kent. And Kent is the man who killed my mother!"

Gunther raised both hands. "Calm down. I'm on your side here."

Abby took a deep breath, glancing around the street in front of the courthouse, at the people coming and going. This was the place where people came for justice, she thought bitterly. On one level she knew she had no right to be so angry. She had more answers now about the murders of her parents than she'd had a year ago.

After Gavin Kent killed her mother, her father fled, thinking that by doing so he'd saved Abby, that Kent would leave her alone. But Kent still burned the restaurant down to destroy evidence, nearly killing Abby and killing an innocent cook, Luke Murphy's uncle. Her father had come out of hiding to try to take Kent to the police, but Cox killed Buck Morgan before that could happen. Then she buried him under tons of concrete in her backyard, where he'd lain hidden for all these years.

Now, at least, there would be one person in jail, sentenced for part of the crime. Abby had hoped Kelsey would finally point the finger at the person responsible for ordering the massacre at the Triple Seven restaurant: California's First Lady, Alyssa Rollins. But after hearing Cox's self-serving confession, it stung like a thousand bee stings to Abby's heart that Alyssa effortlessly slipped through every crack and avoided judgment. She was the real killer, and she would stay free.

She looked at Gunther. "I know you are. This is just aggravating."

"Well, step into my office." He pointed to a street hot dog vendor. "Let me buy you lunch and we'll talk about it."

In spite of everything Abby laughed. "Yeah, that used to be Asa's favorite place to take me for lunch too." Her old partner Asa Foster had been the one to introduce her to the crusty reporter Gunther. "But he did it because he was cheap."

"I resemble that remark," Gunther said with mock insult.

"Thanks for the offer, but I've got some training to get back to, for the cold case squad. Rain check?"

"Sure." He stepped close. "I'd still like to pick your brain about the Triple Seven someday. It's not settled in my mind, and I don't think it's settled in yours either."

Abby cocked her head and shrugged, then continued on to the parking structure.

She'd thought all of this had been settled in her heart and mind a long time ago, but it wasn't, she realized. *I doubt that it will ever be settled. I'm that orphan talked about in the Bible. God is supposed to give me justice. Will he ever deliver?*

CHAPTER

2

"**IS IT POSSIBLE** there are some friends or acquaintances of Kelsey Cox who might know something helpful?"

Luke Murphy considered Faye's question while he studied the crime board he'd memorized. They were both standing in front of his homemade murder board, depicting all the relevant facts regarding the twenty-seven-year-old murders of his uncle Luke Goddard and Patricia and Buck Morgan.

It was a moment before he answered. "I suppose that is possible, but after all these years, why haven't they come forward? I mean, we know she's a killer; she admitted it."

He moved to lean against the corner of his desk. The last bit of writing on the far right corner of the board contained the entry that apparently solved the crime and pointed to the mastermind.

Buck Morgan's letter from the grave says that Alyssa Rollins ordered the gunshots that killed his wife, Patricia, and the fire that killed Luke Goddard in the Triple Seven restaurant. Gavin Kent was the shooter, on

Alyssa's go-ahead. In self-defense Buck killed Piper Shea, a drug dealer who came with Kent, and it was Shea's body that was misidentified as Buck's for twenty-seven years. Kelsey Cox recently admitted to killing Buck Morgan two days after the fire, when he confronted Gavin Kent in the cop's home. Cox and Kent then buried Buck in their backyard.

With all the information he and Abby dug up or had gifted to them, there was not nearly enough to bring about an arrest of Alyssa Rollins for the crime. Kelsey's confession had been the last gift, but it had been a hollow one. Luke had missed the hearing but had spoken to Abby about it briefly afterward. She was angry and disappointed that Kelsey had played the good soldier and stayed quiet about Alyssa. He'd tried to console her but understood that fifteen years for a lifetime deprived of a father didn't seem a fair trade.

Alyssa Rollins remained free and unscathed by anything.

Added to the mix was the fact that she was the wife of the very popular governor of California, Lowell Rollins, who was in full campaign mode running for a vacant senate seat. For a time it had looked like he was a shoo-in for the spot, but recently the woman challenging him had evened things up and the race was now listed as a toss-up.

So Luke and Abby, along with Faye Fallon, a crime blogger from the high desert, were trying to find any proof that could trip Alyssa up and show the world that she was guilty of orchestrating several violent murders.

"Fear," Faye answered, interrupting Luke's musings. "A lot of people have died during your quest for the truth. If there is anyone who knows what really happened, they could be fearful of stepping forward."

Luke grunted in acknowledgment. George Sanders, Gavin Kent, Asa Foster, a couple of hit men—all had lost their lives in just the last year in relation to the Triple Seven.

Faye continued. "Maybe if you found someone now, you and Abby could convince them that there is nothing more to fear. We could dig around in Cox's background, maybe find someone she's close to who knows something."

Luke pondered the thought, then stood and stretched. "I think there's a legitimate avenue of inquiry back in Tehachapi. Remember that dead guy Quinn?"

Faye arched an eyebrow. "I do. He worked for Governor Rollins. They said he was there checking into someone hacking the governor's campaign office. He thought Barone was the hacker."

The last cold case Luke and Robert "Woody" Woods had closed involved Gil Barone. They'd pegged him for the kidnap and rape of a minor ten years previous, but when they closed in, he'd tried to go out in a blaze of bullets, suicide by cop. He'd set a booby trap that had killed Quinn Rodgers, a member of the governor's security detail, but no one knew then or now what Quinn was doing there. In the course of the investigation officers had discovered an extensive computer hacking setup in Barone's garage, and the governor continued to insist that was the reason for Quinn's presence there. His camp seemed to know about the hacking before law enforcement did.

Luke nodded. "Right, but when Woody and I were up there in court on the Barone case, I talked to a couple of investigators. They found no indication Barone hacked the governor's office, campaign or otherwise. He was a prolific hacker, and they're still trying to unravel all the places he got into, but he hacked for profit, not politics."

Luke and Woody spent weeks up in the high desert area of LA at court hearings. Initially it appeared as though Barone was going to fight the charges against him tooth and nail, but after three weeks of legal wrangling, he gave up and confessed, not only to the one rape, but to three more crimes where he also killed the girls—three girls whose bodies had never been found. Currently LA County and Kern County Sheriffs were working with Barone to locate the girls' remains. The hacking charges were still pending. Proving what a sick man Barone was, it seemed he was proud to confess to multiple rapes and murders in order to enhance his reputation in prison.

"What's the governor's official statement on Quinn?" Faye asked.

"To the best of his knowledge—" Luke imitated a highbrow political spokesman—"Quinn was looking into hacking, and the loss of his life was an unfortunate case of wrong place at the wrong time."

"In short, he claims ignorance," Faye said.

"Yep. And he's not said much else. But the interesting thing to me is, when investigators tried to track Quinn's movements in Tehachapi, they found people who said he was there with a woman, one who matches Kelsey's description."

"The plot thickens. Kelsey have anything to say about that?"

Luke shook his head. "She would only talk about the murder of Buck Morgan, nothing more. I'd love to find out what Quinn was into, and if Kelsey was with him, but starting Monday, we've got a cold case to work, and we'll be busy on that."

"It will be your first case working with Abby."

Faye made the comment mildly, but Luke shot her a quick look. True, it had been three months since Abby joined the squad on a temporary basis, and they'd not yet worked together. He and Woody had been tied up with Barone while Abby had been busy building a case against Kelsey Cox.

And he had been dating Faye for that time.

Luke hated to admit it, but as much as he liked Faye and enjoyed her company, he was stuck on Abby. During their first date, Faye had warned him that she sensed this. At the time, Luke thought Abby was still engaged, and he genuinely liked Faye.

"I won't deny that I respect her, and we'll always be connected by the Triple Seven, but that's as deep as our relationship has gone and is likely to ever go," he told Faye, and she accepted that.

Getting back into the dating field after so many years felt a little awkward, but he was willing to put in a serious effort at a relationship with Faye.

Faye had her own baggage as well. She was still hung up on her dead husband, and Luke had realized that soon enough. When Faye spoke in glowing terms about Mitch, Luke didn't feel jealousy, not at all. Instead, his thoughts went to Abby. He admired her and felt attracted to her and couldn't deny the spark he felt when he thought of her.

"What?" He realized Faye was speaking to him. "I'm sorry. I was distracted for a minute."

She moved closer to him. "I asked you if you wanted me to check into this thing with Quinn. Maybe I'll be able to shake something loose. I am a fresh face with fresh eyes."

He smiled and took her hand. "I know you want to help,

but you have your own work to do and you said it yourself—a lot of people have died during this quest."

"Ever the knight in shining armor." She returned his smile but took her hand from his and turned away, back to the board, where she tapped on a portion. "I'll be careful. I know the investigators up in that neck of the woods. They help me out often. I'll work with them, not solo."

Luke realized he couldn't find a flaw with that suggestion; investigators from both Kern County and LA County were all over the case in Tehachapi. Faye should be safe enough. And Faye was a smart cookie. Only after they started dating had he learned that she had a law degree. She'd never taken the bar but had worked as a civilian employee for the FBI, briefly, before she met her husband. She'd quit when they got married. Though four years a widow, she still kept up on legal issues and was a savvy investigator.

"That's a good idea. They might have some more information, a link to follow. I'll have Woody send you a list of names, guys we spoke to and worked with."

"Sounds like a plan. Now I have to get home."

"I'll walk you out." Luke could sense there was something on her mind, much as there was something on his. But neither one of them said anything but good-bye as he gave her a brief kiss and watched her vehicle disappear down the street.

CHAPTER

3

ABBY HATED TO brood but knew that was what she was doing. Kelsey's confession stuck in her mind like an old-fashioned needle caught in the groove of a scratched record. She'd hoped that this trip out of town would help her get the needle unstuck, but the drive to Tehachapi brought to mind a mixed bag of memories for her that didn't altogether solve her problem.

She'd helped Luke and Woody bring down a serial killer in Tehachapi, with a beautiful bit of teamwork between her and Luke. They'd meshed well as partners, and she felt that he understood her in a way no one ever had. But during that time she'd also met Faye Fallon, the woman Luke was dating. She didn't know how she should feel about that. Part of her said it shouldn't bother her at all, but it did.

She had no claim on Luke, she reminded herself when emotions seemed to prickle. When she'd met him, not only did she think he was annoying, she was engaged. Abby had since ended her long-term engagement to Ethan Carver. And she admired Faye. The woman had a lot of courage and class. She was a Marine widow and Luke, former Army Special Forces, a widower. Sounded like a good match.

Her mind kept bouncing silly debates back and forth as if she were arguing with one of her friends, Megan or Jessica.

I'm not engaged anymore, and Ethan is off to the mission field. And I'll be working with Luke. He's been single for over ten years. Why wouldn't he date someone he has a lot in common with?

But Luke and I have a lot in common, and we connect on many levels. Plus, I'm attracted to him in a way I was never attracted to Ethan.

But I like Faye. I should be happy for them.

"Arrgh," she groaned and smacked the steering wheel, working hard to concentrate on the drive. After two months, she'd finally gotten the okay to visit her uncle Simon, a lifer at the state prison in Tehachapi. Thankfully, returning her train of thought to Simon brought up enough nervousness and disquiet to push Luke, Faye, and Kelsey from her mind.

She'd never met her uncle. Simon Morgan was arrested and in prison before Abby was born. And she'd never been to prison to *visit* anyone. As a homicide detective, she'd been to prisons for interviews a few times, but that was official business; this was personal.

Simon had called and talked with Abby on the phone a couple of times; he'd even sent her all the letters her father had written to him, so she felt she had a small window into who he was. But how was this face-to-face meeting going to go?

She exited the freeway and followed directional signs to the prison's visitor parking lot. After getting out of the car, she stopped for a minute and studied what she could see of the California Correctional Institution at Tehachapi.

For some reason this prison was more intimidating than any of the prisons she'd traveled to on official business. High walls, barbed wire, guard towers, and stark-naked landscaping. She wondered if that was just because she was without her gun and badge and any official standing.

The place was busy. There were a lot of people walking along with her as she made her way to the visiting gate. The crowd was made up of mostly young women and children, though there were a few older people. Abby felt out of place and out of sorts. Not because of her age, but more because Simon wasn't a much-missed loved one.

She noted that most everyone had obeyed the dress restrictions that called for modest attire, with no jeans allowed and nothing resembling what the prison staff or inmates wore. She knew anyone who ignored the restrictions would be ushered to a trailer where racks of donated, modest clothing hung. They'd have to change and comply with instructions or go home without a visit.

Some people carried bags and Abby hoped for their sake they'd read carefully enough to know what was allowed. She'd brought nothing with her but car keys and identification. Simon had asked for nothing.

The line of visitors processed quickly, and before long Abby had her visitor pass. She eventually was led to a large room with low stainless steel tables, the kind with round stools attached. The correctional officer directed her to one and asked her to sit and wait.

All around there was steady, muted chatter from the visitors, spatters of Spanish here and there, and the loud clanging of heavy prison doors. Off in the distance Abby heard shouts and catcalls, but they were too far away and muffled for her to make out what was being said. She fidgeted, crossing and recrossing her ankles. To her right, a tatted-up Hispanic man greeted a woman with a small boy in her arms. Only modest displays of emotion were allowed, and after an embrace and a kiss, they sat at the table and began chatting away in Spanish.

Then she saw him. Simon Morgan walked toward her. He looked like an age-enhanced photo of the father she'd lost when she was six years old. She stood as a crush of emotions hit her in the chest like a fastball. It was a couple of seconds before she realized that she wasn't breathing. Swallowing and taking a breath, she stepped forward and took his extended hand. His hand was large, rough, and warm, his grip as tight as she'd ever felt.

"Uncle Simon." Her voice squeaked and she swallowed again.

"Wow," he said, raising his eyebrows. "You are the spitting image of your mother. And I . . ." He stammered and ran a finger under his nose and Abby realized the emotion train had collided with him as well. "I can't tell you how awesome it feels to be called 'uncle.'"

Abby smiled and relaxed. She held his hand with both of hers, squeezing back, and said, "It's really great to finally meet you."

They sat down at the table and began to talk as if they had known each other for years, and not been anonymous relatives for a few decades.

CHAPTER 4

"I LIKE FAYE. She can come to my birthday party if she wants," Maddie said as everyone sat at the table for dinner. "How about you, Grandma? What do you think?"

Luke's gaze snapped from his daughter to his mother, wondering where this had come from. Her birthday was three months past, but at the time her best friend had been away on vacation, so Maddie asked for a party rain check. His mother had warned him she was ready to call in the marker and the party would be scheduled soon. Luke didn't want work to make him miss it.

He still hadn't adjusted to his little girl being a year older, but that thought was overshadowed by something else: had he led his daughter to believe that he was more serious about Faye than he was?

Grace arched an eyebrow, extending her hands so that they could all hold hands while a blessing was said. "She's a sweet lady. But she lives far away."

Luke gripped his mother's hand and bowed his head, not wanting to discuss his and Faye's relationship with Grace and Maddie over the dinner table.

Thankfully his stepfather, James, said a blessing and dinner was served. He hoped that meant the subject was changing, but he was wrong.

"Is she going to move to Long Beach, Dad?" Maddie asked.

Luke cleared his throat. "No, I don't think so. Her life is out in the Antelope Valley." The words hit him as soon as they were out of his mouth. Faye's life *was* over an hour away in the high desert; his was here in Long Beach. Even if Abby weren't occupying his thoughts, would he and Faye ever have a chance?

"Have you two discussed the situation?" Grace asked.

"No, Mom, we've not gotten that serious. I like Faye. I enjoy her company. But I'm not certain I want a serious relationship any more than she does."

"Does that mean that you can date Abby?"

Luke choked on his chicken. After a swallow of water, he looked at Maddie. "Why would you ask that?"

Maddie shrugged. "I like Abby too. And I like her dog, Bandit, so I just wondered. Abby and Bandit can come to my party too."

Grandpa James jumped in to save Luke from further discussion of his love life by asking Maddie about her field trip to the Long Beach aquarium.

Abby was free now. He knew that she'd ended her relationship with Ethan. Was that why she was on his mind so much lately? As he concentrated on his dinner, he wondered at the thrill it gave him to know that Maddie liked Abby. It meant more to him than when she'd pronounced that she liked Faye. But it also meant that he ought to talk to Faye and be completely honest about how he felt.

CHAPTER 5

"I DON'T KNOW how to help you with this thing—this investigation into your parents' deaths." Uncle Simon frowned and played with the plastic water bottle in his hands.

The visit had been going better than Abby ever imagined. Simon was a thoughtful, witty man. He'd earned two college degrees while in prison and could talk about any subject. She thought briefly about how he'd ended up here. While serving a short sentence for a manslaughter charge, he'd murdered a man during a prison riot. And even though she knew what he'd done to merit his life sentence, it pained her that he would never leave the walls of this prison. They'd talked about a lot of different topics during her visit, and as it was nearing a close, they'd circled around to the deaths of her parents, the Triple Seven fire, and Kelsey Cox's confession.

"I didn't think you'd know anything, but were you acquainted with Lowell Rollins and Alyssa before politics entered into it? I was just hoping for some insight there. My friend Luke and I want to keep the investigation open in case something turns up to implicate Alyssa."

"I knew them, sure. Your dad and I were very tight with Lowell before Alyssa waltzed in. She was a piece of work." He drummed the metal table with his fingers, a wistful expression on his face. "For her it was always politics and appearances, climbing the ladder to success. She did what I remember my mom calling 'putting on airs,' acting like she was better than everyone else. The group Buck and I used to hang with, we all thought she was only interested in Lowell because of his money. He inherited a lot, you know."

"Yes, I knew that."

"He even paid for my lawyer."

"I didn't know that."

Simon gave a thoughtful nod. "Yeah, he was never uppity about the cash, never lorded it over us. He was generous, fun, one of us, and a good guy."

Abby had heard all that from Woody. "What about the hit-and-run he and my father were involved in?"

He frowned. "Hit-and-run?"

"You didn't know?"

Simon cocked his head. "Yeah, of course I knew about it. But what do you know about it?"

Abby felt a zing, like an electrical current coursing through her. She'd never thought to look to Simon for clarification on this particular story, but it was possible he could be a wealth of information.

"Supposedly, when they were in high school, Lowell and my father stole a car one night and went joyriding. They hit some man walking his dog and killed him and never said anything."

Brows furrowed, Simon shook his head slowly from side to side. "That's not what happened. I was only a year ahead of those knuckleheads, and in high school your dad and I were tight." He held up his fingers and crossed them. "There was a stolen car and a hit-and-run, but nobody died."

"Then what happened?"

"It was a dare. We were sitting around one weekend—I was sixteen, I think, and your dad and Lowell would have been fifteen." He paused as if trying to remember, tapping his chin with two fingers. "Buck was a little troublemaker at times. He'd gotten suspended for something—I don't remember what—and he was picking on Lowell, calling him a Goody Two-shoes."

"I thought you said they got along."

"Oh, they did. Lowell was like our third brother, and we liked his brother, Louis, too. But that didn't mean we didn't pick on one another. Lowell hated being ragged on. Anyway, Buck dared him to steal a car." Simon grinned. "I chimed in because I thought he'd chicken out. Even Louis said a thing or two. And wouldn't you know it, Lowell does it. He used a screwdriver to start an old Datsun. Made it about a block before he hit a parked car, bailed out, and ran. We laughed until we cried."

It was Abby's turn to frown. "The story George Sanders told me was that they both took the car and killed a guy, then hid the fact. Then my mom found out about it and tried to hold it over Alyssa's head to be able to buy them out of the restaurant. That secret is supposedly what got her killed."

"Sanders . . . Georgie Sanders, the guy who bought the junkyard?"

"Yes."

Simon laughed, and it was a deep, masculine laugh that made Abby grin.

"That's rich. Sanders was always a blowhard, and he was

always trying to gain an advantage over people. He didn't know what he was talking about. Either that, or he knew what Alyssa wanted him to know."

"Alyssa?" Abby was confused. "Why would she peddle such a story to him?"

"Misdirection maybe. She might have made up a story to gain Georgie's confidence for something. Or maybe it was her way of casting a shadow on Buck. Why?" He held his hands out, palms up. "That woman was always conniving, planning and twisting things. It's entirely possible Alyssa is the one hiding a deep, dark secret. Probably told that story to Georgie back then for some reason that makes no sense now."

Simon grew serious. "I know that you know your job, but you should look into her background. She came from somewhere on the central coast, Temple something, and as I recall, she was cagey about her background. Her maiden name was Arndt, I think. I remember Buck teasing her about originating from Hicksville and calling her Alyssa the airhead. She didn't like it, being teased; had no sense of humor. And she never liked questions about her past, where she came from, or her family."

"It's entirely possible Alyssa is the one hiding a deep, dark secret." Those words stung Abby, sent her mind churning, and she grabbed on to the idea as if it were a lifeline. What if it were Alyssa whose dark past included a serious crime? The story of the hit-and-run death was supposedly the secret her mother had used to pressure Alyssa. But the only people who knew exactly what her mother said to Alyssa that day in the Triple Seven were dead, except for Alyssa.

She thought about Simon's suggestion for a moment, trying to remember what she'd read in the file about Alyssa. There wasn't much. Excitement smoldered inside. Was this an avenue that could bring her and Luke to the final act of the Triple Seven investigation?

"That is an idea—"

A jailer indicated time was up, visiting was over. Abby and Simon stood.

"I can't believe how fast our time went," she said.

"This was great," Simon said as he took both of Abby's hands in his. "I hope that you will come back."

"I will; I will." She leaned forward to give Simon a hug, surprised at the tears that threatened. Simon was as close to her father as she would ever get on this side of heaven.

CHAPTER

6

ABBY SNUGGLED ON THE COUCH with her little black-and-white dog, Bandit, munching on Oreo cookies and drinking milk. The conversation she'd had with her uncle about Alyssa Rollins replayed in her mind. She wanted to talk to Luke about it, but knowing that he was dating Faye made Abby reticent to phone him.

She and Luke had made an informal agreement a couple of months ago to work on Alyssa's background, looking for anything incriminating. And this information did concern the Triple Seven, so the conversation she'd had with Simon eventually won out. She'd call, but in the morning.

The drive out to Tehachapi, the visit, and the drive back had literally taken the whole day, and Abby was exhausted. The cookies and milk helped her wind down. After finishing the last Oreo and draining her glass of milk, she picked up the dog and headed into the kitchen to drop off the glass. Abby carried him the rest of the way to the bedroom, rehearsing what she'd tell Luke.

"This could be the jackpot road. We may find something at the end of it in Alyssa's past to finally put the woman away."

Abby smiled as she imagined him agreeing. Talking to Luke always brightened her day.

The bright imagination faded when she remembered she had to tone it down. He belonged to someone else.

———■▶———

First thing in the morning, Abby phoned Luke's home only to be told by his mother, Grace, that he was out for the day.

Grace said she'd give Luke the message but suggested, "Try his cell if it's important."

Abby thanked her, but she did not dial Luke's cell number for the same reason her heart sank upon learning that Luke was not at home on a Saturday morning; she was certain he was out with Faye. She hung up with some of her enthusiasm blunted.

She called Woody. Next to Luke, he was the best sounding board on anything related to the Triple Seven.

"Alyssa back then?" Abby could see in her mind's eye his forehead scrunching as he thought about it. "It's funny that you ask me about Alyssa's past. Faye called a couple of days ago and asked me about the investigators up in Tehachapi, 'bout that thread that connects to the governor, to their investigation, the dead employee Quinn."

"What?" This information rocked Abby back on her heels.

"Yes, I guess she's helping Luke with that. Gonna see if they can find out what Quinn was doing there since they know that he was not looking into hacking. They think Cox was there with Quinn as well. I was able to tell her a few things, give her a couple of names."

Abby's head pounded at the idea of Luke asking Faye to help with the Triple Seven case.

"I wish Asa were still alive," Woody said wistfully. "He'd be a big help concerning both Alyssa and Cox. But I'll ask around." Asa had been Woody's partner before he was Abby's, and he had been tight with her parents and the crowd that hung out at the Triple Seven.

"Thanks, Woody."

"Sure. I'm taking Zena to obedience this morning. I'll talk to you later."

Abby hung up and sat at her computer, smiling in spite of Faye. Zena was the rescue dog Woody had adopted a couple of weeks ago. He'd lost both of his old dogs three weeks apart. Abby and Bandit had met Zena and she was a cutie, all wiggling butt and floppy ears. The rescued Lab mix was the light of Woody's life right now, really helping him to heal. She even made him look younger.

But as Abby fired up her laptop, the whole concept of Luke and Faye working on the Triple Seven together still stung. *Should it sting?* she wondered.

Of course Luke and I are forever connected by the murder, but that doesn't mean no one else can help us. I just want the right people to face justice, finally.

It was a monumental task, but eventually she was able to turn her attention back to Alyssa Rollins. She began to do a little searching into the First Lady's background. Abby used only public sites. To tap into a law enforcement site, she'd have to justify her search, record the reason she had a "need to know." There was no legal reason strong enough right now, no probable cause that would stand up in court for her to put a law enforcement stamp on this quest for information.

She didn't find a lot other than what had been put out

officially by the governor's political machine, and Lowell had been in politics for thirty years. His first political win had been for Long Beach city councilman, a few months after her parents' deaths. From there he'd climbed the ladder: mayor of Long Beach, state representative, state attorney general, and finally governor.

As Simon thought, Alyssa's maiden name was Arndt. She hailed from the town of Templeton, California, a place Abby had never heard of. When she looked it up on Google Earth, she saw that it was between Atascadero and Paso Robles in the central part of the state.

Abby spent several hours clicking here and there. She could not find Alyssa's yearbook picture, but she found an archived article about her that featured a picture captioned "Senior picture from high school." The article was a puff piece about the duties and responsibilities of the governor's First Lady. Alyssa had been a dignified and admired First Lady, low profile. Abby had been living in California when Lowell was elected to his first term as governor. She remembered many glowing articles about Alyssa and her work on behalf of Special Olympics and ending poverty in California.

Abby studied the senior picture. Alyssa did not look happy. She had a hard look, a grim set to her mouth. In researching Lowell Rollins, she'd read that he and Alyssa met in college. Alyssa never received a degree; instead she became Lowell's publicist and eventually his wife, dropping out to work on his campaign.

Abby looked at her notes and knew what she'd do at this point in a police investigation. She would be talking to people—classmates, people Alyssa grew up with—trying to find out what they remembered about Alyssa Arndt. Templeton wasn't that far from Long Beach—maybe four hours, five tops. She got up to stretch, wishing Luke would call back. Busying herself with making a pot of strong coffee—the stronger the better to help her think—Abby picked up the newspaper to pass the time while it brewed.

An article on the front page caught her attention. She'd been avoiding coverage of the senate race because she didn't want to think of Lowell Rollins as a senator. But this article made her smile. The Golden State governor was in trouble. His challenger had overcome a ten-point deficit and the race was dead even. Some polls showed Rollins trailing.

"Yes," Abby said with a clap. If he lost the senate race, a political life would be pretty much over for him. There were term limits in California, and this was his last term as governor.

Abby decided to follow the race more closely.

Another article caught her eye. Walter Gunther was retiring. He'd not said a word about this the other day. Abby's brows crunched in dismay. He'd been a reporter when the Triple Seven burned down, almost twenty-eight years ago. The article said he had a total of thirty-five years with the paper.

She liked Gunther and she'd miss him. On a whim, she picked up the phone and called him.

"Gunther," the gruff voice answered on the second ring.

"You're bailing on us?"

"That you, Hart? Indeed I am. Looking for greener pastures, pastures where computers no longer exist."

Abby laughed. "You sound like Woody. I still can't get him to look up the news on a computer."

"Smart man. I'm going to find a world where people still use cursive writing and turn, not tap, the pages of the book they're reading."

"Sounds like a retirement home," Abby said, snickering.

"Ha-ha."

"Gunther, I'm going to miss you. Will you at least let me cash in that rain check and buy you lunch?"

"A late lunch. I need to eat, but I've a desk to clean out."

"Pick a time and spot."

"I'm low maintenance. How about the Long Beach Cafe around one thirty?"

"Great burgers. I'll see you there."

"Look forward to it."

After she hung up the phone, Abby realized that Gunther could possibly be a great source of information on Alyssa Rollins. He'd said he was interested in what she was doing the other day. It surprised her that she'd not thought of it earlier, and then she wondered if he'd mind if she picked his brain at lunch.

With that new thought she gathered up her notes and worked on what she'd ask Gunther, eventually realizing that for a bit, she'd forgotten that Luke hadn't yet returned her call.

CHAPTER

-7-

DURING THE LONG drive out to Faye's home in Lake Los Angeles, Luke thought hard about what he was going to say to her. It was raining in patches. He'd go through one cloudburst; then it would clear and repeat. Kind of like his mind: clear, then cloudy, and over again. During the weeks of their dating, they'd been alternating trips; this Saturday it was his turn to head out her way for a lunch date.

He hadn't strung Faye along. They had fun together, shared common interests, but neither one of them had talked about getting serious. He did enjoy Faye's company, but it would be best to come clean with her on how he felt about Abby. Luke realized he was more excited to be starting his first official task force case with Abby than to go on this planned outing with Faye.

After an hour and a half of soul-searching about exactly what he was going to say to her, when he pulled up in front of Faye's house, his mind went blank. All he could do was pray that he'd find the right words and that nothing he said would hurt her.

"Hi, Luke." Faye met him on the porch. "I'm so sorry; something has come up. I probably should have called you so you could have turned around before you got here, but I've been hung up instant messaging with the victim's family trying to sort things out."

"What is it? What's wrong?"

She held up a Missing poster. "I've been blogging about this woman for a week. I think I told you about it. She's from Littlerock, and she went missing two weeks ago."

"I remember you mentioning that. Supposedly she went on vacation."

"That was what the ex-boyfriend said. The sheriff just called me. They found her car abandoned on the Angeles Crest Highway. I'm heading up there to find out what's happening."

"Wow." He stepped forward. "Faye, I'm so sorry. I know you've been praying she turns up safe. This doesn't look good, does it?"

She shook her head as the tears fell, and Luke pulled her close, letting her cry on his shoulder. This news was clearly hitting her deeply, and he had no problem trying to comfort her the best way he could.

After a moment she pulled away to blow her nose and wipe her eyes. "You are so sweet. Thank you for letting me vent a bit."

"No problem. I know this is rough for you. The other day we prayed that she would be found safe. Do you want me to come along?"

Faye sighed, shook her head, and shot him a dazzling smile. "You've done enough right now, being here." She dabbed her eyes again. "I was really hoping all would be well with this woman. She leaves behind a two-year-old little boy."

"I understand completely." Though Luke wanted to be straight with her about their relationship, this probably wasn't the best time to bring it up.

She gripped his hand in both of hers. "You are the sweetest man I've met since my husband died. But we're not really going anywhere as a couple, are we?"

Luke smiled sadly. She was a smart lady and he'd underestimated her. "I think today is a perfect illustration of why not. You have your world out here and—"

"You have your world in Long Beach," she finished for him. "We've tried to make a go of it, but in reality, never the twain shall meet."

"I guess not," Luke agreed.

Faye rose on her tiptoes and kissed his cheek. "It's trite, but I still hope we can be friends."

"I hope so too."

"And I do want to help you on the Triple Seven case, if you'll let me."

"You bet. I'm not sure where the new cold case will take us, but I'll be in touch."

"I talked to Orson this morning. He was secretive about where you're going. He likes leaving you in suspense."

Luke smiled at that. Agent Todd Orson and Faye were good friends. Orson had introduced them when he asked Luke and Woody to help her with the ten-year-old rape case that ended with Gil Barone's arrest. Luke knew that they spoke often. They were both involved in the Wounded Warrior Project and worked together on a lot of fund-raisers.

"If you couldn't get the location out of him, then I know that I won't until Monday."

"Thank you again, for everything." She moved toward her car.

"No problem."

"You be careful with whatever type case they hand you."

"Right back at you, Faye. Take care," he called as she climbed into her SUV.

CHAPTER

8

LUKE'S CALLBACK CAME as Abby was on her way to lunch. She pulled over so she could give the conversation her full concentration.

"Hi, Luke. I hope I didn't interrupt anything."

"Nope. I just got home. What's up?"

"It's kind of a long story, but it concerns the Triple Seven. Are you busy? I'm on my way to buy lunch for Gunther, and I was going to pick his brain on this as well."

"Just so happens, I'm starved. My lunch date was canceled, and now I'm free and intrigued."

Abby grinned, happy things worked out. "Great, I'm on my way to the Long Beach Cafe now."

"I'll meet you there."

Abby arrived at the restaurant first. Gunther parked next to her right after.

"Long Beach won't be the same without you, Gunther," Abby said when the reporter got out of his car.

"That's sweet of you, but you'll stop missing me as soon as you meet my twentysomething replacement, I'm sure."

"Not likely." Abby's head turned as she saw Luke's truck pull into the lot. "I hope you don't mind. I asked Luke to join us."

Gunther shook his head and opened the restaurant door. "Murphy? I don't mind. I like the guy. I'm really just an old romantic at heart. I'm kinda hoping you two get together. I can't help it. I like him better than that Ethan fellow."

Abby took a step back, frowning. "What? When did you meet Ethan?"

"At Asa's retirement party."

Abby slapped her forehead. "I remember." She wanted to ask what he didn't like about Ethan, but Luke stepped up and more than anything she wanted to change the subject. Talking to Gunther about her and Luke's relationship was not on her to-do list. But on that list was finding out what Luke had asked Faye to look into regarding the Triple Seven. *How can I fit that in?* she wondered.

"Hey, Gunther!" Luke nodded to Abby and grabbed Gunther's hand. "I hear you're headed for white sandy beaches."

"Only if it's in my grandson's sandbox."

Luke chuckled. "No big plans, huh?"

"Like I told Abby here, I only plan to get as far away from technology as possible."

The trio found a table inside the restaurant. After ordering drinks—iced tea for Abby and Luke and coffee for Gunther—Luke asked, "Seriously, what are your plans for retirement?"

Gunther sipped his coffee and made a face. "Make good coffee for myself every day."

"You sure are cagey," Abby said, shaking her head.

"I really have no plans. My daughter wants me to move back east, New Jersey to be exact." He pretended to shiver. "Too cold for me. I might head east, but in this state. Maybe Hemet or Palm Springs."

"Heat."

"Yep, my old bones demand it. Now, let's get to something interesting. What are you guys working on?"

Abby looked at Luke, then quickly glanced away, suddenly feeling betrayed because of the thing with Faye.

"We get a new case Monday," Luke said. Abby saw his brow furrow. He wasn't any more certain about what Gunther was referring to than she was.

"Not what I meant. The Triple Seven. I know you can't let that case go. Woody tells me that you went out to see your uncle Simon, Abby. What did he have to say?"

Abby fiddled with the straw in her tea. "We had a good visit. Never thought I'd say this about a guy in prison for life, but he's a nice guy."

"Now who's being circumspect? Don't beat around the bush. Did he have anything to say about your parents' deaths? That's what you asked him about, isn't it?" He pointed at Abby with his right hand and Luke with his left. "I know that you two are still working on that case. After Abby's reaction to Cox's confession, I'd bet my pension you already have something in the hopper. I covered the fire and the murders twenty-seven years ago, and as I ride into the sunset, I'd like to hear that the case is closed completely. I sincerely hope you'll let me in on the intrigue."

"I . . . ," Luke began, "uh, we have talked about continuing to search for any evidence still out there." He looked at Abby. "We haven't had a chance to discuss this yet, and it may sound off subject, but Faye and I were talking about the Barone case and that guy Quinn, the one who worked for the governor."

Was that what he and Faye had talked about? How could

Abby forget Quinn? She'd practically tripped over his dead body when she and Luke arrived at Barone's house.

"Is there anything new about why he was there?"

"There is. The investigators looking into his death have talked to people around town who remembered seeing him in Tehachapi the day before the thing with Barone blew up, and they say he was there with a woman."

This was news to Abby and she forgot about Faye. "It was Cox, wasn't it?"

Luke nodded. "She fits the description. I think we should look into Quinn and Cox. Find out if they were there together, and if so, where'd she go after he was killed? They both worked for the governor, but his official statement about Quinn's death said nothing about Cox."

Abby held Luke's gaze, his clear hazel eyes alive with interest and curiosity. This was important, at least as important as what Simon had told her.

"Even if it wasn't Cox with Quinn, where did his partner go after Quinn was killed? If they were there on legitimate business, you'd think a partner would call the police. Not disappear—"

"Unless she was up to no good."

Gunther tapped the table. "Hey, you two, don't forget the guest of honor."

Luke grinned. "Sorry, Gunther."

"That is interesting information. But you lost me on how it connects to the Triple Seven."

Luke and Abby exchanged glances. Gunther didn't know about Abby's letter, the one where her dad said that Alyssa Rollins ordered the Triple Seven massacre. Cox had also said as much to Abby when she was burning papers in her town house and nearly killed herself and Abby. Following Cox did involve the Triple Seven.

"Kelsey Cox connects," Abby said. "She worked for Governor Rollins, and so did the dead guy Quinn." Not yet ready to let Gunther in on her father's letter. It was irrational, she knew, but the letter was her only communication with her father, and right now she wanted to keep it private. It would never be used as evidence; there was no chain of custody and no way to authenticate it.

Gunther considered that, then said, "Okay, I can see a tiny link. I mean, Cox confessed to killing Buck Morgan, and her boyfriend claimed to have killed Abby's mom, so it makes sense that she was more involved in the Triple Seven than we know." He motioned to Abby. "This road could lead to Governor Rollins. I know that crook Sanders pointed a finger at Rollins as being involved in the Triple Seven, but in nearly thirty years there's not been any evidence connecting him to the crime. If that's where you're going, good luck."

"Not him, his wife." She sipped her tea.

"What?" Gunther's bushy eyebrows arched.

"I don't believe that she is the quiet, dutiful wife she's portrayed to be."

"Your evidence?"

Thinking carefully, she said, "If you read the statement Sanders gave, remember the part about the supposed hit-and-run that my dad and Rollins were involved in when they were kids?"

Gunther and Luke both nodded.

"According to him, my mom threatened to tell the world the truth about the incident, and that's what got her killed. Well, Simon told me the real story behind the hit-and-run, and it's not what Sanders said." She related what Simon had told her, watching for Luke's reaction.

"Whoa." Luke frowned. "Why would the story change to something that makes Lowell look more guilty?"

"Simon thinks that was a smoke screen. He doesn't care much for Alyssa and thinks she might have embellished the story to protect herself."

"What?" Luke stared at her. "Protect herself from what?"

"He's not sure, but he thinks Alyssa is a conniver and that the lie worked to her advantage for some reason. He thinks, and I agree, that I—we—need to look into Alyssa Rollins's past." Abby slowed down; this was what she'd been eager to tell Luke. Luke knew about her father's letter. How much would she have to explain for Gunther?

Then Gunther surprised her. "Your uncle is a perceptive man," he said.

"So you think that Alyssa is evil as well?"

Gunther leaned back. "Evil? Ahh, that's a strong word. Alyssa is an interesting animal, but as far as implicating her in the Triple Seven murders . . . As I recall, when Sanders told the story, he pointed the finger solely at Lowell."

"I think it was a misdirection for some reason," Abby said, intrigued that he could believe Alyssa was hinky without even knowing about the letter. "I believe California's First Lady is hiding something."

Gunther studied her for a minute. "I reviewed that transcript of the Sanders interview and noted the bit about the hit-and-run. I looked up several hit-and-run reports from the time period, but it would have been impossible to connect something like that to Lowell. The idea that your parents were killed because your mom was threatening to come forward with that story . . ." He made a face as if he'd smelled something bad. "Makes no sense. Your mom and dad were killed for something far more serious than that canard. But Alyssa Rollins?" He shook his head, not totally convinced.

"You bet Alyssa Rollins," Abby said, looking from Gunther to Luke. Luke didn't appear convinced either. "That's why I think we need to peel back some layers, find out about Alyssa before she became Mrs. Rollins. I want to find the secret she's hiding, if there is one."

"There may be something there," Gunther said. "And she might be hiding a secret. But where we part ways is that the secret is so serious she'd kill over it. She's never been a headline grabber, but I know there is something in her past that she doesn't want anyone to know."

"Her past, not Lowell's? You know this how?" There was the zing again. Gunther was, in his own way, cementing what Uncle Simon had said. He might not think it was a serious secret, but Abby knew it was; she felt it in her bones. As well as she knew Gunther, she wondered why he hadn't told her this sooner.

"I was subbing on the government beat when Lowell ran his first campaign. He lost that one, and it was well before the Triple Seven burned. Then later, when he was doing much better, mostly because of Alyssa, I went up to Templeton to do an article on her—just a puff piece, mind you—and I did find out that she didn't have it easy. There was something there, but before I could get very far, I got pulled from the assignment and called home."

"Why?" Luke asked.

"Boss said it wasn't important. She wasn't the candidate, and

Lowell was losing. His line was that I was taking too much time on it." He shrugged. "Later I learned that he'd been asked to pull me off the assignment."

"By who?"

"I don't know. I was a youngster then. I wanted to keep my job. I shut up and was eventually sent back to the police beat that I loved. But come to think of it, even later when Lowell did win, she was never controversial or nasty in public. It can't be any big thing—maybe a romance that embarrassed her, something like that. I do have a file of what's been written about both of them, and I have a few of my own notes. I'd be happy to separate out what's about her and give you what I have to look at."

Abby jumped at the offer. "Yes, I'd like that."

"How about we go through the notes together tomorrow after church?" Luke asked.

Abby smiled. "Great idea."

Their meal came, and the banter went back and forth, mostly with Luke and Abby asking Gunther about his long career. They enjoyed several of his funny stories.

She gave Gunther as much attention as she could, but inside, she looked forward to tomorrow and working with Luke. She realized how strong the hold, the hope, was that this was the lead she'd been waiting for, the lead that could finally bring Alyssa Rollins down and bring Abby the justice she'd been looking for since she was six. It was a heady realization, and Abby prayed with all her might that it would pan out.

CHAPTER

-9-

THE NEXT DAY Abby found her thoughts occupied more with her chance to talk to Luke than with the contents of the material from Gunther. She'd picked up two file folders of the reporter's notes after lunch the day before. Gunther stubbornly believed that there had to be a hard copy of everything, and she and Luke had agreed to sift through it all together.

When his knock came, she was trying to think of a way to bring up Faye's involvement in the Triple Seven investigation. She really just wanted to know how much Faye would be doing.

"Hi, Luke, glad you could make it."

"Sure. I promised you a while ago that we'd work on this. Sorry it's taken so long to get around to it." He smiled and Abby felt the familiar flutter of butterfly wings in her gut. He always did that to her. He hesitated at the door, so she gestured him inside.

"We've both been busy. I divided up the stuff." She pointed to the coffee table. "Two piles of information; take your pick. I'll sort through what's left."

"Great." He stepped inside and started to say something, then stopped.

"Something wrong?"

He sighed. "No, not at all, but sometimes I admit to feeling defeated on this case, like we'll never fully resolve everything, and I'm not usually that much of a pessimist."

She closed the door and moved toward the couch. "Me too. But at least we have a possible lead here. I pray that every lead will eventually give us something solid."

He nodded and went to the table and opened the top folder of the pile on the right. "I'll tackle this," he said as he sat on the left side of the couch.

Abby sat next to him and picked up the remaining file. "I've got this. Now let's find something juicy."

———————•

"For a short visit, Gunther sure took a lot of notes," Luke observed after reading a portion of the reporter's files. It would take time to go through everything.

He was leaning over the notes on the table while Abby had grabbed her stack and settled back on the couch, tucking her feet up under her. She was wearing a fresh, light scent. He didn't know if it was perfume or the smell of shampoo in her hair, but Luke would catch a whiff of a pleasant smell when she moved. He found himself wishing that she'd sit closer. Sometimes it was hard to concentrate on the dry reporter's notes.

"She started out wealthy and privileged," he commented after skimming through the next few pages.

"I saw that. Privilege ended when her father died," Abby said, looking his way and sorting through a different folder of notes.

"Yikes. He killed himself. Her dad was a commodities trader; he gambled on some bad deals and lost everything, not only his money but also the accounts of about twenty clients. He hung himself in his home office, and that left Alyssa and her mother bankrupt. They had to move from San Francisco to Templeton to live in an aunt's guest room. At thirteen Alyssa lost privileged private schools and money and was sent to a hick town and public school."

"Stuff like that happens to a lot of people and they don't grow up to become homicidal maniacs. And I believe that is what Alyssa is. Does anything in there hint at a deep, dark secret?"

Luke shrugged. "Gunther talked to a lot of school classmates. Most said that while Alyssa had been in their class, they barely knew her. He has a bunch of notes here about trying to find Alyssa's high school boyfriend, Mike Jez. Supposedly Jez was the only one who knew Alyssa well. Gunther never did find him from what I can tell." He looked at Abby's pile of paperwork. "What's in your stack?"

"Vital statistics. Miscellaneous stuff. She didn't get a high school diploma until later, after she was in Long Beach. A lot of this stuff I found in my own search."

"What? I thought that she met Lowell in college."

"She did. She was there taking general ed courses, but she didn't go far. Not a lot has been written about her past. But what amazes me more is how none of this about her dad and her sad life was ever common knowledge. Usually politicians play up that stuff, rags to riches and all that. The articles I've read about Alyssa, or Alyssa and Lowell, are more concerned with him, never with her."

"Well, she was never the candidate." He sat back and stretched, then relaxed on the sofa facing Abby. He shared such a strong connection with her because of the Triple Seven. Something about her touched him at a deeper level than Faye ever had.

"Take a break?" he asked.

"Sure."

"Abby, I wondered if it bothered you that I asked Faye to help us, to look into the deal with Quinn out in the high desert."

"Bothered me?" Abby shook her head and then looked a little sheepish. "Well, maybe at first. But it makes sense, doesn't it? She lives out that way."

"She does, but this case is ours. I guess that's what I thought you would think, why you'd maybe be a little upset. Faye only wants to help."

Abby took a deep breath. "Thank her for me. Help is appreciated. I was surprised to hear that about Quinn, about him being with a woman when he was in Tehachapi. What could they have possibly been doing out there but watching us? The high desert is no hotbed of political activity. And your girlfriend knows the area and the cops up there better than we do."

Girlfriend? The way Abby said it made it immensely important to Luke for Abby to know that was no longer the case.

"She's not my girlfriend," he said with more heat than he intended.

"Oh? You're not dating anymore?"

"No, we've, uh . . ." Words escaped him. "We've become good friends, but our relationship is not serious. After all, she has her life in the Antelope Valley and I have mine in Long Beach. Neither of us is at a place where we'd move just to be with the other." That explanation felt lame to him, but Luke was stuck with it.

"Oh." Abby frowned.

"We're friends; that's all." As soon as the words were out of his mouth, he was curious if more would be possible with Abby, since they were now both free.

CHAPTER

10

THE EXCITEMENT ABBY felt because Luke was no longer dating Faye took her by surprise. Still, doubt sprouted. He and Faye still had a lot in common—friendship could easily grow into something deeper.

Abby thought about her long engagement with Ethan. She'd known him for years before they'd gotten engaged; they'd been good friends. Was that really the stage Luke and Faye were in, the long friendship before commitment? Of course it was possible that Luke wasn't ready for a serious relationship with anyone.

She prayed that wasn't the case. She related better to Luke than she'd ever related to Ethan, even though she'd known Ethan for so much longer. By the time they broke up, it was obvious that their life interests were far apart. She was ready to move on, and she could admit to herself that she wanted to move on with Luke.

But am I really ready for something serious? Abby wondered. *Ethan and I were better friends before we started dating. I don't want to lose what I have with Luke. Maybe staying professional colleagues is the way to go.*

They spent only a short time together Sunday afternoon. He'd left saying he had plans with his daughter for Sunday night. Considering that they'd get their first case Monday made Abby feel like a kid on Christmas Eve anticipating the morning.

"Hey, you sure are deep in thought." Megan, Abby's best friend since her college days, stomped her foot in front of Abby. "Must be thinking about a man."

"What makes you say that?" Abby stood from the dusty bench she'd been sitting on outside the theater and brushed off her pants, hoping Megan didn't read her as well as Luke could. The last thing she wanted was another lecture from her friends about getting back on the horse after her breakup with Ethan. She, Megan, and their friend Jessica were planning on seeing the new blockbuster about an earthquake, the "big one," hitting California.

"Well, we're going to see a movie with a hunky leading man. It could lead to a wandering mind."

"Actually, I was wondering why my friends are always late."

"Ha, the cop speaks. Are you going to give me a ticket?"

"Why? What did you do?" Jessica sauntered up and tapped Megan on the shoulder.

"Nothing yet," Abby said. "Let's buy our tickets and find seats before all we're left with is the front row, looking up everyone's nostrils."

"Nag, nag, nag." Megan rolled her eyes as they linked arms and headed for the theater.

But Abby felt an earthquake in her own heart when she recognized the couple in front of them in the ticket line.

Luke and Maddie Murphy.

"Hey, I know you." Maddie caught Abby's eye.

"Hi, Maddie," Abby said.

Luke followed his daughter's movement and turned to see Abby. "Hey, Abby."

Was it her imagination or did he seem genuinely happy to see her?

"Hello, Luke." She nodded to Jessica and Megan. "You remember my friends?"

"Sure do." He shook each woman's hand. "Both great volleyball players. Which movie are you guys here to see?"

"The earthquake flick."

"Us too!" Maddie grabbed Abby's hand. "Want to sit with us? Dad, can they sit with us?"

Luke looked at Maddie. "They might have other plans."

"Nope, we don't," Megan offered. "And we'd love to sit with you two. The more the merrier."

In the dark theater, Abby found herself between Luke and Megan. Megan and Jessica both had shot her enough looks before the lights went out that she knew they were matchmaking. She had no energy to be angry with them. Besides, she liked sitting next to Luke. And maybe help in matchmaking was a good thing.

It was an entertaining disaster film, if a little corny, and it held Abby's attention, but occasionally brushing Luke's arm jolted her psyche more than any earthquake could.

When it was over and the lights came up, she knew that finding out exactly how Luke felt about her was nearly as important as finding out the whole truth of the Triple Seven. But would it be as difficult?

CHAPTER

11

THANKFULLY, MADDIE DIDN'T say anything about Abby to Luke after the movie. She was more concerned about earthquakes, and Luke wondered if he'd been mistaken taking her to see the disaster tour de force.

"Would our house fall down in an earthquake?" she asked after they got home and were enjoying milk and cookies before bed.

"No, baby, it's well built. Grandpa built it, remember?"

"Yeah, but if the earthquake is strong like the one in the movie . . ."

"Maddie, that was just a movie. Remember we talked about this before? Movies are make-believe."

"But, Dad, big buildings fell!"

He slid his chair closer and looked into his worried daughter's eyes. "Who made the world?"

"God did, but he made earthquakes, too."

Luke blew out a breath and prayed for wisdom. "Yes, he did, but what did he promise to those who believe in him?" He held out his hand in the form of a hint.

"That he would hold us in the palm of his hand." She put her small hand in his and Luke gripped it tight.

"Right. He is our protection no matter what happens—earthquakes, floods, whatever, God is there with us. You don't need to be scared; you just need to pray and ask Jesus to be with you, okay?"

Maddie threw her free arm around Luke's neck, and he released her other hand so he could hug her. Tight.

"I love you, Mads, but God loves you more. Never forget that."

"I won't," she said into his ear. "I love you too, Daddy."

It did Luke's heart good to hear the tension gone from her voice and to hear her call him Daddy. Once she turned eleven, she'd announced that it was time for just Dad, but he still loved hearing Daddy when it accidentally slipped out. She was growing up too fast; he hoped that the next birthday didn't bring on any more announcements.

"Think you can go to bed now?"

She wiggled out of his grasp. "Yeah, the movie was only make-believe. I live in reality."

He stifled a laugh. "Then go get your pj's on. I'll be in, in a minute to pray with you."

She skipped off to bed and Luke cleared away their snack plates. One crisis averted.

But one was still in a holding pattern. Abby Hart. *Crisis* wasn't the right word concerning her, but Luke knew his feelings insisted he deal with whatever *it* was with Abby. Sitting next to her in the theater, he'd wished he could have thrown his arm around her and pulled her close. He wondered at the shock he'd seen in her face when they met in the ticket line. It was so easy to read her when it came to other things, but as to how she felt about him, he had no clue. Was she still hung up on Ethan? They'd been engaged for such a long time. *Am I foolish to think she'd want to start a new relationship so soon after her breakup?*

The situation was creating its own tremor in his heart and mind. Surely he could navigate this relationship without doing anything stupid. Easy, right?

Lord, he prayed, *help me to figure this thing out.*

"Dad, I'm ready to pray now," Maddie called from her room.

"Be right there," Luke said, glad he had Maddie and this nightly task he loved to do, to help keep his heart from shaking about the other, unresolved issues in his life.

CHAPTER 12

MONDAY MORNING ABBY arrived at the federal building on Ocean Boulevard in downtown Long Beach more nervous than she thought she'd be for her first day on the cold case squad. She saw that Luke's truck and Woody's car were already in the lot.

I'm an accomplished investigator. What's with the jitters?

She knew that she didn't have to prove anything, but it was important to do great work, to show Orson and—she admitted to herself—Luke what she was made of.

It was a good thing her partners were already there, she thought as she walked toward the conference room. They'd calm her down, she was certain. She opened the door and entered the room. Woody was at the table, sipping coffee and reading notes. Where was Luke?

Then she saw him.

He was off to the right, deep in conversation with . . . Faye Fallon.

What was she doing here?

Faye had a familiar hold on his wrist, and they looked so comfortable with one another, close even. Why did that cause turmoil to erupt in her soul? Disconcerted, Abby stepped over to get some coffee, hoping it would help calm her down. But in a short moment, Faye joined her.

"Oh, hello, Faye," Abby said as the blogger reached for a cup.

"Hi, Abby. From the look on your face, I guess you haven't heard."

"Heard what?"

"About Duke. He had a massive coronary yesterday."

Duke Keller, a retired district attorney, was the fourth member of their cold case squad—their go-to admin person. "What? Is he okay?"

Faye nodded. "Yeah, he had an emergency triple bypass and is recuperating. I got a call late last night asking if I could step in for him until a replacement is found. No one wants to postpone the start of your first case."

"I don't know what to say. I'm glad Duke's okay." *But are you qualified to take his place?* Abby wanted to ask but didn't. She wondered if this was Luke's idea, and disappointment pinched. Did he regret breaking up with Faye? If her involvement on the task force was his idea, then she bet he and the beautiful blogger were more than just friends.

Faye chatted on. "Last time we met, you were in homicide. What made you leave that slot? Luke tells me you had a great rep there. Didn't you like it?" she asked.

Abby cast a glance toward Luke, who at that moment finally seemed to notice she was there.

"I loved it, and I still do. But after all that has happened regarding my cold case, I felt the need to help others in any way I can. This is a temporary reassignment, but it will allow me to get in some training working with and for federal agencies."

"But your spot in homicide—what about that?"

"Well, it's still mine when I finish here. The department signed off on me temporarily leaving for two reasons: first, my salary will be paid by federal grant money; and second, it gives them a chance to experiment with a detective rotation through homicide. Bill, my partner, will work with Jack O'Reilly, while Ben Carney, Jack's partner, volunteered to be a training officer to detectives rotated through on a temporary basis. The department has wanted to give this training method a try for a long time. Now they can."

"Sounds like a win-win."

"It is."

"Bill thinks so as well." Luke stepped up, standing next to Abby for a coffee refill. "He likes working with Abby, but Jack is a good guy too. And he thinks that giving all detectives cross–homicide training will be a good thing in the long run." He smiled warmly at Abby. "Faye tell you that she's temping?"

"Yeah, but I'm shocked to hear about Duke."

"Me too. Orson hit us with it as soon as we got in."

Just then Orson strode into the room. "Okay, kids, time to get started."

Abby wondered how Faye would fit in. She and Woody were the two with law enforcement backgrounds, and Luke was a PI. Keller was tasked with putting together what evidence they dug up into a workable package to present to the involved DA. How could Faye fill his shoes?

Everyone took their seats and gave Orson their undivided attention.

"You've all heard about Duke, I assume. We've got a card going around for everyone to sign. The good news is, everything is looking up for him. I just got off the phone with his wife. The bad news is, he probably won't be back to the squad."

He pointed toward Faye. "You all know Faye Fallon. She's agreed to step in and cover for Duke until we can find a replacement. In case you're wondering, Faye has a law degree and worked for a time for the FBI helping agents compile evidence in federal cases, so she is up to the job."

Abby saw Luke give Faye a thumbs-up. And she admitted to being impressed with the "worked for the FBI" line. She'd thought that Faye was just a blogger. But her heart sank. The case she thought would give her more time with Luke was quickly becoming one that would give her more time with Luke *and Faye.*

"Here's the case." Orson moved on and passed out summaries of their cold case. "We'll be up in San Luis Obispo. The victim is Ciara Adessi. She was an undergraduate at Cal Poly San Luis Obispo in 1996 when she went missing."

Abby picked up the flyer, momentarily distracted from Faye and amazed at this fortunate turn of events. San Luis Obispo was not far from Templeton, she'd noticed. This case would take her straight to the right area to investigate Alyssa's past. Would Luke be with her on this?

She looked his way and caught him watching her. He pointed at the summary and gave her a knowing nod. Smiling and working to get her head back in the game, where it belonged, Abby prayed that this upcoming trip would lead to something positive in her personal cold case, as well as for Ciara. Nervousness gone now, she tuned into what Orson had to say.

Orson elaborated on the case. "Five years ago her remains were found in a shallow grave on the edge of some farmland about twenty minutes from the college. We have cause of death as blunt force trauma to the head, but scant little else because she was in the ground so long."

"No suspects?" Luke asked.

Orson shook his head. "For a minute, in 1999, they looked hard at a registered sex offender, convicted and sentenced to death for two San Luis Obispo coed murders, in 1998 and 1999. But in 1996, he was in jail on a different arrest. So, as of now, there isn't a suspect who can be identified with direct evidence. But there are two people of interest. The first is a college groundskeeper, who was also looked at hard at the time."

He passed a photo around. A surly Caucasian male glowered at Abby when she picked up the photo. He had a mop of curly hair, narrow, close-set eyes, and thin, cruel lips.

"Meet Jasper Harkin. He was fired because the scrutiny brought up the fact that he'd lied on his employment application. He'd been arrested once for sexual battery."

"Sounds like a good bet for a suspect," Woody said.

"Maybe, but there were no witnesses who could put him with the girl. They thought they had their man at first. But they could never develop hard evidence, not even probable cause for arrest. Harkin lost his job. He sued the city and the police department for harassment after he got fired. Eventually the city settled and he moved out of San Luis Obispo but stayed close. He bought a mobile home just outside of Atascadero, about thirty minutes from SLO, and still lives there."

"Who was the second person of interest?" Abby asked.

"Ciara's fiancé at the time, Chaz Considine." He passed around another photo. This time a blond-haired, blue-eyed pretty boy looked back at Abby. A hint of arrogance lurked around the eyes, and his smile made Abby think of mockery.

"He was a college kid, local, lived in San Luis Obispo, and had been dating Ciara for about a year. Considine was the last person seen with Ciara, but he's always claimed he saw her into her apartment and then went home. He also had no discernible motive. By all accounts they were happy and looking forward to getting married."

"Sounds like a sticky case," Faye said.

Orson shrugged. "It's a case that needs to be closed. We have limited cooperation from the locals."

"Limited?"

"Yeah, this case is a sore point with the local PD and the community at large. There are notes in the file that might explain why. Bottom line, they want the case closed and will give you all the information and evidence, but egos being what they are, that might be all you get. To top it off, there's the shooting."

He looked around the room at everyone as Abby cast a glance at Woody. Yeah, everyone knew about the shooting. An SLO PD officer had been shot and killed during a traffic stop last week.

"They caught the guy, right?" Luke asked.

Orson nodded. "They did. But the officer's funeral is this week. Just a heads-up in case you want to pay your respects."

"I will," Abby said. "I called earlier and asked our union about this funeral, didn't know I'd be up in San Luis Obispo working. I'd like to attend in uniform with the other officers who are going. The Long Beach Police Officers Association said seven officers are going. They've been approved to take two patrol cars."

"That's fine," Orson said. "I figured as much, so just work it in."

"We'll go, won't we, Luke?" Woody asked. "You got a good suit? I'll take mine."

"Yes, I'll pack a suit."

"Good deal."

Police departments seemed to be losing officers in the line of duty all too often lately. The SLO officer had just stepped out of his cruiser when the driver in the car he'd pulled over jumped out and started shooting. He was killed instantly.

Abby understood and felt their pain. An outstanding Long Beach officer had been murdered in cold blood a few years ago when he and his partner were ambushed while on patrol. A gang member shot up the patrol car with an assault rifle. It was a miracle his partner had survived.

Abby also knew the SLO guys would be hurting and angry. She realized that this might be a tough case to get a foothold on if they had to tiptoe around bruised egos.

"At any rate," Orson said, "you'll head up the coast for a couple of days and see what you can do."

All five of them began considering the evidence and planning their investigation. By lunchtime, they were finished with preliminaries and down to their travel schedule. They'd leave the next morning.

⸻▬▶

Abby arranged for her friend Jessica to house- and dog-sit for her while she was in San Luis Obispo. She'd gotten so attached to little Bandit she almost made the decision to bring him along but knew that would not be fair to him, especially if he had to be locked up in the car for periods of time.

"Don't worry about him," Jessica said as Abby hugged Bandit close to her face. "We're pals. He'll be fine."

"I know," she said, handing the dog over. "I will miss him, though, and I don't know for sure how long I'll be gone."

"No worries. I love it here. Just go catch bad guys."

CHAPTER

13

THE NEXT MORNING, Luke picked up the rental car, so he had driving responsibilities. He stopped for Abby first.

"I didn't know Faye had a law degree," Abby said when she got in the car.

"Uh, yeah." Luke cast a sideways glance her way, not sure where this was going. "She never took the bar, but she had a couple years' experience working with the FBI in West LA before she got married. I think that's where Orson met her."

"So that's why you asked her to work with us?"

"Orson asked. I found out about the same time you did. We've been delayed starting this task force once already, and he didn't want to delay us again. Faye's pretty savvy; she'll catch on quick. And Orson will find a permanent replacement for Duke soon, I'm sure."

"Would Faye want the job on a permanent basis if it came to that?"

"I doubt it. She loves what she does and where she does it. I was kind of surprised she came down here just to help."

It seemed as though Abby had more to say, but Luke was

pulling into Woody's driveway and that ended the conversation. Luke wondered if Abby was bothered by Faye's presence. Yesterday morning he'd been listening to Faye tell him about her case with the missing woman. She was no longer missing; her body had been found in the trunk of her car. He felt bad for Faye, but she was handling it well because the woman's exboyfriend was in custody and there was a lot of good evidence to keep him in jail. He hoped Abby didn't misconstrue anything.

At least Faye wouldn't be making the trip with them to San Luis Obispo. She would do what Duke Keller had planned to do: stay in Long Beach, where she would review cases coming into the squad and be available to answer any legal questions the investigators might have about the case they were working.

On the drive north the topic of conversation swung back and forth between their new case, the funeral, and the old cold case, the Triple Seven.

"So what did your uncle Simon have to say when you went to visit him?" Woody asked.

Luke listened while Abby told Woody what he had already heard. It didn't sound any more plausible the second time.

"I still don't get his reasoning," Luke said. "Why would Alyssa switch the blame for the hit-and-run to Rollins? Innuendo about a fatal hit-and-run like that would damage him way more than if she copped to her own mistake, if she even had a mistake to hide."

"I agree," Woody said. "Sounds like Simon is off base. I know Alyssa didn't want anything—and I mean anything—to damage Lowell. Why even remotely insinuate something that juicy about Lowell?"

Abby sighed and Luke thought she looked slightly irritated.

No, frustrated. Was she grasping at this because she desperately wanted to get something on Alyssa? He hoped the answer was no.

"Simon's line of thought was that Sanders might have been getting close to her secret, so she tossed him that bone to get him off the scent," Abby said. "She didn't want to catch any heat, especially from a lowlife like Sanders. He was a gnat she didn't want buzzing around. She probably feared that if he kept looking into her life, he'd find something, but he'd never find anything in Lowell's life."

She looked from Luke to Woody in the backseat, and Luke bet she could see that neither one of them was buying it.

"Hey, Alyssa may have fed him the lie for a reason then that makes no sense now. And think about it: blowing up the hit-and-run like that, to something that never happened that way, made a rabbit trail," she explained. "Opposition research could go crazy trying to prove it but would not be able to. Meanwhile, whatever was in Alyssa's past stayed hidden."

"So you mean that if people were busy digging into Lowell's and Buck's pasts for the ghost event, they'd miss the real story?" Woody scratched his head, still not completely convinced, Luke thought.

"Yep, her crime stays in the shadows," Abby said. "Because no one is looking for it."

"Okay," Woody said. "I can buy that."

Luke shook his head. "I'm still not on board. I don't mind looking to see if Alyssa is hiding something, but I don't want you to get your hopes up."

"Fair enough," Abby said. "There does seem to be a lot to look into when it comes to Alyssa. Something else comes to mind from my conversation with Simon. I wonder how far that hit-and-run story was even circulated. I don't believe it was ever common knowledge."

"It wasn't," Woody said. "If a story like that was going around back then, I would have heard about it. There's never been a hint in any media stories that Lowell had a skeleton in his closet."

"Only George Sanders knew that story?" Luke asked, now seeing that as odd.

"As far as I know. I don't think it ever came up in the original Triple Seven investigation," Abby said. "Sanders was always a petty criminal from what my uncle said. Maybe there was a reason he needed to be misdirected by Alyssa, a reason like Simon thought, that made sense to her then but doesn't now."

"So you think it's possible that somehow your mother and father discovered what Alyssa was really hiding and that was why they were murdered?" Luke asked.

Abby nodded. "Yes, I do. I mean, we don't really know what was actually said in the restaurant before the shooting started."

Luke briefly met her eyes. He could agree with that. "No, we don't."

"Alyssa is from Templeton, and it's close to where we're going. Maybe we'll have time to ask questions," Abby said. "Take a couple of days for a side trip."

Some surreptitious question asking on the side couldn't hurt anything, Luke decided. If it didn't interfere with the case at hand.

"I might bow out on that side excursion," Woody said.

"Why?"

"Sheesh, I'm missing Zena already. Not going to be a day away from her longer than I have to."

Abby laughed at that, and it did Luke's heart good to hear the sound. But he had something on his mind and wanted to get the question out before they got to town.

"What about the funeral? I've been to military funerals, but . . ."

The car went quiet. He knew enough cops to understand that when one went down in the line of duty, they all felt it, no matter the department, no matter the assignment. But he'd never been to a cop funeral and wasn't sure what to expect. Part of him wondered if it was even his place to go.

"Probably similar. It's a funeral," Abby said, looking out her window. "It will be hard and sad and sad again because of the stories and remembrances."

"I'm not sure if it's my place to attend."

"Of course it is," Woody said. "You're close enough to this brotherhood to belong and to pay your respects."

Abby put her hand on his arm, and their eyes locked. "Just being there, saying you understand and that you respect the job cops do, will mean a lot."

"I certainly do respect all you guys."

"Then bring a lot of Kleenex," Woody said.

CHAPTER

14

THE SAN LUIS OBISPO PD was a somber place, kind of what Abby expected. All the badges she saw bore black ribbons across them and the department flag was at half-staff. The funeral was two days from now on Thursday, and today the grief was palpable. The desk sergeant gave Abby a flyer with the arrangements spelled out. She and the guys planned to attend the church service but not the graveside service. For Abby, the handing over of the folded flag at the graveside, especially if it was to a small child, was always too devastatingly sad.

They'd arrived in San Luis Obispo around 1 p.m., and their first stop had been the police station. The original investigators involved in the case had retired, but SLOPD had copied the pertinent reports and interview transcripts for Ciara's case onto a couple of thumb drives. The interviews that were videotaped were copied to a DVD. There was also a detailed hard copy summary of the case and a box of miscellaneous items, DVDs of copied news footage, and due diligence reports. The desk sergeant told them that since physical evidence was stored in another location, the boxes of physical evidence would not be available for viewing until tomorrow. Physical evidence could not be removed from the station.

For the most part, the reception was cool but cooperative. After the sergeant gave them everything, they received a curt briefing by a young SLO investigator who did wish them luck. When the briefing was over, they gathered the information and put it in the car. They ate a late lunch, then checked in at a hotel close to the college. They were given private access to a small conference room, and there they set up a whiteboard and organized the case materials.

There was a lot to review, so they began with the written summaries and then moved to the videotaped interviews. Particularly distressing for Abby was the autopsy report. Ciara was basically a skeleton, reminding her of her own father's remains. It made her wonder if there was something Ciara had left that the other investigators had missed. Abby's father had left her a letter leading right to his killer. The original investigators in Ciara's case hadn't found any such thing, but maybe if they looked closely, there'd be a clue somewhere, something that would make them as fortunate in this case.

After they felt they had a grip on the written case files, they began to discuss the suspects.

"Harkin's interview transcript comes off as defensive and evasive," Luke observed.

"I agree, but Chaz Considine's bugs me more than Harkin's," Abby said.

"Don't like the pretty boy?" Woody scratched his chin and Abby knew by his expression he didn't like Chaz any more than she did.

"I don't. His mother ran interference for him when the police came knocking. She had him lawyered up immediately, and to me, that means guilty."

"I noticed that." He held up the one-page transcript of Considine's interview. "The police got him to answer a total of three questions before she stopped the interview and called a lawyer. It also says here that the police dog led them to his house, but Mom wouldn't allow them in."

"That's big. And they couldn't get a judge to sign a search warrant. Mom had some clout." Abby glanced over the report in her hand.

"What's he been up to since?" Luke asked.

"There are due diligence reviews, but they concentrate on Harkin; he's the one they keyed on. Nothing current on Considine," Abby said.

"Maybe that's where we need to start, with Considine. Is there any note as to why they weren't as suspicious of him as we are?" Woody asked.

Abby nodded. "They couldn't find a motive. There's a summary of statements made by people who knew the two of them. They never fought. Seemed like the perfect couple."

"Anyone could have said that about any of my marriages at the beginning," Woody said. "By the end murder was an option, but divorce came first."

Luke and Abby laughed.

"Like I said," Abby continued, "I get the impression that Mom was connected, powerful, and wealthy. The lawyers she hired were pricey. I've heard of them; they represented that wealthy kid who was spiking women's drinks with the date rape drug."

"That multimillion-dollar trust fund brat from a couple of years ago?" Woody made a face.

"Yep. Maybe that played into the cops' focus. Mom was adamant she didn't want her son's reputation ruined by specious allegations. She demanded cold, hard evidence before she'd let investigators near Chaz again."

"Whereas Harkin was a dirtbag who lied about his past to get a job. He'd look good as the sick groundhog who killed the coed. Maybe he hit on her and she rejected him, so fearing he'd lose his job, he killed her," Woody said. "After all, people are often murdered for less."

"Hmm." Abby clicked through several websites looking for current information on Considine. She had a need-to-know reason to access law enforcement databases, both local and the FBI's National Crime Information Center, and she quickly found out a lot about him.

"Chaz has been arrested six times since 1996. Three for DUI, and his driver's license is suspended. He's got a battery charge and two domestic violence raps."

"He do any time?" Luke asked, looking over her shoulder.

"No, looks like the worst he got was a sentence to take an anger management class. He doesn't live in San Luis Obispo anymore; he lives in Los Osos."

"That's close," Woody observed, pointing to a map of the area they'd tacked up. "It's here by the water."

"I'd like to talk to both Harkin and Considine," Abby said. "What say we start with Considine?"

"Works for me," Woody said.

"That is assuming he'll talk to us," Luke said.

"Can't hurt to ask. Let's see if his contact information here is current." Abby took out her cell phone and called the number listed for Considine.

After she identified herself, the line went silent.

"Mr. Considine, are you still there?"

He cleared his throat. "Yeah, I'm still here. Why are you calling me now?"

"We're taking another look at Ciara's case. That means reinterviewing everyone we can. You were the—"

"Are you going to talk to that moron who killed her? Horrible Harkin?"

"We're going to talk to everyone. You were the last person to see Ciara alive. Can we meet with you, say tomorrow morning?"

"You're barking up the wrong tree with me, sweetie. Horrible Harkin is your man—ask anyone."

"Like I said, we'll be asking everyone. What time tomorrow will work for you?"

Considine stalled but finally said, "I can spot you a few minutes at breakfast. Place called the Coffee Pot down in Morro Bay. Shouldn't have a problem finding it. Nine o'clock."

Abby agreed and broke the connection. "He's certain it was Harkin," she said with a shake of her head.

"Glad he agreed to meet," Luke said, standing. "Now, let's take a walk around the campus before it gets too dark. Get a lay of the land."

"You two go ahead," Woody said. "I'll order a pizza, and dinner will be ready when you get back."

Abby looked at Luke, glad for the change in pace. She needed to stretch her legs and they needed to visualize the last area Ciara was seen.

Just then Luke's phone rang.

"Oh, hello, Faye." He stepped away from the door to talk. "Yeah, we got here fine. We're all set up and working. . . . What's that? . . . Oh, okay. Give him Woody's number. . . . Great. Talk to you later." He closed the phone and pointed at Woody. "A local reporter called the office and asked about us and the case. He's going to call you and set up an interview time. You up for that?"

"You bet," Woody said.

Luke turned to Abby. "Ready for our walk-through?"

Abby nodded, trying to fight back the resentment. Faye wasn't with them physically, but she was still present. *Why does that bug me so much?* she wondered.

CHAPTER

15

"**GOOD IDEA PICKING** a hotel within walking distance of the college," Abby said as she and Luke made their way across the hotel parking lot.

"You'll have to thank Faye for that," he said. "It was her call."

She nodded and started to say something but stopped.

A stray thought crossed Luke's mind, that Abby was uncomfortable working with Faye. *No*, he told himself, *that can't be it.* He ignored the thought and concentrated on the job at hand.

He liked working with Woody, but right now he wanted to hear Abby's insights on the case. Abby had a keen mind and was a good, thorough investigator. He wanted to solve this case, and circumstances found him happy that the man had decided to stay in only because Luke would be able to listen and watch her process things up close and personal.

Cal Poly was a large, sprawling campus on the north side of San Luis Obispo. They had with them a map of the area, with the pertinent locations marked by the original investigators. Ciara had attended a party at a fraternity the night she disappeared, so they headed to the address of the fraternity to retrace the steps she took back to her apartment.

It was dusk now, but mild and a truly beautiful evening, warm for late January and nice. A surprise impulse to reach out and grasp Abby's hand stymied Luke for an instant, and he was glad when her voice broke his train of thought.

"So what was Maddie's take on you being away from home on this case?" she asked.

"She was okay with it, after I assured her I would not miss her party, and that no earthquake was going to flatten the house."

"Oh, good play, Dad." She laughed, and Luke smiled.

"That movie was something, wasn't it?" she asked. "I could feel the ground shaking even after we left the theater."

They'd crossed the main streets and were on the southern edge of the campus now, an area crowded with student housing, fraternities, and apartment complexes. Ciara had rented at the Foothill Garden Apartments, about a block and a half away from the fraternity.

"It was definitely a great disaster film. I almost regretted taking Maddie, but as it was, we had a talk about whose palm we're in."

"Ah." Abby looked at him, eyes dancing. "Wise man. I want to have kids someday, but I have to admit when I see how much there is in this world to be afraid of . . ." Her voice trailed off.

"You know that we're safe in God's hands. Children are a gift, and I cherish my gift of Maddie."

Abby stopped, the brightness fading from her eyes and seriousness dropping like a curtain over her features. Luke held her gaze and his breath, fighting the urge to pull her close.

"I believe that, and I know it," she said. "But look at the two of us. We both know how painful life can be in this fallen world for kids, even being safe in God's hand. I lost my parents and Maddie lost her mother."

Nodding, Luke said, "Faith is hard sometimes—I don't deny that. But what keeps me sane is the knowledge that even though I might not have all the answers, God does."

Abby looked away. When she turned back, a half smile played on her lips. "Everything works together for good?"

"'For those who are called according to his purpose,'" Luke finished the verse from the book of Romans. "I guess we need to keep doing what we're doing, fighting the good fight, catching the bad guys."

"Works for me," she said with a tilt of her head. She pointed in the direction the map indicated and stepped forward. "Let's try to finish this walk-through before it gets dark."

Luke fell into step with her, feeling a comradeship, warm and strong, and praying for wisdom and insight into this fascinating and capable woman.

When they reached the fraternity, they stopped and looked around.

"It's dense here," Luke said. "If something happened to Ciara here in the street or on the sidewalk, someone would have seen or heard something."

"I agree." Abby looked all around. "And there were probably a hundred partygoers. A lot of people did say they saw her leaving with her boyfriend."

Luke nodded. "She crossed the street with him and headed for her apartment . . ."

Abby finished for him, "Where Considine says he left her and then went straight home. His mother corroborated his story. That information made the cops believe he did not have the time to kill her and dump her body."

"Even if he were responsible for her death," Luke said, "it didn't happen at the party. I doubt he would have done anything with all the people in attendance at the party watching."

"True," Abby said as they checked the map, following the path that Chaz had told the police he'd walked with Ciara back to her apartment. "Let's find the apartment."

They crossed the street to the Foothill Garden Apartments, a large complex that looked to Luke like dorms or public housing. Adjacent and just past the complex, there were a lot of trees, hidden places where a predator could lurk.

"You've been quiet," Luke said after he and Abby had walked wherever they could around the complex.

"I'm wondering what a college groundskeeper would be doing over here."

"Good question. On his way home from work?"

"As I recall, he took care of the pool." She considered the map again. "That's this way, west of here. And he should have been off work and home long before the frat party started."

Luke stepped close and looked where she was concentrating. "Investigators would have asked him if he had business near the apartment complex."

Abby frowned. "Yeah, they should have, and he could have lied. I read somewhere that they believed he probably stalked her, but they had no proof of that."

"His background would make that believable, the background he lied about."

"It would have convinced me," Abby said. "Lying about

something like sexual battery definitely moved the spotlight to him, that's for sure."

"We need to talk to him, get a feel for his veracity."

"Or lack thereof." Abby looked at him and smiled. "Maybe we can try Harkin tomorrow after we talk to Considine. You ready for pizza?"

"You bet. Too dark to see much more now anyway." He saw something in her eyes that intrigued him. "You think of something you might want to share?"

She looked away and did a circle on the sidewalk. "The latest case review made a note that not much has changed here, no new buildings. So we're seeing pretty much what they saw originally. Look around at how close everything is. Those first investigators would have to be blind to miss this. A stranger grabbing Ciara . . . well, I'd scream if a stranger grabbed me."

"People would have heard. Even Chaz said that she wasn't intoxicated."

"Right. I'd bet money that she knew the person who killed her. If Chaz wasn't the guy, there's another suspect we have to find."

CHAPTER

16

WHEN THEY RETURNED to the hotel, they found that Woody had company. The reporter Faye had given them a heads-up about.

"I want you two to meet Josh Federer, reporter for the *Tribune* here in SLO." Woody introduced a young guy. Abby guessed he was in his early thirties. He had earrings in both ears and tattoos covering both arms. She couldn't help but think about Gunther and the contrast with this young reporter.

"He's writing an article about us and Ciara's case."

Abby wasn't surprised he'd gotten to them so fast. Orson had told them there would be some media attention regarding their case; it was big when Ciara disappeared and big when her remains were discovered. Abby didn't mind the media attention. She felt it could only help, especially with a cold case. It might encourage past reticent witnesses to call.

"Nice to meet you guys," Josh said. He had on his head an old-style fedora, with the brim turned up all the way around and a pencil in the hatband. "I read up on your team. Think you can solve this case?"

"We'll do our best," Woody said.

They gave him a good overview, stressing that they had high hopes the case would be solved without telling him exactly where they'd be looking. He knew a lot about it.

"I'm familiar with the case. I was in grade school when everything went down with that sex offender they originally suspected," Federer explained. "He was a monster. It's scary to think that there could be another one like him out there."

"As far as we know, Ciara was this perp's only victim. That doesn't point to a predator," Abby said.

"I guess that makes sense," Federer said, "and it kinda validates my own theory that the boyfriend did it."

"Why do you say that?" Luke asked.

"Isn't it always the boyfriend or the husband?"

"That's where we look first. Unfortunately means and motive often live at home."

There was a knock at the door, and Federer checked his watch. "Well, I'll leave you to it. This will be in print tomorrow and online later tonight. The tip line phone number you gave me will be both places, so you might get calls as early as tonight from those Internet readers with insomnia. Thank you, guys, for your time, and good luck." He tipped his hat and opened the door to the pizza guy standing there with dinner.

"Pizza!" Abby clapped. "I'm starved."

As they dug into dinner, Luke told Woody about the walking tour.

"I watched interviews until the reporter showed up. They taped interviews with ten male subjects regarding Ciara's disappearance," Woody said. "Of the several I watched, Chaz and Jasper were not the only hinky ones. And like we saw on paper, Chaz's was also the shortest."

Abby chewed her pizza and thought about this. "Something in the interviews strike you as odd?"

"Haven't gone through all of them yet, but there's another rich kid who bugs me. A kid named J. P. Winnen."

"That name rings a bell," Abby said. "I remember from the file picture he looked cocky."

"The pictures in the file are much clearer than some of the videotaped interviews," Woody said. "They aren't the high-quality digital stuff we're used to now. In a few of them it was even hard to discern facial expressions. The camera was mounted high in the corner, so it's looking down at the room."

"Why don't we just call the original investigators and ask them their impressions?" Luke asked.

Abby winced. "And tell them they missed something that we found on the first day we had the notes?" She gave an exaggerated shake of her head.

"But they're professionals—"

Woody snorted. "They're also human, with human egos. And we already know from Orson some egos are still stinging."

Luke looked at Abby.

She shrugged. "If it were me—I hate to say it—I'd be defensive. Maybe after a couple of days, if I was certain you'd looked through everything, I wouldn't be prickly. But the first night?" She shook her head. "I want to have more before I bring up something like this. Even though the main investigators have retired, these guys have lived with this case for twenty years."

"I guess I can see your point."

"They took detailed reports and we can rewatch the interviews. If there is really something to move on, we'll call them."

She put the DVD with all the interviews into her laptop. She skipped the first two, which were Harkin and Considine, and started with the third. It wasn't until she got to the fourth interview that she got a strange vibe and understood what Woody meant. When it finished, she looked to Woody and Luke.

"Something about Winnen bothers me too," she said as she got up to sift through some of the paperwork they had in relation to the case.

"Told ya. A snot-nosed, spoiled college frat boy," Woody said. "Said basically the same as everyone else: 'Yes, I saw her at the party. She wasn't drunk. Blah, blah, blah.' But there's something there."

"He contradicts himself. In the first interview he says he didn't see Chaz and Ciara leave the party, but in the second interview he says that he did and they were happy campers."

"I saw that," Woody said. "They accepted his explanation that he was just confused."

Abby found the summary she was looking for. "He said he was Considine's best friend; in fact they were roommates until he pledged the fraternity. When he left for the fraternity, Considine moved back home. Here it is, in one of the due diligence reviews." She held it up. "Considine and this kid, J. P. Winnen, were the only close acquaintances, the only two who knew Ciara well. The others were just partygoers." She looked up at Luke and Woody and saw two blank expressions.

"I'm not following you," Luke said.

"Didn't you see how fidgety this kid was? Doesn't appear as if he ever met the interviewer's eyes. He was evasive and cocky, even more so than Considine. I'm with Woody. We need to dig into this."

The three of them watched the interviews over and over,

Abby wishing she'd been there at the time to press the young men, force them to tell the truth. It was late when they gave up and called it a night. Abby slept fitfully, dreaming of grainy black-and-white murder interviews.

CHAPTER

17

LOS OSOS, WHERE CONSIDINE now lived, was a small, quiet community on the back bay about thirteen miles from San Luis Obispo. Luke drove through Los Osos on the way to Morro Bay, taking the scenic route to the meeting to get a feeling for the place. Overall, it looked like a peaceful bedroom community.

The road bisecting Los Osos eventually curved around the back bay and passed wetlands, cut through a campground, and meandered by a marina before it gave way to Morro Bay. As Luke rounded a curve, the bay and the huge rock Morro Bay was known for came into view, and it was impressive as he dropped down toward the water to Front Street.

Luke found the restaurant without any trouble. It was in the midst of a strand of businesses, restaurants, and gift shops, an aquarium, and a couple of sportfishing outfits on Front Street. Abby saw an advertisement for rental kayaks on the way and thought wistfully how nice it would be to be out on the water on a sunny day. Right now there was a heavy fog shroud over everything.

"Cute place," Woody said as they got out of the car.

Abby nodded in agreement as she pulled on her sweatshirt. It was cold this close to the water, way chillier than SLO. They'd already eaten breakfast, intending to concentrate on the interview with Considine. She was a bit suspicious that he agreed to talk to them so readily. He'd stonewalled so completely when Ciara went missing, and even in the past twenty years there had been no indication that he suddenly became cooperative. Would he be at all helpful?

The restaurant was crowded, and Abby wondered if this was the guy's plan: pretend to cooperate but pick a distracting place so a substantive interview was impossible. She realized as she looked around the quirky, noisy place, trying to pick Considine out, she already didn't like the guy. Time to stop that and be objective.

"Is that him?" Luke pointed to the far side of the restaurant. But it was a table of two men, one bent down talking earnestly to the other, who appeared be listening but who was looking out the window at the street.

"Can I help you?" A pretty young woman stepped up with menus.

"We're supposed to meet someone."

"Oh, you must be here for Chaz." She gestured with the menus. "That's him over by the window, with J. P. He's expecting you." She moved on to the people who'd walked in behind them.

Abby looked at Luke. "Good call. You think J. P. is J. P. Winnen?"

He arched an eyebrow. "Let's find out."

The three of them threaded their way across the restaurant. Considine saw them and tapped J. P. on the shoulder. He looked up and met Abby's gaze with narrowed eyes. There was nothing current in the file about him, but she'd bet money he was a cop or ex-military because of the hard, appraising stare he gave her.

J. P. stood as they reached the table. "You guys must be the out-of-town cold case people." His body language was tense and his territorial tone suggested he didn't have much respect for them. His bald head shone and his thick neck and tight biceps said he was a powerful man. Abby thought odds were good he pumped iron and wondered if the acne dotting his face was a sign that he abused steroids.

Woody introduced everyone, but Considine didn't stand and Winnen made no effort to shake hands.

Abby gave him her own steely cop stare and decided she wasn't going to let this chance encounter go to waste.

"You were interviewed regarding the disappearance of Ciara as well, weren't you?"

"I was at the same party." Placing his hands on hips, he gave her a cold look of disdain. "Along with about a hundred other people."

"But you were considered a suspect, just like Mr. Considine."

"Your point?"

"You're someone we'd like to speak to as well. Your taped interview shows that you were less than cooperative back then. Why was that?"

A muscle jumped in his jaw, and Abby felt Luke tense at her shoulder. J. P. Winnen definitely had anger management issues.

"I was a kid, a stupid kid." His tone was clipped now, as if it was taking monumental effort to maintain control. "I've grown up, and I've got nothing new to add to that interview. You have a problem with that, talk to my boss. She's the chief of police here. I'm a cop now." He looked down at Considine. "I've got to get to work. Remember what I said, Chaz." He turned and pushed his way past Luke and Woody, offering Abby a glare that said, "I dare you to stop me."

She said nothing and let him go, mentally etching his name on her suspect list, cop or not.

"He's okay," Considine said. "Just protective. Doesn't think out-of-towners should investigate our crimes." He cleared his throat. "I mean, local crimes."

Talk about a Freudian slip, Abby thought as she cast a glance at Luke, who cocked an eyebrow. Abby and Luke sat across from Considine while Woody sat next to him.

"Thanks for meeting with us," Woody said. Abby noted he was using his best "I'm an officer and your friend" voice.

"No problem. It has always bugged me that Ciara's killer wasn't caught. She was a cute girl, a nice girl. I would have married her." He drained his coffee and then raised his mug. "Shelia, more coffee." Then to Abby and Luke, "You guys want coffee?"

Abby shook her head and took note of Considine's countenance. Gone was the pretty boy face and the cocky smirk. The years had left him with a receding hairline and a potbelly. His eyes were bloodshot and she saw a slight tremor in his hands. In spite of all the coffee he'd probably drunk, she could still smell the alcohol. She bet he'd easily blow over the legal limit if she had a Breathalyzer here with her. And she was certain he hadn't had a drink yet this morning. He was still drunk from the night before. A functional alcoholic, she decided.

"What was it Mr. Winnen told you?" Abby asked as Shelia poured coffee.

"Huh?" He gulped the strong-smelling brew.

"Winnen said to remember what he told you," Luke said. "What was that?"

Considine waved his hand as if fanning away a foul smell. "Nothing about this. What were you going to ask me?"

"What else can you tell us about the night Ciara went missing?"

"Okay, but first, are you, like, going to talk to Harkin as well?"

"Yes."

"Then I'll tell you what I remember. But I know he's the killer. And you're wasting your time with me, but I guess it's your time to waste."

CHAPTER

18

"**DO YOU WANT** to drop in on Harkin like we talked about?" Luke asked as they reached the car outside the Coffee Pot.

Abby was still stuck on the talk with Considine and let the question fall to Woody. They'd learned nothing new from the man. He'd stonewalled twenty years ago, and today he talked in circles. Kept insisting they'd be married now if Ciara hadn't been taken from him. Abby was even more convinced he was hiding something. There was a faint aura of deception on the taped interview with the guy and now, two decades later, it was obvious that something was eating away at him.

Was he their killer? After all this time they'd need to find a strong motive and some solid proof or get an unambiguous confession in order to prosecute.

Her thoughts were drawn back to Kelsey Cox in a rush, and her weak confession stirred familiar anger inside. As always, Abby tried to mellow by reminding herself that Cox would at least serve time in prison. But was it really fair that because of the passage of time the best they could get was partial truth and not the whole story? What would they be able to get for Ciara?

"I'd like to go over the physical evidence," she heard Woody say. "It should be ready by now. I'll look it over and see if I can get out some discreet inquiries to the locals. Why don't you drop me at the PD and I'll do that while you two visit Harkin."

Luke looked at Abby. "Sound good to you?"

She smiled. "Yeah, it's a good idea," she said to Woody. "Glad we brought you along."

Woody gave her a raspberry for that comment and they all laughed as they got back in the car.

"Think Woody will get people to talk?" Luke asked after they dropped Woody off and were on the way to Harkin's property in Atascadero. They'd discussed the interaction with both Considine and Winnen on the way back from San Luis Obispo and agreed that it would be a good idea to get the San Luis cops' impressions of both men as adults, twenty years later. Woody planned to ask around tactfully about J. P. and Chaz while he looked over the physical evidence.

"Oh yeah," Abby said. "Trust me, cops are gossips. For people who deal with facts and hard evidence all day long, they're certainly not reticent to pass on juicy, unsubstantiated gossip about their own. And Woody will have cachet because of his time on the job, even though we're out-of-towners. If he finds someone close to his generation and gets them to talk, he'll learn everything there is to know about J. P. Winnen."

Luke frowned. "Really?"

"Yep, when I was a rookie, one of the first things Woody warned me about was the gossip train. He said a PD was like a Peyton Place. Between the cops, the dispatchers, and the civilian employees, everybody's business was everybody else's, so be careful."

Luke laughed. "Bill never mentioned that to me."

"Bill probably stays out of it. I did my best, but Woody likes to sit around and tell war stories, and that invariably winds down into gossiping about who did what with whom and where."

"Learn something new every day." He glanced at her and his gaze met her dazzling smile that made his heart skip a beat. Things had been going so well during this trip. And this case invigorated him. He'd always enjoyed working by himself but was pleasantly surprised how great it was to be part of a team, a good team. The hope—no, he realized that it wasn't simple hope; it was confidence. He had confidence in himself and the team. They'd get answers—he was sure of it.

GPS told him how to get to Harkin's place. The man had purchased five acres off of Highway 41 and put a mobile home on it. Luke remembered reading in one of the due diligence reports that Harkin had fenced the place in and become a hoarder, living like a hermit surrounded by piles of junk. He found the highway easily enough and exited the freeway.

"Think we should have called him?" Abby asked.

Luke shook his head. "I've found that surprise often works better. Not always, but I think the odds are in our favor. Besides, all the current reports said he's become a hermit, so I bet he's home."

Abby nodded. "I saw that. The last time anyone spoke to him he complained that he was a marked man, that he couldn't go anywhere or do anything without people looking at him as if he were a cold-blooded killer."

"Did you find anything in there about how he supports himself? I doubt the settlement money has lasted this long."

"I saw a line in the last due diligence report that he applied for disability and lives on that. Slow down. I think we're coming up on it now." Abby beat Garmin by a second. Luke liked to listen to her voice more than the annoying mechanical one.

He turned off the highway and the blacktop gave way to dirt road. Garmin told him that they had three quarters of a mile to go. The drive ended at a large wrought-iron gate plastered with No Trespassing signs. There were several big satellite dishes on the roof.

Luke pulled off to the side and parked the car. "Looks like he's got an intercom set up. Let's see if he answers."

He noted the terrain as he got out of the car. Oak trees and dry scrub brush lined the driveway that ran up to a double-wide, weathered mobile home. The path to the front door was clear, but on either side, piles of rusty junk were layered. There were old cars, several refrigerators with the doors removed, chairs, benches, and stacks of other stuff that Luke couldn't identify.

"Eww," Abby said. "This reminds me of one of those reality shows."

"Sure does." He hit the intercom button and stepped aside for Abby to speak. "You might have better luck, says the male chauvinist who thinks this guy will more readily speak to a woman."

"I must be a chauvinist too, because I agree."

The intercom crackled to life. "Who's there?"

"Investigator Abby Hart to speak to Jasper Harkin."

"Investigator?" Then silence for several seconds.

"He's coming out onto the porch," Luke said.

Abby stepped next to him for a better view of the porch. "He's changed," she said.

Luke grunted in agreement. On the interview tape Harkin had been rail thin. The man stepping off the porch of the mobile home was obese, huge. He used a cane to climb down the stairs and then gingerly sat his bulk on a motorized wheelchair before heading their way.

He reached the gate and squinted at Abby through the bars. "What do you want?"

"I want to talk to you about Ciara."

"I'm done talking about that."

He started to turn around when Abby surprised Luke by saying, "What if I told you that I know you didn't do it?"

ABBY HELD HER breath while Harkin slowly turned back toward them.

"You're just saying that. Everybody thinks I'm guilty. Everyone hates me." His fat chin quivered, and for a moment he reminded Abby of a child hurt by kids on the playground.

"I don't know you," Abby said. "All I know is what I read in the reports, and I don't believe you're Ciara's killer."

In the chubby-cheeked face, his eyes blinked and he moved the chair as close as he could to the gate. "So what do you want with me? Can you make people stop hating me?"

"I want to hear, in your own words, face-to-face, what happened that night, the night Ciara disappeared."

He looked from Abby to Luke. "Just who are you people?"

Luke explained, and both he and Abby showed him their IDs.

"From Long Beach? Investigating crimes here?" He sighed and spit off to the right. "Maybe I'd have a chance with someone who's not from here, someone objective."

He steered his chair sideways and keyed in a combination. The gate opened. "Come on up to the house. I'll talk to you."

Abby and Luke followed Harkin into the mobile home.

Woody settled into his chair, evidence spread out in front of him. He sipped the station coffee, which was pretty good, and considered what was before him. Everything that had been with the body was bagged and tagged. After being in the ground for years, it was in bad shape. There was no chance of retrieving DNA off of anything. The body had been wrapped in a blanket and tied with rope and duct tape. Harkin's main responsibility had been the pool, and the blue rope found with the body resembled rope used on different pieces of equipment in the aquatic center and present in the college caretaker's shed. Badly decayed, the blanket was possibly of the type sold at various local retailers at the time. The tape was common gray duct tape.

The original investigators noted that what was telling was what was not present: earrings and an engagement ring.

Woody leafed through the paperwork. Considine had been the last person to see Ciara and he'd given a description of her, saying that she'd been wearing a ring he'd given her and unicorn earrings, which had been a birthday gift from her mother. No jewelry at all was found with the body.

The door to the conference room opened and Woody looked up. A gray-haired fellow in the uniform of a police volunteer stepped into the room.

"Investigator Woods?"

"Call me Woody. Can I help you?"

"Dean Axelson. You can call me Axe. That was my nickname when I was in the harness here." He closed the door.

"Axelson?" Woody shuffled some paper. "You were one of the originals on this."

"That I was. Spent thirty years here, retired two years ago, and then couldn't stand the quiet, you know?"

"I do, I do."

"I came back to work as a dinosaur. I set up those rolling speed checks you see around town now."

Woody knew the term *dinosaur*. In Long Beach it referred to a retired officer who came back to work part-time in a non-sworn capacity. It was probably the same here.

"I got my own form of dinosaur gig working with cold cases," Woody told him as Axe took a seat.

"That's what I heard. And they gave you Ciara's case. I hated to leave without closing that case. It was one that stayed with me."

Woody tried to read the guy. Was he angry that someone from another agency was working his investigation?

"You know, we're not here to step on any toes. It's not the glory of closing a case that we're after. We want closure for the family."

Axelson shrugged. "I'm glad you're here, actually. This tore up that girl's family." He lowered his voice and leaned close to Woody. "Politics in this city tied our hands. You won't have that problem."

"I do know that this destroyed her family. My boss tried to contact the mother." Woody flipped pages. "Dad is deceased; mother doesn't want to talk to anyone until the bad guy is in custody."

"If I can help at all, let me know."

"You can help—thanks. We had a couple of questions about your main suspects."

Axelson held up his hands. "Uh, I'd like to do this in another venue. Can I buy you lunch? Or stop by your hotel room?"

"I get you. I've got about another half hour of stuff to look through and notes to take and I don't have a car; my partners do."

"How about I stop back by in half an hour and lunch is on me."

"Great, thanks."

Axelson got up and left the room. Woody debated calling Abby but didn't want to interrupt anything she and Luke had going with Harkin. He considered Axelson's offer of help. The man had written a lot of the reports Woody had already read through. He could be a big help, but he obviously didn't want anyone at the station to hear what he had to say.

Politics, Woody thought. *That's what usually gums up the works.*

Woody hated politics.

CHAPTER 20

GIVEN THE STATE of the outside of Harkin's home, Luke braced himself for what they might find inside. Harkin didn't move real fast after he got off the chair and ambled up the steps with his cane. His bulk barely fit through the door.

Once inside, Luke was taken aback at the order there. There was still clutter on a monumental scale, but it was neatly stacked and organized. There were a lot of collectible-type toys and sports memorabilia, some in packages, some not. Everything was clean and dust free, and the mobile home itself neat with a fresh smell. There were also stacks of Twinkie boxes and assorted packaged cookies. And a huge flat-screen TV—at least sixty inches, Luke thought—took up half the living room.

Luke wondered about the tack Abby was taking with Harkin. Did she really believe that the man was completely innocent? Already he'd decided to stay quiet because Harkin seemed to be responding to Abby and he didn't want to interrupt the rapport.

Harkin settled his bulk into a large recliner, directly across from the flat-screen. "I can't offer you a seat. I never get visitors, so I'm not set up for them."

"That's okay," Abby said. "We won't be here long. Mr. Harkin, we're here to listen to your side of this story. You've been the main suspect for years. I saw your taped interview, but I'd like to hear it in person. Where were you the day Ciara disappeared; do you remember?"

Luke watched Harkin, amazed at how all the extra flesh distorted his features. The picture in the file was of a thin man, with narrow, close-set eyes and a sharp chin. The man seated before them was round, with folds of flesh and many chins.

"I'll never forget that day. I left work at 6 p.m. on the dot. I rode my bike to work back then and it was a nice evening, so I took the long way home and stopped off at the train station first."

"The train station—why?"

Harkin shrugged. "I used to like to watch the trains. I lived on the other side of the tracks, on George Street. I rented a room from a nice, older couple."

Luke considered this, trying to remember how far the train station was from the school. He made a note to check everything out on a map.

"How long were you at the station?"

"Until it got dark."

"Did you talk to anyone?"

"No. I just smoked a few cigarettes and rode home. My room had a private entrance, so the Garcias couldn't say when I got home."

Luke worked to keep his features blank, but something wasn't adding up. The guy in front of them didn't look or sound like a conniving sexual predator.

"Why did you lie to the university about your past arrest?"

Luke asked, noting Abby was just as interested as he was about an answer,

"I wanted a job. I knew they'd never hire me if they were aware I'd been arrested in Santa Barbara, where I lived before. I loved it there. After my arrest I couldn't get hired to pick up dog poop. I moved here and wanted to start over, so I took a chance and lied. I had good years at that job. No black marks. But after Ciara disappeared, they dug into everyone's past and found me out."

"One of the reports noted that in Santa Barbara you didn't work for the university but near it. They speculated that you had a thing for college girls, that you stalked them, and that's why you came to SLO, to Cal Poly, to hunt college girls," Abby said.

Luke observed that the guy didn't seem upset by the question. He looked down at his feet and seemed, if anything, chagrined.

"I admit I made a big mistake. And yeah, I did like looking at the college girls—forbidden fruit and all that." He hunched his big shoulders and Luke saw his eyes water. "I never stalked them. Never. I admit I went too far with a girl who said no, but she wasn't a college girl. She was my own age and you can check; I pleaded guilty to sexual battery, got community service, and did it all."

"I did see that," Abby said. "Do you think that's the only reason the police concentrated on you?"

"What do you mean?"

"Well, did you know Ciara?"

"Not at all. I worked in the aquatics center. The only students I saw on a regular basis were the ones who swam. I don't think I ever saw Ciara until the Missing poster was plastered everywhere. I'm sorry she's dead, but I might as well be dead also because of her. Everyone hates me. They all think I did it. I don't have a life anymore."

—————————▶

"Do you really believe he's innocent?" Luke asked Abby after they climbed back into the car to leave.

Abby sighed. "I do. I understand why they were so quick to pounce on him. But he's right. His arrest was minor—misdemeanor sexual battery—so he wasn't even required to register as a sex offender and he served no time."

"He lied."

Abby looked at Luke. "Do you think he's guilty?"

He considered her question for a minute. "Where there's smoke, there's fire. But I will admit he sounded sincere, and I can't see him as a cold-blooded killer."

"Add to that, he's been on everyone's radar all these years. If he were a stone-cold killer, I'd think there might be other victims, but there's nothing that would indicate any other victims."

"That we know of."

Abby shook her head. "Something else is going on here." She looked down as her phone buzzed with a text. "It's from Woody. He wants us to meet him at a restaurant."

"He say why?"

Abby chuckled. "Give him time. You know how long it takes him to text."

Luke laughed. "I gotcha."

"Here it is," Abby said after a few minutes. "He wants us to meet him at a place called Frank's Famous Hot Dogs. I'll input the address into the GPS."

"Nothing else?"

"No, just that it's about the case."

"Hope it's something to go on."

"Amen to that."

CHAPTER

21

THIRTY MINUTES LATER they pulled up to an old-fashioned diner-type place called Frank's Famous Hot Dogs.

Abby could see Woody and another man seated at an outdoor table. The weather change was dramatic. Where Morro Bay had been foggy and cold, in Atascadero and here in SLO it was pleasant—sunny and seventy-five degrees.

"There he is." She pointed.

"Looks like he found a friend," Luke said.

Abby shot Luke a smile as they got out and joined Woody.

Woody gestured to the mystery man. "This is Axelson, one of the original investigators."

Axelson stood. "Woody has told me all about you two." He extended his hand. "Detective Hart." He shook her hand and then turned to Luke. "Mr. Murphy."

"The Axe here has a lot to tell us about the investigation," Woody said. "Do you want to eat now or later? I've already eaten."

"I'm not that hungry." Abby turned to Luke. "But I could handle a Diet Coke."

"I'll grab us a couple."

He went inside, and as Abby sat down, she noticed Axelson's uniform.

"You're retired now?"

"Two years. Told Woody here I got tired of sitting around doing nothing, so I came back. Did you get any new information from Harkin?"

Abby glanced at Woody, not certain about this new guy. Sometimes she was too suspicious; it was hard to take the offer of help at face value. But Woody's expression said that the SLO cop could be trusted.

"He said the same thing that he's been saying for twenty years. Can I ask you something?"

"Shoot. I just want to help."

Luke returned with the drinks and Abby took a sip before asking.

"Harkin seemed to be your only strong suspect—at least he's the one the due diligence reports mention. Why?"

Axe cocked his head, a thoughtful expression on his face. "Can't say that I was ever certain it was him. At first, it seemed he was a good bet. He lied about a prior arrest; he was shaky in interview. You saw it?"

"I did, but he could have been nervous because he knew he was going to lose his job."

"Right, but we thought we had our man. He fit the profile: loner, prior arrest for sexual crime. And a couple of girls came forward to complain about the way he looked at them at the pool. There just was no hard evidence. We started surveillance, he got fired, and it all went downhill from there."

"He won a big settlement against you guys for harassment," Luke said.

Axelson's features hardened. "He didn't win; it never went to trial. The city caved, paid him to go away. That's different from winning. We had a chief back then who folded like a cheap suit." He paused, body language stiff, obviously upset. "Look, at the time, that crime was our most urgent to solve, but it became like the perfect storm of bad luck and bad decisions. Factor in politics and the case goes unsolved."

"I get you," Abby said, casting a glance at Luke and hoping he understood that often cops' hands got tied for stupid reasons.

"What about Considine?" she asked.

"There's a piece of work. And he's long been my pick for prime suspect. I'm sure you read that the dogs picked up Ciara's scent near his house. We wanted to search it, but his mom shut us down. Got the warrant quashed because Ciara was Chaz's girlfriend. Of course her scent was there; she'd been to the house often."

Abby nodded. "You're saying that you're sure it's Considine?"

"I'm saying that he needed to be pressed more at the time. If we could have gotten him alone in an interview, we might have gotten something from him."

"His mom wanted hard evidence."

Axelson snorted. "We had no crime scene and no body for fifteen years. Chaz knows more than he's said—a lot more. The problem was at the time, after the fiasco with Harkin, no one wanted to press him. And Considine's mom is well known here. She's a bulldog as a defense attorney, and she had the money to hire a great team for her son. The prosecutor was gun-shy; he'd okayed the surveillance on Harkin, and all that got him was the city bowing to pressure and paying the creep off. Basically our hands were tied; we couldn't do our job." He leaned forward. "You guys won't be hamstrung, though. You can press Considine."

"Where is his mother now?" Abby asked. "I'd love to talk to the woman."

"Oh, she's around, and knowing her, she'll step up and give you a call when she hears that you're working the case. She might even orchestrate a press conference and warn you to stay away from her baby."

Abby thought about that for a minute. "We talked to Considine this morning. We also met Winnen."

"J. P. Winnen?" Axelson arched his brows. "His nickname is Just Plain Whiner."

"He was Considine's best friend when Ciara disappeared. I think he might have some involvement here. Was he looked at in any way?"

"Everyone was looked at. Winnen's a jerk, but I never pegged him for a killer. I know they were friends, good friends. Mama Considine even paid for his lawyer, but he waived his rights and talked to us. Could he have had a role in Ciara's murder? Maybe. I do know that he is the one who originally pointed a finger at Harkin."

"What?" Abby's ears perked up. "I didn't read that in any report."

"You won't find it. One of the bad decisions I'll always regret. Winnen called us about a week after her disappearance. He brought Harkin to our attention. He was on the swim team.

He said he was familiar with Harkin and told us that he didn't like the way the guy looked at women when he was around the pool. We'd been looking at students and frat boys; we only checked into Harkin because of that tip. And then the other complaints came in. When we found Harkin's prior arrest . . . well, you know what happened next."

Abby nodded. They thought they had their man.

"You didn't write it down?" Woody asked.

Axelson put a hand to his forehead as if he had a headache. "We began an investigation into Harkin thinking it was a dead end—you know, rich kid pointing a finger at the workingman. But the arrest and the lie made us decide he was guilty, and I hate to say it—we weren't going to give Winnen the credit. And after everything went right rudder, to say we only investigated Harkin because of a tip another suspect gave us would have made us look more inept than we already did. It was just a mess all the way around."

"You call J. P. Winnen a whiner," Abby said. "Why is that?"

"His reputation since he became a cop. He claims that he decided on law enforcement because of Ciara. He was a polisci major at first. Supposedly her disappearance made him decide on a life of public service." Axelson cursed and made a face.

"You don't believe that?" Woody asked.

"Not for a minute. The guy is too self-serving. The law enforcement community around here is relatively small. We train together and work together often. Winnen whines about training—too much or not enough—he whines about the workload, on and on. Once we had a homicide barely outside his jurisdiction. Thing is, other officers on scene bet money that

Winnen moved the body over the line before calling it in so he didn't have to deal with it."

"Isn't that malicious gossip?" Woody asked.

"Maybe," Axelson conceded. "But gossip or not, the fact that a lot of guys thought it happened should tell you what the general consensus is about Winnen."

CHAPTER

22

BACK IN THE conference room at the hotel, after the meeting with Axelson, Abby, Woody, and Luke reviewed all the notes on Ciara's murder. To cover every base, they phoned and interviewed everyone they could, but some who'd been involved the first time around were unavailable or didn't want to have anything to do with the new investigation. The ones they did talk to had nothing new or different to add. The few they couldn't get ahold of Abby marked down to call later.

Abby was reasonably sure that those who refused were simply fed up with the concept of being "witnesses" and were done talking about the case. Nothing of consequence was gleaned from any of these reinterviews, and for her, Winnen and Considine were shaping up to be the money suspects. Abby watched and rewatched the interview tapes. They all wondered if they would be hearing from Mrs. Considine.

The tip line did ring, and one call raised their hopes sky-high. The woman calling wouldn't give her name, but she swore that she'd known Ciara and that Ciara was going to break up with Considine the night she was killed.

"That's news," Abby said after Woody told her and Luke about the call. "That would have been motive back then. No one at the time had said there was even a wrinkle in the relationship."

"I tried to get more from her," Woody said with a shrug. "But she gave me all we're gonna get."

"She sound legitimate?" Abby asked.

"She didn't sound crazy. Says she was a good friend of Ciara, and she knew this at the time, but Chaz's mom threatened her."

"I think we need to talk to the mom. Enough of waiting for her to call; we need a preemptive strike." Luke began to shuffle through paper to find contact information for Constance Considine, while Abby googled her.

"I've got it," Luke said. "She has an office not far from here."

Abby picked up the phone and was about to dial when there was a knock on the door.

Woody answered, and from where Abby was sitting, she saw a tall man in a suit.

"I represent Mrs. Considine. She'd like to have a word with you."

"With me?" Woody shoved a thumb in his chest and Abby had to hide a smirk. He was using his best "I'm just a dumb cop" voice in response to the man's condescending tone.

"She wants to speak to the entire cold case squad."

"Oh, thanks for the clarification. She's welcome here anytime."

"She wants you in her office."

"Not convenient right now. Maybe she should call and make an appointment." Woody started to close the door, but the man stopped him.

"I don't think you understand." He took one step into the

room, and Luke and Abby both stood as the atmosphere turned tense in a snap.

The man gave them a stare Abby felt was meant to intimidate.

He pointed to each of them. "Mrs. Considine is a busy woman. Right now is good for her."

Abby wanted to talk to Mrs. Considine, but she was not going to be intimidated. And she wasn't sure exactly what the woman was trying to prove with this type of power play. Was this the way the woman operated twenty years ago? Was that how she shut everyone up?

Luke stepped forward. "Like Investigator Woods explained, we're busy."

The man focused his laser stare on Luke. It was pretty useless because Luke gave one right back. They were both the same height and weight, but Abby would put her money on Luke.

"Do you people not understand English?"

"We understand fine," Luke chuckled. "Maybe you don't speak it so good. And maybe Mrs. Considine shouldn't be so heavy-handed."

The man started to reach into his jacket, but Luke stopped him. "Hold on there, bucko. Both my partners are armed. Don't be trying something stupid."

"I'm reaching for my phone." He pulled out his phone and punched in a number.

"They're all here, refusing your invitation." He listened briefly, then ended the call. "Mrs. Considine will be here momentarily." He backed up and stepped outside the room.

Abby and Luke exchanged confused glances. *What was all that about?* she wondered.

In a couple of minutes a striking woman, almost regal,

walked into the room. She was of average height, but the way she carried herself made her seem taller. Her dark hair was held back in a tight bun, and the dark-green skirt, matching shoes, jacket—all perfectly accessorized with classy pieces of jewelry—said money.

"Hello. Am I addressing the so-called cold case squad?"

———✦———

"It was a test," Considine said after everyone was settled around the conference table. Woody had quickly covered up their board and anything else they didn't want the woman to see.

"What kind of test?" Luke asked.

"Twenty years ago the police department here was intimidated because a predator won a lawsuit. They stopped trying to build a case against the animal who killed Ciara because they were afraid. I wanted to see if the same was true of you."

"I take it you realize now that we're not easily intimidated?" Abby asked.

"Yes. I believe you have a chance to finally put the right man behind bars."

"By right man, you mean Jasper Harkin."

"Yes. My son is innocent. Initially, when I heard you'd spoken to him, I was angry. But he has nothing to hide. He didn't kill Ciara. And for future reference, he is represented by legal counsel and has been advised not to make any statements without counsel being present."

"If he's innocent, why not let him talk to us?"

"Because, young lady, I'm not stupid. Twenty years ago Chaz was emotionally devastated by Ciara's disappearance. I was not going to let a hardened police officer take advantage of his mental state and put words in his mouth. And now, twenty years later, my son has never gotten past losing the love of his life. He's still fragile. You will not speak to him again."

The woman started to stand up.

"Did you threaten people twenty years ago not to tell the truth about Chaz and Ciara's relationship?" Luke asked the question evenly and calmly, and Abby wished she could have given him a high five. He struck a nerve.

Considine sat back down. "Young man, I think that you should remember who you're talking to before you make such accusations. Don't make the same mistake the police department did."

"What's that?"

She recovered and stood again. "They pestered the innocent and let the guilty go free. Harkin is your man, and if you are as smart as you seem to think you are, you will pursue that line of investigation."

Her man opened the door for her, and just like that, she was gone.

"Wow," Abby said. "I can so see her intimidating witnesses and telling people to shut up."

"Me too," Luke and Woody said at the same time.

"We can only hope the anonymous woman calls back," Luke said. "And that we can figure out how to convince her there's nothing to be afraid of."

By late Wednesday night, Abby was on overload with the case, but Luke was coming to see things her way.

"I'm with Abby now," Luke said. "I'm sure it's not Harkin."

"Me too," Woody said.

"It's Considine or Winnen." Abby circled their names on the board. "At the very least they know something they're not saying. The 64 billion dollar question is, how do we prove it?"

"We need a confession, but what would make either of these guys confess?" Luke said.

Abby said nothing. She knew all too well that a confession didn't always seal the deal. At least it didn't always mean that the whole truth would shine through.

"Some kind of pressure, stakes raised to the point that it's more important for them to confess than to stay quiet" was Woody's thought.

About midnight, there was a knock on the conference room door. Abby opened the door and saw two of the other Long Beach officers who planned on attending the SLO officer's funeral.

"Hey, don't you cold case guys sleep?" one of them asked.

Abby stretched. "I didn't realize it was so late. You guys just get here?"

They nodded.

The group went over the itinerary for the funeral the next day. The uniformed officers would meet up at the SLO police station in their patrol cars while Luke and Woody would drive straight to the church. The patrol cars would caravan to the church from the station. The LB officers had noted that there were black-and-whites in the hotel parking lot from out of state.

"We talked to a couple of them when we checked in," one of the guys said. "We'll have a mini caravan to the police station from here."

Abby said she'd be ready, then begged off to get some sleep. She knew the next day would be trying and difficult.

CHAPTER

23

LUKE STAYED UP with Woody and the other Long Beach officers for a little bit before heading to bed. They talked about the funeral and what to expect. It would be huge and emotional. Luke wished he were riding with Abby but understood how important it was to her to show solidarity in uniform.

The next day they all shared a light breakfast at the hotel and then he watched the uniformed officers climb into their black-and-whites. The out-of-state officers were from Utah and Nevada. Four patrol cars left from the hotel lot that morning. Luke was sorry to see Abby go. She looked awesome in the dress uniform, and he'd have been proud to stand next to her. The uniformed officers would march into the church in formation. Both Abby and Woody had attended police funerals before, and Luke knew that on a certain level they were grieving right along with the San Luis cops.

"Cuts a chunk out of your heart with a dull knife and no anesthesia when a fellow officer falls like this," Woody had said.

"It could have been anyone," Abby had said at breakfast. "We've all made traffic stops; we know how vulnerable you are at the moment you approach the driver. You don't know what he or she was doing before you saw them. The driver of the stopped vehicle has every advantage."

Luke understood what she meant. The officer who'd been killed had pulled over a man for running a stop sign, little knowing the man had just killed his wife. That fact wasn't discovered until long after the officer had died. The shooter had nothing to lose and came out of the car firing a handgun. It made Luke ill to realize how easy it was for anyone to kill a cop, if that was what he'd determined to do. He was glad that Abby worked out of uniform most of the time, and in a position where he'd be able to help her and hopefully keep her safe.

———▶■—

Abby hated funerals, especially cop funerals. This was her third, and they were always so tragic, so hard. There were hundreds of cops from all over the country in attendance. The guys she'd ridden with were all younger than her, but they completely understood the solemnity. The other cops staying at the hotel, the ones from Utah and Nevada, were seasoned guys, and like Abby, they'd been to funerals before.

"Too many funerals," one had said, and Abby agreed—way too many.

They arrived at the police station, or rather a couple of blocks away, as there were already several dozen police cars lined up. They took a position in line and waited for the signal to move. Besides black-and-whites, there were blue-and-whites, solid blues, solid whites, and green-and-whites. It was quite a collection of different-style patrol cars.

When the procession began moving, it was a four-mile trek

through town to the church. Abby had read that the service would be held at the largest church in town, picked to handle the crowd expected. There were fire trucks parked along the route, and at one point a ladder truck had raised its ladder to hold a huge billowing American flag. There were also citizens along the route, waving, holding signs for the deceased officer saying, *RIP* and *God Bless*.

When they arrived at the church, they filed into the parking lot with all the other cop cars, then walked to the side of the sanctuary, where they were asked to line up in formation. Abby hadn't marched in formation since the last funeral. But since they'd done a lot of formation work in the academy, she was not clueless about it.

While they waited for the official order to begin to march in, she looked around at the diverse crowd. Of course Morro Bay PD was represented, and she saw J. P. Winnen. He didn't see her right away, but when he did, he scowled and then looked away.

Abby let it go as the order to attention was barked out and then the order to march was given. They marched into the church solemnly and smartly. The next hour was emotional and draining. The large framed photo of the grinning man, child in each arm, broke Abby's heart. The eulogies for a young cop cut down in the prime of life, leaving a wife and two small children, were heart-wrenching. The bagpipes playing "Amazing Grace" were haunting and profoundly sad. Abby cried openly, as did many around her. It was, as Woody had said, like having a piece of your heart cut out.

She also caught Winnen watching her once or twice and wondered what was up with that. The funeral was no place to pull him aside and question him, but she wished she could do just that.

When it was over and they left the church, Abby found Luke and Woody. The other Long Beach guys were going to attend the graveside service and then head home to Long Beach, so she caught a return ride to the hotel with her partners. It was quiet in the car and for that Abby was thankful. She wanted to change and take a shower and pray for the hurting widow and her children and ask God to keep her fellow officers safe in a crazy, dangerous world.

———————

About an hour after the service, when they were back in the conference room looking over the Ciara case, Luke's phone buzzed. "It's Orson. I e-mailed him a summary of our progress earlier." He put it on speakerphone. But it wasn't Orson; it was Faye. For some reason Luke felt his face redden and hoped Abby didn't see.

"Hello, Luke. Orson gave me the summary to review. It looks like you've made some good progress, but you might be rapidly approaching an impasse on this one."

"You're on speaker, Faye."

"Hi, Faye," Woody said.

Abby echoed the greeting, then added, "We just got started. I'm not conceding impasse."

Luke saw the stubborn set of her jaw. Or was that irritation?

"I'm not trying to blunt your enthusiasm. We have faith in you. And I know you'll keep digging. I also know that you weren't planning on coming home for the weekend until Saturday. Orson wonders if you'd mind coming back tomorrow and consider taking on another case unofficially, one you'd be working on in the same general area. He has studied everything Luke sent him and thinks you can work both cases at the same time without too much trouble. In fact, the first one might help you work the second one."

"Okay by me," Woody said. Luke knew he was anxious to get home to Zena.

"What's the case?" Luke asked.

"A guy who murdered his family and has been a fugitive for fifteen years. He's on the FBI's ten most wanted list."

Abby piped up. "That's not in the guidelines for our cases. Technically, the case isn't cold—they know who did it, and he's in the wind. If he's fled and a warrant is issued because he fled prosecution, isn't that FBI or US marshals' responsibility?"

"FBI, but this is a special case. Orson wants it clear—this would be unofficial. Basically you'll be doing some knock-and-talks asking questions. And the reason he wants you all back in Long Beach tomorrow is to meet the victim."

"All of us?" Abby asked.

"Yes. He thinks it's important for you to meet the victim face-to-face, hear her story, and listen to her thoughts. In either event, whether you take this on or not, you'll be free to head back up on Monday. If you do decide to help with this case, you can kill two birds with one stone, to use a famous cliché."

"Will you e-mail us information on the case?" Luke asked.

"Uh, no, Orson wants you to meet the victim and commit to the case before giving you all the information. She's here. She came into the building looking for Orson because she'd read about the Barone case and the good job you and Woody did there. This is not a normal case and not a normal intake, but we bet you'll agree when you meet her that it is a case worth looking at. I hope asking you to be here a little early is not a problem. I know that Luke at least will want to touch base at home before returning next Monday."

"True enough on Luke's account," Woody said. "But I've got a pretty lady waiting for me at home as well."

Luke and Abby snickered at that.

"Oh, great." Abby threw her hands up. "That must mean that I'm the only one without a life."

They agreed to head back to Long Beach a day early. Faye rang off and the three of them sat around the conference table discussing this new wrinkle.

"She said it *may* help us with this case," Abby said. "I wonder how on earth it would do that."

24

WHEN ABBY WENT back to her room after the call from Faye, she was tired but couldn't shut down and go to sleep. For the hundredth time she wondered why it pinched so much that Faye was on their team. And now she'd started giving orders, taking over from Orson to a certain extent.

Slapping her forehead, Abby tried to stop her thoughts from going where they were going. If Duke were still with them, Orson might have delegated to him just like he delegated to Faye.

"I have to stop dwelling on her," she muttered. "And Faye or no Faye, I'm not ready to go home yet."

She missed Bandit, but she was fully engaged in this investigation and she didn't want to leave. *No, that's not it,* she thought. *I want to get to Templeton and get started investigating Alyssa. I'm close; I can feel it.*

She looked at the clock. It wasn't yet 9 p.m. Not too late to call Gunther.

"I think I'm staying," Abby announced to Luke and Woody as they met for breakfast the next day.

"Staying? Why?" Luke looked at her as if he didn't believe what she'd just said.

"I can keep working the case." She looked from Luke to Woody. "I'll keep everything we've done so far up on the board and maybe add to it. And you can leave me the tip line phone."

"But that's not the main reason you want to stay, is it?" Luke asked.

Abby saw something in his face. Surprise? Disappointment? Hurt? *Why? Faye is waiting for you.*

"No, not the only reason. I talked to Gunther last night. Apparently our conversation with him at lunch the other day rekindled his investigative reporter gene. He's interested in closing the Triple Seven. He wants to try to set up some interviews for today. He plans on taking the train up here and talking to people. Seems like a good time to get a leg up on asking around about Alyssa's background."

Both men looked at her appraisingly.

"Hey, I e-mailed Orson and he's okay with it. Since I'm the only one without a life, I also cleared it with Jessica. She's fine to stay at my house and look after Bandit over the weekend."

"We'll be back Monday," Woody said. "But be careful. I like Gunther, but he's not really qualified to act as a backup."

"We're just going to talk to people."

"What's the rush?" Luke asked with a frown.

Why does it bother you? Abby thought but didn't ask. "No rush. Just taking advantage of the situation. And Gunther is really interested in finding out if Alyssa is hiding something. He may not be a cop, but he'll be a help, and he's a good interviewer," she explained, hoping to wipe the frown away. It didn't work.

Luke looked away, toying with the food on his plate.

"What's wrong?" Abby asked.

"Huh? Nothing. . . . No, that's not true." He sighed. "I guess I thought looking for evidence of what Alyssa may have done was something the two of us were going to do."

Abby's brow furrowed. "It is, but I didn't think that you were on the same page as me. Didn't you say that Simon's theory didn't make sense?"

"Yeah, I guess I did. But I'm still agreeable to checking into Alyssa's background after we're finished with this case."

Now Abby was torn. She would rather be checking leads and talking to people with Luke, but she didn't want to wait. She felt a sense of urgency that she didn't completely understand, and she didn't know how to explain it to Luke. Finally she said, "Gunther said he would try to set up two interviews with people he didn't talk to when he was here years ago. He's got a plan. Hopefully we can get a line on that missing boyfriend. I'll wait for you to get back before I do any follow-up, any physical search for him."

"What are you going to do about a car?"

"Drop me off at the rental place on your way out of town."

He nodded, but Abby still felt something more bugged him.

There was no time to find out what was bothering Luke as the three worked to leave Abby with clear "so far" pictures of their two prime suspects and Harkin. Woody penciled in a picture of Considine showing how much the disappearance and murder of Ciara had impacted him. He was from a wealthy family, dad was deceased, and he'd gotten good grades and was studying premed.

A year after the girl's disappearance, he dropped out and went to work for his mom. Constance Considine was connected to a lot of wealthy people who owned diverse businesses around the county, and she got him different jobs with several of her friends' companies. It appeared as though he was hired as a favor to her. Considine went from job to job, never lasting very long at any of them. He'd racked up the arrest record Abby had noted already, and now was unemployed, apparently living off a sparse allowance from a fund his mother had set up years ago.

Abby did the same for Winnen and found a different trajectory for his life. There was a newspaper article from the day he graduated from the police academy. In a brief interview, like Axelson had indicated, Winnen said it was Ciara's disappearance that gave him direction. He'd been floundering in school, hating his major. But the contact with the police and the search for Ciara had altered his perspective. He switched majors and eventually entered the police academy with the intent "to make the world safer for women like Ciara."

Luke put together a picture of Harkin that only showed how pathetic his life had become. The cash settlement had given him a comfortable cushion to buy some land and a little privacy, but he was basically a hermit, confined to his home for fear of suffering some kind of reprisal if he stepped out into the world where he believed everybody hated him.

"The crime affected everyone, as brutal crimes usually do," Abby said, wiping her eyes after reading an article about Ciara's parents. Her father had committed suicide after her remains were found and her mother became as much of a hermit as Harkin. She resided on the coast, in a small town called Cayucos.

Abby felt for the woman. Part of her wanted to be the person who knocked on her door to give her the good news—that the person who murdered her daughter was now locked up.

This murder destroyed more lives than just Ciara's, and Abby prayed that they'd be able to bring someone to justice and apply a little salve to the open wound.

CHAPTER

25

"YOU'VE BEEN AWFULLY quiet since we dropped Abby off," Woody said to Luke as they passed through Santa Maria on their way south.

Luke blew out a breath and wondered if he should talk to Woody about Abby. After a couple of seconds he said, "I guess I don't like the idea of her staying up there by herself."

"She's a big girl. She can take care of herself."

"I know, but . . ."

"Why don't you tell her how you feel?"

"What?"

"Don't give me those innocent eyes. You got a crush on the girl the size of Mount Rushmore. Are you going to keep it to yourself forever?"

Luke shook his head. "Look, Woody, we have a connection to a cold case, and I admire her as an investigator."

"Only a connection to a moldy cold case? That's all?" Woody snorted. "In a pig's eye."

"She just broke up with a guy she's known for years and been engaged to—"

"Just why do you think it was so long without a final result? He wasn't the man for her. If you step up to the plate, she wouldn't say no."

Conflicting emotions washed through Luke like a flash flood on a dry plain. Part of him wanted to grin and accept Woody's insight as great news, but when Abby decided to stay in San Luis Obispo, she threw him off. He had thought they were a team and that together they would look into Alyssa. Out of the blue she called Gunther? He didn't know how to process this, and he felt a little discomfort. He was attracted to her, but what if she wasn't interested?

"You sure about that, Woody? I mean, Abby is a capable, independent woman. What if I disappoint her?" The question sounded lame even to him, but he couldn't put the words back in his mouth.

"Holy moly, are you dense or what? You want to spend the rest of your life alone? As for not wanting to disappoint someone, that is weak, cowardly, and you're no coward. Men disappoint women, women disappoint men—that's life and the gospel according to Woody." He hung his head, shaking it before he looked up.

Luke didn't like being accused of being dense, but he couldn't deny that the pain of his first marriage made him cautious. He'd certainly disappointed his first wife. Yet he didn't want to bring that up with Woody, opting to try explaining his reticence a different way. "But Faye—"

Woody cut him off. He wasn't having any of it. "Pull up your big boy pants and tell Faye that you're stuck on Abby. Love is blind, isn't it? She's as hung up on you as you are on her. Step up and open the door. I know she won't close it in your face."

Luke looked at Woody and got a great "What are you waiting for?" glare.

He said nothing, concentrated on driving as he tried to sort out all the feelings swirling through him. He'd been attracted to Abby from day one, been devastated to think she'd marry Ethan and that would be the end of it.

Woody is right and wrong about one thing, Luke thought. *I am a coward. I'm afraid I'll make my move and Abby won't be interested. I need to pray about this and then step forward. Then maybe I'll figure out a way to move close to Abby and not fail.*

CHAPTER

26

AFTER ABBY FINISHED with the rental car company, she stopped to get a cup of coffee. Luke and his reaction to her staying were on her mind. Maybe he and Faye were just friends. It made her doubt the wisdom of her decision to stay and work with Gunther. She'd worked with many different partners while on the PD—some good partners, some not so good. Luke was an outstanding partner all the way around. Was it wrong to take this step without him? She tried to ignore the voice telling her that she should wait; there was no rush.

She paid for the coffee, then got back in the rental car and checked the tip line phone for messages. There were two. One from another man saying that aliens kidnapped Ciara. "The truth is out there," he assured her. The second was from a woman who said two words—"Oh, my"—and then hung up, leaving Abby to hope it was the same woman Woody talked to and that she would call back.

She'd no sooner put the tip line phone away than her personal phone rang. It was Gunther telling her he'd scheduled two interviews and that he'd be on the northbound Amtrak train with an arrival time at SLO around 3 p.m.

It was time to compartmentalize her life. Luke and questions about her future with him needed to be locked away for a time. Ciara was also on hold, unless someone with real information called. Abby made the shift back to Alyssa and her past. Since she had time before the train arrived, she traveled to Templeton and drove around to get a feel for the town but recognized it had changed quite a bit since Alyssa had lived there forty years ago.

Templeton was between San Luis Obispo and Paso Robles, which were both bigger towns. A lot of the area was still agricultural, and there were many wineries, the hills dotted with vineyards. There were also olive trees and a couple of places that made olive oil. Downtown was quaint. Obviously the wine production business was big, as was the catering to tourists and wine tasting.

After she believed she had a good handle on the area, she made her way back to San Luis Obispo and the train station. Hopefully Gunther's arranged meetings were with people who knew Alyssa well enough to generate leads, leads that would help them dig up what it was that Alyssa wanted kept hidden.

Abby refused to entertain the possibility that there was nothing here and Alyssa was above suspicion.

The vintage train station, with its Spanish-style white stucco and red tile roof, reminded Abby of time past. She had probably seen something like it in an old movie. She was a few minutes early, so she parked the car and strolled into the waiting room. She saw a sign on a wall that said something about Lowell Rollins, but she quickly looked away, trying to ignore it. Her insides churned at the thought of him being a senator.

Inside the station, she realized security was not the same here as at an airport. She could continue straight through and wait on the platform. Abby had never ridden a train. She remembered Ethan telling her about the trains he rode in Europe and how much he enjoyed it. Now, out on the platform, seeing travelers waiting and a conductor standing close by, she wondered if Gunther enjoyed the ride and if it were something she'd like to do in the future.

The train station also brought to her mind the story Harkin had told, about him stopping by on his way home the night Ciara disappeared. She looked around the platform and realized she could picture that; she could see him over at the edge of the building, his bike leaning against him while he lit a cigarette and waited for a train to roll through. She liked to think she could read people, something that had been hugely advantageous in her career in homicide. She just didn't read *killer* in Jasper Harkin.

After a few minutes she heard the warning whistle and an announcement that the train would be arriving shortly. It was a bit thrilling to see the big engine approach the station, then continue on through slowly before coming to a stop. It was a long train and Abby knew from listening to the announcements over the PA that there were sleeping cars and coach cars. She also noted the train would continue on from here with an ultimate destination in Washington State.

Gunther was the last person to step off the train. He had with him a small duffel bag in his hand and a sour expression on his face.

"Good afternoon, Gunther. Didn't you have a nice trip?"

"The trip was fine. Old age just kicked in with some stiffness.

Even though my reporting days are over, this little excursion is energizing and I hope we find something."

"Me too. We can get straight to the interviews, right?"

He nodded. "Yep, and these are two people I didn't talk to on the last trip. I only talked to people in her graduating class when I was up here before. This time I contacted a former teacher who is in an assisted-living home but still very sharp mentally, and a woman who graduated the year after Alyssa but knew her."

"Sounds like a plan. What about her high school boyfriend?"

"Might not have any luck with him. I couldn't find information on him. One of the women said that he's a transient, appears from time to time. No telling when the next time will be. Apparently there's a large population of homeless people who live in this part of central California. I couldn't help but notice that there were a lot of homeless camps along the railroad tracks all the way up from LA. Finding him will be a needle in a haystack."

Abby thought about that. This whole case—the twenty-seven-year-old murders of her parents and Luke's uncle—could be called the same thing: the search for a needle in a haystack. But she would never give up trying to learn the whole truth.

"All we can do is try."

CHAPTER

27

KELSEY COX YAWNED and wondered if she'd ever have a moment of peace and quiet in her life again. Or even a simple good night's rest. There was no such thing as quiet in the jail. Not in the Long Beach city jail, and certainly not in the LA County jail. It was never totally quiet, even at night. She heard noises at night that she'd never be able to identify. Even being safely tucked away in isolation—a luxury after being rushed and punched several times by a gang member who was certain Kelsey had arrested her baby daddy—she never experienced complete silence.

What would state prison be like?

She'd been waiting for days for the tap, the guard coming to tell her that she'd be on her way out of Long Beach to the place that would be her home for the next fifteen years. Finally, this morning it had come. Kelsey was ready, and resigned, for the next chapter in her life.

Shackled and sitting on the bus, no one next to her, waiting for the transport to pull away from the Long Beach jail, Kelsey considered that next chapter. Her lawyer had intimated that Governor Rollins would be in a position to grant her a pardon, that Kelsey had been a loyal employee and deserved consideration.

Kelsey realized she didn't care. She hadn't implicated the governor or his wife in anything not because they weren't guilty but because at the time she'd accepted the plea, she feared them. Their reach was long, and unlike her lover Gavin, who'd taken his own life to avoid prison, Kelsey was not ready to die.

But sitting in jail and enduring an irksome delay had changed Kelsey's perspective. She should have been gone days ago. The LB city jail was simply a holding pen for unsentenced prisoners. Kelsey had been sentenced. She knew that Alyssa Rollins had to be behind the delay; she was the only one with enough juice to force the governor's hand. The question was, why? The idle time had given Kelsey occasion to think; it made her consider that she was simply a pawn in a game being orchestrated by Alyssa. What Alyssa didn't know was that Kelsey, in part, had accepted the plea deal because she didn't want to play Alyssa's games anymore.

The bus, which had been idling, was shifted into gear. Kelsey looked out the window as the vehicle pulled away from the city jail and headed toward the 710 freeway.

So Alyssa couldn't delay her any longer.

Is she finished with me? Kelsey wondered.

Gunther had scheduled the visit with the old teacher first because the assisted-living facility where she lived was in San Luis Obispo, not far from the train station. They found the place easily, situated on a beautiful, shady, tree-lined street. It looked more like a residence than a facility.

"This is nice," Gunther commented. "Maybe I should retire here."

"You're not ready for assisted living already, are you?"

Gunther shrugged. "Having someone else take care of my every need? I could handle that."

They asked for Esther Dorne and were directed to the backyard. There they found a white-haired woman under a tree in a lounge chair reading a suspense novel by DiAnn Mills, one of Abby's favorites.

"Mrs. Dorne?" Abby stepped forward.

The woman looked up, eyes bright and alert. She closed the book on her lap and smiled. "Mr. Gunther and Detective Hart, I presume," she said but stared at Abby.

"That's us." Gunther pulled a couple of plastic chairs over, and they sat on either side of the lounge. "You're looking well, Esther. May we call you Esther?"

The woman nodded, but before Gunther could continue, her eyes bored into Abby.

"We've met before." She raised a twisted finger toward Abby. "I'm sure of it."

"Uh," Abby stammered, "I don't think so. I've never met you."

"I'm sure of it," she repeated. "I may be old, but I never forget a face."

Abby held her hands up. "I can't help you. I really have never seen you before."

Esther shook her head in bewilderment. "It will come to me. I know it will."

Abby and Gunther exchanged glances. Abby shrugged.

"Are you ready for some questions?" Gunther asked.

Still studying Abby, she said, "You bet I am. Retirement has been so boring." She rubbed her hands together and turned to Gunther. "I'm ready to stir up some trouble."

Abby tried to forget the weird perusal and fought to keep from smiling at the woman's spunk. "What makes you think we want to stir up trouble?"

Esther raised one eyebrow. "Alyssa is in politics now. I imagine all the good stuff has been written. You must want the bad stuff."

"We just want background, true background. Is that bad stuff?"

"Some is. Alyssa was not a happy child."

"You remember her clearly?"

"I do. I remember most of my students, but Alyssa became famous in this state. I remember Alyssa mostly because the tragedy that touched her life made me notice her more than others and try to help her more."

"Are you referring to her father's suicide?"

"I am. Do you know it was Alyssa who found his body? He hung himself in his study. She went looking for him and found . . ." She grimaced. "No child should see that kind of thing."

"I agree," Abby said.

A strange look came over Esther, and Abby leaned closer as fear spiked. Was the spry old woman having a stroke?

"Are you okay, Esther?"

Esther waved her away. "Yes, yes, I just had the strangest

sense of déjà vu—you know, that you and I had this conversation before."

After a deep sigh, Esther continued. "Let's see, where was I? Alyssa's father's suicide. It changed everything for the poor girl. From what I understand, she was living in a mansion in San Francisco, the Nob Hill area, attending an expensive private school one week, and the next sharing a room in a relative's house in a small farming town in the middle of the state. It was quite a fall."

"You taught her in high school, correct?" Gunther asked.

"Correct. I taught English literature. She was a poor student. I could tell she didn't like to read. Generally, though, she showed up every day."

"Do you know what she was like outside of class? Did she have a lot of friends? Was she involved in any extracurricular activities?"

"She did not have many friends, no. As for other activities . . . well, she was shy, withdrawn, sad. I never saw her fit into any particular group. Every school has them, you know: cliques, circles. Alyssa didn't have one. And some girls were mean to her; there was quite a bit of bullying that went on. We tried to keep an eye out, stop it, but you know how kids can be mean, really mean."

"Didn't she have a boyfriend?"

"Oh yes, but not until her senior year. When she met Mike, the bullying stopped. I'm sure he stopped it. He was really her only friend. They were very close. I think that the romantic in me wanted them to get married and be together forever." For a second she seemed miles away. She snapped herself back to the present. "But something happened that changed everything."

"What?" Gunther and Abby asked at the same time.

"I don't know, but it made Alyssa leave school without graduating, and it broke Mike's heart. You really need to talk with him. Mike can tell you a lot more about Alyssa than anyone can."

CHAPTER

28

THEY SPENT A FEW MORE minutes with Esther, but the woman had no idea why Alyssa left. She would have graduated if she'd completed her finals, but she was a no-show. Her mother was asked about it, but she was no help. The woman had given up on life after her husband's death. Eventually she was placed in a nursing home, where she stayed until her death. Esther said she didn't believe that Alyssa ever came back to visit her mother.

Abby was just about to put the car in reverse and leave the care facility parking lot when her phone buzzed. It was Bill, her partner in homicide. Heart skipping a beat, she immediately thought the worst: that something had happened to Luke and Woody on their drive down.

"I have to answer this," she told Gunther as she left the car in park. "Bill, what's wrong?"

"Whoa, sorry you think I'd only call you when something is wrong." He paused and Abby started to relax. Everything changed when he continued.

"And doubly sorry, because something is wrong. Kelsey Cox escaped from custody."

"What? How is that possible?"

"There was a crash on the 710, city of Commerce. What I'm hearing is that there was lot of chaos, a fire. One of the drivers in another car was killed, and in all the confusion, four prisoners slipped away and Cox was one of them."

Abby frowned and had to think for a moment. The city jail only held prisoners for a short period of time, unless they were sentenced to city time, and that only happened with male prisoners. There was no long-term female prisoner detention. "Why wasn't she transferred right after her plea? Why a week later?"

"I can't answer that. . . . Uh, wait . . ."

Abby could hear the crackle of the radio in the background.

"Looks like three of the escapees are back in custody." There was another long pause. "But Cox is not one of them. I'm sure she'll be caught quickly, but I just wanted you to know."

"Thanks, Bill."

Luke and Woody were almost to Long Beach before the radio broadcast a breaking news story.

"What did he just say?" Woody asked as he turned up the radio.

Very clearly the newsman announced an escape from the jail bus.

"What? Escape to where?" Luke wondered, knowing there wasn't anywhere to run to in the area mentioned.

As the story continued and the names of the missing prisoners were mentioned, he tightened his grip on the steering wheel.

"Kelsey Cox?" He cast a surprised glance at an equally

surprised Woody and wondered what the calamity would mean to Abby

"She'll be caught. Don't sweat it," Woody said with conviction.

"She pleaded guilty. No one forced her to admit to the crime. Why run now?"

"Maybe she just realized how tough fifteen years will be and wanted to see how far she could get. It won't be far."

Luke relaxed his grip on the wheel and conceded that he had to agree with Woody. In the age of electronics, helicopters, and heat-detecting radar, a jailbreak was foolish. Back east there had been a sophisticated prison break when two men had tunneled out from the largest maximum-security prison in New York. Sure, they were on the run for a few weeks, but they were eventually caught. One was killed, the other taken back to jail. Even if Kelsey could evade for a while, where would she go?

All Luke could do was shake his head. Kelsey Cox couldn't be a danger to him or Abby anymore . . . could she?

CHAPTER

29

"SHE'LL BE CAUGHT. It's no big thing," Gunther said after Abby told him what was going on.

Abby had to sit for a minute to digest the information. "I can't remember when I heard of an escape from the county bus."

"It's happened once or twice. They get caught fast, and now Cox will be on all the freeway boards, as if she were an Amber Alert. She won't get far."

Abby looked at Gunther, who gave her a reassuring nod.

"I hope you're right," Abby said, still trying to process whether or not she should be worried about Cox running around free. The question about why it had taken so long for Cox to be transferred out of Long Beach nagged. That should have happened the day of her plea. The longest Long Beach city jail could keep unsentenced female prisoners was ninety-six hours. While Kelsey had been in the county jail before her plea, she was transported back to Long Beach for her day in court and should have been sent to a state intake facility and eventually to a state prison to serve her time. Was this special treatment that she was allowed to stay in LB so long?

After some reflection, she decided there was nothing to fear. Gunther was right. Unless this escape was planned and financed carefully, there was no way Cox could stay free. And Bill had said it was a traffic accident. No worries. The woman would be back in custody soon.

"What did you think of Esther?" Abby asked the reporter as she put the car in reverse.

"She was enlightening," Gunther said as they left the parking lot.

"Not really," Abby disagreed. "She was vague. She liked the *girl* Alyssa, but I'm not sure that will help us with the *woman*. In fact, when I was doing my own research, so much written about Alyssa is vague, spotty."

"You're right about that. She carefully controls media stuff. Guys who write about the governor tell me that. But Esther was certain that Mike Jez is the one we need to talk to. He's the key."

"Maybe so. I hope the old classmate can give us a line on him."

Barbara Stevens was the classmate next on the list, and Abby and Gunther pulled up to her modest house on a hill above the college a few minutes after leaving Esther.

Stevens met them at the front door. Obviously from Abby's mother's generation, Barbara wore glasses that seemed to settle on her pudgy red cheeks, and a flowered blouse that looked very summery. It wasn't summer but might as well have been. The January day was bright with sun.

Abby and Gunther identified themselves and she opened the door. "Please, come in."

They were led into a living room straight out of the seventies in Abby's opinion; at least the yellow shag carpet and the flowered couch made Abby think of *That '70s Show*, which she'd seen on TV Land.

And Barbara gave Abby the same strange look Esther had.

"You think we've met before?" Abby asked, beating her to the punch.

"Yes. Have we?"

"Not to my knowledge. Unless maybe I arrested you in Long Beach?"

Stevens laughed. "No, that's for sure. Sorry; maybe you just have one of those faces."

"Or maybe I look like someone you've talked to before about Alyssa?"

Gunther shot her a look, but Abby had an idea, and she decided to play it out.

"That's it!" Stevens exclaimed, pointing. "You look just like that lady reporter, the one who came to talk to me years ago. She said she was working for *Life* magazine, but I never saw an article about her visit."

Abby gave Gunther an "I'll explain later" look and cleared her throat. "What did that reporter ask you?"

"Well, I don't know that I remember exactly, but I'll give it a try." Stevens held her hands together in front of her with an expression of eagerness on her face.

"It was odd, you know—Alyssa wasn't in politics then. This reporter showed up at my class reunion. She talked to several people. When she found out I knew Alyssa, she wanted to know all about her. She said that Alyssa was doing something special in Long Beach, I remember that, and I told her everything I could about Alyssa. I was happy to help, because I was happy for Alyssa, that things were looking up for her. Now I follow all the news concerning Governor Rollins. He has my vote for senate."

Abby kept her expression and tone neutral upon hearing that news. "Did this reporter say exactly what Alyssa was doing?"

"It had something to do with a famous restaurant in Long Beach. I don't remember specifically. I just know that I never saw an article in *Life* about Alyssa. I talked to that woman for most of the reunion party and never saw a word in print."

"Have you been in touch with Alyssa since you graduated?" Abby asked. "Did she ever attend a class reunion?"

"No, to answer both of those questions. I'm gifted at math, always have been. Alyssa was one of several girls I tutored, but we weren't close. In fact, she wasn't close to anyone. I felt sorry for her; that's why I remember her so well."

"Because her father was dead?" Gunther asked.

She pushed her glasses up on her nose. "That, and she wasn't very popular. I was a year behind, but I still saw how she was bullied, made fun of. Until Mike started dating her, everyone picked on her."

"We've heard she was bullied. Exactly how was she bullied?"

"Other kids—actually it was other girls, mean girls—called her a ragamuffin, made fun of the clothes she wore, how her hair was done, all of that. She was poor; that was obvious. Her clothes were never in fashion, and as for her hair . . . it looked like she cut it herself. And some of the girls in her class were vicious. In fact some people would say one of the meanest girls got her just deserts."

"What do you mean by that?" Abby asked, interest piqued.

"It was a big story here, at least the biggest I remember. I was a junior and it was the most sensational story of my life so far.

And I do remember that the *Life* reporter was very interested in it; she even wanted directions to the dry well. You see, Sheryl Shepherd was a cheerleader, a popular girl, but so mean and so conceited. Not many escaped her sharp tongue. Anyway, she disappeared and died two months before graduation. Fell into a dry well, couldn't get out, and starved to death. Or to be precise, it was dehydration that got her. It was almost two weeks before anyone found her. She was one of the meanest to Alyssa. Really tormented her, even after Mike came into the picture. I think it was because Sheryl was jealous of Alyssa's relationship with Mike."

Abby made a mental note to look up the story about Sheryl in news archives.

"Is it possible for us to see that dry well?" Abby asked.

"No, I'm afraid not. The farm was sold and subdivided years ago; it's a housing tract now."

"Did you know Mike?"

"Everyone knew Mike. He was the most popular, best-looking guy in school and by far the nicest. I even had a crush on him. He was the high school quarterback, voted most likely to succeed . . ." Her voice trailed off and sadness fell over her face. "It's such a shame, really. He escaped the draft but still ended up like one of those sad Vietnam veterans you used to read about all the time."

She paused to wipe her eyes. "What happened to Mike after Alyssa left him is tragic. He was never the same. It broke his heart. That's why he's in the place he is all these years later."

"You mean homeless."

"Yes." She wrung her hands. "The poor man. For years he's lived on the street or in homeless camps around the area. His family disowned him. They're very wealthy, but they stopped giving him money years ago. Not that long ago, they up and relocated to Arizona. He's destitute. It's a horrible situation."

"I heard a rumor that he lives somewhere in San Luis in a homeless camp," Gunther said. "Do you have any idea where we might find him?"

"I've heard from friends that he does show up in town from time to time." Barbara chewed on her bottom lip. "You might try the Christian fellowship on the edge of town. They feed the homeless, so they might know where Mike is, if he's still around."

"Do you have any idea why Alyssa left Mike? She left school at the same time. Did something happen between them?"

"I only remember rumors. Some of them were wild. One was that Mike was too devastated by Sheryl's death, that Alyssa accused him of having a thing for Sheryl." She shook her head. "It's been a long time now. I don't recall anything that made sense. It was just sad."

CHAPTER

30

"WHAT WAS THAT ALL ABOUT?" Gunther asked Abby as they left the Stevens residence.

"I think my mother may have been the reporter who visited Esther and Barbara. That's who they're confusing me for."

Gunther put a hand on her shoulder, stopping her progress to the car. "Your mother?"

"Yeah, I never had any idea that she came up here before today. But the way those ladies looked at me, it makes sense, doesn't it?"

"I guess if it was your mom up here snooping contemporaneous to her being murdered, you might be right. But be careful you aren't stretching here, okay? There's no way to know for sure."

"There is if we discover the secret."

He gave her a grudging nod and they got into the car.

Abby took a minute to check her phone for any alerts regarding Kelsey before she put the key in the ignition.

"That was really stupid of her, you know," Gunther said.

"What?" Abby looked up from the phone.

"Her escape. I know you're checking up on Cox. She murdered your dad, I get that, but she just voided her plea and will face more charges. It was stupid for her to escape. You really shouldn't be that concerned." He considered this. "But am I sensing that it's tied up with why you're so interested in Alyssa, and why your mom was up here thirty years ago?"

Abby nodded. "Cox and Alyssa are connected in a lot of ways."

"Hmm. I came up here mostly out of curiosity and, okay, a little boredom, and because I really resented being pulled home early all those years ago. And like I said, the Triple Seven is near and dear to my heart. You've livened up my life with all of this conjecture about our dear First Lady. Why are you so sure?"

"The story Cox told in court was a watered-down half-truth. Gavin Kent confessed to killing my mother, and it's generally accepted that he set the fire that destroyed the restaurant and almost killed me."

"No way to prove that or question him."

"Right, but there is more. The reason my dad was in Kelsey's backyard the night she killed him was that he was trying to convince Gavin Kent to come clean about what happened in the restaurant. He wanted them both to go to the police, to confess to their crimes and point the finger at the one who ordered the carnage. It wasn't Lowell from afar. It was Alyssa Rollins in person. She was there that day. *She* ordered the killing, the fire."

From the look on Gunther's face she knew she'd shocked him.

"I have a letter my dad wrote, after the Triple Seven fire. He spells out most of what happened that day, and Alyssa was at the center of everything. I know my mom must have discovered something Alyssa wanted hidden, and that's what got her killed."

"Sooo . . . ," Gunther said after a minute, thoughtful expression on his face. "No wonder you're so certain there's a dark, horrible secret to be unearthed, one that will nail Alyssa. Hopefully for murder or worse. Then you'll have revenge for your mother's death?"

"Not revenge. Justice. Alyssa is evil. It's time she answered for her crimes."

All the way back to the hotel Abby explained to Gunther what she knew and what made her want to find out everything she could about Alyssa Rollins.

"I'm even entertaining the thought that Alyssa is the one who sprung Kelsey from jail."

Gunther laughed at that. "Lowell is in the middle of a tough campaign. If Alyssa has done all the stuff you think she's done to get Lowell to this place, why would she screw it up now with something so blatantly stupid?"

"Desperation."

He considered this for a moment. "Well, if she did spring Cox and it has something to do with this big secret out there, it must be a huge secret."

"That's what I think."

"What about Lowell? You don't think he's pure as the driven snow, do you?"

"I don't know. He's the wild card in all of this. My dad liked him, thought a lot of him, but lately he's creeped me out. You know that he asked me to come work for him."

"Really? That's not too surprising as I think more about it. You're competent; he'd want competent people around him.

But you're not muscle—no offense—so that almost makes me think he just wanted to keep you close so he'd have an eye on you."

"Eww. Thanks for making me feel even more creepy."

"Sorry, but my money is still on him, not Alyssa, to be the real bad guy. He's the one with all the power."

CHAPTER

31

LUKE AND WOODY made it back to Long Beach around 3 p.m. Kelsey Cox still had not been recaptured, and the freeway system was a mess. The highway patrol had shut down the northbound side of the 710 because of the accident, the death of one of the drivers, and the subsequent search, and they still had it closed. The southbound side was slow because of looky-loos, and that would make them late for their meeting with Orson and the woman he'd talked about on the phone.

Tapping on the steering wheel, frustrated with the slow-moving traffic, Luke turned to Woody. "Why don't you give Orson a call? We'll probably be at least half an hour late."

"Sure thing."

While Woody called Orson, Luke wondered about Kelsey Cox. The area where she escaped was industrial, gritty. He couldn't see how she'd evaded everyone; she'd stick out like a sore thumb in the area wearing an orange jumpsuit and sporting blonde hair.

Woody hung up chuckling.

"What's funny?"

"I think Orson is sweet on this new victim."

"Orson is a professional."

"Not saying he's not being professional; just saying that he seems to like this woman."

"We'll see," Luke said, not willing to let on that he was curious. When they finally made it past the tie-up, he stepped on it, keeping to barely legal speeds.

When they arrived in the conference room, Orson was by himself.

"Well? Where is she?" Woody asked.

Luke stayed quiet because he could see that his friend and boss was unsettled. Luke had served with Orson overseas and had known him to be unflappable even in the hottest firefight. But something had him antsy and Luke wondered if it was, indeed, the new victim.

"She's in the ladies' room. Glad you guys could finally make it."

"Not our fault." Luke held his hands up. "Blame the CHP. Better yet, blame the prisoner break."

"The what?" Orson looked bewildered.

"Haven't you watched the news? Some prisoners escaped from the county bus."

Orson shook his head. "I've been busy *working*, not watching TV or playing on the Internet."

Luke rolled his eyes and was going to continue the ragging session when Faye walked in.

"Hi, Luke, Woody." She turned to Orson. "Here are the copies you requested. If it's okay with you, I want to head home for the weekend."

Luke noticed the way Orson looked at her and heard the tone of his voice.

"Thank you, Faye. You've been such a big help. Drive carefully."

Faye looked at Luke. "Sorry we didn't have much of a chance to visit, but you know how bad traffic can be this time of day."

"It's bad already because of the escape."

"What?"

"Yeah." Orson stood. "Luke just told me. Someone escaped from the jail bus. You might want to wait until tomorrow to go home."

Faye frowned. "I better go call Caltrans. Maybe I'll be back in a minute."

Luke didn't watch her go; instead he watched Orson. It wasn't the victim Orson was sweet on. But he didn't have a chance to talk to his boss about it.

As soon as Faye left, the door opened and another woman walked in.

Luke had to bring a hand to his chin, praying that shock wasn't obvious on his face. The woman looked like a Photoshop before and after. The left side of her body was normal. Luke saw a foot, leg, hand, and half of a normal, unscarred face. But as she moved into the room, he saw a hook where her right hand should be and a prosthetic limb where the right leg would be. It was metal, something like what he'd seen on soldiers who'd lost a limb, with a tennis shoe where her foot would be. Long, dark hair barely hid the twisted scarring on the right side of her face.

Was this woman a veteran? Luke wondered. Was that why Orson was on edge? She looked like some of the guys he knew who'd been maimed by an IED. A second, uninjured woman walked in behind her, a woman who looked to Luke as if she were a helper or a nurse.

Orson cleared his throat. "Luke, Woody, I'd like you to meet Victoria Napier. Fifteen years ago her husband tried to kill her. He did kill their children, twin boys aged six, but his attempt on Victoria failed."

"It's a pleasure to meet you both." Napier extended her left hand and Luke shook it. Her voice was harsh, hoarse, as if her vocal cords were damaged. Up close Luke could see the scarring on the right side of her face clearer, and he noted that her ear was gone; her hair hung over a lump of scar tissue.

"I can't hear out of the right ear," she said as if she sensed Luke's perusal. "Or see out of the right eye. But my hearing and sight are perfect on the left." She turned to Woody and shook his hand.

"Stuart Napier shot Victoria, their two boys, then set their house on fire," Orson explained as they took their seats around the conference table. "Victoria almost died several times. She eventually survived with the serious injuries you can now see. It was five years before she was released from the rehab hospital. Stuart disappeared without a trace after the crime."

"And for the last ten years I've been looking for him. I didn't die like he wanted. And I won't go quietly. I must find him and see him punished for the sake of our boys. They deserve justice."

Orson passed out the FBI wanted poster on Stuart Napier.

"He disappeared from Florida," Woody observed. "What makes you think that he's in California?"

"One of the things we fought about in the weeks leading up to the day he murdered my children was moving to California. He'd been a wine-making hobbyist for years. He wanted to try his hand at wine making on a large scale. Wanted to sell everything in Florida and buy a vineyard in California. I've made my way across the country, painstakingly checking vineyards and wine-growing operations. I know that this is where he'll be found."

Now Luke's jaw almost dropped for an entirely different reason. Talk about grasping at straws. He cleared his throat. "Excuse me for saying, but wine grapes are grown all over the world. Why, he could be anywhere after all this time. I—"

"Mr. Murphy, are you married?"

"I'm a widower."

"Oh, well, sorry to hear that. My point is that Stuart and I were married for fifteen years and I know him very well. First of all, he's a germaphobe—neurotic about it, really. He would not go to another country because he'd be afraid of the water or the food or of catching something for which he was not vaccinated. Second of all, he's obsessive compulsive, meaning since he had the vineyard idea on his mind, there is no way he could deny that compulsion. He's working at a vineyard somewhere, I know it."

The intensity in her voice rocked Luke back.

"Even if I concede that point, there must be thousands of—"

"Approximately eight thousand in the country—3,674 in California alone."

"That's a lot of ground to cover," Woody said.

"It is," Napier conceded. "But in ten years I've been able to pare it down."

Orson spoke up. "On her own, using private resources, Victoria has been through almost every vineyard in the country and parts of Southern California. Her search has taken ten years." He emphasized the last two words and Luke heard the compassion in his voice. "The FBI has given her minimal help. They think . . . uh, well—"

"It's okay. They think I'm nuts," Victoria said, a tight smile on her face. "Consumed with grief. The sad widow is crazy—that's their opinion." The smile disappeared, replaced by intensity that was serious—more so because of the disfigured face.

Luke winced.

"I'll find him," she whispered. "I'll find him with or without your assistance. It will take me longer without help, but I'm determined. I'll find him if it's the last thing I do."

CHAPTER

32

ABBY AND GUNTHER arrived at the Christian church Stevens directed them to as the office was closing for the day. They found a secretary at the Mid State Christian Fellowship who knew exactly who they were talking about.

"Padre Mike."

"Padre?" Abby asked.

She nodded. "That's what the homeless community calls him. He ministers to them, kind of like a lay pastor."

Gunther frowned. "You mean he's not crazy or shell-shocked or drug addicted or an alcoholic?"

She laughed. "No, not at all. Mike . . . well, Mike is different, I'll grant you, but he's sane. At one time he did have an alcohol problem, but that's long past from what I know. Pastor Terry lets him use the shower we have in the back office area from time to time. And he comes to visit the food pantry now and again. He's just a nice guy."

"Any chance you know when he'll be here next?"

"You just missed him. He was here last Saturday with a

couple of guys who needed some medical attention. He might not be back for a while."

"Where did he go? Where does he stay?"

"That I don't know. Pastor might. He'll be here on Sunday for services, or on Tuesday if you want to talk to him in private. I just help Padre Mike when he's here. I don't ask questions about where he's been or where he's going."

The file Orson gave them started with a profile of Stuart and Victoria Napier. Both were very accomplished individuals. Stuart had a PhD in theoretical physics and Victoria in neuroscience. They'd had their own business as high-level consultants for years before the crime and did great financially. Victoria was extremely well-off in terms of money to spend. Luke could see how she could afford to spend ten years on a single-minded search. It made him wonder how Stuart could support himself and stay off the grid. If he'd fled after a brutal murder spree, how did he survive to make his way across the country to a vineyard in the middle of California? And stay hidden for fifteen years?

The FBI files made available to them showed that there had been no activity on Napier's Social Security number or credit cards in the last fifteen years. At the present time, all of his known credit accounts had long since expired. There was speculation in his file that he committed suicide by fleeing into the swampy area in Florida adjacent to the home he shared with Victoria and that his body would likely never be found. Also in the file was a copy of a letter Victoria had written telling the agent in charge that there was no way Stuart would kill himself. He was narcissistic and averse to pain.

In the profile drawn up by the FBI, Luke noted the words *cocky, shrewd,* and *manipulative.* They also believed that if Stuart was still alive, it was likely that his murder of the boys and the attempted murder of Victoria was planned, and that he'd already set himself up with another identity before he pulled the trigger. They'd tried to rebuild his life just before the fire, to determine whether or not there was a pattern to his behavior that would give them a clue about where he'd gone, but the home and all of his records were completely destroyed.

The motive they ascribed to the killing chilled Luke to the bone. *"The suspect expressed boredom with his situation for approximately two years before the murders. He was tired of his wife, tired of his kids, and no longer challenged."*

You annihilate your family because you're no longer challenged?

After reading the profile, he turned the page to the crime scene photos. It was difficult to look at the gruesome photos. Luke didn't study them all that closely. Victoria's husband had shot his children, shot Victoria, and then set the house on fire by exploding a barbecue propane tank. Victoria was barely able to drag herself from the house. As it was, her clothing caught on fire, causing third-degree burns over 70 percent of her body. She was not expected to live, but after amputations, surgeries, and much physical therapy, she walked out of the hospital on her prosthetic with only the help of a cane.

She still had issues to deal with, one of which was damage to her respiratory system that made her tired if she spoke too much or was too physically active. The woman with her was a nurse who watched her very carefully. Once Victoria briefed everyone, she excused herself to go back to her hotel and rest until the next day. After she left, Orson must have noticed that Luke and Woody were quiet.

"Okay, spill. What's the problem?"

Luke looked at Woody, who indicated that he could go ahead and speak up.

"Her story is compelling," Luke said, "but . . ."

"It's a waste of time?" Orson asked, sitting across from Luke at the table.

"I hate to put it that way, but why is she so sure this guy has been making wine for fifteen years? You have to admit that it's off the wall."

"I agree it sounds strange, and the FBI has blown her off. They just don't believe her theory about her husband."

"But you want to send us?" Woody asked.

Orson sighed. "You guys are already working in an area filled with vineyards. And if you continue through the file, you'll see that she's pared it down to a list of fifteen specific vineyards in that area. That's all. It will take two, three days tops to check these places out. I'm not sending you to Napa. She's working on her list for Napa and she's going there on her own. I just want you to spend some time in the San Luis Obispo, Paso Robles vicinity, checking with wineries, asking questions. If she's right about her husband, it's possible you'll glean a lead we can turn over to the federal team handling this case."

A pained expression passed over Orson's face. "Look, I hate to do this to you, but I've been asked by a friend to take a look at this case, to get this woman off his back. I know that sounds harsh, but she's like a dog with a bone and she's not their only case. They don't have the manpower to follow her whim."

Luke and Woody exchanged glances.

"Besides, Faye thinks she's been through so much, and she's worked so hard all by herself for ten years. She thought you'd want to help Victoria out. I can still tell her no."

Luke looked up at the ceiling and then down to the folder of photos he'd closed. It was the photos of the two little boys that decided him. "No, don't tell her no. I'd like to help if I can." He turned to Woody, who nodded.

"We can ask questions," Woody said. "It won't be a problem."

"Did you tell Abby all of this when you talked to her last night?" Luke asked.

"No, she was fine with getting the story from you two when you get back up there. And I told her I thought you guys were making great progress on Ciara's case."

Orson pointed to a box. "That's the information on the Napier case that Victoria has compiled on her own. A lot of it is her insight written down over the years. Particularly interesting is the visit she made to a vineyard in New Mexico a few years ago. She's certain that was Stuart's first stop. She believes he did grunt work there in order to be able to put something on his résumé. In the file is a possible alias he's using. Shuffle through it; I think you'll see that though her theory sounds odd, she's taken copious notes and drawn up a plausible line of reasoning as to why we'll find her husband at a vineyard somewhere."

"She's definitely an interesting victim," Luke said as he stood and took the lid off the box.

"She's a genius—I mean, a real genius. So is her husband. They met when they were both members of Mensa."

"Mensa? That's the high IQ club?" Woody asked.

"Yep, to become a member you have to score in the top 2 percent on an intelligence test, generally an IQ above 130.

But Victoria told me that both she and Stuart tested at over 150."

"He's that smart and he murdered his kids?" Woody arched an eyebrow. "I'd say somebody needs a retest. Sounds pretty stupid to me."

CHAPTER

33

"**HOW LONG HAD** you planned on staying?" Abby asked Gunther. She'd already decided to stay through the weekend and go to church and talk to the pastor on Sunday. Gunther had booked a room in the same hotel.

"Late tomorrow morning. I might be footloose and retired, but I don't see myself running down a homeless guy living in a camp somewhere. I'm inclined to let you and Murphy chase that man down."

Abby was disappointed on one hand, but the mention of Luke was a plus any way she looked at it. She and Luke would find the guy; she was sure of it.

"You'll leave tomorrow? You came all this way for just a few hours."

"It was a nice ride. Always wanted to do a little train travel. And I'm a loose end; it's you who has work to do. I'd just be twiddling my thumbs for the weekend, no article to write. I figure we'll have time to visit the library and look up that tragic accident before I leave. I know you think that Alyssa murdered the poor girl. That will be a story if it could be proved."

175

"There must be proof out there or else my parents would still be alive."

"Makes sense. After we visit the library, if you'll drop me at the station, when I get home, I'll do a follow-up for you, if it's okay with you. I'll also see what I can find out about the prisoner escape."

"Let me double-check, see if she's still running." She clicked the news on her phone, but there was no mention that Cox had been recaptured. "I hate to see you go, but that's a good idea. If she is still loose by the time you get back to LB, you'll know she had help."

"But if I were to play devil's advocate, if the Rollinses did spring her, how do you know they didn't just spirit her out of the country?"

"Somehow I don't envision that."

"Fair enough. Now how about some dinner? I'm starved."

Abby was hungry as well. They found a restaurant in San Luis Obispo called the Apple Farm and talked about the interviews they'd conducted and a little about Alyssa and Lowell. When the current subject was exhausted, Abby had a question for him.

"Gunther, the other day at lunch, you made a comment about Ethan, about how you liked Luke better than Ethan. What did you mean by that?"

"Just what I said. Ethan was a nice guy, but he didn't complement you like Luke does." He gave a wave of his hand. "I don't mean say nice things; I mean that you and Luke just seem to fit. You mesh right. Ethan . . . well, I just couldn't see you with him. His personality didn't fit yours. I can see you with Murphy."

"Oh, thanks." Abby considered his words, elated by them, really. She could see herself with Luke as well.

They were almost finished when Abby's phone buzzed and she saw it was Bill again.

"I need to take this." She stood and walked outside to answer the call. "Hi, Bill. Anything new?"

"Yeah, there is. I thought I'd fill you in on the latest with Cox."

"I'm sure curious why she did this. Kind of stupid, don't you think? Have they caught her?"

"No, not yet, but dogs found her jumpsuit tossed in a storm drain. There's no sign of her and the dogs lost the scent. They know now that she had help to escape. She's still on the run."

Abby had to think about this for a minute. "Thank you for the update."

"No problem. I'll try to call you when I can, but I'm going to be sucked into this investigation. There are so many questions being asked right now that it would make your head spin."

"I understand. Good luck with everything."

Abby rejoined Gunther at the table. "My partner, Bill, in Long Beach," she explained. "He tells me they now have evidence that Kelsey had help escaping."

Gunther raised an eyebrow. "Curiouser and curiouser. You're sure Alyssa was involved?"

Abby gave an exaggerated nod.

He wiped his mouth with a napkin and then gave Abby the most serious expression she'd ever seen from him. "I can't fathom that Alyssa would be foolish enough to be involved in this escape, but if that woman is desperate enough to do this, and as evil as you think, you'd better be extra careful. Desperate is dangerous."

After dinner, back at the hotel, Abby switched on the news, not numb exactly, but fumbling to understand exactly what this meant to her personally.

Kelsey Cox was officially a fugitive, on the run and wanted by the FBI.

Would Alyssa really send her after me?

Abby paced her hotel room and reviewed her relationship with the retired deputy chief. She'd been a sergeant with LBPD when Abby was hired twelve years ago. They'd clashed immediately, and many officers told Abby that Cox was jealous of other female officers, wanting the spotlight to herself. That was fine with Abby, who wanted no spotlight at all. She only wanted to do her job and put bad people in jail. Cox's career trajectory took her down a different path than Abby's and they only crossed once in a while. The last time they crossed at work, when Abby was working homicide and Kelsey was a deputy chief, was when information came to light about the cold case involving the murders of Abby's parents nearly three decades before.

Cox was adamantly against Abby investigating the cold case. And it was only through a tragic turn of events that Abby learned how Cox's onetime fiancé, Gavin Kent, was involved in the murder and fire at her parents' fashionable restaurant all those years ago. Kent confessed to killing her mother just before killing himself.

After the revelation, Cox retired from law enforcement and went to work for Governor Rollins, taking the job left open by Kent's suicide. Later, when the body of Abby's father was found buried under tons of concrete in the backyard of a house once belonging to Cox, evidence pointed to Cox being the killer. And only a week ago, Abby had listened to Cox's censored confession.

Now the woman was a wanted fugitive.

I can't see her being a danger to me, Abby thought. *I don't understand why she escaped, but then I don't really understand the woman at all. She was a cop, for heaven's sake, and she dishonored the badge. She killed my dad, covered for Gavin, and when she gave a partial confession, she covered for Alyssa.*

Abby folded her arms and stared at the TV, which she'd muted after the item about Cox ended. It defied logic, but Alyssa Rollins had to be the one who helped Kelsey Cox, even though her husband could have simply pardoned the woman.

Abby could think of no one else who would have the resources and the reason. But what the exact reason could be escaped Abby. Was this to keep Kelsey quiet? Or was this a reward for faithful service, just to let her free and maybe get her out of the country? It didn't make sense. Kelsey had implicated no one but herself in her confession, and her sentence wasn't that long. Kelsey retired at fifty-five. If she did the full fifteen, which was doubtful, she'd be out at seventy. It was more likely she'd be released around age sixty-two or sixty-three.

Not able to sort any of it out, Abby got ready for bed, hoping that the morning would bring clarity and capture to the issue of Kelsey Cox.

CHAPTER

34

THE NEXT MORNING, Abby got a call from Luke.

"Just wondered what you and Gunther were up to today."

"Gunther's going home, but we did get a good lead yesterday." She explained about Padre Mike and that she planned on going to church for Sunday service and talking to the pastor afterward. She didn't mention Sheryl's death; she wanted to read everything she could about that tragedy before she grabbed hold with both hands.

"You really think there's something there?"

"I do. I think my mom came up here thirty years ago asking the same questions that I'm asking." She explained about the two women from Alyssa's past recognizing her.

"It could just be a coincidence. I can't see it being any more than that. But be careful. It bothers me that Kelsey is loose."

Abby didn't know what to say to bring him around to her way of thinking about her mother and Alyssa, so she went with him to the subject of Kelsey.

"I'm cautious." Abby rubbed her forehead, remembering the fight she and Kelsey had had prior to Cox's arrest. Cox had set her town house on fire while burning proof. Abby wasn't sure of what, but she believed it had something to do with her parents' murders. And Kelsey and Abby had come close to dying in the fire. It was Luke who saved Abby's life. So in the end, she could agree to disagree with him on one point.

"I know how dangerous Kelsey can be."

"I know that you do," he said. "I'm a little uneasy about her being unaccounted for. We'll see you fairly early Monday, okay?"

"Good."

"Any calls on the tip line?"

"Nothing substantial. The woman Woody talked to has not called back."

Luke told her to look for an e-mail from him about their new case, and then he said good-bye. She checked her e-mail and saw that he wrote a brief note about the new victim, a note that raised Abby's eyebrows about this job. The e-mail also included an attachment with all the information on the case. Abby scanned it and questioned Orson's reasoning that they'd handle the case. It looked like busywork. She hoped the guys would have more information to share on the issue when they got back.

She and Gunther found a small diner near the main library for breakfast. Over four-egg omelets, he said, "We need a librarian older than dirt. She'd remember that accident with the cheerleader and probably a lot of gossip from back then."

"I think that statement is disturbingly sexist," Abby said.

It was fortunate for them that the library opened early on Saturdays.

"Our luck is good," Gunther said as they walked inside. The librarian behind the desk was an older woman.

Abby hoped Gunther was prescient.

"Hello there," Gunther began the conversation. "We're looking for some information on local history. Have you lived in
San Luis Obispo a long time?"

"All my life." The woman smiled. She had an embroidered
name tag on that said Norma. "What do you need to know?"

"Can you remember anything about a tragic accident,
around May or June of 1969? A Templeton High School girl
died after falling into a dry well."

Norma tapped an index finger against her lips. "I do remember that. It was all anyone talked about at the time. I'm not
remembering her name."

"Sheryl Shepherd," Abby said.

"That's right." Norma brought her hands together. "It was
tragic. She was only seventeen. Not all the news from that far
back is available by computer search. That's what you want,
correct? News articles about the incident?"

"Yes, a news article would be great."

"What do you remember about it?" Gunther asked.

"I remember that almost the entire town was out looking
for her." She pointed to a room off to the right. "We do have a
file of local news clippings, but I'm not certain you'd find what
you're looking for there. Come this way to where we keep the
microfilm files." They followed her and she showed them the
microfilm machines and how to search for specific stories, but
she ended up searching for them. Abby loved librarians.

"The more I think about it, the more I remember about that
tragedy. It was so odd. Sheryl knew her way around the area.
She'd grown up on a farm. There was no reason anyone could
think of that she would be so careless as to fall into the well like
she did. It was fenced."

"The well was fenced?"

"Yes. It was a hazard to livestock as well as people. The farmer fenced it in to prevent tragedies like Sheryl's."

She pulled a file for them and put it in the machine. When she had the story on screen, she shook her head. "I thought there would be a picture of the well so you could see the fence. The best anyone could deduce at the time was that Sheryl had been playing on the fence and for some reason had slipped and fallen into the well."

"A teenager playing like that?" Abby asked.

"Like I said, it was a guess."

Abby thanked her and sat down to read the story. She saw that there was a way to e-mail a copy, so she sent one to her account, one to Gunther's, and one to Luke's. She had enough information now to tell him that she thought this was the secret Alyssa was hiding.

Gunther kept talking to Norma. "Everyone was certain that it was an accident? No doubts?"

"There was some talk, but you know, it was a different time back then, simpler. Now killings are common; people hardly blink an eye. And this was a farming area. We didn't have the drug problems that were prevalent all over the country. People respected one another. There were no murders here and certainly not of innocent high school girls."

"But there was talk?"

"Sure. Her mother didn't believe Sheryl would be so careless. She wanted to believe that someone had pushed Sheryl. But who? The girl didn't have any enemies."

Abby thought of the bullying and bet Sheryl had a lot of enemies.

"Does the girl's family still live around here?"

"I don't believe so. I know her father died shortly after the daughter. People thought it was grief. And I believe Mrs. Shepherd is deceased as well."

Gunther thanked Norma and then pointed to his watch.

Abby got up and they left. She drove him to the train station, a little sorry to see the crusty reporter leave.

"I'm going to see what favors I can call in about Kelsey Cox's escape and the search," he said before getting out of the car. "I may even put a bug in someone's ear about Alyssa, that she might be someone to look at."

"Be careful. You yourself said desperation is dangerous, and she's vicious."

"I can be discreet. Don't worry."

"I'm still surprised that Kelsey would go along with something so stupid. You saw her in court—she looked beaten, resigned to jail. Why blow the plea?"

"Must be something in it for her," he said with a shrug. "Let me know if you find Mike Jez."

"I will. Have a good trip."

After the train pulled out of the station, she went back to the hotel to type up a short summary of what she and Gunther had discovered, the information from the two ladies and the librarian. Once finished, she closed the file and set it all aside.

It was time to return to Ciara's case for a review. She phoned a couple of people they'd not been able to get ahold of their first day. She gained no new information and needed a change.

Around lunchtime she turned on a news report for an update on Cox. It was big news in LA, and all the lettered law enforcement agencies were out in force. Taking a chance, she phoned

Bill to see if he had any more information about Kelsey and the search. She got his voice mail and left a message. About an hour later she got a text from him.

Will call you as soon as I can. This is a mess.

After that, needing to stretch her legs, she went for a jog around downtown San Luis Obispo. She used the time to pray about both cases and about Luke, a man she couldn't stop thinking about, a man she wished was by her side right that moment.

CHAPTER

35

LUKE HAD READ most of the notes Victoria Napier had written down, her complicated explanation for why she believed her husband was working at a winery somewhere. A man named Sam Fischer worked at a winery in New Mexico for a year right after the murders and fire. Victoria was certain Sam Fischer was an alias and that the man was Stuart. On her search she'd reached the place some six years after Fischer had already left. There was no picture of him in the file, only a generic description that could have been Stuart. Victoria had written pages about why she was certain that it was her husband. The FBI had looked for him, but Sam Fischer disappeared as completely as Stuart had. Turned out the Social Security number he used belonged to a teenager who died in 1950.

It might have been Stuart, Luke conceded, but the trail was very cold by the time Victoria found it, and it was colder now.

The tale of Sam Fischer further confirmed for Victoria that she was right about Stuart and that he was still employed at a winery somewhere. He was not running his own operation. And she didn't believe he'd be doing anything to draw attention to himself. She postulated that he'd find a job that would give him some authority, where he worked outside but was not in the public eye. As Luke read the different job titles associated with a vineyard, he learned something new. He had no idea there was so much involved in growing wine grapes.

Stuart was most likely a vineyard manager or a viticulturist, someone who actually tended the grapevines, took care of the technical aspects of grape growing, Victoria wrote. The pages of notes were carefully written, and it was obvious the woman put a lot of thought into every word. Victoria reduced the situation to a mathematical formula on probability, factoring in the human element of obsessive-compulsive disorder, Stuart's preference in climate, and the fact that the central coast winery business was big enough to satisfy his ego and small enough to cater to his need for privacy.

"They make very good wine," she wrote. "But the area does not have the same reputation as a place like Napa, California."

Her certainty that Stuart was hiding in plain sight in a vineyard somewhere in California was almost unsettling.

Luke wondered if the fact that she was so certain and so single-minded was partly because she was a genius. He'd run into many smart people who could easily become myopic over a pet project. But then again, chasing the man who murdered your children could not be classified simply as a "pet project."

The situation made him think about the word *obsession* and reminded him of Abby and the search for her parents' killers. She was obsessed for a time, but he'd watched her wrestle with that and eventually give it over to God. He was sure that Abby was still in that place of surrender and peace. Still, he couldn't help wondering if it had been a mistake to agree to help her look into Alyssa's past. What if Abby began to push too hard, if she lost her balance and let the desire to bring Alyssa to justice overshadow her again?

What if she became like Victoria?

No. He shook that thought away. Abby was no longer obsessed, but Victoria was obsession on steroids.

He forced his thoughts back to the Napier case. He didn't mind visiting the vineyards she'd listed; he understood why Orson and Faye wanted them to help. Victoria deserved help, not only for the fact her two children were dead, but also for the solo effort she'd put in on the search for her murderous husband.

Luke pushed the file away and stood to refill his coffee cup, wondering where Woody was. They were due to meet with Victoria in a few minutes this morning, and then after the meeting Luke promised to take his daughter to a father/daughter church party at the beach. Woody's pep talk in the car on the way down had stuck in his mind. It was time for him to step forward and tell Abby how he felt, let the chips fall where they may. Luke had never been afraid to take a chance before and resolved to shelve any cowardice and test the waters where Abby was concerned.

The door opened and Woody stepped in, humming.

"You're in a good mood this morning."

"And why not? Hard-charging coworkers, interesting cases, and a beautiful woman waiting for me at home."

"Ha. I'm glad I know that that's your dog."

"Zena is wonderful. She makes me laugh. I miss Ralph and Ed—they were good dogs—but I'd forgotten how much energy a young dog has. It's contagious."

"I'm glad you're happy."

Luke could hear Orson in the hallway, and a second later, he and Victoria came through the door. Luke changed back to investigator mode, having written down a number of questions to ask the woman, in order to get a better grasp on the man they would be looking for, Stuart Napier.

—————➤

"How did your wife pass, if you don't mind my asking?"

Luke looked up at Victoria, surprised by the off-topic question. "Uh, no, that's okay. . . . Um, she was killed in a car accident."

"Was it recent?"

He shook his head. "It was almost eleven years ago now."

"Oh, my, and you're still single. You must have loved her very much."

"It's, uh . . . it's complicated. I had a baby daughter to raise, so I've been busy."

"Oooh, a little girl." She put her good hand on her chest. "I so wanted a little girl. I loved my boys, but I wanted a little girl."

Luke nodded, not sure what to say. For some reason the woman made him uncomfortable. He hoped it wasn't because of the disfigured face, the sightless eye, and the scars. Maybe it was her intensity. The stare of her one good eye was disconcerting. Woody was up refilling his coffee cup and Orson had left to take a phone call. Victoria's nurse was on the other side of the table reading a magazine.

"I find it hard to believe the reason you're still single after all these years is simply because you've been busy."

"It's complicated," Luke repeated, wanting to change the

subject. "Can you tell me why Stuart did this to you? What was his motive?"

"Isn't that in the file?"

"It is, but I want to hear it from you. Why would he do such a thing?"

"He asked me for a divorce and I told him no. He threatened to leave, and I told him that he'd never escape his responsibilities. We—the boys and I—became a problem for him. He saw killing us all as a solution to his problem."

"Why not divorce?"

"Because he'd still have to deal with us. Child support, custody, all of that would have been an anchor to him."

"Wow, cold." Luke couldn't wrap his mind around it.

"That's why he must be caught. For all I know he's killed again."

True, Luke thought. He went back to his notes. "Is it possible that Stuart will be bearded now?" He thumbed through the stack of pictures they had, computer-generated guesses of what he'd look like with various disguises.

She made a curious clicking noise with her mouth that he'd heard before from her and shook her head. "I doubt it. He always saw facial hair as unsanitary."

"Is it possible that being on the run has changed some of his perceptions?"

"No," she huffed, now clearly annoyed with him. "Have you ever known anyone with an obsessive-compulsive personality? They don't change."

He wondered at how she could switch from conciliatory and helpful to angry so quickly and was about to ask another question when the nurse cleared her throat.

"I think perhaps that it's time to rest, Mrs. Napier."

Victoria shot her a stern look but then nodded in agreement. "I'll admit it, I am tired." Turning back to Luke, "I hope I've helped. And I hope that you'll call me if you have any more questions about Stuart."

"I will." She got up and he stood as well, a wave of relief rolling over him as she left the room. It was the obsession that was disconcerting.

Woody sat down and sipped his coffee, watching her go. "She's on a mission," he said.

All Luke could do was nod.

A minute after she left, Orson came back into the room.

"She add any more to what she already told us?" Orson asked.

"Not really," Luke admitted. "But she is certainly sure that she knows her husband."

"The call I took," Orson said as he sat down. "It was from a friend in the bureau. I have a surprise for the team."

"Yeah?" Woody asked. "What?"

"I'm going to be joining you guys in SLO town," Orson said.

"What? Checking up on us?" Luke asked.

"Yes and no. I have a friend assigned to the FBI's resident agency in Santa Maria. I'm using this as an excuse to visit him. I'll head up your way after the visit, maybe help you out, since I've given you extra work."

Luke started to say something and Woody stopped him. "Never say no to extra help."

Luke laughed. "I was going to say it would be good to have Orson around."

"Kiss up."

Everyone laughed.

CHAPTER
36

KELSEY WAS TOLD to eat some breakfast and she did. Lately, doing what she was told was so much easier than trying to think for herself. Ever since the moment the firefighter had cut her leg shackles with bolt cutters and pushed her from the scene of the bus crash into thick bushes off to the side of the freeway—telling her to hurry, that someone was waiting—she decided that following orders was better than giving them. She'd been pushed right into the arms of a driver who unlocked her cuffs and shoved her into the backseat of a sedan with darkly tinted windows. Even as he pulled away, he barked orders at her.

"Change your clothes fast. There's a bag next to you. When you're finished, throw that jumpsuit to me."

She'd complied, discarding the ugly prison jumpsuit for some jeans and a sweatshirt and tossing him the suit. That was the only time the vehicle had slowed. He'd lowered his window and flung the jumpsuit from the car and then sped away. A short time later he'd tossed the shackles out in a different place. Then he'd driven on back streets for about an hour before pulling into a small garage, closing the door behind the car, and letting Kelsey out of the backseat.

He showed her to a small bedroom and told her to get some rest, leaving her, closing the door, and locking it behind him. Kelsey asked nothing, said nothing. But her mind churned with a sobering realization. *Alyssa is not finished with me yet.*

She sat on the bed for a long time, trying to enjoy the silence and wanting to sleep but unable to with all the thoughts spinning in her mind. One question kept repeating itself: *How is it I find myself in this position—all control of my life taken out of my hands?* She gingerly touched the bruise on her cheekbone, still tender over a week later, from the punch the gangbanger had given her in jail. Kelsey doubted that she had really arrested the woman's baby daddy, but it was no use explaining. Fellow inmates and Alyssa Rollins were surprisingly alike in one regard: they heard only what they wanted to hear.

For some reason thinking of Alyssa brought Abby Hart to Kelsey's mind. That day in court Hart had been so angry. Kelsey knew that Hart wanted her to rat out Alyssa Rollins, spill the beans on the psychotic wife of the governor. Hart had no idea how dangerous Alyssa really was, no idea how her husband figured into everything.

I really thought I'd be free of them, finally. I would have been happy to quietly serve my time. Why am I here?

There was no answer for her in this small, quiet room.

After a while fatigue won and she fell on the bed and into the first sound sleep she'd enjoyed since her incarceration. Her driver had woken her up to feed her breakfast in the room, then left her again a few minutes later. It didn't escape her notice that the bedroom and bathroom windows were barred. Unease began to grow. She had been prepared to settle into a state prison full of known dangers. But this was a prison of unknowns. After what she believed were two days—figuring time was difficult—the driver had let her come out of the bedroom to the kitchen.

For the first time she paid attention to her surroundings. The house was small, probably somewhere in East LA, she guessed. Like the bedroom and bathroom, all the windows were barred. Outside the faint sound of mariachi music resonated. From the road noise, they were near the freeway.

She thought of the big oaf Quinn. He'd been mindless muscle, ready to spring into action for whatever Alyssa had in mind: campaign, security, murder—it didn't matter to Quinn.

But it mattered to Kelsey. She didn't see herself as Quinn, and she didn't want to. She doubted that Alyssa had sprung her for an altruistic reason. And if it had been Alyssa, Kelsey bet that she would be expecting a Quinn-like attitude in return. Alyssa had yet to make contact. As she chewed the food the driver had put in front of her, she knew that she'd soon hear from her rescuer.

And when she did, she'd learn the price for her freedom. Could she pay it?

CHAPTER

37

THE CHURCH WAS PACKED. Abby had a hard time finding a seat. It was nondenominational like her own home church, so she felt right at home. Pastor Terry was young and engaging. Abby enjoyed listening to him. His message was about forgiveness, how it's needed for the simplest and smallest irritations to the largest insults and hurts.

After the service she waited until he'd finished with the people in his congregation, those who'd come forward to speak to him or to ask for prayer, and then she approached him and introduced herself.

"Ah, you're one of the people looking for Padre Mike." He held her hand in both of his. "I'd love to talk to you about him. Are you in a hurry?"

"No, not a big hurry, but—"

"Good, then join us for lunch. I'm famished and my kids are waiting to eat. I don't want to short you. We have lunch here on the campus on Sundays."

Before Abby could answer, a boy about ten or eleven, Luke's daughter's age, ran up and grabbed Pastor Terry's hand. "Come on; it's time to eat."

Terry let the boy drag him off and Abby followed.

Lunch was a table full of homemade dishes, a potluck. Terry explained while he and Abby made their way through the food line, filling their plates, that this was how the staff fellowshipped after service every Sunday.

"We break bread, we talk about the church, but mostly we relax. Let our kids play, and just be good friends."

It was a relatively young group of people and a lot of small children. Terry introduced her to everyone, which included his wife and two boys. Abby felt comfortable with the group and she was glad Terry had asked her to lunch. It made her miss her home church, and Luke, a little less.

"So you want to find Padre Mike," Terry said as they sat and began to eat their meal. "What do you want with him?"

Abby nodded, her mouth full of a wonderful-tasting chicken casserole. She swallowed. "I would like to talk to him about something that happened a long time ago in Templeton, where he grew up."

"He's not in trouble?"

"Not at all."

Terry chewed his food and looked ready to ask another question. When he swallowed, he asked, "What's the whole story? Can you tell me that from the beginning?"

"It's complicated."

"That's okay. I've got food. I'm ready for a good story."

His wife brought him a cup of coffee, and Abby put her fork down. She told him everything, from the Triple Seven murders to the escape of Kelsey Cox.

"That's the story, and since I'm up here working on Ciara's murder case, I wanted to find him and ask him a few questions."

He stared at her in amazement. "Wow. That's incredible. You really think the First Lady of California is basically a murderer?"

"I don't know that I could prove she ever pulled a trigger, but I do believe she ordered my mother's murder. And then when my dad got away, she ordered the restaurant burned down, which resulted in the death of another man. Since then, I believe she's ordered more people killed to cover her tracks."

"Sounds like a movie. What about the governor? I met him once when he was here in SLO on the campaign trail a few years ago. For a politician, he really seemed sincere."

Abby thought a moment before answering. "I really don't know about him. My father thought a lot of him; they grew up together. I've always known him to be nice. But the cop in me asks how could he not know that his wife was a monster?"

"Unless you're wrong about her."

"I don't think I am."

He held her gaze and she saw concern there, concern that made her wonder if he thought she was too wrapped up in this. *I'm not going overboard,* Abby told herself.

"You know, sometimes when people are hurt by others, or victimized like you have been, they hold on to the hurt too long. Even more than getting justice, there is a fear of letting go of the hurt, because then what would they have? The hurt has become a part of them and it's scary to let go."

"I understand what you're saying, but that's not me. I'm simply following a viable lead." For a second she wavered. Was she getting too swept up again? It had happened before.

No. She pushed the thought from her mind.

"Back to the Padre," he said, changing the subject. "He's an interesting guy. He doesn't stay in any one place for long. He does return to spots, but he moves around a lot. And sometimes the police move the spots themselves when they break up a camp. He sees the homeless community as his mission field and himself as an old-fashioned traveling evangelist."

"So he's not crazy or impaired in any way?"

Terry laughed. "Mike's probably more sane than you and I. I don't know if you know much about the homeless—"

"I've dealt with them at work. Most of my contacts with the homeless were with drunks, addicts, and mentally unstable people."

"Maybe some. But Mike ministers to families, broken people, veterans, runaways, and the occasional mentally unbalanced. He moves in and about a transient population. He doesn't try to change them. He just brings them the gospel. He helps a lot of people. It's possible he'd be able to help you, and I might be able to find him, but it wouldn't be quick. Mike could be in Salinas or Santa Maria or just up the road—I'm not sure."

"Is there a homeless camp that you know of, one close that I could visit and ask around?"

"I wouldn't advise you to visit those places by yourself."

"My partner will be here tomorrow. I don't have to go alone."

"I've only visited one. Mike took me to a runaway girl once. I was able to talk her into coming home. This one is behind a shopping center—not close to it, but behind. But you should probably ask a county deputy about the place before you go; it might have been broken up by now. I'm not sure that if you find anyone, they will be much help to you . . . but you never know."

He drew her a crude map and Abby thanked him. She stayed a little while longer, enjoying the company and eating ice cream. But she wanted to visit the camp. It was torture to wait for Luke.

CHAPTER

38

MONDAY MORNING LUKE AND WOODY got off to a late start. Maddie wanted to be sure that Luke would be back on Thursday for her belated birthday, and then Grace, his mother, asked him to help with some last-minute party details. After all that, Woody took extra time to explain to his dog sitter how Zena's routine went.

Once they were on the road, Woody and Luke discussed Ciara's case and the power Orson believed they had to try to trick one of their suspects into confessing.

"We can do just about anything as long as we get consent, as long as the two suspects don't refuse to talk to us or scream, 'Lawyer,'" Woody told Luke.

"By that you mean we can bluff them, try to force them into a corner?"

"Exactly. We just have to think up something foolproof the first time out. We're not likely to get a second chance. Plus, Faye thinks we can use the Ciara case as a cover for the Napier case."

"How?"

"By using it to search for Stuart. We can make up a possible witness to the body dump. That could be the cover story for getting into wineries, telling them we're looking for a farmworker. We can develop a profile and work it up as an anonymous tip."

"I like that idea," Luke said. "Good for Faye. But as far as Ciara's case, it will be a challenge to come up with something that would force one of our suspects to confess to a murder that they have, for all intents and purposes, gotten away with."

"Um . . . we'll just have to be sneakier."

———▶■▶———

Monday, after a quick complimentary breakfast at the hotel, Abby's curiosity got the better of her. Taking the map, she got in the rental car and prepared to follow the route penciled out for her by Pastor Terry. She knew she should wait for Luke, but it felt like she had ants in her pants. She was so close to finally getting something on Alyssa. At the last minute, instead of following the map, she took Terry's advice and decided to ask local law enforcement first. She found the sheriff's station and went inside to ask about homeless camps in the area in general and this one in particular. There was a field deputy on the desk because of an injury who was familiar with the camp and who knew Mike.

"He helps us out from time to time," he told her. "In fact, once he helped us catch a killer. Around here we like the Padre."

"He's not in any trouble. I just want to talk to him."

"Well, unfortunately, there are a lot of homeless camps in the county. And they're fluid. They don't stay in any one place too long. This hand-drawn map you have is to one of the camps close to town, behind a shopping center."

"It's still there?"

"Yep. It's been quiet and peaceful, no complaints lately."

He explained that there were two ways in; the easiest and most traveled was a walking path that started at the back side of the shopping center parking lot. That was the path people with shopping carts or discarded strollers often took.

There was also a roundabout, drive-in way. It required a little hiking, but it would bring her to the camp from the back side, so she could watch the area, look for any trouble before actually walking in. He thought that would be the safest way to go. He also cautioned her not to go by herself.

"I'm armed," she said. "And I would take every precaution. Most likely I'll wait for my partner."

Abby thanked him and left, realizing as she got back in her car, she couldn't stop herself if she tried.

"The hurt has become a part of them and it's scary to let go."

Abby shook Pastor Terry's words from her mind and started the engine. Her phone chimed with a text from Luke telling her that he and Woody were on their way. She looked at the time and calculated how long it would take for them to get here. Two and a half hours tops. She could wait that long, couldn't she?

I'll just take a look, she thought, *in order to get an idea of the place. The deputy said I could see the whole camp and decide if I want to walk right in.*

Following the deputy's directions was not complicated at all. He'd clarified Terry's handwritten note. It was a drive across a bumpy dirt road through some uninhabited terrain before she got to a reasonable access trail.

She parked her rental car where the road ended at a locked gate. Once out of the car, she hiked a well-worn path that took her through dry brush and old oak trees. All along the path was scattered evidence of human incursion: trash, paper, and an occasional discarded, broken, rusty shopping cart.

The terrain was mildly hilly, and Abby climbed up to the crest of a small incline before heading down. She could see the makeshift tents and shelters below. There were a lot of people milling around by the tents; the size of the camp surprised her. The deputy was right. From here she could view the whole situation and make a rational decision about whether or not she would approach. But it was a cluster of people off to her right, away from the tents, that caught her attention.

A man was being bullied. Thoughts of just "taking a look" dissipated as Abby started down toward the camp. As she got closer, she counted three against one. A homeless man guarding a shopping cart was in the center of three kids, teenagers. It looked as if they were trying to take the cart and, in the process, peppering the homeless man with profanity and rocks. The boys were all cleanly dressed; there was no indication that they were also homeless. She winced as the shabby man turned his back, holding on to the cart for dear life.

"Come on, you stinky old man. What are you hiding in there?" the tallest of the teens said.

Another one circled around and wrenched the cart from the man, eliciting a howl from him and chortles of laughter from the teenagers. The man fell to his knees and the three boys jerked the cart out of his reach and dumped the contents everywhere.

With the old man on his knees, helpless, Abby stepped forward. "Hey, what's going on here?"

The boys all turned her direction.

"What's it to you?" The tallest bully adopted a belligerent pose Woody liked to call "chicken chested" and advanced toward Abby.

She squared her stance and lifted the corner of her light jacket to show the butt of her gun and badge. "I'm a police officer. Back off from the man and his possessions."

The tall boy stopped moving forward the same time a second boy sneered and said, "Possessions? It's all trash."

"Then why'd you have to dump it and take it away from him?"

From the corner of her eye, Abby saw people from the tent area moving their way. Suddenly she wondered at the wisdom of confronting the boys, especially if the homeless people saw a reason to confront her. She couldn't physically subdue all of them. If they didn't want to listen to her, or if they were given to more violence, the only force option she had was her firearm. Did she want to get into a shooting over a cart of trash?

The three boys started moving her way again as the old man scrambled on all fours toward his scattered belongings.

"You're not a cop." The tall one made a fist and thumped his chest. "I know all the cops here. That's a toy badge. What are you doing with a gun?"

Abby thought that with his attitude he certainly did know every cop in the area. She pulled her phone from her pocket. "Why don't I dial 911 and let someone sort this out?"

That stopped them again and Abby pressed the three numbers, thumb hovering over Send.

One of the other boys put a hand on the tall kid. "Hey, this is boring now. Why don't we find something else to do?"

"Nah, maybe we should just take that gun away from her."

He took another step forward, but Abby saw his eyes flick toward the tent area. Three or four figures were closer now, and they seemed to be concentrating on the altercation.

Indecision flashed in the kid's eyes and he looked toward his smaller friend. "Aw, you're right. This is boring and these people stink. Let's get out of here before we catch a disease."

He spit on the ground toward Abby and then turned away, waving his hand in a dismissive fashion. The other two fell into step with him as they left, taking a trail away from the camp, but a different trail from the one that brought Abby to the spot.

She realized she'd been holding her breath and turned toward the tent people. They'd stopped their progress toward her but were still watching. There were two men and a woman. Putting her phone away, she nodded toward them, then went to see if she could help the man who was putting his "treasures" back into his cart.

Keeping an eye on the watchers, Abby approached the man. "Are you okay?"

He mumbled something she didn't understand and continued picking up his belongings.

Abby helped him right his cart, noticing cuts on his grimy hands. The man appeared to be in his sixties, painfully thin, balding, and wearing jeans too big for him, tied with a rope. The polo shirt he had on looked as though it hadn't seen a washing in a month, and the odor confirmed that. Abby had seen many homeless men like him in Long Beach when she worked patrol. She never liked to deal with them, not because of the grime and the stench, but because the majority of those who attracted police attention needed medication for some illness or another and they refused to take it. That was generally why they were homeless. Trying to reason with people who had untreated mental issues was pretty much impossible.

"It's jelly; it's jelly," the man said.

"What?" Abby asked. "Are you missing something? Did the boys take something from you?"

"It's jelly; it's jelly."

Abby wasn't certain what he was saying, and she knew she'd not get any information from him about Mike Jez. She continued helping him put everything in his cart and pull it back up onto the path the boys had dumped it from.

"Hey!"

Abby's head jerked up to see a figure running toward them. On alert, she stepped back to be prepared.

"What are you doing to him?" the out-of-breath man asked. About the same age as the shopping cart man she was helping, this man was dark-skinned—Hispanic or Indian.

"I'm not doing anything to him. I was helping him get his things together."

"You a cop? Is he in trouble?"

"I am a cop, and no, he's not in trouble."

"Then what are you doing here?" He faced her with his hands on his hips, brow furrowed.

"I'm looking for Padre Mike."

"Padre Mike? Is he is trouble?"

"No, nobody's in trouble. I just want to talk to him."

The first homeless man gestured to the second man. He handed him something and pointed to Abby.

"What? You sure?" he asked. The grimy man nodded and the second man took the object. "I don't know what you did, but Jelly likes you."

"Is that his name, Jelly?"

"That's what we call him. Me, I'm Ham. We're buddies, Ham and Jelly. He wants you to have this, so you must've done something good."

He held out his hand and Abby had to fight the fear that Jelly wanted to give her a filthy present from his cart. But when she looked into Ham's hand, she saw a small geode, a stone cut in half to reveal beautiful crystals inside. It wasn't grimy; in fact it looked as if it had recently been polished.

"Oh, that's beautiful," Abby said, "but it's his treasure."

"Don't matter. He wants you to have it." He pushed the stone closer and Abby took it.

"What happened here?" Ham asked.

She explained about the boys.

Ham slapped his forehead. "I know those boys. Man, I never should have left Jelly. We was down at Mickey D's and they were trippin' on us. They must've followed us back here. Thank you for helping Jelly. Now, what do you want with the Padre?"

"I just want to talk to him about something that happened a long time ago, something he might know about." She pulled out a business card and wrote down her cell phone number. She handed the card to Ham. "I'll be here for a few days. He can call me at this number or check in at the church if he wants to be certain I'm on the level. I know Pastor Terry."

"Pastor Terry? He's good people." Ham took the card and read it carefully. "You're from Long Beach? Padre's never been to Long Beach, I'm sure." He frowned.

"This happened here. Well, not here, but in Templeton, where he went to school. A long time ago. I really want to talk to him."

Ham nodded. "I'll see what I can do, but I ain't promising nothing." He turned to help Jelly push his cart to where the tents and makeshift shelters were. Abby watched them go. Then she put the geode in her pocket and headed back up the trail the way she'd come.

When she reached the rental car, she stopped abruptly as if she'd hit a wall. All four tires were flat as pancakes.

CHAPTER

39

ABBY WALKED AROUND the car, all the while noting her surroundings. There was no one in sight, yet all four tires had obviously been slashed. She could see the damage to the sidewalls. Was this the work of the boys? She doubted that. They had left in the other direction. Perplexed, she took out her phone and called AAA for a tow. After a long wait that only caused her anger to simmer, they told her it would be forty minutes before a truck could get there.

She put the phone away and leaned against the car, glad that the day was a comfortable temperature. But she was thirsty and her stomach growled with hunger. Anger at the tire slasher gave way to anger at herself.

I never should have come out here by myself, she thought. *This really could have gone bad—way worse than four flat tires.* The bleak, deserted landscape served to heighten her angst. Was this because of the Ciara case? Was Alyssa responsible? Or was it something random?

She heard the car about the same time she saw the dust cloud approaching. There was a light bar on the roof, Abby saw that much, so she knew it was a patrol car. She stood up to greet the approaching law enforcement officer, her eagerness turning to caution when the car pulled to a stop and she saw that it wasn't a sheriff's vehicle. It was a Morro Bay police car, and J. P. Winnen was behind the wheel.

Tense now, Abby folded her arms and waited while he parked and got out of the car.

"Run into some trouble, Detective Hart?" he asked as he walked toward her, hooking his thumbs in his belt. It wasn't a smirk on his face, but it was close.

"I'd report this," Abby said, "but you're a long way out of your jurisdiction."

"Any suspect info?"

"No."

"Then I doubt the sheriff's department will be able to help either."

"You obviously came looking for me, Officer Winnen. What is it you want?"

"I was just curious as to what a bunch of human debris living in a homeless camp had to do with Ciara's murder."

"That information is available on a need-to-know basis, and you don't need to know."

She saw the muscle jump in his jaw as his features clouded with anger, and she wondered at the wisdom of antagonizing him out here in the middle of nowhere. But she was equally angry and didn't like the feeling of being watched or followed.

He brought a hand up to his face and looked away for a moment before turning back, eyes narrowed. "What is your problem? I did a little research on you and your team.

Out-of-towners and FBI—it would show good sense to be on positive terms with local law enforcement."

Barely contained anger from the man.

"We are on good terms with San Luis Obispo PD. And the only problem I have is that Ciara's case has gone cold and a murderer is still out there free." She gestured toward his patrol car. "I also have an issue with someone following me."

He spit off to the right. "I found you because the deputy you talked to at the station is a friend of mine. He said you were interested in the homeless. Again, what does the homeless camp have to do with Ciara?"

"That's none of your business."

His face turned red. "You'd better be careful. Today it's flat tires; tomorrow it could be something worse."

"Is that a threat?"

"Warning. This is my home field, not yours." He spun on his heel and stomped back to his patrol car.

A few minutes later Abby watched his dust cloud recede and tried to make sense of the visit from a man she was quickly moving to the top of her suspect list.

CHAPTER

40

LUKE AND WOODY arrived back in San Luis Obispo about three in the afternoon. Abby wasn't at the hotel, and Luke puzzled about where she might be. She didn't leave a note of any kind. He sent her a text telling her they were at the hotel and did not get an answer right away.

"She might be out of range somewhere," Woody said.

"By herself? I hope not." He powered up his laptop and rechecked his e-mail. Nothing. Anxious, he checked his spam folder and found a message there from Abby. She'd sent it Saturday and there was a link attached to a large file, so he guessed that was why it was weeded out to spam. He clicked on the link and saw a copied newspaper article. They had a portable printer with them, so he printed it out.

The article was from a Templeton newspaper and it was dated May 1969, around the time of Alyssa's high school days. Obviously Abby and Gunther had dug up something.

Local Girl Found Dead

The search for Sheryl Shepherd ended in tragedy
yesterday when the 17-year-old high school cheerleader's
body was found in a dry well. She'd left home two
weeks ago, telling her mother she was meeting with
friends. When she didn't return home that night, her
parents called the sheriff's office. A search began almost
immediately when it was learned that she never met
with her friends. High school classmates joined the local
search and rescue to no avail.

A local farmer rounding up his cattle checked out
the location of the well when he saw buzzards circling.
It's not known why Sheryl was in the vicinity of the
well, but it does appear as if this was a tragic accident.
There is no sign of foul play. The theory is that Sheryl
fell into the well and was not able to climb out.

Police believe that Sheryl most likely succumbed
to the elements. Funeral services are pending a routine
autopsy. Her parents request in lieu of flowers donations
be made to the local Salvation Army.

Abby had not written any explanation for the story, and
Luke wondered why she'd sent it.

He checked his phone, but she'd still not responded to his
text.

"I'm worried too," Woody said.

"You can tell I'm worried?"

"Like there's a neon sign over your head."

"It just seems like she would have left a note or at least sent a text." All Luke could see in his head was the maniacal look in Victoria Napier's eyes. Was Abby becoming so wrapped up with the Triple Seven again that she did something unsafe?

As if on cue his phone chirped with a text.

Parking now.

CHAPTER

41

MORE THAN SEEING LUKE, Abby wanted a shower. It wasn't just being around the grimy homeless men or the dust from her hike down to the homeless camp. It was also waiting an hour for a tow truck and getting dirty from the ride in the rig back to the rental office, where a big hassle awaited. The only bright spot was the arrival of a sheriff's deputy with the tow truck. Someone—she was sure it was the teenage boys—had called 911 about a woman with a gun at the homeless camp. Luckily, the desk deputy she'd talked to earlier had heard the call and radioed to his colleague about Abby and her mission.

The deputy was more helpful than Winnen had been, and Abby wasn't nearly as creeped out by his visit as she had been by the Morro Bay cop. She knew there could be many reasons why Winnen was so far out of his jurisdiction. He could have had a court appearance in San Luis; he could have been running an errand, going to training—any number of things besides looking for her. Her gut, though, told her that he was simply following her. But why?

The deputy took a report about the damage to the tires

and told her that he knew Padre Mike and worked the homeless camps. He also knew the boys she'd confronted. They were local bullies and tended to pick on the homeless wherever they found them. They'd been counseled often to stay away from homeless people. The deputy decided they obviously needed another warning.

"I wouldn't put slashing tires past them," he said. "All four is overkill, though."

Abby doubted the boys had slashed her tires. At the same time she was sure that it wasn't random or coincidental. She was thankful for his help, and he promised to contact her if he came across Padre Mike.

Starving by the time she received a new rental car, she asked the attendant for the best pizza place nearby. She didn't see Luke's text until she was back in the hotel parking lot.

Hungry, tired, and grimy, she knocked on their door, bringing with her a pizza.

Luke opened the door, and in spite of all the bad the day had brought, she got the familiar rush, the flush to her skin, and the increased heart rate that seeing him often did to her.

"Hey, sorry I'm late." She extended the pizza. "Here's a present to make up for it."

He smiled and took the pizza from her. "I'll admit I was worried, but I'm glad you're here now."

Something in his tone bugged Abby. Why was he worried? *I can take care of myself.*

Fighting irritation she knew was because of the flat tires, Winnen's visit, and the prolonged day, she stepped inside the room to greet Woody. Luke set the pizza on the little hotel table while Abby excused herself to wash her hands.

"So where were you?" Woody asked. "I hope you weren't running around chasing down leads on your own."

Abby almost snapped. "I was looking for someone," she said, voice tight, drying her hands and heading for the pizza. After a couple of bites she calmed down and told him about Padre Mike and the homeless camp she'd walked to. The expressions on both their faces stopped her from mentioning Winnen.

"You went down there by yourself?" Luke's tone was sharp and he stared at her, aghast.

"I'm a big girl," Abby said a little more forcefully than she wanted to. But fatigue and irritation were a powerful combination. "I have a gun and I handled it fine."

"That's not the point." Luke frowned. "I thought this was something we were going to work on together. I thought you'd know better than to run off by yourself."

"Know better? What I know is that I'm not a child." Abby set her unfinished pizza slice down, appetite gone. "I'll follow leads however I see fit."

"It's not smart to put yourself in jeopardy like that. It's reckless."

They stared at one another, Abby itching to throw something back at him.

Then Woody stood. "Hey, you two, calm down. We're all on the same side. Abby, Luke cares about you and he was worried—so was I, if the truth be told. You're not in Long Beach now. You don't have your radio and backup at your beck and call. Didn't I train you better than to try to bite off more than you can chew?"

Abby stood. "Yes, you trained me. You trained me to take

care of myself, and I resent you questioning my ability." She left them the tip line cell phone before she stomped toward the door. "Now if it's okay with my two guardians, I'm tired and I'm going to bed."

CHAPTER

42

"MAYBE SHE FELT ganged up on," Luke said after Abby stormed out of the room. But in his heart was a real fear that she was letting the case take over. He'd already thought the lead she was following—this idea that Alyssa was hiding a horrible secret—was weak. Abby had put herself in real jeopardy chasing a phantom.

"Could be," Woody agreed. "But she really took a risk. She's lucky she only got flat tires."

Luke sighed, working to calm down. After all, Abby was not Victoria. Was he overreacting? "Tell me the truth, is it something you would have done in her position?"

"I, uh . . ." Woody looked at Luke, expression sheepish. "I hate to tell you the things I got into alone when I was a youngster."

"Exactly." Luke shook his head. "I don't like what she did, walking into an unsafe situation all by herself, but maybe both of us jumping on her like that was over the top." He sat down on his bed and texted his daughter good night, all the while trying to understand the stark fear that had gripped his heart when

Abby nonchalantly told him about confronting multiple people out in the middle of nowhere and then having her tires slashed.

He realized that he couldn't try to suppress the feelings he had for Abby any longer. He'd overreacted because of them and it was time he told Abby how he felt.

Luke was up early, hoping to smooth things over with Abby before breakfast and explain why he'd reacted the way he had. But when he looked out the window, he saw that she'd been up even earlier. She was dressed to run, and she hit the bottom step and headed out of the parking lot at a brisk jog.

"Man," Luke moaned as he hurried to put on his own running gear and catch up to her.

"What's going on?" Woody asked, eyes still half-closed with sleep.

"Go back to sleep. I'm going to try to catch Abby." With that, he was out the door and down the steps. Luke had brought his running clothes hoping to get in a workout or two because he'd not been able to hit his cardiovascular training very hard lately. The months of test taking and working to clear his business calendar had meant that he'd not been to the gym regularly or made many basketball games.

His breath came fast after crossing the parking lot and reaching the sidewalk. He looked right first and saw nothing. Turning left, he saw Abby a few blocks down, moving at a fast clip.

"Thank you, Lord," he muttered under his breath as he started running, glad Abby had chosen to start her run downhill, not uphill.

He eased up his stride about a block before he reached her,

to give his breathing an opportunity to slow. He also prayed she'd stop when he did get to her because he wasn't sure how much longer he could keep his pace up. Putting on a burst of speed to keep from being caught at a red light, Luke pulled within a stride's length of Abby.

"Abby!" he huffed.

She jerked around, startled, slowing somewhat.

He pulled even with her. "Please, I want to talk to you."

She frowned, pulled up, and stopped. Hands on hips, breathing hard, she faced him. Luke bent over, hands on his thighs, and waited for his breath to ease.

"Thanks," he breathed and noticed Abby watching him with an unreadable expression. Fear bit that she wouldn't accept his apology. As soon as he could, he straightened up. "I wanted to explain."

Besides the fact that she looked totally unaffected by the seven- or eight-block run down the hill, her brows furrowed. "Explain? You and Woody treated me like a child."

This was not going well. Luke realized that she was still mad.

"I'm sorry if it seemed like that—"

"It was like that."

"Abby, I can't speak for Woody, but I was afraid for you. I care about you—a lot—and I don't want to see you become so wrapped up in the Triple Seven investigation again that you put yourself in danger needlessly." Luke spoke fast so that she couldn't interrupt again.

They stared at one another. Abby looked away first.

"I know that you're not a child. I know you are an incredibly awesome investigator. I don't want . . ." He was going to say that he didn't want to see her become like Victoria, but

Abby wouldn't know what he meant. "I don't want that case to consume you again. At one time you yourself were afraid of that happening."

She took a deep breath and Luke could see conflicting emotions cross her face. "You're right. I don't want that either. You don't owe me an apology." She waved him off. "I owe you an apology for acting like a child. I'm sorry. I realized . . ." She stopped and for a second Luke thought she was going to cry.

"Realized what?"

"Maybe it was getting to me. I know I shouldn't have put myself in that position." She stomped her foot and he saw the tears. She gave an angry sweep with her hand at one eye. "We're so close to the end of the Triple Seven, to finally holding Alyssa accountable. I feel it. I also feel like someone trying to grab a brass ring that keeps getting pulled away. I don't want to be obsessed. I . . ."

Luke couldn't let her finish. He stepped forward and took her into his arms, holding her close and letting the tears fall on his shoulder.

CHAPTER

43

ABBY FELT DANGEROUSLY comfortable in Luke's arms. But a niggling of fear rambled across her mind. She let him hold her until long after the tears of frustration stopped because it just felt right. His heart was beating rapidly at first, but it slowed to a steady and strong pace, and he was warm from his jog. His arms felt like a solid and safe place to be. But they were standing on a street corner in the middle of downtown San Luis Obispo and she needed to be clear about where he really stood with Faye, and those realities shook her from her musings.

She sucked in a breath and pushed out of his embrace to wipe her eyes. "Sorry about that. I'm okay now."

"I wasn't complaining," he said with a half smile. The warmth in his eyes made her blush. "Do you want to finish your jog or tell me why you think you're getting obsessed again?"

"Better not keep jogging. You'd never keep up," she teased.

"Ouch." He seemed glad she was getting her feet back under her.

She folded her arms. "I shouldn't have gone looking for Mike by myself. I know better. And when I got there, first thing that happened was I had a confrontation. But it was like I couldn't stop myself from going. And then J. P. Winnen showed up."

"What?"

Abby nodded. "He showed up there right after I phoned AAA. I was so out of sorts yesterday. I'm sorry I couldn't go into it. But he truly creeped me out."

She watched Luke's face and thought she saw irritation streak by, but now there was only concern and support.

"We rattled his chain. He's keeping tabs on us."

"That's what I thought. It just confirmed for me he's someone we need to look hard at."

"It does for me as well. Why don't we talk about it on the way back to the hotel, at an easier pace." He held out his hand, but she hesitated to take it.

"Luke, I need to know about you and Faye."

Luke sighed. "We really did call it quits. I had nothing to do with asking her to take Duke's place. That was all Orson."

Abby felt a little bit of anxiety loosen in her chest. "Okay, thanks for that. Maybe I shouldn't have wondered, but I did."

"It's okay. I probably would have felt the same way if Ethan showed up to work on this case with us."

"That won't happen." She laughed and took his hand. "He's in Africa."

On the walk back, holding hands, shoulder to shoulder, she gave him more details about the confrontation at the homeless camp.

"Teenage bullies," she said. "But it could have been worse." She felt Luke squeeze her hand, and the rough strength there sent a shiver through her.

"Do you think the kids flattened your tires or Winnen?"

"I doubt it was the kids. The deputy thought flattening all four tires was overkill for the kids, and I agree. Winnen was trying to send a message, scare me, I'm sure of it. I think he flattened the tires."

"But he had to know doing that would make us suspicious."

"He's cocky. I've run into guys like him before. He's an in-your-face, I-dare-you kind of guy."

"And the warning?" Luke shot her a concerned glance that she didn't miss.

"I'm thinking a bluff. But we still need to be careful."

"I'm glad you said that. You shouldn't have gone alone."

A spark of anger flared—Abby wasn't sure why—and she tried to pull her hand free from his, but he held tight. She stepped around to face him and stopped, wanting to tell him that she wasn't a child, when she saw the laughter in his eyes. She should have heard the tease in his voice.

Immediately all her anger was defused. He was right; she'd already admitted that. What was it about him that seemed to set all her emotions alive at once?

She grinned and he chuckled. "Very funny, Luke Murphy, pushing my buttons like that."

"It was a low-hanging curveball; I had to hit it out of the park." His gaze changed to serious, and she felt the tug on her hand as he pulled her close, neck bent, holding her eyes with his. "I don't want to lose you, Abby. Not to carelessness, not to anything."

Abby melted into him as his lips brushed hers. He let her hand go and pulled her into another tight embrace.

"Promise me we'll be a team on this from now on," he

whispered, his warm breath tickling her ear. "If we're a team, I can keep you safe."

"I promise," Abby said, voice unsteady, breathing his scent, feeling safe and secure in his embrace. "And if we're a team, I can keep you safe."

He kissed her head, then grasped her shoulders, gently pushing her back to look at her, his smoldering hazel eyes holding hers once again.

"Thank you." He grasped both her hands and brought them to his lips and kissed the knuckles. "We'll see that justice is served. I promise you that."

They continued walking hand in hand. Abby knew the best thing for her to do was to trust Luke and to work with him, not strike out on her own. He was right; together they would find justice for their shared cold case.

After a long silence, Luke cleared his throat. "You know that I'm still having a difficult time with this whole Alyssa secret thing. But I do want to hear more about why you think your mother might have been up here thirty years ago."

"It has to do with something Uncle Simon said. When we met for the first time, he said I was the spitting image of my mom. The last time he would have seen her, she was probably my age. And both of those women said that they recognized me. Do you think that's only a coincidence?"

"In spite of my doubts, I guess I'd have to say no." He frowned. "Do you think she found Padre Mike?"

Abby stopped. "I don't know. I hadn't thought that far down the road. It's possible. I do believe that whatever my mother found here is what got her killed."

"Is that why you sent me that article about the girl in the

well? Do you think Alyssa had something to do with that?" His tone carried a hint of incredulity.

"I do. I thought that the story about Sheryl Shepherd was more than an odd coincidence. Alyssa left town a week after that girl was found dead. And Sheryl was one of the girls who bullied Alyssa."

They started walking again.

"But the article said that there was no sign of foul play. It might be as hard to find out the truth there as it would be to find the hit-and-run your uncle said Lowell did."

"It's a thread. I want to pull it."

"Of course you do."

"Luke, there is something here—I feel it. Can't you trust me?"

"I do trust you. But you and Woody have often pointed out the danger of tunnel vision. I don't want you to get that when it comes to chasing this faint maybe of a lead. The victim in our new case is chasing a phantom of a lead—it's made her a little crazy. I think you'll see that when you look over the files."

"Fair enough. I'll keep things in perspective."

"That's all I ask." They were silent of a moment, until Luke changed the subject. "I talked to Bill earlier. He said you called him."

"I did. He didn't call me back."

"He's busy helping with the escapee search. Said he'd call you when he had a few more details. Did you hear the latest about Kelsey Cox? Besides the jumpsuit, they found cut leg irons and open handcuffs."

Abby wasn't surprised. "That's more hard evidence she had help escaping. Gunther said it was stupid for her to run and I agree. She's blown her plea deal. But I can't believe that she is any danger to me, or you for that matter."

"I think that's a safe bet, but I wanted you to be up to date. Once you sift through the new case, we'll all be on the same page."

They were almost to the hotel parking lot.

"Both of these cases need our full attention; the Triple Seven can wait." She stopped, took her hand from his, and held it out for a shake. "Deal?"

"Deal." He gripped her hand and smiled a brilliant smile that made Abby want to jump into his arms again. But then she saw a worried Woody heading right toward them.

"Hey, you two, don't do that to me again. I had no clue what you were running off to."

Luke chuckled.

"Where did you tell him you were going?" Abby asked.

"I really didn't tell him anything."

The look on Woody's face made Abby freeze and the smile faded. "What is it?"

"She called back—the tipster. She gave me a detailed statement. Swears Ciara was going to break up with Chaz, give him back his ring. Mrs. Considine paid her off to keep quiet. Wanted to be sure she never told the police that story."

"She give her name?" Luke asked.

"No. She's still afraid. She says Mrs. Considine is evil and has a long reach. I tried to explain that we wouldn't let the woman intimidate her. But I think this is important. Chaz and his mother went to considerable trouble to keep the narrative under control. There's something there. It's up to us to prove it."

CHAPTER 44

THEY WERE A TEAM in more ways than one, Abby thought as she showered and changed for the day, feeling as though the smile would never leave her lips. She couldn't deny her strong feelings for Luke, and now she knew he felt the same way. Abby could still feel the warmth in her body from Luke's hug, feel the caresses on her shoulders from his strong hands.

Abby knew that the rest of this trip would be a success as well. Everything was on track.

"Looks like you took my advice," Woody said when Luke got out of the shower.

"I guess I did," he said with a smile. "I'm not a coward."

"Didn't think you were."

Luke whistled while he got dressed, Abby on his mind. He thought of all the things about her that attracted him: her heart, mind, strength, will, and tenacity. Unfortunately, he realized that some of those qualities were a double-edged sword. He truly believed this thing with Alyssa was a dead end. What would he do if Abby couldn't, or wouldn't, let it go?

——————▶

The smile he gave her as he opened the restaurant door for her sent shivers up her spine. Abby tried to shelve her feelings. There was too much going on. The best thing to do would be to close this case with an arrest, and that was what she prayed for. After they were seated and had ordered their breakfast, Luke and Woody told her about Victoria Napier.

"She's absolutely certain her husband's up here working at a vineyard somewhere?" Abby frowned. "Sounds like a long shot."

"It does," Woody conceded. "But Orson was asked to give her a little help, and it's just fifteen wineries. I don't have a problem with it. He plans on joining us to help out."

"Let's work out the details of our new DNA story," Luke said. He turned to Abby to explain. "Woody and I decided on a fake DNA test story to plant in the paper. Something along the lines of a new, sensitive test for the evidence related to Ciara. We're hoping this will make our suspects nervous, force them to do or say something that will catch our attention."

"Good idea."

"We have to sell the deception for it to be plausible," Woody said.

Abby nodded. "I've used deception before, like telling half of a crime team that the other party is spilling their guts. Sometimes it works. I'm hoping that Chaz, in an alcoholic haze, will be convinced we're closing in on him."

"Well, I reread the inventory of items found with her. If

the blanket found with Ciara belonged to Chaz, it's plausible if there were a new test, we would find his DNA. If it belonged to Ciara, it won't put a fire under anyone and we'll be out of luck."

"Her mom didn't recognize the blanket as being hers. Refresh my memory. What else was found with her body?" Luke said.

"Duct tape, the blanket—partially decomposed—and blue rope," Woody said. "How about our false story is along these lines? There's now a method to test the blanket for DNA, and a sample has been sent out for that purpose."

"You've put a lot of thought into this," Abby said with a smile.

Woody grinned. "Yes, I have. That reporter who talked with us when we arrived here, Josh Federer—maybe he'll plant the story."

"We'd have to let the girl's mother know it's a ruse," Luke said.

"Agreed. But let's leave the PD in the dark."

Luke raised his eyebrows. "You think they're dirty?"

"No, not at all, but Winnen is a cop. He'd have no problem contacting someone at the sheriff's department, or San Luis PD, for information. If he's not the guy—" she hiked a shoulder—"there will just be some hurt feelings. But we won't be tipping off a suspect. We will have to sell the reporter, though. I know Gunther would do something like that; not sure about the guy here."

"I'll sell it to him," Woody said. "I can be convincing." He tapped the table, smug expression on his face, and Luke and Abby laughed.

CHAPTER

45

RIGHT AFTER BREAKFAST, Woody set up an appointment with Josh Federer. Luke and Abby settled in to review all of the recorded television news footage from when Ciara went missing and then fifteen years later when her remains were found. There was a lot of footage, but it was important to review. Sometimes news camerapeople recorded important things accidentally.

The twenty-year-old news footage showed a younger Mrs. Considine in all her glory. She gave several interviews extolling her son's virtues, telling everyone that Chaz and Ciara were in love; he never would have done anything to hurt her. She strenuously refused to let him be interviewed unless there was hard evidence against him.

"She sure was intimidating back then," Luke said. "Even on a small screen."

"But her actions make everything circle back to Chaz." Abby chewed on her bottom lip, frustrated and wishing she'd been in on this case since the beginning. Because Mrs. Considine shut down all the attempts to interview Chaz by himself and then stopped the one interview in which she did sit down with him at the station, there was nothing much to play with regarding his statement. Their conversation at breakfast last week hadn't really added anything workable.

Winnen was another matter. He'd given two taped interviews and had called the police with tips at least twice. The first time was what the retired cop had told them about, the one not officially recorded, but the second time was recorded. In the second call he talked about all the women he knew who complained about Harkin and promised to give the cops names. And because Abby believed the two men were in some way connected, she was certain that if they got to Winnen, they would get to Chaz, or vice versa.

One point Luke found interesting was the timing of Winnen's calls. First the tip that Axelson had told them about, the call about Harkin. Then, after the PD had begun to focus on the pool maintenance man, Winnen called in to give the names of two coeds who claimed Harkin had disturbed them by the way he looked at them. The coeds were two people the team had not been able to reconnect with. Was the anonymous caller one of them?

"Did he know about Harkin's past? Is that why he called in the tip?" Abby wondered out loud. "And did he line up the girls to pile on to Harkin, keep the cops going down that trail?"

"Wouldn't be the first time guilty people tried to misdirect the police," Luke said.

"In the first taped interview, he says that he didn't see Chaz and Ciara leave the party but remembers that they were already gone when he left," Abby noted.

"Yes, and in the second interview, he says he did see them leave and gave a time of 12:15." Luke sifted through the transcripts. "When he's asked about the discrepancy, he claims that he just forgot, that he had a brief conversation with the pair and saw that they weren't fighting or anything."

"They pressed him on that, and he stuck to his second story. But I'd still be curious about the change," Abby said.

"Maybe they were curious at the time, but the next day they had Harkin to look at."

"Could be, and they obviously got tunnel vision when it came to Harkin. It happens."

"I can agree with that," Luke said. "Like you said, it was truly an impediment to the investigation not being able to interview Considine. My money is on him knowing a lot more than he ever said."

"Well, then let's pray that our ruse works and we scare him to open up." She closed the files on Ciara and moved to the Napier case.

"Victoria Napier's formula for finding her husband is so complex it makes my head spin," she said after reading through some of the paperwork. "But the story is compelling. What a monster this Stuart Napier is. And to disappear so completely." She shook her head.

"She's something in person," Luke said. "So intense. She's convinced that she will find him and she plans to keep looking until she does."

"She does appear to be a mite focused. After the work she's put into locating the guy by herself, I hope that he is eventually found. I can't imagine driving all over the country, walking into vineyards, looking for her killer husband. Just think, suppose she'd found him? Came face-to-face with the killer of her children? It would have been ugly."

For lunch, they decided to take a drive. Woody left to meet the reporter Federer, so it was just Abby and Luke. They drove to Paso Robles and stopped at a deli near a park across from city hall. They picked up sandwiches and drinks and located a free table in the park.

To Abby, Luke seemed to want light conversation, but she drew him back to the Napier file, the images still fresh in her mind. The case had touched her; she understood why Orson wanted to help.

"I can't help but put myself in that position, if I were the investigator called out to that horrible scene."

"Would you have done anything different?"

"No, I guess I wouldn't have. I mean, there wasn't much to do but study the death and destruction, hoping for any clues to catch the killer. He certainly disappeared in a masterful way."

"I agree. He had to have planned it."

"Either that, or he's dead."

"Victoria is convinced he's alive."

"She seems pretty courageous. She almost died three times."

Luke chewed a bite of sandwich and considered that. "Courageous, maybe," he said after he swallowed. "Obsessed certainly. To be honest, she made me a little uncomfortable."

"I understand her, I think. Those were beautiful little boys. And the damage to her physically is horrendous."

"Yeah, maybe, but there has to be a point in any investigation where the victim must step back. This search has consumed her whole life. That's not healthy."

Abby looked away and felt a pinch in her soul, as if Luke

were talking to her and not referring to Victoria. And Pastor Terry's words still rang in her mind.

"The hurt has become a part of them and it's scary to let go."

"She lost so much," she said after a minute. "I see why she is so determined to find the man who took it all away." She toyed with her lunch. If Luke was referring to her, she would ignore it and bring up what else was on her mind. "Which brings me to the elephant in the room. This morning, when . . . well, when—"

"When you and I . . . ?"

"When we hugged. What was that? I mean, are we taking a serious step in our relationship?"

His clear hazel eyes held hers and Abby felt her heart jump in her chest.

"I hope so. For a long time I've been attracted to you. But I wasn't certain if you were over Ethan. I—"

"I am, Luke, and I'd love to take a serious step with you . . . once we're done with this case and home again." She reached across the table with her hand.

He grasped it. "That makes me very happy, Abby. And I—"

Luke's phone buzzed and the spell was broken. "It's a text from Woody. The reporter will help us out. They were already going to run an in-depth story about the squad, so they'll add the DNA test."

Abby wanted to know what he was going to say and felt irritated by the interruption. But shelving her angst and the question for another time, she gave him a thumbs-up. "Outstanding. We'll put this case to bed—I know it."

She wanted the moment back but could be patient for the time being.

CHAPTER

46

THE RUSE HAD to be more elaborate than Abby expected or wanted. In fact, Woody spent most of Tuesday afternoon coordinating on the phone with Faye in Long Beach. Orson had joined them after lunch and he was also part of the powwow.

Since Ciara's disappearance and murder had been such a big case in San Luis Obispo, they had to expect legitimate news inquiries. So Faye would field calls, pretending to be the DNA lab attempting to extract DNA from the sample they sent. It was also Faye who contacted Ciara's mother, through an attorney, and relayed that the woman was behind the idea. Abby actually liked it that Faye talked to Ciara's mother. Faye understood the kind of loss the woman felt. Faye's husband had been murdered; she knew how to speak to a woman who had suffered such a loss.

As to the ruse, Abby knew that sometimes if you made a thing too complicated, it wouldn't work. The story the reporter planned to run with was short and straightforward, and she hoped that would ensure success. Faye had a brief script and a dedicated phone line. Was this simple enough?

"All we can do is wait and see if Considine or Winnen takes

the bait," Abby said after the story appeared on the Internet news site.

"And I've been thinking about that," Orson said. "I think Woody and I should conduct a little surveillance on Considine. It's no use putting a tail on the cop, Winnen. But if we sit on Considine for a bit after the story runs, we might be able to tell if it's rattled his cage."

"Sounds like a plan," Woody said. "Luke and Abby can start visiting wineries, and we'll sit on Considine. I'll have the tip phone with me, and I'll call them if anything happens on either front."

"Good idea," Luke said.

"I agree, great idea. But I think we need a ruse for the vineyards as well," Abby said. "I don't think we can walk into a winery and tell them we're looking for a wanted killer."

"Woody and I talked about that," Luke said. "We can be looking for something else."

"Right," Woody said. "My idea is that we create a witness to Ciara's body dump. He can look like Napier, and since we've already been in the paper as looking for her, it's not out of the ballpark."

"Well, we've already made up a DNA test." Abby stood, energized by the idea, a plan forming in her mind. "That is an idea. They employ a lot of seasonal workers in the vineyards. Why don't we say we're looking for a farmworker who possibly saw something?"

"New information comes to light," Luke said. "We can describe Napier as our elusive witness."

"An anonymous tip. It's plausible someone would call the tip line with something like this. Our tip number is out there for anyone with information to call, so to say we got a call on that line is not too out of the ordinary. But I don't think we should feed this fake witness search to the press. I think it should only go to the individual vineyards when we tell them who we are and what we're trying to find—a witness, nothing more." Abby wrote this down on the whiteboard.

"They are sure to have already seen the press coverage about the cold case and the new DNA test," Woody said.

"Exactly. So this inquiry at their vineyards, in their minds, will not have anything to do with finding a suspect hiding there. We just want to talk to people, see if there is anyone around who may know the fictional worker we are going to invent."

"All the while looking for Stuart Napier."

"But we do have to be careful, mindful that Napier is dangerous," Woody said.

"I agree, but he's also hiding," Luke said. "Nothing we've given to the press mentions the Napier case. Orson says we are unofficially looking into it, so I would think unless we tip our hand . . ." His voice trailed off.

"And the fugitive realizes we're looking for him, we should be fine."

Abby and Luke gave each other a high five. Then all of them moved to the map, setting pins down for the vineyards Victoria had listed. They drew up an orderly schedule for the vineyards. They also had to devise a strategy about what to do there, something that wouldn't alert Napier, if they did find someone who might be him.

Anything they thought was a lead would mean they immediately notify Orson. He would forward the information to the proper authorities. It was not up to the cold case team to take down a wanted fugitive.

CHAPTER

-47-

AFTER THEY CALLED it a night, Orson grabbed Luke's arm. "Can we take a walk?"

Luke looked at his boss and friend and could tell there was something serious behind the request. "Sure."

He followed Orson out into the hotel parking lot. Abby had already gone to bed and Woody was on the phone with his dog sitter.

"What's up, buddy?" Luke asked.

"I want to ask you a personal question." He faced Luke with his hands in his pockets. "I just wondered about . . . Faye. I mean . . . are you two . . . uh . . . ?" Orson was uncharacteristically tongue-tied.

"Faye? We're not dating anymore, if that's what you're asking."

Relief flooded his friend's face. "I was hoping you'd say that."

"I thought you were sweet on her."

Orson's face reddened. "I was about to ask her out when you jumped in. Good thing we didn't have to fight about it. I'd have kicked your butt."

"Oh yeah?" Luke raised his fists in a mock fighting posture.

"Yeah," Orson said, doing the same, then dropping his fists and holding his arms outstretched. "But I wouldn't want to mess up that pretty face in the middle of a case." He grinned.

Luke extended his hand to shake Orson's. "I think you'll be perfect for her, my friend."

They shook, shared a brotherly hug, and went off to their separate rooms. Luke found himself happy for both of his friends, really happy.

The next day their fake DNA story ran in the paper, along with the in-depth story about the cold case squad itself, why it started, its success so far and plans for the future. It was a great story, adding to the initial story Federer had written about the squad looking into Ciara's murder. It even generated some phone calls to the dedicated tip line. Unfortunately, most of the calls they received that morning were not helpful. Two more people called saying aliens had kidnapped Ciara, and what happened to her was a result of their failed tests. A couple more callers claimed they were certain horrible Harkin was a serial killer with more bodies buried under his junk.

Orson and Woody headed for Los Osos to conduct surveillance on Considine while Abby and Luke left early to start on the winery search.

Their first stops were to the wineries located in and around San Luis Obispo. On the list Victoria had composed, there were seven in the SLO area. A website for wine tasting in San Luis Obispo said that the bulk of vineyards in the area could be visited within a fifteen- to twenty-minute drive in any direction. They weren't doing any tasting; they were just asking questions.

The biggest problem with their cover story was the fact that grape harvest time was long past. It was now late January; grapes were generally harvested in late summer and early fall. The majority of migrant workers were gone. At the first vineyard they visited, the owner told them they'd never find the guy they were looking for.

"From twenty years ago?" He shook his head.

Abby embellished the story. "The tip we received said the man is still working in the area, and he's here now. We just have to find out where."

"Well, good luck to you." He studied the description they'd drawn up of their "witness." "No one close to this works here, but I think I may have seen this guy. Just can't help you with where."

Abby left him her card and he promised he'd call if he remembered where he'd seen their man before.

They left the tasting room and headed back to their car. It was Luke who saw him first. Abby felt him stiffen next to her.

"What is it?" she asked, glancing at Luke. He was looking straight ahead. She followed his gaze and they both stopped.

J. P. Winnen was leaning against their car. He was in civilian clothes: cargo pants, T-shirt, baseball cap.

"What are you doing here?" Luke asked.

"Wine tasting. My turn. What does this place have to do with Ciara?"

Luke started to say something and Abby nudged him to stop. She could feel his anger and didn't want to hit Winnen with it yet.

"Why, good news," Abby said brightly. "We got a tip. There was a witness to the dumping of Ciara's body. We're just trying to find him."

Winnen paled noticeably, and a muscle twitched in his jaw. "How is that . . . ?" He rubbed his chin. "You're sure?"

"Yep," Luke said, following Abby's lead. "The tipster was genuine, the tip gold. We're working a hot trail right now."

Winnen seemed to gather himself. He straightened up and moved away from the car. "Wow, I guess that is great news. Great news."

"It is," Abby said with a smile.

"What's the deal with this new DNA test?"

"You can read all about it in the newspaper."

He hiked a shoulder. "Yeah, yeah, but is it the real deal? We're all on the same team here; I want this guy caught as bad as you guys. Maybe more. If I can help . . ."

Luke shook his head. "We have everything under control. Don't you worry. We're close to wrapping up this case with an arrest." He smiled. "Enjoy your wine, Officer Winnen."

As they drove away, Abby said, "He's got ants in his britches, don't you think?"

"I do." Luke laughed. "We really rocked his boat."

She didn't mind the wild-goose chase much anymore and couldn't wait to tell Orson about the contact with Winnen. She phoned him and let him know.

"That's great." Orson was equally enthused. "We didn't even have to circulate that story. He was nervous enough to keep tabs on you."

"Yep," Abby agreed as she ended the call, at that moment happy to have something to do while they waited to see if anything popped with their DNA story. She'd rather be moving than sitting and watching Considine. And she was beside Luke while they drove through beautiful countryside. The winter had been mild, and the drought in California severe, but in December and most of January there had been some rain, so wildflowers were poking their heads out of the ground in a lot of places.

By late Wednesday afternoon, they'd covered six of the seven vineyards in SLO. At a couple of places they ran into workers fearing that they were immigration. Orson's direction on that had been clear: *"We're not immigration. So if someone is illegal, we'll just forward the information to the proper place. But make sure that's all it is. Our fugitive is cagey and resourceful. We need to turn over every rock."*

Abby and Luke worked hard to assuage immigration fears, and they usually got people to start talking. They would ask about the guys they worked with and around, and conversation flowed. In spite of the good conversations, the only interesting information they'd collected was that men at three of the vineyards mentioned a neighboring vineyard manager who everyone thought was quirky.

"He speaks Spanish too well," one man said. "Says he's Mexican but talks like a Spaniard."

"That guy obviously made an impression," Luke said.

"Yep, too bad we're not looking for a Spaniard pretending to be a Mexican."

CHAPTER

48

THEY WERE ON the way to the last vineyard of the day before Abby had to drop Luke off at the train station when her phone rang. He'd taken a cue from Gunther and was taking the train home tonight, to be in Long Beach Thursday for Maddie's party and returning on Friday.

"It's Pastor Terry. Maybe he's found Mike."

She eagerly answered the call as Luke sat back and watched her. Her excitement was off the charts.

"We can meet with him tomorrow," she said, holding the phone down. "What do you think?"

"I won't be here tomorrow."

She slapped her forehead and asked Terry if Mike would be around until Friday.

He could tell by her face the answer was no.

"Me taking an hour out of the day tomorrow won't hurt anything," she said.

"Abby, we agreed: first things first. I don't want you to go by yourself."

"Woody, maybe?"

"Then you're pulling him away from the job he has to do. Maybe this just wasn't meant to be."

She went back to the phone and he could see the irritation in her body language. "Terry, I'll call you back."

The look on her face confirmed Luke's worst fear. She was letting this pipe dream consume her.

"Luke, you don't really believe we're going to find Napier. I will be very careful if I meet with Mike."

And what if Mike says something that leads you down a rabbit hole? he thought. But said, "I'd really prefer you leave it alone. We can try to find him again when our cases are finished."

He saw the anger simmering, but this was as important to him as it was to her. He did not want her to become Victoria.

"I don't want to lose this chance."

Now Luke's hackles rose. He would be leaving shortly for Long Beach. Woody was busy. He could see her going to talk to Mike without him.

"Abby, I didn't say that I wouldn't go with you. I just want to wait."

"Well, I don't want to wait. He's in the area—who knows where he'll be when we finally finish with this search." She threw her hands up in the air.

Luke bit back what was on his mind as they pulled into the winery parking lot. Why couldn't she see that what she was doing was exactly what she said she wouldn't?

They went into the tasting room of the seventh winery and followed the script, but he could feel the ice forming around Abby. *Oh, Lord,* he prayed, *she's letting it consume her. Please help me know how to snap her out of it.*

They met briefly with Woody and Orson at the hotel when they went to pick up Luke's belongings for his trip home.

"We saw a lot of activity at Considine's house," Orson told them. "Winnen visited him early, and then later a couple of guys dropped by who looked like lawyers."

"We might just catch two birds with one stone," Woody said. "I wondered if they both had a hand in Ciara's murder."

Abby tried to put her snit with Luke away after hearing that it was looking like Considine was nervous and felt pressed, along with Winnen. But Padre Mike was on her mind. She felt like the brass ring was in her grasp and she was not going to lose her focus this time—this time she would grab it and hold on.

Driving Luke to the train station was an excruciatingly quiet ride. After a frosty drive she walked him to the platform.

Trying to brighten the mood, she said, "Maybe we'll wrap this up by the weekend, find Mike, nail Alyssa, and get on with our lives together."

His jaw was set and she could tell that he was still upset. "Abby, what about us being a team? Keeping each other safe? If you go looking for this guy by yourself, you blow all of that off."

Abby's own frustration flared. "The man isn't dangerous. He's just a transient, hard to find. What about striking while the iron is hot?"

"What about honoring first commitments first?"

"I will honor my commitments," she said through gritted teeth. "But you know how important this is. This could be the nail in Alyssa's coffin. Isn't that worth something to you?"

"Maybe not. I just can't buy into this fantasy that this one man holds the key to bringing down a woman like Alyssa Rollins. It's flimsy. You're pinning your hopes on a phantom wish, not hard, cold facts."

Abby turned on her heels to leave, but Luke grabbed her arm. She looked at him, angrier than she could remember being, but his expression stopped her from saying a word.

"Abby, please, I care about you. I don't want to see you obsessed and eaten alive by this case. We may never have total justice where the Triple Seven is concerned this side of heaven. Let it go."

She jerked her arm from his grasp. "You sound just like Ethan!"

Luke stepped back as if struck, but Abby couldn't stop herself.

"That's all he could say about my parents' case: let it go. For your information, I'm not obsessed. This might just be my last chance."

"Then you're lying to yourself. And to me." He turned and climbed onto the train, leaving her seething on the platform.

CHAPTER

-49-

THE TRAIN WAS passing Santa Barbara when Luke's phone rang. He prayed it was Abby, but caller ID told him that the prayer was not answered. He answered it, trying to sound unaffected by the turmoil in his heart.

"Hi, Faye. It's kind of late. Is everything okay?"

"Yes, sorry to call so late, but I have information I think you'll find interesting. Can you talk now?"

"Yeah." He explained to her where he was. "Someone call you about the DNA who sounded shady?"

"No, no, it's not about that. I've actually still been doing a little work on your case—you know, looking into the incident in Tehachapi."

"Oh, wow, I'd forgotten about that."

"You've been busy with other stuff. I've stayed in touch with the investigators out there, looking into Quinn and what he was doing in Tehachapi the day he was killed."

"What have they found?"

"He was there with Kelsey. I suggested they show her picture to the hotels in the area and they got a positive ID at one."

"They were there overnight?"

"Yes, and they visited Barone's shop. They had business with the man; we just don't know what. But there's more. A retired sheriff's deputy who lives in Lancaster contacted the lead investigator yesterday. He claims that Kelsey called him and asked him to do some surveillance for her. She wanted him to keep an eye on Abby Hart and the PI who was with her."

Luke felt as if the train had just gone into a dark tunnel. He had to process this information. He and Abby were being watched for Kelsey Cox?

"Luke, are you still there?"

"Yes, I'm just trying to understand what that means. I can't believe that surveillance was set up for any good reason. Does this guy say why she wanted him to watch us?"

"No. All he says is that he was just supposed to keep an eye on you while you were in the high desert and she would be in touch. Her escape shook him up, I think. He's asking for protection."

"Well, I'm not sure what to say other than thank you for the information."

"Sure. I hope it will end up helping you in some way. Is everything okay, Luke?"

"Everything is fine. I'm looking forward to Maddie's party."

Faye said good-bye and left Luke with his thoughts. He didn't know what to make of the information Faye had given him. He was tempted to call Abby but didn't.

For the rest of the way back to Long Beach, Luke replayed the argument with Abby, the reason he didn't feel like he could pick up the phone and tell her what he'd just learned. He was angry that she couldn't see what this thing was doing to her.

And for her to accuse him of being like Ethan really stung. She was too good an investigator to fall for such a weak lead in someone else's case, but completely blind in this instance that involved Alyssa.

Every way he looked at it, trying to figure why Alyssa would lie and implicate Lowell to cover her own misdeed just didn't make any sense. He realized that if this Padre Mike did have information that could torpedo Alyssa, he'd owe Abby a huge apology. And he didn't mind that—he'd apologize. He was missing Abby already and hating the fact that the very case that brought them together now seemed to be tearing them apart.

Abby partnered with Woody for Thursday's search, leaving Orson to stay on Considine. He said he was sure the man was cracking. She and Woody moved their vineyard search to the Templeton/Paso Robles area on Thursday, hoping by Friday they would finish the last few on the list.

Abby nursed her anger as if it were a newborn puppy, not wanting to let it go. How dare Luke accuse her of lying to herself. She wasn't lying—not really. In trying to prove that fact to herself, she attempted to enlist Woody, convince him she was right and get him on her side. He wasn't having any of it. He didn't want to talk about it and he wasn't taking sides.

Fidgeting before dinner, Abby checked and rechecked her phone, not certain if she wanted to hear from Luke or Pastor Terry.

"You look excited," she observed when Orson joined her and Woody for dinner Thursday night.

"I am. I'm sure that DNA ruse made our man nervous. I

talked to Faye and she's had several calls, a couple from news agencies but also a couple that seemed to be people testing the waters. Considine is shaky."

"But our tip line has gone quiet," Woody said. "I was hoping that lady would call back."

"Patience."

Abby said nothing. She was excited to see things wrap up because she wanted to move on to Mike Jez.

With or without Luke.

Without just about broke her heart, but Abby kept stoking the anger, thinking about anything but Luke and the look on his face before he got on the train.

The only thing that nagged at her a bit was Kelsey Cox. The woman was still on the run. Did that have any ramifications for her?

"What's up tomorrow?" she asked Woody.

"I've got three on the list, and the last one has the best name. It's called the Dancing Purple Grape. Maybe we'll get lucky."

CHAPTER

50

IT HAD BEEN a few days since her rescue, and Kelsey wondered if that was still the right word for what had happened to her. She began to consider her predicament. Yes, she'd hated the clanging, noisy, smelly jail, and the fear that the other prisoners would discover she'd been a cop and she'd find herself outnumbered somewhere in a horrible situation. But what opportunity had she been given by being pulled out of the frying pan?

She'd slept enough and thought enough to know that maybe she hadn't been done a favor. She thought about Alyssa and Lowell and the truth she knew about the couple. She knew that Alyssa ordered the killing of Abby Hart's parents. And that while Lowell had no idea about it at the time, when he found out about it later, his response was "Alyssa always does what's best for me."

Kelsey felt sick about what she had done for the couple over the years. What Gavin had done for them over the years. He killed himself in order to avoid implicating them.

Kelsey would never do them that kind of favor.

It began to make her angry. She'd kept her mouth shut about

what she knew and made a deal with the prosecutor she could live with, and now that deal was history. Kelsey could never hope to remake it.

She paced and wondered what options she had. There was no phone in this house, no way for her to communicate with the outside world, and she wasn't even sure exactly where she was. Maybe if she walked into a police station and turned herself in, just maybe she'd find mercy.

She heard a car outside. A few minutes later the door opened and the driver walked in.

"Good, you're up. It's time to go."

"Where to?"

He stared at her as if she had no right to speak. "You'll see. Now let's go."

***

Kelsey sat in the backseat of the car as Los Angeles gave way to Long Beach. She wondered if he was going to take her to the governor's house in the Naples area. But he didn't exit the freeway until he got to the airport off-ramp. He didn't go to terminal parking; he went around to the private plane portion of the airport. The area was gated, and he stopped to enter the proper code and the gate swung open.

He parked next to a hangar and got out. When he opened the door for Kelsey, she hesitated.

"Come on. I'm not going to carry you."

She got out, squinting in the bright morning sun.

He pointed to a small jet. The words *Micro Solutions* with a business logo were painted on the side. She remembered that the company was a big donor to the governor.

"That's your ride."

Kelsey looked at him, blinked, and when he got back in his car and closed the door, she walked to the plane and climbed the steps. She ducked to enter the main cabin, and there was Alyssa Rollins.

"Kelsey, how nice to see you, my dear. Orange was never your color."

She was trying too hard to sound lighthearted, Kelsey thought, as she sensed something was wrong.

Kelsey didn't know what to say. She wanted to turn and run and be free of this woman forever.

But then from the back of the plane came Lowell Rollins.

"Well, get in here, sit down, and buckle up. We're taking off." He was angry—and Kelsey didn't miss the glare he shot Alyssa. Was there trouble in paradise?

Unable to stop herself, Kelsey sat in the first available seat and put on the seat belt. A few minutes later the jet was airborne and there was no question she was squarely in the center of the fire. The only question was how hot it would get.

⸻

"My wife went to a lot of trouble to secure your release, Kelsey. Against my advice and judgment." His tone was tight and clipped, and Kelsey knew what the problem was. Alyssa had probably acted without his knowledge or consent when she sprang Kelsey from jail. Maybe at one time he thought she always knew what was best for him, but clearly not now.

The governor moved to sit next to Kelsey once the plane reached cruising altitude.

Not knowing what to say, Kelsey simply said, "Thank you."

She found talking to the imposing man difficult. His manner was mesmerizing. Where she might have been able to say no to Alyssa, she couldn't say no to the governor. But she wanted to. Part of her wanted to scream, *"I just want to get off this ride!"*

"There is something we'd like you to do for us."

Here it comes, Kelsey thought, *the pound of flesh.*

"Alyssa and I have a couple of private fund-raisers to attend in San Francisco and San Jose. We're going to drop you off in a little place called Paso Robles. Are you familiar with the town?"

Kelsey nodded and found her voice. "It's near Hearst Castle."

"Yes, it is. We want you to find someone for us." He handed her a manila envelope. "Who we want you to find and where to look is in that envelope. There are also instructions on what to do when you find him."

She took the envelope. Lowell started to get up.

"What then?" she asked.

"What?"

"After I complete this, this, uh . . . mission. What then?"

"This plane will take you wherever you want to go. There are several beautiful places on this planet that have no extradition treaty with this country. You've been a good soldier, Kelsey. Your service will be rewarded."

He bent and patted her shoulder and then went back to where he'd sat when the plane took off.

Several minutes passed before she opened the envelope and poured the contents on the seat next to her. She saw a new California driver's license with her picture and a new name. She was now Helena Cooper, and her photo had been altered to give her black hair. There was money, keys to a car, black hair dye, and some typed instructions.

The instructions surprised her. It wasn't what she expected. After she'd read them a couple of times, she put everything back in the envelope and put it on the seat. She didn't want any of this. She didn't want to follow the instructions and she didn't want to spend the rest of her life in exile in some third-world nonextradition country.

There had to be a way out of the fire, and Kelsey pledged to herself that she would find it.

CHAPTER

51

"YOU'RE LYING TO YOURSELF."

Abby Hart couldn't get the four words out of her mind. Even two days later, after the initial sting had faded, she felt the burn. And it was as much the person who'd said them as the words themselves. It was a phrase that made her consider leaving a job she'd committed a year to and not looking back. She would leave and never have anything to do with Luke Murphy ever again.

He questioned her judgment about the lead she wanted to follow.

"It's flimsy," Luke had said. *"You're pinning your hopes on a phantom wish, not hard, cold facts."*

Abby's thoughts swirled with justification for jumping on the lead. *Why can't he trust me to know when something is worth following?* Even as she nursed hurt feelings, indecision crossed paths with indignation. Luke was generally so perceptive, and she trusted his instincts.

"Wow, maybe I should rethink my retirement."

Woody snapped into her train of thought, brought her back

to the here and now, their current case. She knew he wanted to keep her mind off of Luke and on the job at hand.

She swallowed her bruised feelings and tuned in to Woody.

He was relaxed in the passenger seat, shades on, gray hair a bit longer than when he was in uniform, looking more like a tourist than a cold case investigator.

"What, you want to grow wine grapes?" she asked.

"Maybe. It's beautiful here, like a paradise. Seems like a place to put your feet up and relax."

The bumpy dirt road they were bouncing down right now was hemmed in by rows and rows of bare grapevines. Abby inhaled and exhaled a calming breath and looked around her. It *was* beautiful; she couldn't argue with that. And this week alone she'd driven through more vineyards than she thought existed and hadn't tired of them yet. Though the vines were winter bare, they were intriguing in their perfect uniformity. The picturesque garnish on the scene were the wildflowers dotting the hills, serving to paint a beautiful landscape. Yes, she had to agree with Woody that as a backdrop to a murder investigation, the rolling hills of Paso Robles were inviting and a bit intoxicating without even a sip of alcohol.

This vineyard, the Dancing Purple Grape, was just outside of Paso Robles. It was the last on a list of fifteen that the cold case squad had been asked to check into. After this final winery, they'd be done with the good deed and she'd be free to pursue her lead—sans Luke.

Why can't I feel relieved? Blinking away Luke's handsome face from her thoughts, she sparred with Woody.

"Oh, come on. Are you saying you'd be happy to sit around and do nothing?"

"Just saying that when I see this kind of countryside, it makes me consider the road not taken."

Abby forced a smile and pulled over as they reached the lot carved out for the vineyard manager's residence. Majestic oaks randomly towered over the small home, a bit of chaos in the midst of the uniform rows of grapevines, and it created a story-book kind of scene that was totally appealing.

"This looks like a fairy-tale cottage, one you'd see painted on the cover of a kids' book." Abby turned toward Woody. "Trouble is, in those books something bad often lives in the cottage."

Her partner laughed. "Think an ogre lives here?"

"If this were fairy-tale Grimm, you can bet that's what we'd find."

When Sergio opened the door and surprised them, all Abby could think was *Welcome to fairy-tale Grimm.* The dog was the smart one, running away at the sight of the bearded fugitive.

Now Sergio, otherwise known as Stuart Napier, was threatening to kill them. Given what he did to his own family, Abby knew he was deadly serious . . . despite the claims he was making.

"Victoria's the killer, not me. I can't let you tell her you found me." Napier jabbed the gun toward Woody. "You. You have a gun as well—I can see it. Very carefully give it to me."

"Look, son, it's the end of the line now; don't you get that?"

"Don't argue with me! *Give me the gun!*" Napier was near hysterical and Abby feared the gun in his hand would go off by accident.

She touched Woody's arm. He turned to her and she could see the worry in his eyes. She gave a slight nod.

He turned back to Napier. "Okay, okay." Woody slowly reached to his belt, took out the small automatic he carried, and handed it to Napier. Napier snatched the gun and put it in his pocket.

Woody said, "If you're not the killer like you claim, why not just come in with us? We can protect you from Victoria."

"You're not smart enough, and you don't know her like I do. I know she's told everyone that I'm the monster." He waved the gun. "Do you both have handcuffs? Let's see them. Put them on the kitchen table."

Abby and Woody both complied.

"Now keys and cell phones."

Once they had placed the items on the table, Napier shut their phones off and ordered them back to the entryway, to a decorative support column off to the right of the front door. Napier pulled Woody aside and handcuffed him first. Abby knew now that her own cuffs were going to be used against her, and she wondered if it would have been better to go with plastic restraints like Luke carried. If nothing else, they might have been more comfortable. Thinking of Luke pinched her heart as the image of love and concern in his eyes flashed in her memory.

Napier turned his attention to her. He handcuffed Abby and pushed her down on the couch. Abby was numb with the realization Luke had been right. How could she have been so blind? Obsession with getting Alyssa had dulled her senses to everything else. This guy was hinky from the get-go and she hadn't seen it. Even the dog running away like he had should have kicked her instincts into gear. Her lack of attention to detail might very well have signed her and Woody's death certificates.

Woody shot her a look that said, "Stay calm." Napier pulled him back toward a support column and ordered him to sit. It was difficult for Woody to get down with his hands behind his back, but when Abby leaned forward to protest, the gun was quickly pointed her way. Napier half pushed, half helped Woody to the floor.

Was there a way out of this without either of them getting hurt?

"Now, you, girl, stay quiet." He backed up, gun pointing first at one, then at the other. "Both of you stay quiet and still. I'll be right back."

Inside, Abby felt relief as Napier left the room. Securing them like he was, it seemed as though Napier meant to leave them and flee.

Woody had the better view of Napier's exit than Abby, as her back was against the couch.

"Where did he go?" she asked.

"Out the back door, I guess." He cleared his throat. "This is a tad embarrassing."

"I was just thinking that. But if we make it out of this only red-faced, I can live with it." She'd have a chance to apologize to Luke, to admit he was right and she was wrong.

"You said it. Never expected to be shanghaied by the guy."

Abby heard the guilt in his voice and knew the real guilt lay with her. "This isn't your fault. I was preoccupied. This guy wasn't right from the minute he opened the door and I ignored it. I could have said something."

Woody sighed. "Maybe you're right; maybe not. I just can't help thinking I should've done something different. Thirty-five years on the job, never let a suspect get the drop on me. Maybe I should retire completely."

A door closed behind her. "Is he coming back?"

Woody nodded. "He's got something in his hands."

"Okay." Napier put something odd-looking down by the door, then walked to the kitchen table and grabbed a set of car keys. He had Abby's gun in one hand and the keys in the other. "I've been preparing for this eventuality. Girl, I know that there's a handcuff key here somewhere."

"It's Detective Hart."

"Whatever." He found the key and looked from Abby to Woody. "I'm undoing him for a minute, to change his position. I don't want to hurt anyone, but I've investigated this gun; I know how it works. There's no safety, just a first pull double action, so I'm not afraid to use it."

He held Abby's .45 up as if to prove his point.

"We're not going to give you any guff," Woody said. "It's not our job to hurt you, just see to it you're caught."

"You aren't smart enough to hurt me or catch me." He pointed with the gun barrel and said to Woody. "I want you to be secured to the column."

"Whatever, sport. Just get it over with."

Napier bent down, flashing Abby a warning, then uncuffed Woody and recuffed him to the column.

"What now?" Woody asked.

"Listen to me," he said. "I told you—I'm not the killer; Victoria is. But I'm desperate. If forced or pressed beyond my limits, I will kill either one of you or both of you."

"We get you," Abby said. "We won't try anything."

He jammed the gun into his waistband and picked up the strange item he'd brought from outside. The top of it looked like half of a pair of giant handcuffs, the bottom part like a rectangular locker the size of a shoe box, but not as thick. Uneasiness engulfed Abby as the item looked familiar, but she couldn't remember why.

"Bend down a bit," he said to Woody as he opened the top hinge on the thing in his hands.

"What are you going to do?" Woody asked, without moving.

"Just trying to make sure I have time to get away." He jammed his fist into Woody's stomach.

"Hey!" Abby struggled up from the couch as Woody crumpled over with an *oof*, and Napier quickly attached the odd item around Woody's neck. It clicked locked and a red light on the box now resting on Woody's chest began blinking.

A wave of sick revulsion stumbled Abby as she realized what the thing was; she'd seen something like it in training.

An improvised explosive device.

"You sit back down!" Napier stood and pulled the gun from his waistband and jabbed it toward Abby.

"What are you doing to him?"

"Just what I said: making sure I have time to get away to a safe place. I have a plan B and I will execute it." He held up a handwritten note so Abby could read it.

This is an explosive device. Any attempt to remove it will result in detonation. It can only be removed by inputting the correct combination. One mistaken number will result in detonation. It must be exact. Trying to cut it will result

in detonation. I will give you the correct combination only
when I am certain I am free.

For a second Abby couldn't speak. She remembered why the
device had looked familiar. It had to do with an attempted bank
robbery at a PNC Bank back east a few years ago. A man wearing a similar device had robbed the bank only to be stopped by
police a short distance away. The man was handcuffed, placed in
front of the patrol car, and officers moved back to a safe distance
while they waited for the bomb squad. The bomb exploded on
national TV three minutes before the squad arrived. Abby had
seen the unedited footage of the device exploding into the man
when she was in an advanced officer-training course. It was an
image that stayed with her. The blast blew a five-inch gash in
the man's chest. The concussion killed him almost instantly.

Napier taped the note onto the front of the device.

She inclined toward Woody. "Are you okay, Woody?"

"I'm breathing, if that's what you mean, but this ain't no
way to be stuck."

"You can move around," Napier told him. "The device is
very stable until you try to take it off. I will give you the correct
combination, but only when I'm sure I'm safe."

"Get safe quick, will ya, pal?" Woody said, and Abby heard
the tension in his voice.

"What are you going to do with me?" Abby asked.

"Girl, you're coming with me."

CHAPTER

52

THE PLANE LANDED at a small municipal airport. Kelsey's hair was still a little damp from a quick dye job in the plane's restroom and she wasn't all that certain she liked it black.

"This is where we part company." Rollins sat down next to Kelsey again once the plane stopped taxiing. "We're continuing north and will be taking the train back down south after the fund-raisers. I'm campaigning through the center of the state. We plan on making a stop in this area by Sunday." He stared at her. "I expect our request to be completed by then."

"France," Kelsey said.

"What?" He frowned, and Kelsey gave herself a brownie point for knocking him off his game if only for a moment.

"That's where I want to go. They seldom extradite."

He threw his head back and laughed. "Of course, of course. I told you, wherever you want to go. When you get off the plane now, you'll find a car waiting and a cell phone that goes directly to me. I want to hear immediately when the job is completed."

"And the plane? Will it be here to take me to France?"

"Yes, definitely," he said smoothly and she knew he was

lying. "I told you that Alyssa and I are taking the train back down south; we won't need it. She hates this part of the state, but it can't be avoided. The plane will be at your disposal."

By this time the exit door was open and he gestured for her to leave.

Dismissed, Kelsey stood, taking with her the envelope she'd been given, and exited the plane as Helena Cooper.

A tall, dark-skinned man Kelsey knew, DelRey Mackenzie, was at the bottom of the stairs. He'd worked with Gavin, and Kelsey had never had a problem with him. She also knew that whatever Rollins did, DelRey would agree with and get behind. He was not going to question her status as fugitive.

"Hey, Kelsey, color looks great on you." He approached and shook her hand, then handed her a cell phone. He pointed to a black SUV with tinted windows. "There's your ride. I'm the point guy here, setting up security for this leg of the train ride." He handed her a card. "If you get in deep weeds, call me, but only if they are really deep weeds, got it?"

"I understand, DelRey. Perfectly." She took the card and continued to the SUV.

By the time she'd familiarized herself with the car and started the engine to leave the airport, the governor's plane had begun to taxi back toward the runway for takeoff.

CHAPTER

53

ORSON DROVE A LITTLE TOO FAST; but then, he was behind schedule. He'd thought Considine was ready to break, so he'd stayed in Los Osos a tad longer than he should have. Considine was cracking, but it was a slow breakup. He'd taken a trip to a liquor store and come home with a box of bottles. Orson figured he'd be there for the rest of the day. Now, he feared he'd be late for his lunch with Woody and Abby. And Woody was on a time schedule; the early lunch had been set so that he'd be sure to have enough time to pick Luke up today. But Orson also drove fast because it bothered him that both Woody and Abby seemed to have turned their phones off. He could see one of them shutting off a phone but not both. Abby especially was great about answering her phone and checking in when she was supposed to.

For some reason this last vineyard bothered him. He'd not shared his concern with Woody and Abby, not wanting them to think of him as overly protective, so this silence bugged.

"Argh," Orson groaned, suddenly sorry he'd taken on this case, even if it was a favor for a friend. Talk about a cluster of problems if they did find the guy.

"I'm getting sappy in my old age, or maybe I just can't say no to Faye," he muttered. Talking to himself had become a habit. Instead of taking the off-ramp that would get him to the restaurant, Orson sped up, deciding he'd see if Woody and Abby ran into any trouble at the last vineyard on their list.

When he exited the freeway, he watched for their rental car, certain he was overreacting but unable to stop himself. He was sure he'd see them going the opposite direction and then turn around and follow them to the restaurant, make up some lame excuse, harangue them about turning off their phones, not tell the silly story that he was worried about them.

His GPS directed him to turn onto a dirt road, but the big sign for the Dancing Purple Grape Vineyard tipped him off first. He'd only been on the road for a few minutes when he saw another car coming his way at high speed. It could be Abby and Woody's rental, but where was the fire?

He slowed and pulled as far as he could to the right, which took his car partway into a ditch. The vehicle coming at him didn't slow, and he felt his jaw drop when he saw the strange bearded man in the driver's seat—and Abby in the passenger seat.

What was going on?

Where was Woody? he wondered as the vehicle flew past, kicking up a cloud of dirt. Turning around as quickly as he could, spitting out more dirt as his rear tires spun before catching, Orson took off after the speeding vehicle.

He caught the car as it came to a stop when it reached the blacktop. Before Orson could decide what action to take, the driver's door of the car ahead of him flew open and the bearded man stepped out. He raised a handgun and began firing.

His windshield exploded, and Orson reflexively threw his arm up in front of his face. That was when it felt as if his arm exploded.

Crying out, the searing pain leaving him breathless, Orson fell across the passenger seat, knowing he was helpless but unable to move through the pain mist in his brain to draw his weapon with his off hand. He thought of Faye and wished he'd told her how he felt.

The shooting stopped and he waited for the final bullet, certain he was minutes away from a kill shot. But time ticked by without the deathblow coming, and the pain he felt went from excruciating to simply agonizing. He opened his eyes to take stock of the situation and saw immediately that his right arm was a bloody mess; his right hand hung uselessly.

Gritting his teeth, he tried to grip the steering wheel with his left hand, nearly passing out as the movement affected his busted arm. He pulled himself up to look out the shattered window and saw nothing.

The car with Abby in it was gone.

CHAPTER

54

SHUTTING OUT HIS PERSONAL, internal turmoil, Luke could say that Maddie's party yesterday had been great. Luke and his mother had taken Maddie and six of her closest friends to Knott's Berry Farm. Maddie loved the place and so did Luke, in spite of tired feet from running after seven 12-year-olds all day. When he kissed her good night, he knew the day had been a success.

"I'll be gone before you get up in the morning so you get a double kiss, good night and good-bye."

Maddie had hugged his neck. "Thanks for the best party ever. When will you be home?"

"Couple of days." Luke tucked the blanket around her neck. "I hope we'll wrap everything up over the weekend."

"Okay. Be careful." She sighed as Luke watched her eyes get heavy. Even when she was a baby, once she was in bed, she always fell asleep quickly. He'd waited until her breathing was steady and regular, then kissed her forehead and tiptoed quietly out of her room.

Luke yawned now as the train rumbled up the coast. He

hadn't been able to sleep as planned. His day had started when his stepfather dropped him off at the bus station in Long Beach at 5:45 a.m. He took the LAX shuttle to the Amtrak station in Santa Barbara. All told it would be a little over seven hours before he arrived back in San Luis Obispo. Briefly he'd thought about switching to air travel; he'd arrive much faster. But a look at the flight schedules and the prices had dissuaded him. The only hurry was his personal issue. He'd not spoken to Abby but knew that Woody planned on picking him up.

He wondered what waited for him back in SLO. Was Abby still mad? He wanted to settle this thing with her. He was no longer mad, just concerned. Was there anything he could say to convince her that she was letting the case get the better of her?

Luke started to get antsy a little after 12:45 p.m. He checked and rechecked his phone. He'd texted Woody, who should be finishing lunch with Orson by now. Why wasn't he responding? *Maybe I should just call,* he decided.

He'd just begun to punch in Woody's number when his phone rang with an unfamiliar number. But it was an 805 area code and that was correct for SLO, so Luke answered.

"Hello?"

"This is Deputy Revel, San Luis Obispo County Sheriff. Whom am I speaking to, please?"

"Uh . . ." Taken aback because he'd been expecting Abby or Woody, Luke cleared his throat. "This is Luke Murphy. What can I help you with?"

"Mr. Murphy, you're a member of the cold case task force working here in San Luis Obispo, correct?"

"Yes, I am." Luke's hand went numb. Had something happened to Abby? "Is there a problem?"

"I'm afraid there is. Where are you right now?"

"On a train, about to pull into the station at SLO. What is going on?" Luke fought the panic in his voice.

"There's been an incident at a winery called the Dancing Purple Grape. I don't have all the details yet. We have an FBI agent en route to the hospital trauma center with a gunshot wound and there's a lot of confusion about what exactly happened."

CHAPTER

55

"**I THOUGHT YOU** said you weren't a killer!" Abby struggled against the restraints. Napier had cuffed her to the seat belt to be certain she didn't attempt to get out of the car. She tried in vain to look around and see if Orson was okay. She was sure that was who Napier had shot at. Orson must have been on his way to find her and Woody.

"I told you that I'm desperate. That man made a U-turn to come after me. He was a threat."

"Convince me you're not a monster. You just shot a man in cold blood. Turn yourself in."

"No. No. No. She won't win this. She won't. I'm smarter than you and smarter than her." He slowed the car and Abby watched as he appeared to be steadying his breathing, calming himself down.

She and Woody had turned off of Highway 46 to reach the Dancing Purple Grape, and that was where Napier went, back to the highway. He made a right onto Route 46, heading away from Paso Robles.

"Where are we going?"

He shook his head. "I planned for this. She won't catch me; she won't."

Abby started to say something, then stopped. There was no talking to the man. She instead concentrated on where they were going so she would know what to say if she found help or got to a phone.

I have to think my way out of this. She worked to remember what she'd read about Napier. He was a genius, he was obsessive-compulsive, and now he was desperate. She glanced across the car and saw him drumming on the steering wheel—not randomly, she realized. He was tapping out a rhythm. Trying to watch without him knowing she was watching was tricky. He was tapping twice with his index finger, six times with the middle finger, then four with his ring finger, and then back to the index finger.

Was that a birth date? A combination? She thought of the thing around Woody's neck and began to choke up.

Oh, Lord, she prayed to herself, *please help me find a way out of this.*

He shook his head. "I planned for this. She won't catch me; she won't."

Abby started to say something, then stopped. There was no talking to the man. She instead concentrated on where they were going so she would know what to say if she found help or got to a phone.

Wide-awake as fear exploded in his gut, Luke struggled for words. "Who . . . ? Orson got shot?"

"Don't have a name yet. There's also an investigator at the winery with an IED attached to his neck. We're still trying to sort things out. Can you clarify anything?"

"IED?" Luke nearly passed out. They were in central California, for heaven's sake, not Iraq. "I told you, I'm on the train, and we'll pull into the station shortly. Investigator Robert

Woods was going to pick me up. Where is he? And where is Abby?"

"I'll make sure someone is there to pick you up. Your questions will be answered then." He disconnected, leaving Luke hanging and ready to explode.

He had to conclude that it was Woody who had a bomb around his neck because of the pronoun used. And it had to be Orson at the hospital with a gunshot wound. So where was Abby?

They must have found Napier. The train slowed, but they were not yet to the station. Luke grabbed his backpack and got up to stand by the door. He was ready to bust out a window and run to the station. The porter told him that it would be twenty minutes before the train pulled into the station and stopped.

Unable to do nothing, Luke pulled out his phone and called Victoria Napier. He needed to know what they were dealing with.

"Victoria, it's Luke Murphy."

"Ah, Mr. Murphy." The husky voice came across scratchy. "What can I do for you?"

"I want to run a hypothetical situation by you." Luke swallowed and tried to keep the worry and fear out of his voice. "Say we do run into Stuart—how's he likely to behave?"

"Behave? What do you mean?"

"Well, is he likely to give up? Or is he a fighter? I mean, he's described as armed and dangerous on the FBI flyer, and I believe that. But if we actually find him, will he realize it's a lost cause to try to flee?"

"Have you found him?" Scratchiness gone, Victoria barked the question.

"I didn't say that. I'm just asking a—"

"He's dangerous, extremely dangerous—I thought that was clear. You should shoot first and ask questions later."

After the conversation ended, Luke fidgeted. He knew Faye needed to know what had happened, and maybe if she was at the Long Beach office, she could get some help up here for Orson.

He punched in her number only to reach her voice mail. He then called the office and was told that they had already been notified and that Faye was on her way to the airport and would be there soon.

He put his phone away, feeling a little better that the wheels were already turning. He prayed to fight the dread and the fear that seemed to be filling him. Clenching and unclenching his fist, he tried to imagine what could have happened. All three of them were experienced officers. He wondered why they were all together and how Napier—if it was Napier—had gotten the drop on them.

Luke stopped that train of thought. Blame wasn't necessary; rescue was. Mostly his heart ached because of the promise he'd given to Abby: to keep her safe, to take care of her. Even angry with her, he would have stopped a bullet for her in a heartbeat.

We're a team.

As soon as the train hit San Luis Obispo and the door opened, he was off and searching for whoever the deputy had sent for him. But it was another twenty minutes before he saw a San Luis Obispo Sheriff's car. He ran into the parking lot and waved the car down.

"Are you looking for me?"

"You Murphy?" the deputy asked.

"That's me. Can you tell me what's going on?"

"I can't. My instructions were to take you to the hospital. You'll have to get your information there." He jabbed a thumb in the direction of the passenger seat.

Once Luke got into the car, the deputy said, "I didn't mean that the way it sounded. I would tell you what was going on if I knew. I know that an FBI agent was shot. He's at the hospital, but talking, so that should ease your mind. Feds are on the way up here from Santa Maria. I don't know much else. I'm supposed to stay with you until someone who is in the know gets here."

"Thanks. If you hear anything more, please let me know." Luke felt relieved at the news about Orson.

"Will do."

When they arrived at the hospital, there was a large police presence all over the place. No media yet. Probably too early, he thought. He followed the deputy into the ER, where everyone was busy.

"We have a report-writing room over here." He pointed. "Let's wait in there and stay out of the way."

Luke nodded, not wanting to sit and wait, but not knowing what else to do at the moment. He paced the small room while the deputy listened to the radio.

After about half an hour the deputy stood. "Agents just arrived. So hopefully you'll get answers soon."

He radioed to someone and a few minutes later a harried-looking man wearing a Windbreaker emblazoned with *FBI* opened the door to the small room. He walked in and the deputy left, nodding to Luke as he did so. The agent was Nordic-looking, tall, blond, and trim, wiry, and worried, Luke thought.

"Luke Murphy?"

"That's me."

"I'm Skip Purcell. I used to be Orson's partner before he took your gig."

They shook hands. "He's mentioned you. Were you the friend he came up to visit?"

"Yeah, we had a great visit a couple of days ago."

"How is he?"

Purcell shook his head. "I just got here. I have someone else looking into that. I want you to tell me what you know."

Luke shrugged. "Not much. I was on the train, coming from Long Beach, when all this happened. I just got back. No one can tell me what's up with Woody or where Abby is."

Purcell ran a hand down his face. "Woody—that would be Robert Woods?"

"Yes."

"He's at a vineyard with an IED around his neck. The device appears stable, but there is a threatening note attached. The locals have called any and all bomb squads who can come to help. As for Abby Hart, she's been snatched."

"Snatched?" Luke felt an icy chill radiate through his whole body.

Purcell nodded. "I expect she's a hostage of this fugitive, Napier."

"Hostage?" Now things were surreal. "Has he made demands?"

"Not yet." He put his hands on his hips and gave a deep sigh. "Orson and I talked a little bit about Napier, his wife, and the search. He really didn't think you'd find anything."

"To be honest, neither did I," Luke said.

There was a knock at the door. "Skip." A female agent stuck her head in. "Press is all over the place now. The hospital gave us a room upstairs to use, close to where Orson will be brought to recovery but away from the press."

He motioned to Luke. "Let's go upstairs."

Luke nodded, anxious to find out more about Abby and Woody.

They took the elevator to the third floor. Once they got off, the woman led them to a small room off the waiting area. Two more agents were in the room. One was on the phone, while the other was clicking through TV news stations with the sound muted. They all looked like Purcell, tense and worried. The door closed behind them, and when Purcell's phone rang, he gestured for Luke to have a seat.

"Okay, what can you tell us about this Stuart Napier?" the woman asked and three pairs of eyes bored into him.

"You must know more than I do. He's one of your fugitives. How is Orson?"

The agent playing with the TV spoke up. "A bullet shattered his right arm. According to the docs, he was stable when he got here. The damage to the arm was so bad that they needed an orthopedic surgeon to work on it immediately."

"And Woody?"

"Your turn. Stuart Napier."

"All I know about him was what was in your file and what his wife told me."

"Victoria Napier?" Purcell asked as he ended his conversation.

"Yeah, she met with us, with Orson. That's the reason we said we'd help her out."

"By chasing down an armed and dangerous fugitive? Is that

in your job description as cold case detective?" The agent with the TV remote was condescending and snarky.

"We were just going to ask questions, hopefully shake up a lead—"

"Instead you stuck your hand in a hornets' nest and we have to clean up the mess."

"And what was your approach? Let him go and get away with murder?"

"All right, all right." Purcell held up his hand and stepped between Luke and the other agent. "This isn't solving anything. Where is Victoria now?"

"In Long Beach, I think. The last time I talked to her that's where she was. What about Abby? What about Woody?"

Purcell shook his head. "Not my biggest concern right now. Several bomb teams are set up. There's a command post at the Dancing Purple Grape winery."

"Then there isn't anything for me to do here."

"I'd like you to be available for questions."

Luke thought about that for a second. He wanted to see Orson, but he was in the doctor's hands. He wanted to know about Abby, but again, if she was a hostage, the FBI would handle it. He had no control over anything right now and it drove him crazy. He needed to talk to Woody, find out what happened.

"I'll give you my cell number, but I can't sit around here and wait without knowing what's going on with Woody." He pulled out one of his business cards and shoved it toward Purcell.

"I wish you'd hang out here in case we need to ask you something." Purcell wouldn't take the card.

Luke left it on the table, then turned and exited the room.

He phoned for a rental car once he reached the lobby. Deftly moving to avoid any press, he waited outside for his ride.

The sun was fading by the time Luke got off the highway and drove in the direction of the winery. Bright lights lit up the road and he passed what he decided was Orson's shot-up car. The front windshield was gone and the car was catawampus in a ditch. There was a CHP cruiser standing by as a tow truck was just starting to drag the car on board. After that, he only made it as far as the Dancing Purple Grape gate. A San Luis Obispo County deputy manned the gate, which had crime scene Do Not Enter tape strung across it.

Luke explained who he was to the deputy and again had to wait for a radio conversation. After several minutes he was given the okay to drive back. The deputy opened the gate for Luke to proceed through.

Steeling himself, Luke drove down the road to a cluster of police vehicles from several different organizations; he saw an SLO County bomb task force vehicle and a couple of plain vehicles that were obviously police cars. He found a place to park and continued in on foot. At the center of another patch of bright lights was a small house. Woody had said they were going to talk to the vineyard manager; was this where he lived?

"You Murphy?" A man with *FBI Bomb Tech* on his jacket approached well before he reached the house. Behind the agent Luke saw a huge vehicle stenciled with *Bomb Squad Mobile Team*. He felt sick to his stomach.

"That's me."

"I'm Agent Van Horne. Mr. Woods has been asking for you.

But we can't let you go into the house." He gestured to the mobile operations vehicle. "You can see him and talk to him from in there."

Luke stepped into the vehicle, a fully operational tactical office. There were TV screens on one wall with all the major news outlets on. There was radio equipment and phone banks—almost everything manned. In the back of the vehicle, he saw four men with *Bomb Squad* on their jackets in a huddle. The agent pointed to a video screen. Luke stepped close and peered at the screen.

There sat Woody, his friend and partner, on the floor, some kind of device around his neck. Next to the screen was a copy of a note. Luke read it and would have vomited if he had anything in his stomach. That a guy sick enough to latch a bomb around Woody's neck had Abby was an impossible truth to swallow.

CHAPTER

56

KELSEY WAS DRIVING along the coast when she heard the news come over the radio. An FBI agent had been shot and a cold case detective was missing. She had to pull over to the side of Highway 1 in order to hear the entire news flash. Ever since she'd left the airport, she'd been driving around, enjoying the feeling of being free. She made an attempt to find the person Rollins wanted her to find, but it was only halfhearted. She knew Rollins was never going to fly her to France—or anywhere, for that matter. In fact, she was a big liability to him now.

Abby Hart was missing, kidnapped by a fugitive. Kelsey wondered how she should feel about this news and realized she didn't feel anything. At this stage of her life she doubted that she'd ever feel anything again.

But this news was something unexpected. Kelsey speculated if she truly would be cut loose and if the plan she'd been given would be shelved. This thought made Kelsey pull back onto the highway. If her orders were canceled, what did she have? She was a fugitive from justice. To be back in jail now meant more than fifteen years.

She glanced in the rearview mirror and still didn't recognize herself. The black hair dye was a simple change that made her a new person on the outside. The picture on the fake CDL, under the name Helena Cooper, was still close enough to be her, but no one walking by her on the street would see Kelsey Cox.

Her phone buzzed, and she jumped. It was the burner phone DelRey had given her. Kelsey answered.

"You're in place?"

"Yes, but have you seen the news—?"

"I don't care about that. You're in position. I want you to proceed with the plan. You have enough money?"

"Yes."

"Then call me when it's done. And hurry." The connection was ended.

Kelsey set the phone down. Running a hand through her hair, she tried to think. She was in the fire now and she wanted out. She'd exchanged one prison for a different one, a kind of living purgatory. Was there any way out of this? After a minute she realized that there was. There was nothing to gain by doing the governor's bidding. Nothing.

The realization was so freeing Kelsey laughed. Rollins had given her freedom. And she was going to use it to benefit her, no one else. She made a U-turn and headed back to San Luis Obispo. She had to come up with a plan fast, and finally she felt alive enough to do that and complete it.

Napier started getting paranoid almost immediately.

"Someone is following us. How did they do that? Girl, who is it?"

Abby looked behind them as best she could but couldn't say that anyone was following them. "I don't know what you mean. There's no one I know behind you."

"I don't believe you." He began making turns, driving erratically. Finally he pulled onto a dirt road, in a rural area. He relaxed slightly, but for what seemed to Abby hours, he drove around and around on dirt roads or two-lane country roads until finally hitting the blacktop again. It was about a mile before Abby saw a road sign. They were back on Highway 46, but she was so turned around she had no idea exactly where they were. The only thing she was sure of was that Napier seemed certain he'd shaken the "tail." All Abby could think was if only there were a tail.

They continued on Highway 46 for another hour, and daylight began to fade. Napier said nothing to Abby; he simply drove and kept tapping out that number sequence, either on the steering wheel or on his thigh.

Abby had not driven this east/west highway before, but she knew from looking at a map earlier in the week that it would eventually hit north/south Interstate 5. When they passed a sign that said Lost Hills, she knew the interstate was close.

But Napier didn't reach the interstate. They drove through a bleak landscape with old oil drills, bare fields, and dilapidated buildings. He passed a grocery store and turned right into what looked like an industrial area.

She couldn't imagine where he was going until he turned again and stopped in front of a locked gate. The gate blocked the entrance to a storage facility, one long closed from what Abby could see. There were tumbleweeds piled around and dandelions growing up through broken and crumbling asphalt,

297

rusted containers, and a weathered For Sale sign with only the *r*, *s*, and *e* truly readable.

Napier got out and worked a key into the padlock and opened the gate. He had to kick the ground at the bottom of the gate to get it to swing, but after a few kicks he had it open enough to drive the car inside. Once inside, he hurried and closed the gate behind them.

He drove the car between rows of storage units to the back of the yard. Here, he parked just before the last two units. The yard backed up to a bare hillside. Abby despaired. She wanted to get away and find help, but from where?

He got out of the car again and opened both units. The doors were the metal roll-up type, like garage doors. One was empty from what Abby could see, but there was a car in the other, covered. Napier opened Abby's door.

"Okay, girl, time to get out." He uncuffed her hands from the seat belt, let her stand, and then quickly cuffed both hands behind her back.

"Look, I'm not going anywhere. I want the combination to the IED. I'm not letting you out of my sight." She stretched as best she could, stiff from the ride and hungry and thirsty. She'd also need to use the restroom soon and wondered how Napier would handle that.

"Better safe than sorry, as they say." He pointed to the unit with the car inside. "In there, now. I'm going to get your car out of sight."

He pulled a dusty chair out from the side of the unit and Abby sat. When it looked as though he was going to cuff her to the chair, she protested.

"Where would I go?"

He stared at her for a long minute and then nodded, leaving without attaching her to the chair.

He pulled the rental car into the empty unit and closed the door and locked it. While he was doing that, Abby looked around at her surroundings for anything that would help her get free. The cuffs were rubbing her wrists raw and her shoulders were stiff from being held in one position. She couldn't see much. It was dark in the unit and now dark outside. There looked to be boxes stacked in the back of the unit.

Napier stepped inside and pulled the door down as he did so, plunging them into complete darkness.

Abby fought rising panic. "What are you doing?"

"You'll see," he said. Then she heard him count out a sequence of numbers. "One, two, one, two, three, four, five, six, one, two, three, four."

There was the sound of him opening something, three or four clicks, and lights switched on—bright, overhead shop-type lights—causing Abby to blink at their brightness.

"That's better," he said, rubbing his hands together.

CHAPTER

57

"**I CAN TALK TO HIM?**" Luke asked.

"Yeah." The agent pointed to a small mike. "He can hear us. We wired everything so we can talk back and forth."

"Woody?"

His friend looked up. "That you, Luke?"

"Yeah. Are you okay?" It was then Luke noticed that Woody was not alone. There was a dog beside him, looked like a shepherd. He had his head on Woody's thigh and Woody was gently stroking him.

"All things considered. Any word on Abby?"

Luke looked at the agent, who shook his head.

"Not that I've heard. What happened to you guys?"

"Oh, I must be getting old. He got the drop on us. Then after he trussed me up, he ran off with Abby."

"Did he say anything? Was he planning on using Abby as a hostage?"

"I don't know. He didn't say hostage. He did say that he wasn't the monster; his wife was. But his actions kinda make me doubt that. I hear Orson went down."

"He did. He's in surgery but okay, from what I've heard. Stuart claimed Victoria was the monster?" Luke frowned. "What, so he's been hiding all this time because he's innocent?"

"That's what he said, that he's afraid of her. Wanted to make sure we wouldn't tell her we'd found him."

"That makes no sense. After what he did to you, to Orson, and to Abby, now the whole world knows we found him."

———

Napier whipped the cover off of the car, and Abby coughed at the dust cloud it caused. Under the cover was a clean, older model Camaro. He lifted up the hood and began to fiddle with the battery, eventually hooking it up to a battery charger. She could see clearly now, and in spite of the dilapidated outward appearance of the storage facility, this unit had power and plumbing; there was a sink on the other wall. She could also see what appeared to be a portion of a counter. This unit could have been a one-room apartment but for the car in the middle of it.

"You've had this car hidden here for fifteen years?"

"Not quite that long, but yes." He spoke without looking at her. Now he was busy digging through the boxes at the back of the unit. "I knew Victoria would get close. I had to be prepared. It took her longer than I expected."

"That's because you almost killed her."

He dropped the box he was looking into and rushed to get in Abby's face. "I did not kill my children and try to kill Victoria. She did it all."

Abby could only lean back so far. His breath was harsh and bitter-smelling. "She tells a different story. Why don't you tell me what happened?"

He straightened up and began to pace. "Of course she'd tell a different story. That's her conniving, manipulative way. She'd started struggling with depression. Nothing in this world challenged her anymore, she said. It was a drag being around her."

He waved his hands as he talked and paced. "I told her she needed medication, she needed to deal with the problem, but she wouldn't listen to me. She never listened to me. She wanted a suicide pact."

"Suicide because of depression?"

"That's what I said." He pointed frantically at Abby. "She just moped all day long. I was fine. The boys were fine. Who demands that someone who is fine commit suicide? Who does that?"

He began tapping again. "I didn't know what to do. I'd never seen her that way. At first I agreed with her plan just to get her off my back, but then I couldn't go through with it. I loved my boys. I couldn't leave them. That's what I told her. I couldn't leave them."

He stopped tapping, shoved his hands into his pockets, and faced Abby. His face was ashen. "That was when she killed them. Shot them both while they slept. She said I had no excuse then. I . . . I was appalled, shattered, disbelieving. I went for her throat. We struggled, the fire started, the gun went off, and I ran. She screamed after me that she'd kill me."

He stood a few feet away, shoulders slumped, looking defeated and lost.

Abby swallowed. She needed Woody's "I'm a police officer and your friend" voice. "Then turn yourself in. Tell the truth. The more people you hurt, the less you'll be believed."

A hand came out of his pocket and he began tapping again.

He shook his head. "No. They'll believe her. They'd never believe me. I'm not going to hurt you. As soon as the battery is charged, I'm just going to disappear again. I have money and a plan. I'll leave you with the combination for the device and tell your colleagues where they can find you."

With that he resumed digging through the boxes at the back of the unit.

"What can I do to help?" Luke asked. Van Horne had left the mobile operations vehicle and there was another agent with Luke.

"Nothing. This is ours now."

"But Woody and Abby are my partners. I have to do something."

He shook his head. "You're not even a cop."

Luke looked around him at all the assorted law enforcement personnel, their faces basically telling him the same thing. But he couldn't just watch things play out on the monitors.

He left the trailer and started toward the house where Woody sat. A deputy tried to stop him, but Luke shoved him aside. The deputy then tried to grab him, but Luke knew control holds better than the deputy did.

"You can't go in there. That thing could detonate," the deputy said as Luke twisted his wrist so tight it made the man stand up on his tiptoes.

"He's my friend. I want to talk to my friend, touch him, pray with him. You'll have to shoot me to stop me." He let the man go and shoved him away.

The deputy's hand went to his gun. "You can't go in there."

Luke ignored him and continued into the house. The gun didn't go off.

His friend was seated on the floor, leaning against a pillar. Luke knelt next to Woody and put a hand on his shoulder. The dog looked up and his tail thumped the floor.

"Hey, partner, how are you really doing?"

Woody looked at him, fatigue evident in his face. "I'm okay, Luke. Worried about Abby, but okay. They undid the handcuffs before they backed out and left me. Told me I could move around a bit, but I just want to sit here. And I've got my friend here to keep me company."

"Did the bomb guys take a look at the device?"

"Yeah, they did. They took X-rays of the thing with a nifty little gadget. They've been back a couple of times. They're good guys, especially Van Horne, but none of them want to be responsible for blowing my head off. The note said they couldn't disarm it, but they told me they'd keep trying to find a way to disarm it. The quickest way would be to find Napier and get the combination."

"I'll work on that. I promise. I want to pray with you before I go."

"Have at it. . . . You know, it's funny." He patted the dog. "My buddy here knew there was something off about Napier. As soon as the guy opened the door, he tucked tail and ran. It was only after Napier left that he came back and sat down here with me. I don't want him to get hurt, but I . . ." He stopped and Luke could see that he was getting emotional.

"Lord, I lift my friend Woody up to you, Woody and his new buddy, praying for their safety and for Woody to have complete peace in this crazy situation. Help him to stay peaceful and steady until we can disarm this device, and help me find the person responsible. Amen."

"Thanks, Luke. I've listened to Abby enough over the years. I know I need what you two have, what you talk about all the time. It hasn't fallen on deaf ears."

"Glad to hear it. And God isn't deaf ether. Call on him."

Woody gave as much of a nod as he could with the device around his neck. "One more thing. Napier said he was prepared for this, that he had a plan B."

"Like maybe a hiding place?"

"Could be. A fugitive would be wise to have a backdoor escape plan. Someone who knows him well might be able to help you figure out where he is. Did these guys call his wife?"

"I don't know. They haven't said. At least they aren't telling me much."

"It would be the place to start."

Luke nodded, squeezed his friend's shoulder, and stood to leave.

"Luke . . . if this doesn't go right . . . if, well . . . you know . . . Will you look after Zena?"

Luke swallowed a lump, unable to look directly at Woody. "Of course I will, but you're going to be fine. I promise."

58

ABBY DIDN'T BELIEVE for a second that Stuart Napier wasn't a cold-blooded killer. He'd not hesitated to shoot Orson, and she doubted his story that he was the victim in all of this. She wished she'd talked to Victoria herself and that she knew a little bit more about what made Stuart tick.

He placed two boxes on a table next to the car. He pulled a towel, a container of hand soap, and two large bottles of water out of one of the boxes and put them on the table. Next he placed two towels, two tubs, and two more towels on the table. He took off his shirt and hung it on a hook on the side of the container.

He poured water into the tubs, squirted soap all over himself, and began to wash his arms and chest in the first tub. When he was finished, he rinsed off in the second tub, then dried off using one of the towels. Then he went back to the first tub and began to trim his beard using scissors. When he'd cut it as close as he could, he lathered up and shaved.

The end result still didn't make him look exactly like the wanted poster Abby remembered, but close. His dark hair was a good disguise. Dried off, he opened the car door and took out another shirt and put it on. He seemed to have forgotten Abby was in the room as he started humming and straightening up everything he'd just used.

———————⬤▶

Luke left the little house to face an angry deputy rubbing his wrist.

Van Horne stepped between them.

"You're lucky, Murphy. Lucky I don't place you under arrest right now," the deputy said.

"He's my friend and my partner," Luke said before turning to Van Horne. "What are the chances you'll get that thing off his neck?"

"We're working on it. I hear you talked to Victoria Napier."

"I did."

"What did she tell you about her husband? How on earth did you find him here?"

Luke put his hand on his hips and took a deep breath. He had to get the emotions out of it, the concern for Abby and Woody. He wanted them both safe, and he needed to think clearly.

"She worked out a formula, something she made up, and plugged in what she knew about her husband, and then she gave us a list of wineries to check out. This was the last one on the list."

"Where is she now?"

Luke shrugged. "I don't know. Maybe still in Long Beach?"

Several officers interested in what he had to say surrounded him.

"We've tried to find her and haven't had any luck."

"I talked to her today." He pulled out his phone and read the number he had for Victoria. The officers exchanged looks.

"Murphy." An agent came out of the trailer with a cell phone in his hand. "Purcell at the hospital wants to talk to you."

Luke took the phone and asked Purcell, "Is Orson all right?"

"He came out of surgery all right. Faye Fallon is here with him now. We're waiting for him to come around. I need some information from you. Where is Victoria Napier?"

"I just told your people here I have no idea."

"Agents just went to her hotel. She's gone, packed up and left. The number we found for her on Orson's phone is not a good number. Do you have a way to contact her?"

Luke's head began to spin. What was going on here? All the men were looking at him now and the man on the phone wanted Victoria Napier. Where had the woman gone?

Abby rubbed her wrists; one was bleeding after being rubbed raw. Napier had released her to use the bathroom. There was one in the back of the storage unit. She showed him the raw marks and the bloody wrist.

"There's nowhere for me to go. Besides, I'm sticking with you until I get that combination."

He considered this and then directed her to sit back down in the chair. She complied and watched him work. She fantasized about picking something up and hitting him over the head with it. She was reasonably certain she could move fast enough. But what if she hit him too hard? Or suppose she did turn the tables on him and he refused to help? It was aggravating beyond belief.

He had survival food in the back of the unit and he was organizing batches of it and putting it in the trunk of the Camaro. He also had clothes and shoes, which he was stacking in the backseat of the car. She glimpsed a lot of cash and some fake IDs. He really had planned for this. Every so often he'd check the progress on the battery charger.

Abby yawned, not sure what time it was, but knowing it was going to be a long night. All she could do was pray for Woody and Orson. Thoughts of Luke caused shame to bubble up in her gut. She was mortified that the last conversation they'd had was an argument. And he'd been right. She'd gotten tunnel vision because of Alyssa. She couldn't let go because she didn't want to let go.

What was it Axelson had said about the lack of progress in the early days of Ciara's murder investigation? The perfect storm of bad luck and bad decisions. That was Abby's life at the moment. But as she sat and prayed, she felt stronger, more secure. God was in control, and an escape opportunity would present itself. She just had to be ready when it did.

CHAPTER

59

VAN HORNE GRILLED Luke for several more minutes about Victoria, but there was nothing more that Luke could tell him. Finally he was released to return to the hospital and see Orson.

He drove back down the dirt road with a heavy heart, not certain what to do. The FBI agents at the hospital had made it clear that they didn't want his help, and the officers here were ready to arrest him. He had to find Abby, but he had no idea where to begin looking. He'd left the Dancing Purple Grape vineyard and was almost back to the freeway when his phone rang; there was no caller ID. Thinking it was one of the agents, he pulled over to take the call.

"Hello?"

"Luke, can you talk?" The raspy voice was unmistakable.

"Victoria, people are looking for you. Where are you?"

"Closer than you think. I need your help."

"With what?"

"I know where Stuart is, and I want you to help me catch him."

Napier turned off the light that had illuminated the storage unit, plunging them into darkness. He turned on a small flashlight and brought the handcuffs back to Abby.

"I'm going to sleep. You have to be restrained."

Abby was too tired to argue with him. He didn't cuff her to the chair, just hands behind her back.

"I'm going to take a nap. The battery will be fully charged in an hour. At that time I will leave and then call and tell them where to find you."

"The combination?"

He shook his head. "You'll get that when I feel safe."

He climbed into the back of the Camaro for his nap. The flashlight went out and the darkness in the unit was total. All Abby could hear was the hum of the battery charger. She was exhausted, but to try sleeping on a folding chair with her hands cuffed behind her was impossible. She knew that she was flexible enough to slip the cuffs, to move them in front of her, and that was what she decided to do.

Sliding off the chair to the floor with an *ooof*, she lay still for a minute and listened, wondering if she'd disturbed Stuart. There was no movement from the car, so she folded her knees under her and stretched her hands under her butt, grimacing at the pain from the stretch and from the cuffs. It hurt, but it was totally worth it. Once she had the cuffs in front, she bent from the waist, head on her thighs and took deep breaths, trying to ignore the burning in her wrists. After a minute she relaxed, wondering if she could sleep like this. Certainly her shoulders thanked her for the move. It was then that she heard the noise.

A shoe scraping the pavement outside the door.

She turned her head. It was faint, but it sounded as if someone was walking outside the unit. She strained to hear. They were footsteps going back and forth, she was sure of it. She could see nothing inside the unit but was fairly certain that Napier wasn't stirring. She prayed that he couldn't hear what she heard.

Napier had locked the unit where he hid the rental car, but he couldn't lock this unit, not from the inside. Anyone could pull the door open.

Someone was out there. Who was it? And was her rescue imminent?

———————

"Victoria, where are you?"

"I hired a plane immediately after your call and flew up here. Right now I'm at a park in downtown Paso Robles, across from city hall."

Luke knew the spot. A few days ago he and Abby had had lunch there. He pulled back onto the road and headed for the park.

"A lot of people are looking for you."

"Bureaucrats. They won't let me help. They would only tie my hands."

"I think you're wrong. Stuart shot Orson. The FBI is here in force. They won't let him get away."

"Are you on your way here?"

"Yes, I'll be there in a couple of minutes."

"Did you tell the FBI that you found me?"

"No, I haven't had a—"

"Well, don't until we've had a chance to talk."

"I really think the sooner they know, the more help they'll be."

"I won't talk to them, and I won't talk to you unless you promise not to call them."

Luke frowned. What was up with her? "Okay, okay, I promise." He slowed as he reached the dark park. "Where are you? . . . Oh, I see."

There was a dark Land Rover stopped near the bathrooms with its lights on, and he could see the interior light. Luke pulled his car into the space next to it and got out. The driver's door opened, and a man Luke had never seen before—a big man who looked like a bouncer—nodded his way, then opened the back door, gesturing for Luke to get in.

Luke complied. Victoria was there with a computer on her lap and a distorted smile on her face. There was no sign of her nurse. The door was shut behind him, and the driver climbed back behind the wheel. Before Luke had a chance to say anything, the Rover pulled away from the curb.

"Where are we going?"

Victoria turned the computer toward him, and he saw a route highlighted on a map.

"I've found him. I know where Stuart is. Now we're going to catch him."

Luke remembered what Abby had said about the prospect of Victoria actually coming across Stuart at a winery. She'd said whatever happened, it would be ugly. Was that where they were going now? To an ugly confrontation?

CHAPTER 60

ABBY SLID CLOSER to the door, cupping her hands over her ear and putting them close to the corrugated metal, praying Napier didn't hear her. The person had stopped moving. Was he still out there?

Barely breathing, Abby moved closer to the side seam, a small crack where she could feel a slight breeze.

"Is somebody there?" she whispered.

Scrape, scrape.

"Who's there? I need help."

"Detective Hart?"

Abby nearly jumped out of her skin at the sound of the answering whisper. "Yes! Who's there?" So intent was she straining to hear someone speak she didn't hear Napier get up until he was right next to her.

She looked up to see a gun pointed at her head.

"Shush," he hissed as he stepped back and grabbed the door handle with his free hand and pulled. As soon as the door was up, he began firing.

"What?" Luke stared at Victoria Napier. "How could you know where he is?"

"Because I know him. When I heard about the incident here, I began searching. He would have a backup plan, a hiding place, and I found it."

Luke sucked in a breath, working to control the seething anger within. "The incident? Orson has been shot, Abby kidnapped, and Woody has a bomb around his neck. I think that's a little more than an incident."

"I know, I know, and I understand your anger. Why do you think I brought you along? You get to catch him. You get to save the girl and catch the bad guy. Don't you want that?"

"Of course I want that. But I want it the right way."

"The right way is the way that succeeds."

Luke stopped himself from saying any more. The look in Victoria's good eye was bracingly cold, borderline maniacal. She held all the cards. He didn't have any options here but to go along and pray that she was right and that they would find Napier. He wanted Abby back and safe, and Woody himself had postulated that Napier had a hiding place. Kudos to Victoria if she really had found it.

He wasn't armed, had never wanted a concealed carry permit, and he knew that Napier was armed and not afraid to shoot. The survivalist in him looked around the car, wondering if Victoria had a plan to confront her husband.

Working to calm himself, he pointed to the computer. "Where is he?"

"I guessed that he would have an escape plan, a place to run to if he felt I was close. When he ran away with Detective Hart like he did, I knew he was not simply fleeing aimlessly."

"And?"

"I did a public records search for property."

"But he'd be stupid to use his name on a property purchase."

"You're right; he didn't. He purchased it under the name of a fake corporation. BHL Investments. I've found it: a storage facility in a place called Lost Hills."

"How?" Luke frowned. "How could you know that?"

"The facility was bought ten years ago and never used again. I've read through pages of records. He bought it, kicked everyone out, then closed the place but never used it for anything. He used the initials BHL, the second, eighth, and twelfth letters of the alphabet. He's been obsessed with the numbers two, six, and four for as long as I've known him. Two gets us the letter *B*; add six, and we get *H*; four more and we're at *L*."

"Suppose you're right, and he is there. What do you plan to do?"

"What I've told you," she said, sounding like a teacher lecturing a dense student. "Let you rescue the girl and catch the bad guy."

Victoria resumed studying her computer, and Luke sat back, wondering if she were certifiably 5150, police slang for crazy. He prayed for Abby, that she was safe and would stay that way until Napier was caught. Then he prayed for himself, for the wisdom to do the right thing if Victoria was, in fact, leading them to the fugitive.

CHAPTER

61

THE GUN'S REPORT was deafening. Abby smelled the acrid odor of gunpowder, heard a man's grunt of pain, and pushed herself to her feet. In the filtered moonlight she could see Napier pointing the gun at a figure on the ground, and she leaped forward, ramming both of her hands into his side, knocking him off his feet. The gun went flying into the darkness, and Napier hit the ground with a groan. Abby was more concerned about the downed man. She turned toward him as Napier flailed to get up.

It was J. P. Winnen, in civilian clothes, writhing in pain on the ground.

Abby knelt at his side, trying to determine how badly he was hurt. He cursed and moaned.

"Winnen, stop moving. Where are you hit?"

"It's bad, I think."

"What are you doing here? How did you find us?" She saw blood, but it wasn't excessive. Was it possible he wasn't hurt that bad?

He curled up in a fetal position, moaning, gasping. "I . . . I put a tracker on your car. Wanted to keep tabs. I . . . ahh . . ."

"All right, all right, it doesn't matter. Do you have a phone so I can call help?"

Behind her she heard Napier try to start the car, but it wouldn't turn over. Napier was going to flee.

The combination!

"Winnen, do you have a gun?" Frantically she checked his waistband but did not see a weapon. The Camaro motor was cranking over and over but not catching. She turned toward the car but knew she couldn't leave Winnen to chase down Napier.

"Pocket," Winnen said, voice weakening.

Abby had to lean close to hear him as the motor caught and Napier goosed it several times. The car inched out of the space. Abby checked his pocket and retrieved, not a gun, but the phone. She punched in 911.

The Camaro pulled out of the unit and accelerated by the time Abby reached a 911 operator.

"What's the nature of your emergency?" rang in her ears as the Camaro's taillights turned a corner, out of sight.

All she could think about was Woody on the floor with an IED around his neck and no way to get it off.

"Will you let me call someone so we have backup?" Luke asked.

Victoria glared at him. "I have all I need with me. I'm giving you the chance to be a hero. Can't you just be grateful?"

Luke blew out a breath and said nothing. They drove in silent darkness for about forty-five minutes. Luke checked his phone for messages. There were several calls from Purcell. Even as he considered how to call the agent back, he felt Victoria's gaze boring into him.

"You will not call the bureaucracy. They will only slow us down."

"I didn't call anyone. I'm just checking messages."

"We're almost there."

Luke put his phone away and paid attention. They were in an industrial area; he'd seen a sign for Lost Hills a little while back and bet they were close. The driver stopped at a gate and turned and spoke to Victoria.

"It's locked. Do you want to proceed?"

"Yes, yes, hurry."

The driver got out and checked the padlock. Luke leaned forward to watch what the driver was doing. He retrieved a crowbar from the back of the Land Rover and broke the lock, then pushed the gate open. He was not quite back in his seat when Luke heard the gunshots. Five of them.

For the first time since he became an investigator, Luke wished he had a gun. He started to get out of the car, but Victoria grabbed his arm.

"Stay in the car." She dropped his arm and pulled a handgun from the seat pocket in front of her.

The driver jumped back in his seat and accelerated through the gate as another car came screaming around the corner of a row of storage units. The lights blinded Luke, and he put his head down as the driver of the Land Rover cursed and slammed on the brakes. The other car was coming too fast and hit them head-on. The impact jolted Luke. Since he wasn't belted in, he slammed into the back of the driver's seat even as the driver was thrown back by the air bag.

The front seat recoil snapped Luke into the backseat. His head hit the headrest hard, and he blacked out for a moment. When he came to, he had to shake the fog from his mind. Victoria was mumbling, but she appeared to be okay.

"I want to kill him," she kept repeating.

The driver was moaning and moving around. Luke stepped out of the car on shaky legs. He opened the driver's door.

"Are you okay?" he asked the driver.

"I think so."

"Can you call 911?"

"Yeah. I will."

Luke left him and walked around to see who hit them. In the back of his mind he thought it must have been Napier.

The man behind the wheel of the other car was a bloody mess. He had not been wearing a seat belt and his face had shattered the windshield. He wasn't moving, and there was no one else in the car. If this was Napier, where was Abby?

Luke knew he had to find her. He started off into the darkness, in the direction the speeding car had come.

CHAPTER

62

ABBY HAD TO repeat herself three times before the operator understood what she was saying. When she finally got the message, the operator said that help was on the way. Abby put the phone down and tried to ascertain how Winnen was doing. She heard a crash in the distance but ignored it and concentrated on Winnen.

Not good. She still didn't see much blood and knew he could be bleeding inside.

"Winnen, medics are on the way. Hang on."

He moaned. "I can't. . . . I have to tell you. Phone. Record."

Abby stared at the man on the ground. She knew what he wanted. She'd asked for such a thing twice in the course of her career. Asked a dying man for a dying declaration. A confession to clear the conscience before death.

She grabbed his phone and searched for a recording app. As she searched, he started talking. "I followed you here. I was going to leave you. But I remembered the funeral. I couldn't leave. . . . You're a cop. . . ." He coughed.

"Take it easy, Winnen. I found the app. This is Detective

Abby Hart, recording a conversation at the request of J. P. Winnen. Is that what you want, Winnen?"

She put the phone to his mouth and he whispered, "Yes."

"Did you kill Ciara Adessi?"

"No. It was Chaz." He collapsed into a fit of coughing, grimacing in pain. "I helped him bury her body. He said it was an accident. I didn't want an accident to ruin his life."

He faded out, and Abby checked his pulse. It was weak. She wasn't going to prod him for more.

She heard footsteps rapidly approaching and looked around for the gun Napier had dropped. There was a flashlight app on the phone, and as soon as she activated it, she saw her gun and leaped up to grab it, pointing toward the sound. A dark figure appeared.

"Abby!"

"How?" It didn't compute as Abby let the gun lower, pointing at the ground. It was Luke.

"Abby, thank God!" He grabbed her in a bear hug she couldn't return because her hands were still cuffed in front of her. She didn't care. She leaned into Luke as the sound of sirens rent the air, and she knew this part of the nightmare was over.

———————

Chaos didn't completely describe the scene in the storage yard when emergency services began arriving. Winnen was the first to get scooped up by paramedics, but Victoria Napier needed transport as well. It looked as though she'd broken her collarbone. And she barely cooperated with the medics. She was screaming about Stuart. She recognized the Camaro, said Stuart had looked at the car a few days before he shot her, but told her that he didn't buy it. She was insisting she be allowed to chase him. Abby was convinced that if she had two good arms and legs, she'd have been off and running after Stuart.

Stuart Napier had disappeared. Even though when Luke had checked on him, he'd been out cold, apparently before the medics arrived, he'd run off into the night. But the Camaro bore witness to the fact that Stuart didn't get off scot-free. The windshield was shattered and there was blood and hair present; he was obviously hurt badly. The local police were coordinating with the FBI on the phone and a police dog arrived to help in the manhunt.

Abby was glad when the ambulance doors were closed and Victoria was gone. But the word *obsession* rattled her brain. She wondered if she'd looked that maniacal to Luke when she put him on the train two days ago. She watched him handle the emergency responders, explaining everything he knew. Ramrod straight, military posture, and an appealing, confident way about him. Abby knew she loved him and couldn't for the life of her figure out how she'd let herself be swept in the opposite direction, away from him.

We're a team. She vowed that they would be again and she wouldn't let anything come between them, not ever.

Besides Luke, Victoria's driver was relatively unscathed. The Land Rover's air bag had protected him. Abby's wrists were treated on scene, and then a California Highway Patrol officer sent by the FBI to drive Abby and Luke back to the Dancing Purple Grape picked them up. Abby was glad it wasn't a debate. The FBI had jurisdiction over her debriefing, and she didn't even mind riding in the back of a patrol car. At least Luke was with her.

But worry for Woody hit her like a punch.

"How is Woody? Did you see him? Did they get that thing off?"

Luke put his hands on her shoulders. "He was fine when I saw him, tired, but the bomb guys believed that IED was stable. He was holding his own when I talked to him." Luke shared with her what Woody had said about faith.

Sighing with relief, Abby sagged into Luke. "I'm so sorry. I should have listened to you. Maybe if I hadn't been so preoccupied, if I'd been more in tune with the task at hand, I would have recognized Napier, stopped him."

Luke gathered her in a hug. "Abby, don't blame yourself. Woody doesn't."

"You were right. I was blind, obsessed."

He pushed her back and held her gaze. "Forgiven and forgotten." He kissed her cheeks as her tears fell.

"But it's my fault. If I hadn't been preoccupied, thinking about Mike and Alyssa—"

His kiss silenced her. "No more of the past. Only the now, and the future." His warm hazel eyes held her and she relaxed into him.

The highway patrolman cleared his throat. "I'm ready to go if you two are."

Abby wiped her eyes as Luke told him, "You bet."

They climbed into the back of his white CHP cruiser.

"Have you ever ridden in the back of a patrol car?" Luke asked.

"Only with a prisoner," Abby said, leaning against him. "I can't imagine what Woody is going through with an explosive device around his neck. He really didn't mind your prayer?"

"Nope."

She was about to say something else when the officer driving them interrupted to say he'd received a radio transmission.

"The search dog just caught the fugitive, Stuart Napier," he said. "Found him hiding in a Dumpster at a gas station."

"Hallelujah," Abby said. "Has anyone talked to him? Though I doubt he'll be cooperative. He said that he would not give anyone the combination to the device unless he was free."

"That's not going to happen," Luke said.

"I don't have any more information," the officer said.

Abby closed her eyes. She'd been praying for Woody and didn't want to stop until he was free of the horrible device. *Wisdom, Lord. Wisdom for the bomb techs to take that thing off safely.*

Luke held her hand gently. Though wrapped and treated, her wrists were still raw and sore.

"I met the head bomb squad guy, Agent Van Horne. He's squared away. I trust that he can figure that thing out," Luke assured her.

The sun was up by the time they arrived back at the Dancing Purple Grape. Immediately they were told that Van Horne wanted to talk to Abby.

As she and Luke walked through the row of official vehicles, she hated it that she and Woody had become victims when they were supposed to be on the other side.

Luke pointed out Van Horne when they reached the operations vehicle. The man might have been an inch shorter than Abby, but she was able to look him straight in the eye. There was an aura of above-average command presence around him as he took notice of them. He reminded Abby of a battle-hardened Marine, complete with the Marine-style haircut.

"Detective Hart, glad to see you made it here in one piece." Van Horne extended his hand and Abby shook it. "Can you tell us anything that can help us? I've been on the phone with the agent with Napier, and the guy has gone silent."

"He never told me the combination. But he did seem obsessed with a number sequence." Abby told him about the constant tapping. "Does that help?"

Van Horne shook his head. "Afraid not. I've studied the device as best I can, and from what I can see, there are five numbers needed to disarm it. Those three may be a part of it, but I need two more numbers."

Abby didn't know what to say. After a minute she found her voice. "I want to see Woody, talk to him, hold his hand."

Van Horne hesitated. "First, come into the command post with me. I want to show you something."

Luke and Abby followed him into the vehicle. He led them to the front, where a whiteboard stood. There was a diagram of a device similar to what was around Woody's neck. And there was an X-ray. Abby could see immediately that it was an X-ray of an object around someone's neck. Probably Woody's. They sat in what appeared to be a small planning office.

"You folks ever hear of the Collar Bomber?"

"I have," Abby said, looking to Luke, who shook his head.

Briefly, Van Horne explained to him about the bank robbery and the man with the explosive device around his neck.

"I was on that case, studied what was left of that very sophisticated IED. There have been a couple of copycats in various places around the world since then. In Australia a similar device was locked around a wealthy girl's neck. The makers tried to extort money from the girl's rich parents. Bomb guys got it off."

He leaned back in his chair, expression pensive. "The device on Woody's neck is a copy, or attempted copy, but I don't think it's as well made." He pointed to the board. "An IED is basically four parts: a power supply, a trigger, a detonator, and a main charge, the thing that makes it go boom. To disarm it, I need to cut off the power supply, or stop the trigger from activating the detonator, or break the circuit and stop the detonator from providing energy to the main charge. The combination deactivates the power supply."

"Can you do that another way?" Abby asked.

"I think with this device, stopping the trigger is our best bet. I see a kind of ruse where the combination is concerned. If we did input the wrong number here—" he pointed to the X-ray—"it would go boom."

"But you can stop the trigger?"

"I believe so. I've spoken to Woody about it and he told me to talk to you, that you two were his family. He said that if you agree, he's okay with me trying."

Abby stared at Van Horne. She'd prayed for wisdom, for someone to have the ability to make the device safe without the combination. Van Horne knew his stuff, and she saw his confidence. Luke asked the question at the tip of her tongue.

"You're putting yourself in danger to try this, yes?"

"I'd rather be able to move the device to a safe distance and blow it up. I don't have that option here. But I'll be wearing as much protective gear as possible. Unfortunately there isn't much we can do for Woody. I won't say this is a piece of cake, but I believe that I can do it."

Abby looked at Luke, who squeezed her hand.

"It's okay with me, but can I talk to Woody first?"

"We have him on closed circuit—"

"I want to see him in person."

Van Horne considered this for a moment. "Okay, it will take me a few minutes to get into my suit, but you can't be in there when I get to work. I just don't need the distraction."

"Fair enough."

"No hugging, minimal touching. We think the device is stable, but there's no reason to tempt fate."

She and Luke left the command post and walked across the road to the manager's house. Her head spun with the knowledge that it was not even twenty-four hours since she'd first approached this small house, thinking it charming and enjoying the beautiful weather.

What a difference a day makes.

Abby had to steady herself when she walked into the house and saw Woody sitting with his back to the pillar, the horrible device around his neck. She also saw the dog, the one that had greeted them when they first drove up that morning that now seemed like days ago.

"Hey, kid." He smiled when he saw her and his eyes brightened. "You're okay! So glad to see you."

She knelt next to him, grasping his hand. "I am okay, just a little scratched up. I see that you made a friend."

"Yep, he's a good dog. He's kept me company all night. One of the guys told me Napier is in custody."

"He is. But he won't give us the combination."

"I figured as much. But this Van Horne is a sharp guy, don't you think?"

"I do. I think he can get this off. I told him so."

Woody gave a slight nod. "Good, then this will be over soon, and this thing will be off my neck." He squeezed her hand. "Don't worry about me. The last time Luke was here he told me God wasn't deaf. I took him up on that and we've had a good conversation. I'm okay. No matter what happens, I have peace."

The tears fell and Abby brought his hand to her cheek. "Outstanding. We have to wait in the command post. We'll see you in a few."

"Can you do me a favor? Take the dog with you when you go. I don't . . . Well, just take him."

He smiled and Abby could see his eyes fill as well. She let go of his hand so Luke could shake it.

Abby called to the dog and for a second he looked uncertain. But Woody told him to go, and he got up and went to Abby's side.

"We're still praying for you, buddy."

They left the little house, and a few minutes later, Van Horne went in wearing a full bomb suit, moving slowly and deliberately. They listened from the command post. He had with him a toolbox, and as he opened it, he said, "I believe I can do this, but there's still a risk. And I'm not certain how long it will take."

"Then get started and git 'er done. I'm sick of sitting here staring at the wall."

Luke grasped Abby's hand and the two of them bowed their heads. They couldn't watch because the screen went blank as Van Horne began. She could only trust that God had given Van Horne the wisdom and ability to remove the evil device safely.

She lost track of time and kept her eyes closed until she heard a click and Woody exclaim, "Yahoo!"

CHAPTER

63

BY THE TIME Woody was free of the IED, members of the FBI fugitive apprehension team, those now in charge of Napier, had arrived at the winery. The vineyard's owner was also there, wringing his hands, incredulous at the fact that his star employee was actually a much-wanted fugitive.

The apprehension team interviewed Luke, Woody, and Abby extensively, wanting every bit of their contact with Stuart and Victoria Napier recorded and set down in formal reports. Abby didn't mind. Luke and Woody were safe, there was a lot of coffee available, and someone had brought in a huge plate of sandwiches for lunch. There was also a crisis counselor who spoke to both Woody and Abby. For Abby, it was nice the guy was there, but she'd go to her pastor if she began having problems later on. She knew, even though she felt fine at the moment, trauma could resurface.

She couldn't get a feeling for how Woody was doing, but he did spend a few minutes with the guy. It was well after noon before they were finished. After that, one of the agents drove Luke to pick up the rental car he'd left in Paso Robles.

Abby and Woody stayed in the incident vehicle while the crime scene was breaking down around them. One by one emergency vehicles began leaving, while they talked with Van Horne. The bomb tech was a nice guy, and Abby guessed that he could see how guilty she felt about the whole incident.

"Don't blame yourself, either of you. There's an old saying: 'We don't catch the smart ones.' This guy was smart; we never would have caught him. He had a solid ID and a safe hiding place. They tell me he had a lot more fake IDs and a lot of money in the storage place he took you to, so he was a man with a mission: stay free."

"I understand what you're saying," Abby said. "I can't say it makes me feel better right now, but maybe after a good night's sleep. I do think this proves that he planned his family's killing. He was too prepared not to have."

"I agree with you there. He's not talking, and from what I hear, his wife won't stop talking. That will be a court case to watch."

"Not for me," Woody said. "I've had my fill of the lot of them."

Van Horne laughed. "They tell me Luke is back with your ride. You guys are free to go."

"I'm not going to let the door hit me on the way out." Woody was up and on his way out of the vehicle.

"Thanks again, Agent Van Horne. You be safe."

"Intend to."

Abby followed Woody out to the car. When she got there, Luke wasn't inside.

"He's over there," Woody said, gesturing to where Luke was talking to a deputy. "Said that he had to apologize." He pointed to the dog. "Think Zena would like this guy?"

"I'm sure she would. You want to take him home?"

"The vineyard owner said he's a stray. Workers feed him. Napier hated him. We're about wrapped up here. What do you think?"

"About what?" Luke asked. Abby had seen him shake the deputy's hand before walking back to the car.

"Woody wants to take the dog home."

Luke shrugged. "I've seen dogs at the hotel. It's fine with me."

"Thanks, roomie. I've even given him a name. I think I'll call him Boomer."

Abby laughed and Luke joined her, putting an arm over her shoulder and pulling her close. Abby loved Woody for the light moment.

"You guys ready to leave now?" Luke asked.

"Ten minutes ago," Woody said as he climbed into the back-seat with Boomer hopping in after him.

Luke chuckled and opened the passenger door for Abby.

"What did you have to apologize for?" Abby asked.

"I got a little out of line with that deputy earlier. I couldn't let that stand."

He looked tired to her, but oh, so good. He grasped her hand and bent to give her a light kiss before she took her seat, and the gentle touch was enough to ease all the hurts of the past day.

His phone rang, and as he looked at it to check the number, he said, "It's Faye, but I don't have much battery left. Here goes nothing. Hello, Faye. . . . What's that?" He looked at Abby and held the phone down. "Orson is awake and asking for us. Are you up for a visit?"

"I am," Abby said, feeling a second wind now and not giving a thought to Faye being on the team. She looked in the backseat; Woody and Boomer were fast asleep. "They look comfortable; we can make the visit brief."

Luke told Faye they'd be along in a few minutes.

When Luke put his phone down, Abby realized she'd never turned her phone on after getting it back from the agents at Napier's house. She took it out of the envelope where agents had placed it with Woody's phone and both their keys. She turned it on and saw that there were several messages. She debated for a couple of minutes about just ignoring the messages until tomorrow, but curiosity got the better of her.

The first one was Orson telling her he was running late. It was the next one that got her full attention. It was from Pastor Terry, telling her that Padre Mike was not going to be around much longer. What did she want him to do?

"Call me back and let me know."

CHAPTER

64

LUKE THOUGHT FOR a long minute before responding to Abby.

"I think we should try to meet him." He'd pulled over and stopped so they could talk about it.

"What?" Abby stared. He could see that she didn't believe what she was hearing. "I almost lost you because of an obsession over meeting this guy, which you've even told me you think will probably turn out to be nothing. I think I should just lay it down now and forget it."

"I'll agree that I've been the biggest skeptic. But now that the guy is available, why not talk to him? It may be what you've finally wanted after all these years; it may not be anything. But you'll know, one way or another. And we'll do it together."

She shook her head. "Maybe I'm tired. But I can't help but think about Victoria Napier. Her broken collarbone was practically sticking through the skin, and she was still screaming about getting Stuart."

She gripped his hand. He could see her eyes begin to fill. She held his gaze, and Luke's heart melted at the pain he saw there.

"Luke, I don't want to be that woman. So consumed with

337

the need for revenge, so unforgiving, full of hate. It changed the way she looked."

"Abby, you are so far from Victoria it's not funny. Maybe for a bit there I was afraid that vengeance was on your mind, but not now. Now I see a woman fighting for justice—justice for those who have no voice. Just because those victims are your parents doesn't mean that you're frothing at the mouth like Victoria."

"But it scares me, if there is a morsel there, that I'll want to keep digging. Pastor Terry said people like me can hold on to the hurt and be afraid to let it go—"

He stopped her with a kiss. "You won't because I won't let you. Besides, I've seen your heart in this. You want the truth and you want a court to see the truth and make a judgment. Honestly, if there's nothing here, would you hold on with your fingernails and keep digging?"

Abby sniffled and sat up straighter. "I never thought of that. I've moved forward believing that there is something to find. But . . ." She shook her head, frowning. "I wouldn't like it, but if there is truly nothing here, I'd really have to let go."

"And you would. I know you believe that God has this. You have the faith to let go and trust him for all of it."

He could see a change move over her features. Finally she sighed and smiled. His chest tightened with love for her.

"Luke, you're right. When I look up, let go of the tunnel vision, and consider the whole picture, you're right. I may not ever see Alyssa brought to justice, but God is a God of justice; he's got this whole mess whether I get to see it now or not."

"Amen." He leaned over and pulled her close, relishing her warmth and quiet strength, wishing they were done and on the way home but knowing that they needed to do this one last thing.

"It's okay to call him back and tell him we'll meet with Mike and listen to him, no matter what he has to say." Luke brushed her lips with his.

"I will," she said. "And I love the sound of *we*."

"I'm so glad that you're safe now," Pastor Terry said when Abby called him back. "I probably left that message as you were . . ." His voice trailed off; then he continued. "I told Mike what happened, and he said he'd hang around, wait to meet you. You've been through so much."

"Thank you. I'm okay now, and I do want to meet with Padre Mike." Abby put a hand to her forehead, suddenly unsure of what day it was. A whole lifetime seemed to have passed since she met Pastor Terry. "Uh, what day is it?"

"Saturday." Luke and Terry spoke at the same time.

"That's right. I . . . uh, we can be at church tomorrow. Would Mike come there?"

"I think that he'd rather meet you at the homeless camp. But I'll check with him to be sure and call you back. We've been praying for you. I bet you have quite a story to tell."

"I pray that he'll have something for us," Luke said as she disconnected.

"Me too. What a message to miss. And I haven't even played all of my messages." She listened to the next one and it was nearly as eye-opening as the last. The cigarette-roughened voice of Gunther assaulted her ears.

"Abby, I've got a source telling me a bomb is about to drop

regarding Governor Rollins. You may be right about who sprang Kelsey. They just arrested a firefighter who they believe helped her escape. If Alyssa was behind this like you think, the ceiling is likely to fall in on her soon. They're investigating who footed the bill. Call me when you get a chance. This is really big."

She played it for Luke as he pulled into the hospital parking lot.

"Maybe we've hit the mother lode there. And even if Alyssa is hiding something, this news makes it a moot point."

Abby tried calling Gunther as Luke parked but got his voice mail. All she could do until Gunther called her again was watch a news report. In any event, Abby was now wide-awake. Woody was still sound asleep in the backseat, his arm around the also-slumbering Boomer.

"Think we should wake him?" Luke asked.

Abby shook her head. "He spent hours with an IED around his neck. I think he deserves a rest. Orson will understand."

They quietly got out of the car. As they walked toward the hospital, Abby caught her reflection in a window. It brought her up short. She stopped and brought a hand to her head.

"I'm a mess. I look as if I've been dragged through the dust for miles." She tried to straighten her hair with her fingers, turning around to see Luke chuckling.

"Sorry, sorry," he said, raising his hands. "I think you look great. A little tired maybe, but awesome." He took her arm. "In any event, Orson isn't going to mind."

She laughed and let him pull her along.

They continued into the hospital and took the elevator to the third floor. A tall, blond man with an FBI jacket was waiting for them. He didn't look happy.

"Nice of you to answer my phone calls, Murphy."

Luke threw his hands up. "Sorry, just didn't have anything to tell you. And I was a little busy."

"I'm just glad it's Orson you work for. We might have issues."

"Fair enough. This is Agent Skip Purcell," he said to Abby. "He's Orson's friend."

"Detective Hart, it's an honor. I hear you kept your cool under some tough circumstances."

"I'm here in one piece. How's Orson?"

"Ornery, as always. But they tell me he'll be fine. They also airlifted the officer Napier shot, Winnen, and brought him here. He got out of surgery a little while ago. The San Luis cops might want to talk to you."

Abby nodded. She was prepared for that. Winnen's phone, with the statement she'd recorded, had been handed over to the officer who responded to the storage yard. She'd thought Winnen would die, but the medics told her they had him stable before they left. Now the battle would be if he retracted his statement. But even if he did, they had cause to lean on Considine.

Before they went into Orson's room, Abby stopped and looked back at Purcell. "Can you do me a favor?"

"Depends on the favor."

"Can you check on the progress of another agent's investigation?"

He gave a half shrug. "What's this about?"

Abby told him what Gunther had said about the arrest of the firefighter who helped Kelsey Cox escape.

He shook his head. "You go talk to Todd. I'll see what I can do about this, okay?"

"Okay." Abby walked into the room and saw a worried Faye

there at Orson's bedside, holding the hand that was not bandaged. Seeing the concern in her face made Abby feel bad for all the angst she'd wasted about Luke and Faye. Obviously Faye's thoughts were focused elsewhere.

The injured agent was sitting up, his right arm resting on a pillow and encased in a cast that looked like a torture device, rods poking out here and there. His face brightened when he saw Luke and Abby, but he still looked tired, and Abby bet he was under the influence of some powerful painkillers.

"Hey, it's great to see that you're okay. When I saw that car fly by me, I knew something was off."

"I'm very happy you're all right as well. I feared he hit you but couldn't tell how bad. How's the arm?"

"I got so much metal in this arm now I'll set off every airport screener. But the doctor thinks he saved me. I'll still be able to use the hand. Nothing else but scratches. Oh, and I'm filled up with some awfully good drugs right now, so don't ask me for any secrets or promises." He winked at Faye, and Luke laughed.

"I'll keep that in mind," Luke said. "How much do you know about everything that happened?"

"Faye has kept in touch with Skip. Between the two of them, I'm up to speed. And I'm grateful Woody is okay. Dodged a bullet there." Orson looked chagrined. "I'm so sorry I said yes to that job. Never should have helped her out."

"I'm sorry too," Faye said, "that you listened to my two cents."

"Don't say that," Abby said. "Napier is in custody. It was a backdoor way to do it, but it's all good."

"What about Victoria?" he asked.

"I haven't heard. I know that she was injured, looked like a broken collarbone, but I don't know what's going on with her."

He yawned. "Well, you two get some rest. Thanks for all your hard work. Tell Woody I said the same."

Luke chuckled. "You bet, buddy."

When they stepped out of the room, Purcell was waiting for them, arms folded, stern expression on his face. "I just put my head in a beehive because of you."

"What?"

"Who told you what you told me, about the arrest of a firefighter?"

"I'm not going to get anyone in trouble. What is going on?"

He looked around as if to make certain no one was listening, then pulled her and Luke aside and spoke in a whisper. "I hope it was a law enforcement source because this can't hit the press yet. They did arrest a firefighter for assisting in the escape of a sentenced prisoner. And it seems he's got a conscience; he's singing his heart out. The team is now looking at someone who is close to the governor of the state. Can you believe that?"

Abby nodded. "Yeah, I guess I can."

Purcell shook his head. "It blew my mind. At first they weren't listening to the firefighter until they discovered that there were irregularities in the escaped prisoner's detention. She was held in Long Beach way longer than she should have been. The reason—because the governor's office requested it."

Abby frowned, sure more than ever that Rollins freed Kelsey but wondering at the brazen stupidity of the move. "He could have pardoned her if he wanted her free. It's not like she was waiting for an appeal."

"That's right. It's pretty unprecedented and it lent credence to the firefighter's story. Says he thinks the prisoner was kept in LB to give someone time to plan the breakout."

"Wait." Abby stopped him, head spinning. "If he was paid to cut her free, then—"

"The accident that caused the jail bus to crash was a setup, and someone died in that crash. This thing is bad and getting worse. It's been combined with another investigation, something that happened on that case you were involved in up in the high desert." He pointed at Luke. "Someone on the governor's staff was killed up there, supposedly looking into hacking. They have a CI who says Cox was supposed to pay him to keep an eye on you and Abby, not a hacker."

"And they can connect the governor to this?"

"They're working on it."

CHAPTER

65

"PURCELL REMINDED ME of what I forgot to tell you," Luke told Abby as they stepped into the elevator. "Faye called when I was on the train. She confirmed that it was Cox with Quinn in Tehachapi." He told her everything Faye had told him about what investigators had uncovered.

"This guy was supposed to keep an eye on us?"

"Apparently. For Cox, and to me that means also for Rollins. It makes me believe that they had something in store for us, but it got derailed."

Abby stopped and gripped Luke's hand. "Luke, we are not going to be free and safe until Alyssa Rollins and Kelsey Cox are behind bars. Am I sounding obsessed?"

"Not at all. You're making total sense. We'll figure something out together."

They continued to the car, where Woody was still asleep and Boomer wagged his tail.

"What a silly risk for a smart man to take, if it was Rollins who set up that escape," Luke said as he started the engine.

"I don't think it was him. I'd bet it was her. Alyssa wanted

Kelsey out. I think that if Gunther were here, he would agree that it wasn't too bright."

"If that is true. And what could be in it for Kelsey? She'll never be a free woman. She'll always be a fugitive. And I don't peg her as an assassin."

Abby leaned back in the seat. "Maybe she wants revenge."

Luke reached out and grasped her hand. "Because you caught her?" He squeezed her hand. "She'll never get near enough to you to even think about it."

"Thanks, Luke. But I'm not worried about her. I'm not. I'm tired and I have a headache."

"We're almost all done here. We'll make it to the end."

"Yeah, I know we will." She gripped his hand in both of hers. "I have more messages, but I don't want to think about anything right now other than a shower and sleep." As if on cue, her phone rang. "This is Pastor Terry." She put the call on speakerphone. "Hey, Pastor, will Mike be there tomorrow?"

"Not at church, but he will meet you afterward. Same place I told you about when I first met you. Service is at ten o'clock, so figure about eleven thirty or twelve."

She looked at Luke and held her thumb up. "Great, we'll be there." She disconnected and turned to Luke. "I'm glad we finally get to meet Mike, but I have hit a wall."

"Me too."

A few minutes later they arrived at the hotel. It took some effort to wake Woody up. In the end it was Boomer licking his face that did it. But he came around and Luke, Woody, and Boomer went to their room and Abby to hers.

Luke let Woody shower first, while he used the wait time to call home and talk to his mother, then to Maddie. All is well, he told them. Next, he opened his Bible and prayed that, if in fact the governor had arranged Kelsey's escape, his reasoning had nothing to do with Abby.

CHAPTER

66

THE NEXT MORNING Abby awoke rested but stiff and sore after the ordeal the day before. She'd showered the previous night but enjoyed another one when she got up. After drying off and dressing, she sat on the bed and played the rest of her phone messages. There was one from Jessica telling her everything was fine and one from Bill telling her basically the same thing Gunther had about the investigation into Kelsey's escape. It was a big hush-hush investigation.

She called Jessica and talked with her for a bit, assuring her that she was all right. Abby figured she'd be home Monday or Tuesday but wasn't certain. Jessica was just happy to hear from her.

She turned on the news to see if there was any mention of the escape and FBI investigation, but there wasn't. She'd been told once by an officer who worked on an FBI task force that the reason FBI investigations seemed slow was because they often dealt with cases where developing actionable evidence took years. They were methodical and they had a chain of command that demanded input at every level. They needed all of their ducks in a tight row. But in the case of Kelsey's escape, with the governor of the state's possible involvement, they had a fugitive from justice on the loose. Abby wondered if they'd pick up the pace of the investigation. Until now, Abby knew better than anyone how Alyssa always escaped justice. If she and Lowell had orchestrated Kelsey's escape, had they finally crossed a bridge too far? Or was Lowell even involved? Maybe this was all Alyssa, and that would be the end of her.

Luke knocked on the door about quarter to nine.

"Abby, you up?"

She opened the door. "Yep, and feeling much better today."

"Great to hear it." He stepped forward and gave her a hug. "You ready for breakfast?" he whispered in her ear.

For a good second she simply enjoyed the hug and said nothing. Then, stepping back, she grasped his hands. "Yes, I am. What about Woody and Boomer?"

"Woody was up early. He went to the store and bought some dog food, a new leash and collar, and a dog bed. He's coming—to breakfast and to church. It's cool enough to leave the dog in the car."

"Outstanding." Abby felt light and free at the moment, in spite of a dark and foreboding sky. Her wrists were still sore, and the ordeal of the day before fresh in her mind, but she and Luke were truly a team and she had an expectation of success for wherever things took them today.

The church service was even better today than a week ago when Abby went by herself. She was so glad to have Woody and Luke in church next to her, especially Woody. The memory of the collar bomb still gave her chills. Because of her good mood, she ignored the feeling she had that they were being watched.

It was an odd feeling that caused goose bumps to ripple down her arms. She rubbed them away and dismissed the sensation, chalking it up to simple paranoia, and settled in to listen to Pastor Terry's sermon.

———————▶

"Nice to meet you, Pastor Terry." Luke extended his hand. "Great message this morning." Abby had made introductions. She'd noticed that Woody paid close attention to the entire message and had even taken notes on the back of the bulletin.

"Glad to meet you all. I'm very happy to see that you're okay, Abby." He gave her a pastoral hug. "We prayed for you the moment we heard about what had happened."

"Thank you so much. I'm really okay. The bad guy is in custody. I'm ready to move on. I'm happy that you found Padre Mike."

"Yes, well, there's something a little strange he wanted me to tell you." He frowned and rubbed his forehead. "He called me complaining about some woman hounding the homeless population on Friday. One of his friends was even pistol-whipped by this woman. At first he wondered if it was you, but I told him I didn't think you would behave that way. Now I know without a doubt it wasn't you."

Abby stiffened, suddenly wary. "You're right; that's not my MO, even if I'm talking to a really bad guy." She cast a glance at Luke and Woody, who both looked equally concerned.

"What exactly did this woman want?" Luke asked.

"He said that she was asking for him. Pushing people around, trying to intimidate. She smacked one of the simpler men, a guy people call Jelly, with her handgun and broke his nose."

"Oh no." Abby was angry. "I met him; he was harmless."

"I know he is. Like I said, Mike seemed convinced that it was you. But I explained to him what had happened to you, that you've been up here looking for a fugitive, and that you caught him. I assured him you weren't the type to throw your weight around like that."

"Thank you. Will he still meet with me?"

"He will," Terry said. "It will still be at the same homeless camp I drew you a map to. Do you need another one?"

"No, I remember how to get there. I was there once—that's how I met Ham and Jelly."

"Okay. Mike will be waiting for you this afternoon. He even sounded eager to talk to you."

Abby thanked the pastor, and the three of them left to return to the hotel and dress for a hike and a possible confrontation.

"You think it's Kelsey out there throwing her weight around, don't you?" Luke asked as they drove away from the church.

"Who else would it be? And did Alyssa free Kelsey to go after Mike?"

"If she did," Luke said, "then I owe you an apology because there must be something there for her to risk so much."

———▪▶

Back at the hotel, Abby changed into jeans and tennis shoes. Her gun was scratched up from sliding across the asphalt at the storage yard after Napier dropped it. But it was operational. She loaded it, checked the slide and operation, then slid it into her belt holster. Her phone rang and displayed Gunther's name.

"Hey, Abby Hart, so glad to hear your voice, and so chipper."

"I'm feeling okay."

"You had a rough day, I hear."

"Understatement. I'll tell you about it someday. Hey, where did you hear that information about Kelsey's escape?"

"I can't reveal my sources."

"Ah, well, it's supposed to be secret. You don't want to tip anyone off, do you?"

"I'm not reporting on the story. You're the only one I told. Here I am, inquiring about your well-being, and you jump all over me."

"I'm not mad at you. I was just curious. I will tell you that we heard from Padre Mike." She told Gunther what was she was up to. She also told him what Pastor Terry had said, about the angry woman looking for Mike.

"Hmm, that's something to consider. When I was with you last week and you said you thought that Kelsey was coming after you, I feared you were paranoid."

"But now you think it's possible?"

"Well, let's just say I'm glad you found Padre Mike, but you might not need him. This thing with the escape and what now has been proven to be a staged accident is exploding. I've heard that agents recently mentioned 'interview' and 'governor' in the same sentence."

"That would probably torpedo his senate aspirations."

"You bet. But you know, you found a fugitive and he was desperate to escape and look what he did. If Alyssa and Lowell Rollins are guilty of the escape fiasco, they would be looking at prison time, not just a failed campaign. So be careful—that would make them desperate . . . scorched-earth desperate."

Kelsey was ready to chuck her phone out the window and never retrieve it. Alyssa was driving her crazy, calling every ten minutes demanding an update. The phone started to ring again. Sighing, working hard to hold her temper in check, Kelsey answered it.

"Yes?"

"Have you finished yet?"

"No. But I have them in sight. I'm sure that they'll lead me right to him." It was a half-truth. She did have them in sight, but she no longer cared about the target. For some reason, she wanted to let Hart know what she planned. She doubted that she'd be able to explain her actions after the fact.

"I want to hear the minute you've wrapped everything up. The minute."

"You got it." Kelsey disconnected.

She thought about tossing the phone from the car but decided she might need it.

"I'm going to do you a big favor, Abby Hart," she said as she watched the rental car leave the parking lot.

She thought of the poor, simple homeless man she'd pistol-whipped because he wouldn't answer her questions. He kept saying, "Jelly," and she'd lost her temper. That never would have happened when she was a police officer. She was a professional then; she'd taken abuse and ignored it and done her job the right way.

I've fallen so far that I don't recognize myself anymore, and the black hair has very little to do with it. She pulled out after the rental car, a few car lengths back. There was time. Maybe she could reach Hart another way.

But Kelsey was still conflicted. *Maybe I should just concentrate on my plan, say nothing, and let the chips fall where they may.*

⸻━▶

"We need to have a plan," Woody said when everyone was in the car. Abby had shown them the map the deputy had drawn for her the day she went to the homeless camp. They'd agreed that the best idea was to drive up to the same place Abby had and head in the back way.

"I don't think we should all go together. We should split up. Didn't the deputy show you another way to walk in?" Woody asked.

"You can hike from the back of the shopping center parking lot," Abby said. "What do you have in mind?"

"I say that you two get out of the car at the gate, where the walking path is. Then I'll take the car and drive to the shopping center, find the other path. I'm going to swoop in on you from there. If Kelsey is anywhere around, I'll get the drop on her."

"Sounds like a good idea," Luke said, looking at Abby. "What do you think?"

"Well, Woody is armed, and I'm armed, so I think it's a good division of resources."

"But something is bugging you."

"We don't know how long the walking path from the shopping center will take, and it's really bugging me that we have no idea where Kelsey is and what she really has planned."

Woody gave a wave of his hand. "She was looking for Padre

Mike—I'd bet on it. And she bullied a bunch of unarmed homeless men. That's not us. She can't bully us."

"I agree, but I don't want to be overconfident."

"I'm not being overconfident," Woody said. "I'm just not going to let anyone get the drop on me ever again. And today I have Boomer to look after. Nothing is going to happen to him."

Abby turned to see the look in his eyes and knew it would be bad for Kelsey if she did try to mess with Woody.

They were almost to where they would turn onto the dirt road when Luke spoke up.

"I think we're being followed," he said.

"That black SUV?" Abby said.

Luke smiled. "You noticed?"

"I've been watching."

Luke turned off the main road onto the dirt road.

"The SUV kept on going," he said. "How long until we get to the path?"

"About five minutes."

"So if she decides to follow us, I could meet her coming in while I'm driving out. That will give me something to think about," Woody said as they all climbed out of the car.

Luke handed him the keys. "Call us. You have me on speed dial, so don't hesitate if you have a problem. Be careful, buddy."

"Right back at ya."

Woody climbed into the driver's seat, and the dog jumped up to sit shotgun. Abby and Luke made their way to the gate and onto the path Abby had walked alone just a few days ago.

"We follow the path through the oak trees and crest this small hill and then walk down to the camp. We can see the whole layout, get an idea of how many people are there," Abby told Luke as they walked.

"How many people do you think were there?"

"I didn't go directly into the camp. I saw several people, but only Jelly and Ham approached me."

They reached the top of the small hill.

"I see the camp," Luke said as they stopped for a moment. "And it looks like a pretty good-size encampment. Kind of like the ones that used to get built in Long Beach along the flood control."

"This one isn't that big. Those used to spread out and it would take a couple of days to clean them out when something happened."

"Is that why you guys would break them down?"

"It wasn't always us. Most of the time it was public service worried about health issues. We got involved if they turned violent. They sometimes did, with stabbings and assaults. When they grew in size was when the trouble usually started."

"Let's hope this is a peaceful camp without angry people present," Luke said as they started down toward the camp. "I think we've already got someone's attention."

Abby agreed. She saw the men standing up and looking their way. She saw mostly tents, but farther away she noted a couple of makeshift cardboard shelters. Trees there shielded her view, so there was no way to tell how many people were in the camp.

One man broke away from the group, and she recognized Ham. As she and Luke reached the bottom of the rise, she spoke to him.

"Hello, Ham, remember me?"

He frowned. "Who's that with you?"

"My partner, Luke."

"I know you aren't that lady who hassled us, but who was she? Did you show her the way here?"

"I didn't show anyone here except Luke. What did the lady look like?"

"'Bout your height, long black hair and mean face."

Abby and Luke exchanged glances. "Black hair?" Abby asked.

"Yep. She was all over us Friday."

"I'm not sure what she's after—"

"She wanted the Padre. None of us were going to give him up to her."

"Well, we won't give him up either. We just want to talk to Padre Mike."

Ham turned and waved for them to follow.

CHAPTER

67

INSIDE THE TENT CITY was an assortment of lost-looking people, not unlike the people Luke had seen in Long Beach tent cities. He wondered what threshold law enforcement had here before they broke up the camps. He realized he never wondered what happened to the people, how they lived when their possessions were taken away. Luke knew that a lot of homeless were that way because they wanted to be. But as he looked around at the people—a couple of women, some teens—he bet some just wanted an opportunity to get out of a place like this.

Sitting on a wooden crate set on its end was a leathery brown man with a broad smile, graying hair, and an eye patch covering his left eye. The other eye was a clear, bright blue. Laugh lines framed the eye. He stood as they approached, and he was as tall as Luke, but with a more wiry build.

He addressed Abby. "So you've been looking for me. I'm Mike Jez. People call me Padre." He extended his hand and Abby shook it.

"Detective Abby Hart. So glad that you agreed to meet with

me. This is my partner, Luke Murphy." She looked around at the others, watching. "You aren't what I expected."

He smiled broadly. "I take pride in being what people don't expect."

"How many people live here?" Luke asked.

Padre shrugged. "It varies. Most people move on to something more stable after a while. The police usually clear us out after a time and we move somewhere else. Eventually we make it back here and the cycle starts over."

"You minister to these people?"

"To anyone who will listen, yes. My turn for questions. I'm intrigued as to why two people from Long Beach would be interested in talking to me." He indicated they could sit. There were two lawn chairs near him. He resumed sitting on the box. His manner relaxed Luke, even though he noticed that they'd become the object of a few people's attention and three or four of the campers were watching and listening to them. They weren't close or threatening; they were just listening.

"Actually," Abby said, "I wanted to ask you about a woman you went to high school with."

"Ah, it's what I thought. You want to know about Alyssa."

"I'm not the only one who has come to talk to you about her, am I?"

"You must be her daughter," Mike said.

And Luke saw that even though she had suspected that her mother had been here, the affirmation was still a big surprise to Abby.

"What?"

Mike sighed deeply and looked down at the ground for a minute before looking back up. "I never forget a name or face.

I remember Patricia Morgan coming to talk to me, looking for me in much the same way you have. It wasn't at a camp then. I was living in a halfway house, easy to find. She wanted to know about Alyssa and so you must also."

Abby could only stare for a moment. Looking into Mike's calm blue eye steadied her.

"You remember my mother?"

"I do. It was after I talked to her that I got this." He pointed to his eye patch. "I learned then that it was dangerous to talk about Alyssa, to answer questions."

Abby found her voice. "What did you tell my mother about her?"

"Your mother wanted to know about another girl in our class, a—"

"I know about Sheryl."

"Oh, okay. Your mother wanted to know whether or not Alyssa contributed to her death." He pinched the bridge of his nose, a pained expression coming over his features. "I will tell you what I told her. I don't know. But I believe so. It's what broke us up, what sent me here, indirectly. I loved Alyssa. But how do you love someone you no longer trust?"

"Why do you think Alyssa killed Sheryl?"

He sat back a bit and sighed. "Why is it so important to you, now, after all these years? There's no proof no matter what I think."

Abby stiffened at the phrase she'd heard all too often when it came to her parents' deaths and the people responsible. *"There's no proof."* Guilty but free forever in this world because of those three words.

"I believe that Alyssa is responsible for my mother's death, that she ordered the killing. Whatever secret you told my mother so angered Alyssa that my mother, Luke's uncle, and eventually my father were murdered to keep the secret."

Jez seemed to blanch. He brought a hand to his face and then stood. He looked up at the sky as if to implore God for help, then turned back to Abby.

"Then I am as guilty as Alyssa. The day Sheryl disappeared, she and Alyssa were supposed to meet." He sat back on the crate, deflated, and tears fell. "Alyssa told me she wanted to confront Sheryl about the bullying, make it stop. Sheryl was a bully—I'll give you that."

He paused and drew in a breath, sniffling. "But we all were a lot of things in high school that we grew out of when given the chance. Anyway, I thought it would be a good thing for the two of them to work out their differences. Later, Alyssa told me Sheryl never showed up. But there was something wrong in the way she said it. And when Sheryl came up missing, I asked Alyssa again."

He shook his head and wiped the tears away. "She said that Sheryl got her comeuppance. That no one would have to worry about her again and I should just let it go. I couldn't let it go. What I was thinking horrified me. I joined the search for her and learned that they were searching in a certain area because they'd been told that was where Sheryl was last seen, where Alyssa had last seen her. It was five miles away from where Sheryl was eventually found."

Abby said nothing as she processed what Mike had just said.

He continued. "I believe Alyssa knew Sheryl was in that well and deliberately misled the search parties."

"If the well was fenced and they saw no signs of foul play," Luke asked, "how do you think Sheryl fell in? Did Alyssa push her?"

Jez took a deep breath. "The fence was mainly to keep live-stock out. It wasn't a barrier for teenagers. And Sheryl did have injuries on her body; they just thought it was from the fall. When her body was found, I confronted Alyssa. It was like I never really knew her. I lied to her, told her that I *knew* she'd done something to Sheryl and could prove it. I'd hoped to force her to tell me the truth, to come clean and turn herself in. I was wrong."

"She ran instead," Luke said.

"She did. I haven't seen her in person since that day I lied to her."

"That's what you told my mother?"

"That I lied? Yes. But I wasn't the only one your mother talked to. She also spoke to the coroner about the injuries on Sheryl's body. She wanted to get the case reopened and classified as a homicide. She hoped if I told my story, it would happen. I said I didn't agree, that too much time had passed, but your mother was on fire. She was a woman with a mission. I don't know how much information she had, but it was obviously enough that . . ."

He didn't finish and went silent for a few seconds. "It was after your mother left that three big guys found me and beat me within an inch of my life. I lost my eye then. I was warned not to tell tales about high school."

"Why didn't you come forward?" Luke asked.

"I was in a bad place at that time. Drying out. I'd made such a mess of my life. At the time I thought God was punishing me for the lie I told Alyssa. I know that's not true now, but for a bit I thought I got what I deserved. In the end, the beating actually cleared my head, gave me a new focus. I've been able to take classes with the help of Pastor Terry and others. I eventually earned a theology degree. I was a broken man and I decided that I needed to minister to broken men."

He took Abby's hand and held her gaze with that piercing blue eye. "I couldn't give your mother what she wanted. I couldn't say that I could prove without a doubt I knew Alyssa was a killer. But apparently Alyssa must have felt enough of a threat by my lie that she sent men after me, then went after your mom. For that I'm eternally sorry."

Abby suddenly felt a lump in her throat as she imagined her mother on the hunt to solve a cold case, on fire to do it. It had cost her life.

Now that I have the information she had, what can I do with it?

She felt Luke move toward her and put a hand on her arm. "You okay?" he whispered.

Abby swallowed the lump and nodded, unable to speak for the moment.

"For fifteen years after Alyssa left, I lived in a bottle, unable to live with myself because I stayed quiet about what I knew," Jez said. "Since the Lord found me and lifted me out of the pit, I've spent my life in a sort of penance. I live the way I live now to die to self and bring his Word to people who are lost like I was. But I think I have unfinished business with Alyssa, especially if there were more deaths on account of me."

Abby found her voice. "The murders are not your responsibility. It's all on Alyssa. She had a choice. She chose to kill. I will do my best to see that she faces justice here soon, but I might not be able to. I might have to wait and trust God to deliver justice in his time."

Jez nodded. "That will happen. Will you go back to Long Beach and confront her?"

Abby didn't have an answer. She knew now what had gotten her mother and father killed, but she still had no hard evidence, nothing strong enough to put Alyssa in a cell. She looked at Luke and saw in his eyes that he was with her no matter what she decided to do, and it gave her strength.

"I will go back with what I have and pray about the next step."

"I'd like to go with you. If there is a chance for me to speak to her, I'd like to take it."

"You're welcome to come back with us," she said as she stood. "I can't promise that you'll get any more closure than I have."

"I've learned that there's really no such thing as closure. People learn to live with the hurt, the tragedy, or they don't. I have things to say to Alyssa. Things I should have said years ago. I travel light. Let me get my backpack." He got up and went to one of the tents.

Abby held her hands out to Luke and stepped into his embrace.

"You were right," he said. "There was something here. Sorry I doubted your instincts."

"I was right but going about it the wrong way. I really expected a smoking gun, the thing that would drop the hammer on Alyssa. But Alyssa's been a killing machine based on a lie. There is no proof."

"There was no proof in Ciara's case, but we closed it."

Abby leaned back and looked into Luke's eyes. "You're right; we did." She laughed.

"What's funny?"

"Just that I didn't get what I wanted, but I guess I got what I needed. I feel so connected to my mother right now. I don't feel like the orphan begging for God's justice. I feel like a person who can trust that it will all work out. Does that make sense?"

"I think so. I felt that way after you read me your father's letter. My uncle was in the wrong place in one sense, but in the right place because he saved you. I didn't have to understand everything. I felt that I could trust God with the details."

She frowned and looked around. "But where on earth is Woody?"

Luke started with fear. What happened to Woody? Had he run into Kelsey? He pulled his phone from his pocket, but there was no text, no message. Mike was back, and the three of them started out of the camp.

"Did you see anyone else coming up the path?" Abby asked the man she called Ham as they walked out of the camp toward the shopping center.

"No one else." He nodded to Mike. "Make sure you bring the Padre back to us."

"I'll be back," Mike said.

He led the way, Abby followed him, and Luke brought up the rear.

"How long does it take to get to the end of this path?" Luke asked.

"About ten minutes."

"Is there a chance Woody could have gotten lost?"

"If he found the path, it's straightforward as you can see." Mike waved with his hand. If Woody had found the path, where was he?

The path ran behind a large outdoor shopping center, and Luke could see the rental car long before they reached the parking lot. He increased his pace, and then the driver's door opened and out stepped Woody.

He looked toward them and started forward.

"You'll never believe who called the tip line and has been bending my ear," he shouted, hurrying to meet them. "Kelsey Cox."

CHAPTER

68

ABBY STOPPED SHORT.

"Cox?"

"Yes," Woody said as they all came together. "At first I thought it was a hoax, someone yanking my chain. But the more she talked . . . well, I recognized her voice. It was Kelsey."

"What did she have to say?"

"She talked in circles about different stuff, past and present, and claims—" he pointed to Mike—"that if you're Padre Mike, she was sent here to kill you."

Mike asked, "Is this the woman who was here roughing people up?"

"I guess. Cox says that she was freed from prison and sent here by Alyssa to take care of you permanently."

That news seemed to hit Mike like a body blow. Abby touched his arm. "That's the type of woman she's become." She turned back to Woody. "What else?"

"She said she never wanted to be broken out of custody. And then rambled on about doing you a big favor."

"What kind of favor?"

He shook his head. "I don't know. She wasn't making much sense. If she really is in the area, she could be anywhere."

"Well," Abby said, "I'm betting it was her who roughed up the homeless men, so she is here. But what kind of favor could she possibly do for me?"

"The train station. Rollins," Luke said. "What if she plans to hurt the governor?"

"The train station?" Abby frowned. "Why there?"

"He'll be here today," Luke said. "I saw a flyer on the train. He and his wife are taking the Coast Starlight, campaigning through farmland is what the poster said. It's Sunday; he'll be here sometime today." He checked his watch.

"Alyssa Rollins will be here today?" Mike asked.

"It would be crazy for Cox to try something like that," Woody said. "But then, she sounded crazy."

Abby hit her forehead with her palm. "I don't want either of them dead or hurt. I want them in jail. We have to get to the station. Woody, do you have enough to warn the PD?"

He shook his head. "She didn't say anything specific. And we can't say for certain that she's even here."

"He's right," Luke said. "I think the three of us are the governor's only hope, if Kelsey is going to try to hurt them."

"The four of us." Mike grabbed Abby's arm as she started for the car. "I'm going with you. If Alyssa is here, I need to see her."

"No time to argue. Let's get going."

CHAPTER

69

ABBY HOPPED BEHIND the wheel as everyone piled into the car. Her mind churned with possibilities as to what Kelsey could have possibly meant by "doing a favor" for her. She prayed that they were jumping to conclusions, that Kelsey would not have the nerve to hurt Rollins or his wife.

Woody called the police, but as feared, they didn't believe he had enough for a credible threat. They did, however, say that they would forward what he had told them to the CHP. The highway patrol was in charge of security for the governor.

"Did they say what time the train would be pulling into the station?" Luke asked when Woody hung up.

"They weren't positive but thought it would be any minute."

"I wonder how many people will be there to meet the train and how long the governor plans to be there," Abby said, and she pressed hard on the accelerator, praying that they'd be able to do something if Kelsey was there.

"From what I read when I was on the train, he'll give a short speech, rally support, that kind of thing, then continue on down the coast. His last stop is Santa Barbara."

When she got close to the station, she saw that there were going to be a lot of people. Traffic was thick and slow, and cars were parked everywhere.

"We're not going to be able to get close," Abby lamented as they came to a stop.

"Turn right at the next street. I can get you close on the back side," Mike said.

Abby did as he directed. They headed in the general direction of the station when things began to thicken up again.

"I'd park wherever you can find a spot," Mike said. "It's a short walk from here."

Abby took his advice and parked the car.

They got out of the car and hurried toward the station.

"What's the plan?" Luke asked.

"We should split up. We can cover more ground that way," Woody said. "I'll take the Padre with me and check out the front. Why don't you and Abby take the back."

"If you see her, grab a cop," Abby said. "She's armed, and Kelsey is a crack shot."

CHAPTER

70

KELSEY FELT RELIEVED and calm now that she had made up her mind. She'd bought a *Rollins for Senate* cap and T-shirt and a little American flag from a vendor a couple of blocks from the train station. When she reached the station, she saw San Luis Obispo PD doing traffic control, but she doubted they'd be any closer to the event.

She had the advantage. She knew what the governor's security detail looked like, and she could avoid them. Governors didn't generally rate the same amount of security as presidents. And Rollins preferred plainclothes people, not uniformed, so Kelsey knew she had a chance to be successful.

These types of events were generally hard to control, which was why they were short and sweet. She bet that Rollins would make a brief speech from the platform, shake a few hands with Alyssa at his side, and then get back on the train.

Kelsey guessed he was doing the train trip because he was losing. His competitor had accused him of being out of touch with the state as a whole. She'd read the hits and seen the ads that trumpeted the idea that Rollins only cared about Sacramento. And she also knew that all the bad press he'd received because of the Quinn fiasco in the high desert had not helped.

The train hadn't yet arrived when she got there, and people were milling around outside the station and, from what she could see, on the platform. It was a small station; there wasn't much room inside or out and that bothered her, but she'd deal with it. She started for the front entrance but saw DelRey immediately. That would be a problem. He knew her with dark hair, and she had to stay out of his line of sight.

There was a side entrance that didn't go through the station itself but led out to the platform. Two people she knew as security, but not on a first-name basis, manned it. She changed direction and made her way toward that entrance, blending in with a group of women holding signs that said, *Soccer Moms for Rollins*.

She made it through the side entrance and out on the platform with no trouble. There were no uniformed officers on the platform as she guessed, but there were barriers and armed security standing by to keep people from getting around behind the stage set up for the governor.

It was easy to fade into the crowd. All she needed to do now was to find the perfect spot to wait and take her shot.

Abby and Luke made it to the platform through the front station entrance. She was ready to show her ID if anyone asked, but they both passed inside the station, then out without being asked. The only uniformed cops she'd seen were outside dealing with traffic, and that made her nervous. Kelsey was good; she'd been on the shooting team at the PD for a while. If she got off a shot at the governor or Alyssa, she'd hit her mark.

Oh, Lord, help me get the chance to stop her. It was just a matter of jumping on Kelsey as soon as they saw her.

There were a lot of people, and it was a mostly older crowd. She and Luke squeezed out onto the platform. There was a podium set up on a small stage, where she assumed the train would stop, and the governor and Mrs. Rollins would most likely step from the train onto the stage for him to give his remarks. There were barricades in place to keep people from getting behind the governor. But she knew he'd probably venture into the crowd to shake hands. Would that be when Kelsey would strike?

A train whistle sounded, and Abby asked a man with an Amtrak badge how long before the train arrived.

"Two minutes."

She caught Luke's eye. "It's going to be hard to—"

"Detective Hart! Detective Hart!"

Abby turned at the sound of her name and saw Barbara Stevens waving at her. The woman was dressed in red, white, and blue and holding a *Rollins for Senate* sign.

"Glad to see you here supporting the governor!"

She said more, but Abby couldn't hear it as the squeal of train brakes rent the air and the train rolled into the station.

———

Before the train rumbled past, Kelsey heard someone call out to Detective Hart. She searched the crowd and saw Hart with the PI Murphy.

I should have expected this, she thought. But there was never a thought of aborting her mission. *I have nothing to lose, nothing at all, and I'm going to take my shot no matter what. Besides, Hart won't know me with dark hair.*

She should be grateful, Kelsey thought. *She's finally going to get justice.*

The train arrived, slowing down, eventually coming to a stop. Kelsey saw DelRey push through the crowd and hop onto the podium platform, scanning the crowd. She pulled the brim of her hat down with one hand and waved her flag with the other. The crowd around her began to surge forward. She went with the flow and slipped back behind the barriers when security was distracted by the opening of the train door behind DelRey. The crowd roared.

Kelsey kept waving her flag with one hand while she reached behind her back for the gun in her waistband with the other.

———————►

The crowd pressed in around Luke and Abby. He kept scanning around him but knew they'd do better if they split up. He hesitated to make the suggestion, but Abby beat him to it.

She stood on her tiptoes and whispered in his ear. "I'm moving over to the right. There are too many people."

"I'll go left." He gripped her arm and she looked up at him. "Be careful."

She gave him a tight smile, nodded, then pushed through the crowd to the right of the stage as the door to the train opened. The crowd roared with the chant of "Rollins, Rollins."

Luke turned and looked back toward the station and saw more people filing in. He didn't see any extra security measures and guessed that the cops had not taken Woody seriously.

He turned back toward the podium as Lowell and Alyssa Rollins stepped onto the stage.

Abby saw her. She'd looked back toward Luke when she caught a glimpse of the woman's face behind the small stage. Now she couldn't find Luke. She tried to push through the crowd. Kelsey shifted as a security person approached her, probably asking her to move from behind the podium, Abby thought.

Rollins was at the mike, waving as the crowd cheered. Alyssa was at his side. Abby had to shove through the crowd, getting annoyed glares.

How she wished she had a radio to let Luke know. If she yelled, she doubted he would hear. Ditto the ring of a phone. And it would show Kelsey their hand. She continued forward, staring as Kelsey said something to the security person. Slowly the flag lowered, and Abby saw her shoulder dip, saw the gun come up.

"Gun!" she yelled, surging forward, unable to draw her own weapon because of the crowd.

The first crack of a gunshot silenced the crowd. Abby saw the security person go down. In quick succession Kelsey fired three more shots, and the crowd panicked.

People screamed and started to flee from the gunshots. Abby had to press forward hard to keep from being sucked into the panic. Another crack sounded, and she watched a second security man fall.

The Rollinses went down.

As the people fled away from the stage, Abby was freed from the crowd and able to draw her weapon. At the same time

377

Kelsey leaped up onto the platform, shooting the big security guard Abby had noticed earlier. She grabbed Alyssa Rollins and threw an arm around her neck, pointing a gun at her head.

People were screaming and shouting, and the few security personnel in the crowd scrambled to get them out of harm's way.

Abby yelled, "Police!" and brought her gun up on target as the people between her and Kelsey disappeared, clearing up the sight picture. "Kelsey, drop it and let her go!"

"This is for you, Hart. She's finally going to pay for all the bloodshed." The gun remained pressed to Alyssa's temple.

Abby steadied her aim while moving forward, wanting an open shot at Kelsey, but Cox knew what she was doing and she kept Alyssa well in front of her. Alyssa was clearly frightened.

"I don't want this. Not bloodshed," Abby said. Then she noticed Luke. He'd somehow gotten behind the stage. He was working his way behind Kelsey. He'd have to jump up on the stage to grab her, but maybe if he startled Kelsey, she'd lose her focus on Alyssa.

"Kelsey, your life is worth more than this. Don't waste it on someone like her. At one time you stood for justice."

"I'm toast, no matter what. Your negotiation skills are useless on me."

Abby saw Luke moving in low, but what could he do before Kelsey put a bullet in Alyssa's head?

CHAPTER

71

LUKE SAW KELSEY just before Abby yelled, "Gun!" He started that way, shoving people out of his path. When Cox started shooting, he made it behind a barrier, wishing he had a weapon as he saw security people fall. He saw Rollins go down. The governor fell onto the stage and rolled off, smacking the ground hard. Then Luke saw an opening. The security officer closest to him ran for the fallen governor.

With Kelsey focused on Abby, he could get behind her, maybe distract her enough for Abby to take a shot. He leaped over a barrier and scooted past the bloody governor, pausing for a moment, but there was nothing to be done for the man.

He heard Abby trying to talk to Kelsey and Kelsey not having any of it. He briefly considered his options. But there was no time. He had to act or Alyssa was dead—of that he was sure. Here, closer to the stage, was another dead security guard.

Luke focused on Kelsey. The stage was waist-high; he could easily grab the woman. But if he jostled her wrong . . .

He eased toward her as Alyssa raised her high-heel-clad foot and stomped down hard on Kelsey's foot.

Kelsey screamed and Alyssa wrenched free. Kelsey pointed her gun, but it was Abby who fired, striking Kelsey in the shoulder. She lost her balance and toppled backward off the stage. Luke grabbed for her, but all he could do was slow her fall.

Her gun bounced from her grasp, and despite being hurt and bleeding, she still tried to scramble for the gun. Luke grabbed it first and shoved it into his pocket. He then pulled out some plastic restraints he carried with him. He quickly tied her wrists and was about to check her wound when a San Luis Obispo cop appeared.

"I got this; I got this."

He gave the officer the gun and looked around for Abby.

She was nowhere to be seen.

Abby saw Kelsey fall toward Luke, and her first impulse was to go toward him and help. But Alyssa, showing an agility Abby never would have thought she had, climbed down from the stage and started to run. It wasn't fast—in fact it was almost comical. She had on high heels, but the sight was such a shock to Abby she hesitated a second.

"Hey!" she yelled, holstering her weapon and leaping after the First Lady. She reached her quickly and grabbed her shoulder, spinning her around.

Alyssa faced her with a look of pure fury and raised her arm. The sun glinted off the blade of a knife as Alyssa jammed it toward Abby's chest. Abby shifted, and the blade missed its intended mark but still struck Abby's shoulder and upper arm, jarring her and inflicting stinging numbness that made her left arm useless. But Abby didn't need her left arm. Her anger matched Alyssa's, and she brought back her right fist, behind it the anger and frustration of nearly twenty-eight years, and punched forward, smacking Alyssa square in the nose, feeling the crunch of cartilage.

The First Lady of California went down, falling back into a planter like a sack of potatoes. Security appeared. At first it looked to Abby as though they were angry because she'd slugged the First Lady. But their attitude changed when they looked from the woman on the ground to her.

What was wrong? she wondered as things slowly got hazy.

Panic struck Luke like a bullet. He leaped up on the stage and looked around. He caught sight of Abby at the edge of the platform and jumped down, sprinting for her. He saw her land a knockout blow and Alyssa go down. Elation turned to fear as he reached Abby, and she turned to him, and he saw the blood spurting from her arm.

Abby stared at Alyssa on the ground as dizziness hit. She felt wobbly; then strong arms gripped her, pulled her away. It was Luke, but there was blood, so much blood.

Was Luke bleeding?

Strength fled and she was so weak. "Luke, are you hurt?"

The pain in his eyes pierced her soul, but her eyes were so heavy, Abby couldn't keep them open, and everything faded from her view.

Blood—there was blood everywhere. He held her as her knees crumpled beneath her. She said something he couldn't hear and then fainted away. Luke knew they had to stop the bleeding from the wound in her arm. His surroundings seemed to disappear as he applied the pressure needed to stanch the flow of blood. Her face was so pale. Luke prayed as he had never prayed, and then Woody was there with an improvised tourniquet.

Woody and Mike had to move like football players to get through the station and out to the platform after they heard the shots. People were being herded out, and they were going against the flow. When they got to the platform, the crowd thinned out.

Then Woody saw Abby. It felt like a kick to the gut to see all the blood. He rushed forward and fell to his knees at her side. He saw Mike rush to Alyssa, but at that moment Woody couldn't care less for Alyssa.

He took off his belt because he saw that what Luke was doing didn't seem to be helping. Quickly Woody made a tourniquet with his belt as medics arrived. His face felt wet with tears, and his chest hurt. She was the daughter he'd never had.

"Oh, Lord, it can't end like this!"

For only the second time in his life, as he pressed the wound to stop the blood, he opened his heart and prayed.

CHAPTER

72

ABBY CAME TO slowly and with not a little disorientation. She couldn't move her arm, and she knew she wasn't in her own bed. She struggled to remember what had happened. It came back to her in a rush of disorganized pieces.

Kelsey.

The gun.

Lowell and Alyssa.

She tried to sit up and it hurt.

"Hey, hey, look who's with us." Luke smiled down at her, but he looked so tired, and there was a growth of beard on his face.

She felt his hand on her forehead.

"Welcome back to the land of the living."

"What happened?" she tried to ask, and it felt like a croak.

"You saved the day. Alyssa is fine, but Lowell didn't make it."

Abby closed her eyes for a minute as it all came back to her now completely, not in pieces. "He didn't make it?"

"No, Kelsey was a good shot. She took out four people before she grabbed Alyssa."

"Is Alyssa in jail?"

"Not yet, but that's only a matter of time. It took us a while to clear things up at the train station. But Skip Purcell came down and gave us some help."

"I don't remember any of that."

"Nah, you wouldn't. You were on your way to the hospital when they arrested me and Woody."

"What?"

He laughed. "Long story, but there was a dead governor and a First Lady with a broken nose. It took time for the authorities to sort through everything." He squeezed her hand. "You know, she is responsible for so much death and destruction and a lot that was collateral damage. It's ironic that her husband ended up collateral damage."

Abby sighed. "I'm truly sorry about Lowell, but I'm glad Alyssa will face justice."

"Yeah, Mike is working on her, trying to get her to come clean and confess. I don't know if she's listening, but he plans on keeping it up."

"If I saved the day, you must have saved me."

He smiled and she felt her heart jump in her chest.

"Don't forget Woody. And of course we did. We're a team."

CHAPTER

73

BEFORE SHE WAS released from the hospital in San Luis Obispo, Abby learned that Chaz Considine had turned himself in to police and confessed to the murder of Ciara Adessi. In a gesture to Ciara's mother, he returned the jewelry he'd taken from Ciara and kept all these years.

Abby cried with Ciara's mother when she gave a brief statement to the press saying that she couldn't forgive Chaz, not yet anyway, but she was thankful to have that small piece of her daughter back.

Chaz's mother was still insisting that he was innocent, but according to the paper, he declined her offer for defense. His codefendant J. P. Winnen had almost died a couple of times, but he only ended up losing a kidney. Charges against him were pending.

Abby got an unexpected visitor after the news broke. Jasper Harkin lumbered into her room on his cane, holding a small vase of roses that he placed on her nightstand.

"I can't thank you enough, Detective Hart." He nodded

toward Luke. "Investigator Murphy. You were the only ones who believed in me."

"It's our job to find the truth, Jasper," Abby said. "I'm very gratified that everything came out in the open in this case."

"You gave me my life back. The world looks so different to me today. I hope you're not hurt too bad."

"They tell me that they were able to repair all the damage the knife did." She moved all of her fingers on her left hand, the injured side. "Nothing permanent. I should be fine in a few weeks."

"Glad to hear it." He reached out his pudgy arm and shook her right hand, then shook Luke's. "Get well soon. God bless you both." He wiped a tear from his eye and lumbered from the room.

God has blessed me, Abby thought as she looked at Luke's handsome face. *Beyond my wildest dreams, God has blessed me.*

EPILOGUE

ONE MONTH LATER

THE PERP WALK.

The steps of the courthouse were crowded with press and cameras, waiting for Alyssa Rollins to arrive at the halls of justice. They would record the woman's legal day of reckoning. She'd been ordered to appear in court to face a long list of state charges that would have effectively ended Lowell's political career if he had lived. Federal charges would follow. Abby hooked her arm through Luke's as they walked together past the chaos to get a seat inside the courtroom.

"Do you want to watch her wade through the gauntlet of cameras?" Luke asked.

"No, I'll be content with seeing her walk into the courtroom."

When they got inside, Woody, Padre Mike, Orson, and Faye were already there. Abby wondered about Mike. Alyssa must have really cared for him; he seemed to be the only one in her path who wasn't murdered. From what she'd heard, he'd tried to stay with Alyssa that day, wanting to support her and help her.

But he'd been completely and totally rebuffed. Still, he was on a mission to save her soul, so Abby knew that he would keep trying. Luke and Abby sat down next to them, one row from the front of the court.

Faye, for her part, had helped the FBI link Alyssa to the fiasco in the high desert. She'd been able to prove that Kelsey Cox had been there with Quinn the day he was killed. When confronted with the link, Kelsey had caved and admitted to being there on Alyssa's orders. It chilled Abby to the bone that she'd actually been sent there to kill her and Luke. Cox was now going to be a key witness for both the state and the federal government against Alyssa Rollins.

But the escape was what really sealed Alyssa's fate. She'd left a trail of coconspirators who, now that the governor was dead and couldn't protect her, were ready to turn state's evidence against the former First Lady.

After a few minutes, Abby knew from the commotion she could hear behind her that Rollins had arrived. She turned to watch her walk up the aisle. Alyssa looked frail, broken, walking between two attorneys, arms linked with theirs, and leaning on them. Would she confess? Abby wasn't going to hold her breath.

Abby thought about Jasper Harkin thanking her for giving him his life back. Today she felt as though God was giving her back her life. True, Alyssa would never be held accountable in court for her part in the Triple Seven murders, but she would never be free again; she'd never be able to hurt anyone else again.

As for the fear that when the investigation finally ended Abby would have nothing to hold on to, that was gone as well.

She looked at Luke and returned his smile. Life was just beginning.

TURN THE PAGE
TO JOIN THE CASE
WITH DETECTIVE
CARLY EDWARDS
IN *ACCUSED.*

1

"I SWEAR IT'S AS IF my life is caught in a riptide, Joe." Carly hated the whine in her voice, but the frustration in her life that started six months ago had lately built to a fever pitch. "I feel like there's a current pulling me under, and every time I try to raise my head, I get buried by a wave." Her angry strides pounded an uneven path across the damp beach.

"Don't raise your head, then; you'll just get water up your nose," Joe responded. He walked alongside, dodging the sand Carly's feet kicked up.

She shot him a glare. He laughed, and in spite of her mood she managed a half smile. "What would I do without you? You always try to cheer me up even when I bet you think I'm just whining."

Matching her stride, Joe placed a calloused hand on her

shoulder and said, "Hey, I know this isn't you. Being wrongly accused sucks—doubly so when you can't even defend yourself. I'm not sure I'd have handled the last six months as well as you have if I were in your shoes. If you need to vent, vent."

Carly stopped a few feet from the surf and blew out a breath as tears threatened. Emotions a jumble, she was touched by Joe's unwavering support. He'd been her partner on the force for three years—until the incident six months ago—and they'd been through car chases, foot pursuits, and fights together, developing a partnership that was as comfortable as her favorite pair of sweats. She knew, no matter what, she could count on Joe. She was lucky to have him, and he deserved better than her current bad attitude.

For a minute they were both silent, standing side by side watching the waves churn the salt water. The crash of the surf— a little rougher than she had expected—and the smell of the sea relaxed her a bit as the tableau soothed raw nerves.

Joe broke the silence. "Anyway, nothing will happen until all the facts are in and the litigation ends. Request your transfer back to patrol then. For right now, relax and be patient."

Carly swallowed the tears and dropped her beach bag. "I'm a horrible bench sitter. You know me; when they handed out patience, I stood in the ice cream line."

At that, Joe laughed and Carly was glad to hear it. One of the things that made them a good pair was the divergent way they looked at problems, Carly ready to kick the door in and Joe willing to wait hours if need be. Other officers teased them, labeling them Crash and Control. Carly would jump into things with both feet, while Joe would test the waters first with his big toe.

"I shouldn't dump on you. I'm just frustrated." Carly met his eyes and forced a smile.

"I don't mind listening." He shrugged. "That's what partners are for. You've listened to me enough over the years. We'll work together again." Joe tossed his bag next to Carly's.

Nodding, she bent to pull a towel out of her bag, biting down on her bottom lip, trying to swallow the frustration she felt and embrace the encouragement her partner gave.

"You sure you need to celebrate your birthday with a swim in this kind of weather?" Joe asked, hugging his arms to his chest. "Can't I just buy you a milk shake?"

Glad for the subject change, she followed his gaze to the water. The Pacific was a stormy deep-green color, pinched by small but choppy swells, melding to a gray and overcast horizon. Far to the left, several surfers bobbed on their boards, riding the swells while waiting for a good wave. Though late February, Southern California's mild water temperature made surfing and swimming possible. Dark, cloudy weather didn't bother Carly; it simply mirrored her mood. And for her, water normally made things better—even when it was forbidding and cold.

"It's good training." She looked down her nose at Joe. "You're not going to chicken out, are you? And you can also buy me a milk shake."

"No chicken here. Just giving you a chance to back out gracefully." He peeled off his sweatshirt and rolled his shoulders. "I mean, it could be embarrassing for you, the ocean star, to get an old-fashioned thrashing on your turf by a pool swimmer."

"Ha. I plan to *give* an old-fashioned thrashing. You haven't been training." She pointed to his slightly paunchy stomach before she pulled off her own sweats. The cold air brought on a shiver.

Joe proudly patted his bit of paunch. "This will only make me more buoyant."

Casting Joe an upraised eyebrow, a cop glance reserved for obviously guilty crooks who protested innocence, Carly laid down the swim's ground rules. "Okay, it's a mile and a half to the buoy. Last one back to the beach buys lunch, milk shakes included."

Joe nodded, and they both pulled on their goggles and shook out their arms. She counted, and on three they ran together into the surf and dove into a wave. The cold winter water took her breath away, but Carly wasn't worried, even when Joe pulled ahead. Joe was taller—five-ten to Carly's five-seven—and took longer strokes, but he also carried a good sixty pounds more than she did. In spite of her teasing, it was mostly muscle, which made him denser in the water, not more buoyant. All she needed to do was settle into her stroke. This race would go to the one with stamina.

Carly warmed up fast and swam hard, determined to leave her frustration on the beach. Joe was right; this wasn't her. She rarely indulged in pity parties. But today, as she woke up to her thirty-third birthday, everything in her life seemed to converge in a perfect storm of failure.

The divorce had started her funk; the final papers had arrived two days ago, and reading them abraded Carly's still-raw heart. Now was the time she always imagined she would be starting a family, not filing away the proof that one had disintegrated. Nick had taken so much of her with him that she felt hollow. As good a partner and friend as Joe was, he didn't understand.

And Carly felt like a failure when she faced her mother. No one in the family had ever divorced, until now. Mom's solution was church, as though that would somehow fix a busted marriage. Her roommate Andrea's response was more realistic but even less doable: "Forget about him and find a new man."

Work used to be her respite, a place of security, support, and camaraderie, but lately her assignment in juvenile was more a black hole of boredom, sucking her life away. Compared to LA, a neighbor to the north, Las Playas was a small city, but it had its share of big crime. Carly wanted to be back on patrol, crushing her portion of it. Joe hadn't talked about it, but she knew the entire force was on edge over Mayor Teresa Burke. The popular and high-profile mayor had been missing for four days. Carly wanted to be out in a black-and-white, chasing clues and leads, not stuck inside babysitting juvenile delinquents. She kicked the water with a vengeance.

Carly caught and passed Joe just before the buoy. Ignoring his presence, she made the turn and sliced through the swells with her best training stroke. Her shoulders heavy with fatigue, she pushed harder. She conjured up an image of Joe as a shark bearing down on her heels, his fin parting the water in hot pursuit, a mind game to keep her from slowing.

A local celebrity in rough-water swims, Carly laid claim to a perfect record: undefeated in eighteen races. "Whenever life closes in, retreat to your strength" was an adage she lived by. Lately the ocean was a second home.

The shoreline loomed before she was ready to stop punishing the water. But the ache in her shoulders and lungs forced surrender, and as she eased up in the waves, pushing her goggles off to look back for Joe, she realized she did feel better. The ocean was magic. She'd beaten an imaginary shark in Joe, and even though there were still real ones on land threatening to drag her down, she felt energized by the swim.

Carly glided to where she could float and relished a peace she hadn't felt in a while. She willed it to last. Joe was right on his second point as well—there was no reason to be impatient. Between the buffeting swells and the pounding of her heart, she wondered if she should just take a few days off, get away from her current assignment in juvenile, with all the reminders of what she couldn't be doing, and relax somewhere far away. She breathed ocean air and tasted salt while floating, the water a rolling cocoon, protecting her from life's demands and drains.

Joe soon joined her, and together they treaded water, facing one another.

"Boy," Joe gasped, "you swam possessed. Bet that would have been a record."

Carly splashed her friend, the smile now not forced. "Thanks for the swim. I feel better."

He splashed her back. "My pleasure. Just call me Doctor Joe."

She laughed and it felt good. "Anytime you want a swimming lesson . . ." Carly turned with another splash and kicked for the shore.

"Ha," Joe called after her. "You missed your calling. Instead of a cop, you should be a sadistic swim coach somewhere, yelling, 'One more lap, one more lap.'"

Carly headed straight for her towel as the cool air turned her skin to gooseflesh. Joe followed.

"You need to get back into competition again," Joe said as he reached for his towel. "Admit it, you're half fish."

"I'd like to, but working an afternoon shift makes it difficult." She quickly slid into the comfort of dry sweats and wrapped her thick auburn hair in the towel. "But you're right; the water helps my mood as much as good ole Doctor Joe does."

The shrill chirp of a work BlackBerry cut off Joe's rejoinder. He looked toward his bag. "Yours or mine?"

"Mine." Carly dug the offending device out of her pocket, eyebrows knit in annoyance. The BlackBerry, or "TrackerBerry" as most officers who were issued the phones called them, rarely brought good news. The text message flashing across the small screen read, CALL THE WATCH COMMANDER ASAP, 911, 911. Her pulse quickened with a jolt. *What kind of emergency?*

"Look at this." She showed Joe the message.

"Whoa, I wonder what's up."

Carly shrugged and hit the speed dial for the watch commander's phone.

"Tucker."

The name took her by surprise. Sergeant Tucker was the head of homicide. Why was he answering the watch commander line?

"Uh, Sergeant Tucker, it's Edwards. Did you page me by accident?"

"Nope, you're the one I wanted. We found the mayor and . . . uh, hang on."

Carly could hear muffled voices in the background. Shock brought on by the sergeant's comment about the mayor left her slack jawed. *We found the mayor* coming from the *homicide* sergeant was not a good thing. She'd just been thinking about the woman! Speculation about Mayor Burke's fate had run the gamut among department personnel during the past four days. Now Carly's stomach turned as she guessed at the reality. She repeated the sergeant's words to Joe, who whistled low in surprise.

"You still there?" Sergeant Tucker came back on the line.

"Yes, sir." More questions clouded her mind. *Why is Sergeant Tucker calling me about the mayor's case?*

"I can't tell you much right now. The area is crawling with press. The mayor was murdered. We need you at the command post ASAP."

"What?" Carly's hand went numb with the confirmation of her suspicions. "Uh, sure, where?" *Mayor Teresa Burke was murdered.* This news would devastate the city she worked for. Carly listened as the sergeant told her where to report and broke the connection.

"Earth to Carly, you still with me?" Joe tapped the phone. "What happened?"

"Mayor Burke was murdered, and they want me at the crime scene now."

"Wow." His face registered the shock Carly felt. "What do they want you to handle?"

"Tucker didn't say." She held Joe's gaze. "Why me? I work juvenile invest, not homicide."

"My guess would be there's a minor involved somewhere. But why ask why? Go for it; this will be an important investigation. The fact that they want you says something."

"After six months of telling me to pound sand, suddenly they need me?"

Joe laughed. "You know what they say about gift horses? If you look them in the mouth, they bite! Just go and be the outstanding investigator I know you are." He gripped her arm.

"Stop thinking less of yourself because they've stuck you in juvie. You're a good cop."

"Thanks. You're right, I guess, about doing my best with whatever they've got for me." She shrugged. "At least I've got nothing to lose. Thanks for the swim."

He applauded as she left him at the water's edge and jogged across the mostly empty beach toward home, a block and a half away.

After a quick shower to wash away the salt, Carly took a minute to shuffle through her wardrobe. Juvenile was a nonuniform assignment, the dress code business casual, which for her afternoon shift usually meant jeans and a department polo shirt. But this was a big case. Deciding that she wanted her appearance to scream competent and prepared, she chose a pair of black slacks, a dark-green sweater, and hard-soled shoes rather than the running shoes she normally wore.

A quick glance in the mirror left her satisfied. She double-checked the gun and badge in her backpack on the way to the car, the familiar ritual helping to calm her jumping nerves. But the adrenaline rush was intense.

I'm going to be a cop again. I'm going to do police work, sang in her thoughts. She locked the seat belt across her chest and started the car. A question popped in her mind and zinged her pumped-up nerves like tinfoil on silver fillings.

Why would anyone want to kill Mayor Teresa Burke?

ABOUT THE AUTHOR

A FORMER LONG BEACH, CALIFORNIA, police officer of twenty-two years, Janice Cantore worked a variety of assignments, including patrol, administration, juvenile investigations, and training. She's always enjoyed writing and published two short articles on faith at work for *Cop and Christ* and *Today's Christian Woman* before tackling novels. She now lives in a small town in southern Oregon, where she enjoys exploring the forests, rivers, and lakes with her Labrador retriever, Abbie.

Janice writes suspense novels designed to keep readers engrossed and leave them inspired. *Catching Heat* is the third title in her Cold Case Justice series, following *Drawing Fire* and *Burning Proof.* Janice also authored *Critical Pursuit, Visible Threat,* and the Pacific Coast Justice series, which includes *Accused, Abducted,* and *Avenged.*

Visit Janice's website at www.janicecantore.com and connect with her on Facebook at www.facebook.com/JaniceCantore.

DISCUSSION QUESTIONS

1. Detective Abby Hart knows the courthouse is "where people came for justice," but she still feels frustrated that her parents' case isn't getting its due share. Is there a situation in your own life where justice has not prevailed? Or can you think of an issue in society where justice has failed? What is the best way to respond to situations like that?

2. Abby's visit with her uncle Simon gives her the idea to dig deeper into Alyssa Rollins's past. Why does Luke Murphy have a hard time buying Abby's theory about Alyssa's role in the Triple Seven case? Why does Abby feel so strongly that she's on the right track?

3. Luke reminds his daughter, Maddie, that God "is our protection, no matter what happens—earthquakes, floods, whatever." When have you seen evidence of this in your life? When have you needed this reminder?

4. Luke's heart isn't really in his relationship with Faye Fallon. Why does he continue to try to make it work with

the blogger? Is it okay that he persists, or should he have called things off sooner? How well does Abby handle her feelings about his and Faye's relationship?

5 Constance Considine uses intimidation tactics against those threatening to question or prosecute her son for his fiancée's murder. Is this simply a case of a mother protecting her son, or does it go too far? Does that make you more or less likely to think Chaz is guilty?

6 Abby opts to investigate on her own a few times, ignoring Luke's protests. Do you agree more with Abby, who believes there's minimal danger and she can take care of herself? Or is Luke right to be worried for her safety? Which character do you relate to more? Do you tend to dive in or hold back to assess things?

7 Woody challenges Luke to man up and tell Abby how he really feels about her. Describe a time in your life when you stepped up and revealed your feelings (romantic or otherwise), not knowing how the other person would respond. Would you do anything differently now? Why or why not?

8 When Luke meets Victoria Napier, he sees "obsession on steroids" in the woman and worries that Abby might fall deeper into that mind-set. What similarities do you see between the two women and how they pursue answers? What differences are there?

9 Pastor Terry tells Abby that sometimes after a person has been hurt, "they hold on to the hurt too long. . . . The hurt has become a part of them and it's scary to let

go." How is this true for Abby? Is it true for you or for someone you know? What can you do to avoid holding on to a hurt too long?

10 What does it take for Woody to finally surrender and admit he needs faith? Was there an event or situation in your life that convinced you to put your life in God's hands? If not, is there something that's holding you back?

11 Despite appearing to have something to hide, J. P. Winnen shows up at surprising times, usually to antagonize the cold case task force. What prompts his change of heart late in the story?

12 Padre Mike tells Abby, "I've learned that there's really no such thing as closure. People learn to live with the hurt, the tragedy, or they don't." Do you agree with this idea? Why or why not?

13 Even after confessing and resigning herself to a prison sentence, Kelsey Cox learns she still has a role to play for her employer. What surprised you about the actions she takes at the story's climax?

14 What do you think of the way the author wrapped up the story? The series? Are you satisfied justice has been served? Is Abby? Is Luke?

TYNDALE HOUSE PUBLISHERS IS CRAZY4FICTION!

Fiction that entertains and inspires

Get to know us! Become a member of the Crazy4Fiction community. Whether you read our blog, like us on Facebook, follow us on Twitter, or receive our e-newsletter, you're sure to get the latest news on the best in Christian fiction. You might even win something along the way!

JOIN IN THE FUN TODAY.

 www.crazy4fiction.com

 Crazy4Fiction

 @Crazy4Fiction